PENGUIN CLASSICS

THE PENGUIN BOOK
OF MIGRATION LITERATURE

DOHRA AHMAD is professor of English at St. John's University. She is the author of *Landscapes of Hope: Anti-Colonial Utopianism in America*, editor of *Rotten English: A Literary Anthology*, and coauthor (with Shondel Nero) of *Vernaculars in the Classroom: Paradoxes, Pedagogy, Possibilities*. Ahmad also contributed an introduction to the Penguin Classics edition of *The Housing Lark* by Trinidadian author Sam Selvon. Born in Chicago, she has lived in Amsterdam, Lahore, and San Francisco, and now lives in Brooklyn with her family.

EDWIDGE DANTICAT is the author of numerous books, including *Everything Inside*; *The Art of Death*, a National Book Critics Circle finalist; *Claire of the Sea Light*, a *New York Times* Notable Book; *Brother, I'm Dying*, a National Book Critics Circle Award winner and National Book Award finalist; *The Dew Breaker*, a PEN/Faulkner Award finalist and winner of the inaugural Story Prize; *The Farming of Bones*, an American Book Award winner; *Breath, Eyes, Memory*, an Oprah's Book Club selection; and *Krik? Krak!*, also a National Book Award finalist. A 2018 Neustadt International Prize for Literature winner and the recipient of a MacArthur "Genius" grant, Danticat has been published in *The New Yorker*, *The New York Times*, *Harper's Magazine*, and elsewhere.

The Penguin Book of Migration Literature

DEPARTURES, ARRIVALS, GENERATIONS, RETURNS

Edited with an Introduction by
DOHRA AHMAD

Foreword by
EDWIDGE DANTICAT

PENGUIN BOOKS

PENGUIN BOOKS

An imprint of Penguin Random House LLC
penguinrandomhouse.com

Published in Penguin Books 2019

A portion of the foreword by Edwidge Danticat was published in different form in
"We Must Not Forget Detained Migrant Children" in *The New Yorker*, June 26, 2018.

Pages 284–286 constitute an extension of this copyright page.

LIBRARY OF CONGRESS CATALOGING-IN-PUBLICATION DATA
Names: Ahmad, Dohra, editor, author of introduction. | Danticat, Edwidge, author of foreword.
Title: The Penguin book of migration literature : departures, arrivals, generations,
returns / edited with an introduction by Dohra Ahmad ; foreword by Edwidge Danticat.
Description: New York : Penguin Books, 2019.
Identifiers: LCCN 2019004724 (print) | LCCN 2019010719 (ebook) |
ISBN 9780143133384 (pbk.) | ISBN 9780525505167 (ebook)
Subjects: LCSH: Emigration and immigration in literature. |
Immigrants in literature. | Exiles in literature.
Classification: LCC PN56.E59 (ebook) | LCC PN56.E59 P47 2019 (print) | DDC 808.8/03552—dc23
LC record available at https://lccn.loc.gov/2019004724

Printed in the United States of America
1 3 5 7 9 10 8 6 4 2

Set in Sabon LT Pro

For migrants everywhere

Contents

THE PENGUIN BOOK
OF MIGRATION LITERATURE

DEPARTURES

no one leaves home unless
home is the mouth of a shark

—WARSAN SHIRE, "HOME"

ARRIVALS

And, hungry for the old, familiar ways,
I turned aside and bowed my head and wept.

—CLAUDE McKAY, "THE TROPICS IN NEW YORK"

GENERATIONS

*defining myself my own way any way many
many ways*

—TATO LAVIERA, "AMERÍCAN"

RETURNS

Foreword

One of my earliest childhood memories is of being torn away from my mother. I was four years old and she was leaving Haiti for the United States to join my father, who'd emigrated two years earlier, to escape both a dictatorship and poverty. My mother was entrusting my younger brother and me to the care of my uncle and his wife, who would look after us until our parents could establish permanent residency—they had both traveled on tourist visas—in the United States.

On the day my mother left, I wrapped my arms around her legs before she headed for the plane. She leaned down and tearfully unballed my fists so that my uncle could peel me off her. As my brother dropped to the floor, bawling, my mother hurried away, her tear-soaked face buried in her hands. She couldn't bear to look back.

Even the type of carefully planned separation that my parents chose tore their hearts out. Whenever they were eating, my mother used to say, they wondered whether my brother and I were eating, too. When they went to bed at night, they wondered if my brother and I were sleeping. Even though we spoke to them on a scheduled call once a week, they never stopped worrying and longing for us.

It is perhaps that ache and longing that made my parents take me to visit Haitian refugees and asylum seekers who were being held at a detention center near the Brooklyn Navy Yard when our family was reunited in New York, in the early 1980s. I have continued to visit detention facilities over the years, including ones where children are held, either alone or with their parents. At a children's facility in Cutler Bay, Florida, most of the boys and girls had been detained for so long that they'd transitioned from childhood to adolescence behind those walls. Then there were the Miami hotels turned detention centers, where women and children were being held for weeks or months at a time. Up to six women spent twenty-four hours a day in one room, often with crying babies and toddlers, while armed guards patrolled the halls.

One of the most distressing aspects of migration, for both adults and children, is how invisible the migrant can become, even when being detained, or imprisoned, in our proverbial backyards. When vulnerable populations are kept hidden, or are forced into hiding—which is the daily reality of so many undocumented migrants, immigrants, and refugees—they not only live in the shadows; they become slowly erased and their voices become muffled or go unheard.

That's why it's so illuminating to have a book like this at this particular time, an indispensable anthology full of intimate and deeply moving poems, short stories, novels, and memoirs about what it's like to live on the margins of borders today. This book dares to ask what departures, arrivals, and returns are like, what being "in motion" means at a time when, according to the United Nations High Commissioner for Refugees, 68.5 million of our fellow human beings are coming and going because of war or economic, environmental, or political instability.

The Penguin Book of Migration Literature: Departures, Arrivals, Generations, Returns also explores what home is and can become. Is home the place where we are born, where, as we say in Haiti, our umbilical cords are buried? Or is home the place we die, where we are buried? Or is home the place where we toil in between? The place to which we've sacrificed our youth, our strength, the place to which we have given the best years of our lives? Some of us are born speaking one language and will die speaking another. We are seeds in one soil and weeds in another.

We don't always get to decide where we call home. Many times it is others who decide, gatekeepers, immigration officers, border guards. Is home where, as the physician and poet Oliver

Wendell Holmes Sr. said, "our feet may leave, but not our hearts"? Or is it as the novelist, essayist, and activist James Baldwin wrote, "not a place but simply an irrevocable condition"? Do we define home as where we welcome others in, or as where we keep others out? These days it certainly seems as though the latter is prevailing, but the voices you are reading here will not be pushed out. They will not go unheard.

"Tell us," the novelist Toni Morrison said in her 1993 Nobel lecture, "what it is to have no home in this place. To be set adrift from the one you knew. What it is to live at the edge of towns that cannot bear your company."

These writers more than tell us. They show us. They pull us in and draw us out. They invite us into homes, families, souls.

Human beings have been migrating since the beginning of time. We have always traveled from place to place, looking for better opportunities, where they exist, and no matter how many walls are built, this will not change. After all, raging, seemingly impassable seas have not stopped migrants from leaving places that, as the Somali-Kenyan-British poet Warsan Shire has written, won't let them stay.

As I am writing this, seven thousand mostly Honduran migrants are traveling on foot through Mexico and heading to the United States in what is considered one of the largest "caravans" of US-bound Central American migrants on record. Made up mostly of families, including young children, this group is fleeing poverty, gang activity, and one of the highest murder rates in the world. These people are risking everything, including separation from their children, for the mere possibility of a better life. I wonder what stories they will eventually tell about this journey and others they have been on. I wonder what their children will have to say. Perhaps those who have preceded them, including many of the writers in this book, will set a blueprint for them and open the gates, so to speak, for their voices to be heard.

EDWIDGE DANTICAT

Introduction

Every year, millions of people move to a new country. From war refugees to corporate expats, migrants constantly reshape their places of origin and arrival. It is rare for a single day to pass without news coverage of the many migrations—voluntary and involuntary, documented and undocumented—that characterize contemporary life. Over the past several decades, sociologists, demographers, political scientists, and economists have given their academic views on the causes and effects of migration. For an equally valid and possibly more nuanced perspective, we can turn to literary sources: poems, short stories, novels, memoirs, and graphic novels. For migrants and non-migrants alike, literature renders migrant lives comprehensible and familiar. While one can find origin-specific anthologies (e.g., African, Caribbean, or South Asian diasporas) and destination-specific ones (e.g., Canadian, British, or US immigrant literature), this is the first collection to offer a global, comparative scope. My hope is that *The Penguin Book of Migration Literature* will convey the intricacy of worldwide migration patterns, the diversity of migrant experiences, and the common threads among those varied experiences.

It is the very complexity of the migrant experience that leads me to consider this an anthology of *migrant* literature rather than *immigrant* literature. Definitions can be dry, but they lend clarity, and many of the terms around migration can be loaded and confusing. "Migration" denotes any long-term movement; "emigration" is the act of leaving a place; and "immigration" refers to arrival. So all migrants may be classified as emigrants or immigrants, depending on perspective, but more realistically all migrants feel themselves to be both emigrants and immigrants at once. Yet even the most welcoming and sympathetic commentators in destination countries tend to speak of "immigrant literature" rather than the more holistic "migrant literature." An anthology or university course titled "Immigrant Literature" elides migrants' prior histories, suggesting lives that begin anew in a host country. I wanted to include that sometimes neglected history, which is why I begin this anthology not with arrivals but with departures—and sometimes the decision not to depart at all. Similarly, we end not with assimilation but with the possibility of returns, for homelands always linger even if only on an emotional level.

Besides the qualities of being global and multidirectional, an essential element to note about migration is that it exists in a continuum of involuntary to voluntary. Forced migrations— enslavement, "transport" (i.e., deportation to an overseas prison), trafficking, political or religious persecution, exile, expatriation— formed the world that we know. While slavery might not have traditionally been considered within the literature of migration, I find it critical to consider the full history of people going from place to place. Therefore I have included writers like Olaudah Equiano and Phillis Wheatley, whose insights help us understand the massive forced migration known as the Atlantic slave trade.

Along with the unambiguously involuntary migrations that have shaped our current reality, many migrations fall in a gray area between involuntary and voluntary. Indentureship; war; persecution based on political activity, religion, sexuality, and other factors; lack of economic possibility: this categorical ambiguity defined the second half of the nineteenth century, and continues through the present. Zadie Smith's sensitive novella *The Embassy of Cambodia* and Chris Abani's harrowing *Becoming Abigail*, among other fictional sources, depict women living in a corresponding limbo. In the case of Smith's protagonist, "It was not the first time that Fatou had wondered if she herself was a slave, but this story, brief as it was, confirmed in her own mind that she was not. After all, it was her father, and not a kidnapper, who had taken her from Ivory Coast to

Ghana." Legal trade in human beings may have been outlawed by the end of the nineteenth century, but millions of people still find themselves in Fatou's and Abigail's position. One of the two affecting narrators of Edwidge Danticat's short story "Children of the Sea" writes to her lover, "i thank god you got out when you did. all the other youth federation members have disappeared." The departed lover may have made a choice to leave Haiti, but it was no kind of choice if the other option was death. Similarly, in "An Honest Exit," Dinaw Mengestu's unnamed protagonist tells of his father, who "knew that if he returned home he would eventually be arrested again, and that this time he wouldn't survive, so he took what little he had left and followed a group of men who told him that they were heading to Sudan, because it was the only way out." As Warsan Shire poetically sums up these stories of semivoluntary migration, "no one leaves home unless home is the mouth of a shark." In all these instances, migration is simply not a choice, but rather a matter of survival.

At the other end of the continuum, it's important to recognize that those who have the luxury of choosing not to emigrate are part of the story of migration as well. An example is the heroine of Salman Rushdie's uncharacteristically straightforward parable "Good Advice Is Rarer Than Rubies," who challenges the conventional wisdom that migration will represent a better life. We also need to consider the original inhabitants of destination countries: native people whose land, cultures, and economies bore the cost of these voluntary and forced arrivals. Within this collection, Joseph Bruchac's poem "Ellis Island" stands in for the experience of Native Americans, Canadian First Nations people, Indigenous Australians, Maori, and other indigenous people for whom the migrations of settler colonialism wrought unfathomable and unwelcome change. Further, internal or "intranational" migration (i.e., migration within one country) can be just as transformative and traumatizing as international migration. We see this in the fiction of Charles Dickens, John Steinbeck, Bessie Head, and Rohinton Mistry; Langston Hughes's poetry; and within this anthology in the excerpt from Mohsin Hamid's *How to Get Filthy Rich in Rising Asia*. As

Hamid indicates, even with no change of citizenship status and no risk of deportation, internal migration—especially from rural to urban areas—can be a wrenching and isolating move.

This anthology conveys deep commonalities as well as significant differences across its literary portraits of migration. In listing the common elements, it is not my intention to homogenize or flatten the differences; migrants have a very broad range of experiences depending on race, gender, sexuality, class, language, legal status, and many other factors. However, we will also see meaningful overlaps. First, each of these pieces rebuts existing discourses and stereotypes about migrants and migration; in other words, they each have a strong counterdiscursive function. Some of those discourses and stereotypes include the prevailing notions that all migrants are eager to leave their home countries; that migration is optional; that migration is permanent and unidirectional; that it automatically leads to a better life; and that the ultimate goal of migration is to assimilate to a new place.

The beautiful, dynamic literary texts contained here present a more complex and multilayered picture on all these counts. Whereas sociologists and historians differentiate between "push factors" (namely, reasons that people emigrate, for example war or economic depression) and "pull factors" (namely, reasons that people immigrate to a specific country, for instance employment opportunities or changes in immigration policy), popular media in destination countries tends to focus almost exclusively on the latter. Not much has changed in that respect since Sam Selvon observed in his 1956 short story "Come Back to Grenada": "Them English people think the boys lazy and goodfornothing and always on the dole, but George know is only because the white people don't want to give them work." Invariably, our writers need to concern themselves with what "them English people" (or Australian, Canadian, French, German, or US people) think. In reality, as the excellent documentary *The Other Side of Immigration* points out, migration would be better understood as effect rather than cause.

Relatedly, many of these pieces contest the idea of immigration policy in destination countries as moral or absolute, as opposed to being determined entirely by shifting global power relations. In Mengestu's "An Honest Exit," the narrator's father is cynically advised to "tell them you were fighting against the Communists and they will love you." Often, "push factors" stem from violent interventions on the part of destination countries— France in Algeria and Vietnam; Portugal in Angola; or the United States in El Salvador, Guatemala, Honduras, and Nicaragua—against the popular view of destination countries as saviors or innocent victims.

Third, these pieces dispute the idea that migration is an individual or even a family-based phenomenon, eloquently asserting the collective nature of the endeavor. Witness this heartbreaking passage from Danticat's "Children of the Sea": "Since there are no mirrors, we look at each others faces to see just how frail and sick we are starting to look." Amid the trauma of forced relocation, only migrants themselves—along with the writers who document their collective experience—can validate each other's humanity. We see a similar process in Julie Otsuka's "Come, Japanese!," which tracks the creation of a new collectivity encapsulated in Otsuka's innovative first-person plural "we" narrator.

Finally, when taken as a group, the writings included here counter the primacy of the United States in the rhetorical landscape of global migration. Whereas many in the United States think of ourselves as holding a global monopoly on immigration, other countries host a far greater number of migrants relative to total population. For example, only a tiny proportion of Syrian refugees resettled in the United States—even before Donald Trump's inhumane closed-door policy—compared with Turkey, Lebanon, and other countries. Part of my purpose with this anthology is to break the United States' monopoly on the idea of being a "nation of immigrants." Understanding migration within a global scope helps us observe fundamental differences—legal, political, and cultural—as well as shared elements around the world.

Across the many migration routes depicted here, we can observe many recurring symbols. Foremost among these is the ocean, which looms large especially in the writings that recount

African enslavement, South Asian indentureship, and their generational reverberations. Equiano writes of a terror of the sea that recurs in later writings on migration, especially in the African diaspora; M. NourbeSe Philip echoes him two centuries later with the loaded phrase "perils / of water." Danticat's narrator asserts horrendous continuities across time, asking, "Do you want to know how people go to the bathroom on the boat? Probably the same way they did on those slave ships years ago." The original sin of slavery generated untold wealth for England, France, Portugal, and the United States; pillaged West Africa of its human capital; and contributed to the displacement of the original people of the Americas. These literary pieces remind us that we can't understand contemporary migrations without understanding slavery and colonialism as their precursor and cause. The pieces also assert commonalities across descendants of enslaved and indentured people, as well as refugees. These voyages imperil both physical and psychic survival; they also unite those who suffer through them. As Danticat's narrator observes, "There are no borderlines on the sea."

At the same time that these readings dramatize the many commonalities among migrants, *The Penguin Book of Migration Literature* helps us break apart, or dis-aggregate, the concept of migration. Intersecting categories like race, gender, sexuality, class, physical ability, language, age, and legal status profoundly structure one's experience of migration. For people from Black-majority countries, endemic anti-Black racism can come as a shock. In her poem "Home" (a spoken version of "Conversations About Home," included here), Warsan Shire records the violent and hostile epithets "go home blacks / refugees / dirty immigrants / asylum seekers / sucking our country dry," and worse. In his memoir *To Sir, With Love*, E. R. Braithwaite records how, when seeking employment in London after serving in World War II, "I had just been brought face to face with something I had either forgotten or completely ignored for more than six exciting years—my black skin." Within a xenophobic destination, visible markers of religious faith can be as perilous as dark skin. In Shauna Singh Baldwin's short story "Montreal

1962," the narrator's husband finds that "I could have the job if I take off my turban and cut my hair short." Migrants from particularly marginalized groups undergo a sense of hypervisibility and a pressure to positively represent their entire perceived demographic, as Baldwin, Braithwaite, Selvon, and others of our authors illustrate. At the same time, racism can become an assimilation ritual for non-Black immigrants: solidarity among new arrivals and local communities of color may exist but isn't guaranteed.

Gender, too, heavily influences the experience of migration. Across countries and over time, destination countries have shaped their populations by legislating preferences for specific genders, historically gendered professions, and domestic configurations—for example, single men (as in the case of Chinese workers on nineteenth-century US railroads), single women (as in Filipina nurses around the world), or heteronormative nuclear family units (as in family-based immigration policies in Europe and the United States). Border rape and predatory smugglers may add trauma for all migrants but especially those who identify as female. Further, being a migrant of a gender or sexual minority can make one particularly vulnerable, especially since family-based immigration policies become implicitly heteronormative if a destination country fails to authorize gay marriage. Shani Mootoo's unassuming but complex short story "Out on Main Street" portrays its narrator navigating swirling eddies of racial, national, sexual, and gender identities. Her story guides us past our possibly limited, proscriptive definitions of family and community.

These readings also allow us to observe a further linked set of factors related to social class: namely, income, occupation, education, language, region of origin (country or city), and immigration status (authorized or undocumented, with much gray space in between). In Otsuka's "Come, Japanese!," class status fragments the narrator's collective "we" into "some of us . . . and some of us." As the narrator tells us, "the girls from first class had never once said hello from beneath their violet silk parasols in all the times they had walked past us up above on the deck." Similarly, in "Children of the Sea," one of Danticat's narrators reports that his fellow refugees "get into arguments and they say to one another, 'It is only my misfortune that would lump me together with an indigent like you.'" Tapping into the critical importance of immigration status and employment status, Deepak Unnikrishnan writes of the "Temporary. People. / Illegal. People. / Ephemeral. People. / Gone. People" whose lives differ radically from permanent migrants. The official discourses of migration employ deceptively discrete categories—economic migrant, refugee, asylum seeker, expatriate, student, stateless person, trafficking victim—that in reality overlap and blur. These literary texts bring to life both the significance and the instability of such categories.

The intersectional categories multiply. As our literary texts demonstrate, much depends on when, how, and to where one emigrates. Policies of destination countries—for instance *jus soli* (citizenship by birth location) versus *jus sanguinis* (citizenship by parents' ethnic origin)—significantly affect migrant lives, as do tolerance, or lack thereof, for minority religious practices. Many of the characters we will meet here have been shaped by multiple diasporas—e.g., the Afro-Caribbean Londoners in Selvon's "Come Back to Grenada," and the Indo-Caribbean Vancouverites in Mootoo's "Out on Main Street." As Mootoo's narrator observes sardonically, "I used to think I was a Hindu *par excellence* until I come up here and see real flesh and blood Indian from India." Timing matters as well. Selvon shows how an earlier migration can cushion the impact for later arrivals: "George can't help thinking how things change a lot since he first come England, how now it have so many spades that you bouncing up with one every corner you turn." Djamila Ibrahim narrates the seldom told story of migrant domestic workers threatened by civil war in an already hazardous destination. Depending on the author's perspective and characters' or poetic speakers' experience, we may see isolation or community; dehumanization or empathy; trauma or triumph.

Appropriately for the vast difference in the experiences portrayed, *The Penguin Book of Migration Literature* also encompasses a variety of literary styles and techniques. Here are love stories, coming-of-age stories, school stories, and travel narratives; tight rhymes, gliding free verse, and experimental lyrics; heartrending tales and wryly humorous observations. Just as there is no singular migrant experience, there are myriad ways of writing about migration.

I have divided our literary texts into four sections—departures, arrivals, generations, and returns—with the aim of imparting the full range of the migration experience, from the complex and often ambivalent decision to emigrate; to the act of relocating; to the process of adjusting to a new home; to the lives of migrants' first-generation children; to the backflow of many migrations. While useful, this structure implies a unidirectionality that the readings themselves will helpfully disrupt. Similarly, I have arranged each section chronologically according to the time period during which each piece takes place; again, this organization felt generally useful, but may obscure the historical and aesthetic present of each writer. In other words, many of our writers (like Julie Otsuka, or NourbeSe Philip, to name only two) are deeply immersed in a bygone period yet also informed by the political concerns and narrative innovations of their own time. I hope that readers will keep in mind the many links among and across these chronologically ordered sections.

DEPARTURES

The stories and poems in our opening section present the reasons why people migrate—or don't. As mentioned above, I felt it important to counter a simplistic, unidirectional immigration narrative by acknowledging migrants as people with deep histories—individual as well as collective—that predate their migration, rather than newly created humans whose lives begin on a boat, plane, or desert crossing. We will see homelands portrayed as idyllic (as in Equiano's *Interesting Narrative* and Eva Hoffman's *Lost in Translation*) or hellish (as in Shire's "Conversations About Home"). In the category of voluntary and semivoluntary migrants, many are motivated by misleading myths

generated in destination countries. Otsuka's voyagers believe
that "in America the women did not have to work in the fields
and there was plenty of rice and firewood for all. And wherever
you went the men held open the doors and tipped their hats and
called out, 'Ladies first' and 'After you.'" In his autobiographi-
cal story "Under the Wire," Francisco Jiménez's brother tells
him that "people there sweep money off the streets." Djamila
Ibrahim, in her short story "Heading Somewhere," writes of
"young women who'd left Addis Ababa to work as maids in
Saudi Arabia, Syria, and elsewhere, light on luggage and high
on anticipation for a better life." The protagonist of Marina
Lewycka's *Strawberry Fields* seeks out a scene "just like En-
gland is supposed to be." Poet Dunya Mikhail goes further, to
imagine "another planet / beyond this Earth," free of war,
weapons, and police. Here she shares the utopian strain seen in
many of these readings, including those that depict escape from
the most horrific conditions. These writers can always see a bet-
ter world, even if it lies past the solar system or (as in Equiano
and Danticat) at the bottom of the sea.

This section also conveys the trauma of children left behind,
rarely discussed but seen here in Edwidge Danticat's exquisite
foreword and Paulette Ramsay's epistolary novella *Aunt Jen*, as
well as elsewhere in Lisa Harewood's short film *Auntie*, Hare-
wood's vital Barrel Stories oral history project, and the com-
passionate and illuminating documentary *The Other Side of
Immigration* (all listed, along with many others, in the "Sug-
gestions for Further Reading and Viewing" at the end of this
book). After all, those who stay home—whether by choice or
otherwise—also belong in the complex story of migration.

ARRIVALS

In our next section, many migrants find that their destination
falls far short of the alluring promises that those migrating vol-
untarily, at least, had been given. The women in Otsuka's story
learn that "the letters we had been written had been written to

us by people other than our husbands, professional people with beautiful handwriting whose job it was to tell lies and win hearts." In Baldwin's "Montreal 1962," the narrator observes bitterly that "this was not how they described emigrating to Canada. . . . No one said then, 'You must be reborn white-skinned—and clean-shaven to show it—to survive.'" Migrants find themselves reduced to the labor they can provide, as Emine Sevgi Özdamar's narrator reveals in *The Bridge of the Golden Horn*: "While we were working we lived in a single picture: our fingers, the neon light, the tweezers, the little radio valves and their spider legs." They are beset by nostalgia, as Claude Mc-Kay's poetic speaker conveys in "The Tropics in New York," when, "hungry for the old, familiar ways, / I turned aside and bowed my head and wept." As well as the lost geographies of home, they may long for far-flung family members separated by cost or by law, and for missed milestones like births, weddings, and funerals.

In an environment that is at best indifferent and at worst murderously hostile, there are also compensations. Like the journey, the arrival may be made bearable by other people. Selvon writes: "Long time George used to feel lonely little bit, but all that finish with since so much West Indian come London." Migrants build communities that are not only national, ethnic, and racial, but also affiliative in other, undefinable ways—for example the connection between Punjabi taxi driver Parvez and English prostitute Bettina in Hanif Kureishi's "My Son the Fanatic" (included as part of our "Generations" section but also relevant here). Throughout this section, as Edwidge Danticat explains in her foreword, the concept of "home" undergoes radical redefinition. Turning to Selvon once more: "When he think 'bout home it does look so far away that he feel as if he don't belong there no more." In all these selections, adaptation is gradual and nonlinear, as Unnikrishnan imparts in his staccato line "Acclimatizing. Homesick. / Lovelorn. Giddy." In that process of adaptation, migrants reinvent the seemingly static national identities of both origin and destination countries.

GENERATIONS

The next section contains readings that depict the experience of children and adults with migrant parents. This is another fuzzy category within the discourse on migration, as most commentators use "first generation" while others use "second generation" to denote the offspring of migrants. Both terms are imperfect, in that both erase the previous generations in origin countries; both are also overly clean-cut, in that many migrants travel as children themselves, and thus could make up a "generation .5" or "generation 1.5" (depending on the numbering system). In any case, it seemed important to include the reality of these offspring, whom some writers describe as caught between worlds. In "The Time of the Peacock," Mena Abdullah explores the sensation of control—or lack thereof—over one's surroundings: for young Nimmi, growing up in an Indian family in rural Australia, "the hills were wrong." For Zadie Smith's teenaged Irie Jones in *White Teeth*, not the landscape but her own body is wrong. Mehdi Charef's narrator characterizes protagonist Majid in terms that sum up many first-generation experiences around the world: "For a long time he's been neither French nor Arab. He's the son of immigrants—caught between two cultures, two histories, two languages, and two colours of skin." For Marjane Satrapi, who moved from Iran to Austria as a young adult, "The harder I tried to assimilate, the more I had the feeling that I was distancing myself from my culture, betraying my parents and my origins, that I was playing a game by somebody else's rules." To Shani Mootoo's doubly diasporic Indo-Trinidadian-Canadian narrator, "we is watered-down Indians—we ain't good grade A Indians." Charef, Kureishi, and others dramatize the parent-child conflict that takes its particular shape from the condition of migrancy. In "Green," Sefi Atta's young narrator differentiates herself from the embarrassing "they" of her Nigerian immigrant parents: "'What's it like being African?' my friend Celeste asked when we used to be friends. 'I don't know,' I told her. I was protecting my parents. I didn't want Celeste to know the secret about Africans.

Bones in meat are very important to them. They suck the bones and it's so frustrating I could cry." However, that isn't the whole story: other writers voice a triumphant mood of presence and innovation. Safia Elhillo's elegantly woven poem "origin stories (reprise)" consists of multiplying and competing origin narratives that eventually settle calmly into a strong matrilineal sense of self. Atta's "Green" closes with the exultant sequence "This is it. Me, scoring. My mom looking like she loves soccer. My dad looking like he really loves the President. Three of us, looking like we really belong." Tato Laviera's vibrant poem "AmeRícan" defies a simplistic model of assimilation as cultural loss, insisting that "we blend / and mix all that is good!" By revising "American" into "AmeRícan," Laviera shows how Puerto Rican internal migrants alter their destination as well as themselves, just as Selvon's migrants forcefully transform Britain into Brit'n. Food, music, religion, names, language: every element of both origin and host cultures changes irrevocably as new generations evolve and thrive.

RETURNS

Many of the pieces throughout *The Penguin Book of Migration Literature* emphasize the continual and multidirectional nature of migration, which is not a discrete process but an ongoing condition. Therefore I have also included a brief, one-item mini-section to reinforce that sense of flux. Some of the migrations included here may be permanent, but others (such as those depicted in Unnikrishnan's and Lewycka's excerpts) are temporary or partial. In Laviera's description, "across forth and across back / back across and forth back / forth across and back and forth / our trips are walking bridges!" And even when migrations are physically permanent, homelands still linger on an emotional level. This last section consists solely of Pauline Kaldas's short story "A Conversation," which captures a dilemma common to many migrants and their children. Kaldas's unresolved dialogue stands in eloquently for a number of other literary explorations of migrant returns, such as Chimamanda

Ngozi Adichie's *Americanah*, Naomi Jackson's *The Star Side of Bird Hill*, Tayeb Salih's *Season of Migration to the North*, and Zoë Wicomb's *October*. These works present a multifaceted and composite vision of migration that is more complex than my own table of contents might indicate.

The Penguin Book of Migration Literature contains those poems, stories, and excerpts that I have most enjoyed teaching, and feel most compelled to share with a wider audience. My selections are inevitably subjective and massively incomplete; there is practically an infinite number of other gorgeous and compelling works that I could have included. For this reason I have added a list of reading and viewing suggestions at the end of the volume—print sources as well as film and online materials. Here I have gathered many titles that I would have loved to include but could not for reasons of space. While I aimed for a wide range of migrations and migration experiences, given the breadth of the topic, many significant migration routes do not appear in this anthology. The "Suggestions for Further Reading and Viewing" is more comprehensive, comprising important routes (Europe to the United States; West Africa to France; Latin America to Spain); aspects of the migration experience (sex trafficking; statelessness; long-term detention; family separation at borders); and specific catastrophic events (Russian pogroms against Jews; the Armenian genocide; the Holocaust; the 1947 Partition of India and Pakistan; the 1948 Palestinian Nakba; mass exoduses driven by armed conflict, in Vietnam, Liberia, Rwanda, and Yugoslavia, among other places). Like the table of contents, the "Suggestions for Further Reading and Viewing" indicates the specific migration routes depicted in a particular text or film.

When planning the anthology I omitted some older materials (such as John Winthrop's "A Model of Christian Charity") that would have enriched the collection but that I felt had already been widely circulated elsewhere; Penguin Classics features an impressive collection of historical writings on European exploration and migration, including the travel writings of Marco Polo, Columbus, and Cabeza de Vaca, as well as the *Mayflower*

Papers, to which readers may turn. I steered away, as well, from nineteenth- and early-twentieth-century US-based writings likely to appear in multiple anthologies of US immigrant literature. Many of these, too, are available in Penguin Classics, from Mary Antin's *The Promised Land* to Anzia Yezierska's *Hungry Hearts*.

The writings collected here represent only a sliver of literature on migration. Indeed, one could commit to reading *only* fiction and poetry about migration and still barely scratch the surface of this critical topic. The history of migration, after all, is the history of humanity. Even the supplementary list of suggestions for further reading and viewing is itself necessarily incomplete: migrations will continue; migrants will suffer and flourish; new migration stories will be written, sung, painted, filmed, and coded. I encourage interested readers to visit the website migrationliterature.weebly.com, where I will keep an ongoing list of migration literature to which I invite you to contribute.

In closing, I will turn to our contents pages and ask readers to consider how the bleakness of the first epigraph ("no one leaves home unless home is the mouth of a shark") contrasts with the optimism of the last one ("defining myself my own way any way many / many ways"). It is up to those of us already in destination countries to mitigate the former and ensure the latter—and to act toward better conditions in origin countries—so that all migrations may be as optional and joyous as they are enriching.

DOHRA AHMAD

The Penguin Book
of Migration Literature

DEPARTURES

*no one leaves home unless
home is the mouth of a shark*

—WARSAN SHIRE, "HOME"

OLAUDAH EQUIANO

From
THE INTERESTING
NARRATIVE OF THE LIFE
OF OLAUDAH EQUIANO

CHAPTER I

. . .

That part of Africa, known by the name of Guinea, to which
the trade for slaves is carried on, extends along the coast above
3400 miles, from the Senegal to Angola, and includes a variety
of kingdoms. Of these the most considerable is the kingdom of
Benen, both as to extent and wealth, the richness and cultiva-
tion of the soil, the power of its king, and the number and
warlike disposition of the inhabitants . . . This kingdom is di-
vided into many provinces or districts: in one of the most re-
mote and fertile of which, called Eboe, I was born, in the year
1745, in a charming fruitful vale, named Essaka. The distance
of this province from the capital of Benin and the sea coast
must be very considerable; for I had never heard of white men
or Europeans, nor of the sea . . .

As we live in a country where nature is prodigal of her fa-
vours, our wants are few and easily supplied; of course we have
few manufactures. They consist for the most part of calicoes,
earthern ware, ornaments, and instruments of war and hus-
bandry. But these make no part of our commerce, the principal
articles of which, as I have observed, are provisions. In such a
state money is of little use; however we have some small pieces
of coin, if I may call them such. They are made something
like an anchor; but I do not remember either their value or

denomination. We have also markets, at which I have been fre-
quently with my mother. These are sometimes visited by stout
mahogany-coloured men from the south west of us: we call
them Oye-Eboe, which term signifies red men living at a dis-
tance. They generally bring us fire-arms, gunpowder, hats,
beads, and dried fish. The last we esteemed a great rarity, as our
waters were only brooks and springs. These articles they barter
with us for odoriferous woods and earth, and our salt of wood
ashes. They always carry slaves through our land; but the strict-
est account is exacted of their manner of procuring them before
they are suffered to pass. Sometimes indeed we sold slaves to
them, but they were only prisoners of war, or such among us as
had been convicted of kidnapping, or adultery, and some other
crimes, which we esteemed heinous. This practice of kidnap-
ping induces me to think, that, notwithstanding all our strict-
ness, their principal business among us was to trepan our
people. I remember too they carried great sacks along with
them, which not long after I had an opportunity of fatally see-
ing applied to that infamous purpose.

Our land is uncommonly rich and fruitful, and produces all
kinds of vegetables in great abundance. We have plenty of In-
dian corn, and vast quantities of cotton and tobacco. Our pine
apples grow without culture; they are about the size of the larg-
est sugar-loaf, and finely flavoured. We have also spices of dif-
ferent kinds, particularly pepper; and a variety of delicious
fruits which I have never seen in Europe; together with gums of
various kinds, and honey in abundance. All our industry is ex-
erted to improve those blessings of nature. Agriculture is our
chief employment; and every one, even the children and women,
are engaged in it. Thus we are all habituated to labour from
our earliest years. Every one contributes something to the com-
mon stock; and as we are unacquainted with idleness, we have
no beggars. The benefits of such a mode of living are obvious.
The West India planters prefer the slaves of Benin or Eboe to
those of any other part of Guinea, for their hardiness, intelli-
gence, integrity, and zeal . . .

. . .

Such is the imperfect sketch my memory has furnished me

with of the manners and customs of a people among whom I first drew my breath . . .

CHAPTER II

. . .

I have already acquainted the reader with the time and place of my birth. My father, besides many slaves, had a numerous family, of which seven lived to grow up, including myself and a sister, who was the only daughter. As I was the youngest of the sons, I became, of course, the greatest favourite with my mother, and was always with her; and she used to take particular pains to form my mind. I was trained up from my earliest years in the art of war; my daily exercise was shooting and throwing javelins; and my mother adorned me with emblems, after the manner of our greatest warriors. In this way I grew up till I was turned the age of eleven, when an end was put to my happiness in the following manner:—Generally when the grown people in the neighbourhood were gone far in the fields to labour, the children assembled together in some of the neighbours' premises to play; and commonly some of us used to get up a tree to look out for any assailant, or kidnapper, that might come upon us; for they sometimes took those opportunities of our parents' absence to attack and carry off as many as they could seize. One day, as I was watching at the top of a tree in our yard, I saw one of those people come into the yard of our next neighbour but one, to kidnap, there being many stout young people in it. Immediately on this I gave the alarm of the rogue, and he was surrounded by the stoutest of them, who entangled him with cords, so that he could not escape till some of the grown people came and secured him. But alas! ere long it was my fate to be thus attacked, and to be carried off, when none of the grown people were nigh. One day, when all our people were gone out to their works as usual, and only I and my dear sister were left to mind the house, two men and a woman got over our walls, and in a moment seized us both, and, without giving us time to cry out, or make resistance, they stopped our mouths, and ran off with us into the nearest wood. Here they tied our hands, and continued to carry us as far as they could, till night came on, when we reached a small house, where the robbers halted for refreshment, and spent the night. We were then unbound, but were unable to take any food; and, being quite overpowered by fatigue and grief, our only relief was some sleep, which allayed our misfortune for a short time. The next morning we left the house, and continued travelling all the day. For a long time we had kept the woods, but at last we came into a road which I believed I knew. I had now some hopes of being delivered; for we had advanced but a little way before I discovered some people at a distance, on which I began to cry out for their assistance: but my cries had no other effect than to make them tie me faster and stop my mouth, and then they put me into a large sack. They also stopped my sister's mouth, and tied her hands; and in this manner we proceeded till we were out of the sight of these people. When we went to rest the following night they offered us some victuals; but we refused it; and the only comfort we had was in being in one another's arms all that night, and bathing each other with our tears. But alas! we were soon deprived of even the small comfort of weeping together. The next day proved a day of greater sorrow than I had yet experienced; for my sister and I were then separated, while we lay clasped in each other's arms. It was in vain that we besought them not to part us; she was torn from me, and immediately carried away, while I was left in a state of distraction not to be described. I cried and grieved continually; and for several days I did not eat any thing but what they forced into my mouth. At length, after many days travelling, during which I had often changed masters, I got into the hands of a chieftain, in a very pleasant country. This man had two wives and some children, and they all used me extremely well, and did all they could to comfort me; particularly the first wife, who was something like my mother. Although I was a great many days journey from my father's house, yet these people spoke exactly the same language with us . . .

Soon after this my master's only daughter, and child by his first wife, sickened and died, which affected him so much that for some time he was almost frantic, and really would have killed himself, had he not been watched and prevented. However, in a small time afterwards he recovered, and I was again sold. I was now carried to the left of the sun's rising, through many different countries, and a number of large woods. The people I was sold to used to carry me very often, when I was tired, either on their shoulders or on their backs. I saw many convenient well-built sheds along the roads, at proper distances, to accommodate the merchants and travellers, who lay in those buildings along with their wives, who often accompany them; and they always go well armed.

From the time I left my own nation I always found somebody that understood me till I came to the sea coast. The languages of different nations did not totally differ, nor were they so copious as those of the Europeans, particularly the English. They were therefore easily learned; and, while I was journeying thus through Africa, I acquired two or three different tongues. In this manner I had been travelling for a considerable time, when one evening, to my great surprise, whom should I see brought to the house where I was but my dear sister! As soon as she saw me she gave a loud shriek, and ran into my arms—I was quite overpowered: neither of us could speak; but, for a considerable time, clung to each other in mutual embraces, unable to do any thing but weep. Our meeting affected all who saw us; and indeed I must acknowledge, in honour of those sable destroyers of human rights, that I never met with any ill treatment, or saw any offered to their slaves, except tying them, when necessary, to keep them from running away. When these people knew we were brother and sister they indulged us together; and the man, to whom I supposed we belonged, lay with us, he in the middle, while she and I held one another by the hands across his breast all night; and thus for a while we forgot our misfortunes in the joy of being together: but even this small comfort was soon to have an end; for scarcely had the fatal morning appeared, when she was again torn from me for ever! I was now more miserable, if possible, than before. The small relief which her presence gave me from pain was gone, and the wretchedness of my situation was redoubled by my anxiety after her fate, and my apprehensions lest her sufferings should be greater than mine, when I could not be with her to alleviate them. Yes, thou dear partner of all my childish sports! thou sharer of my joys and sorrows! happy should I have ever esteemed myself to encounter every misery for you, and to procure your freedom by the sacrifice of my own. Though you were early forced from my arms, your image has been always rivetted in my heart, from which neither *time nor fortune* have been able to remove it; so that, while the thoughts of your sufferings have damped my prosperity, they have mingled with adversity and increased its bitterness. To that Heaven which protects the weak from the strong, I commit the care of your innocence and virtues, if they have not already received their full reward, and if your youth and delicacy have not long since fallen victims to the violence of the African trader, the pestilential stench of a Guinea ship, the seasoning in the European colonies, or the lash and lust of a brutal and unrelenting overseer.

I did not long remain after my sister. I was again sold, and carried through a number of places, till, after travelling a considerable time, I came to a town called Tinmah, in the most beautiful country I have yet seen in Africa. It was extremely rich, and there were many rivulets which flowed through it, and supplied a large pond in the centre of the town, where the people washed. Here I first saw and tasted cocoa-nuts, which I thought superior to any nuts I had ever tasted before; and the trees, which were loaded, were also interspersed amongst the houses, which had commodious shades adjoining, and were in the same manner as ours, the insides being neatly plastered and whitewashed. Here I also saw and tasted for the first time sugar-cane. Their money consisted of little white shells, the size of the finger nail. I was sold here for one hundred and seventy-two of them by a merchant who lived and brought me there . . .

The first object which saluted my eyes when I arrived on the coast was the sea, and a slave ship, which was then riding at anchor, and waiting for its cargo. These filled me with astonishment, which was soon converted into terror when I was carried on board. I was immediately handled and tossed up to see if I were sound by some of the crew; and I was now persuaded that I had gotten into a world of bad spirits, and that they were going to kill me. Their complexions too differing so much from ours, their long hair, and the language they spoke, (which was very different from any I had ever heard) united to confirm me in this belief. Indeed such were the horrors of my views and fears at the moment, that, if ten thousand worlds had been my own, I would have freely parted with them all to have exchanged my condition with that of the meanest slave in my own country. When I looked round the ship too and saw a large furnace or copper boiling, and a multitude of black people of every description chained together, every one of their countenances expressing dejection and sorrow, I no longer doubted of my fate; and, quite overpowered with horror and anguish, I fell motionless on the deck and fainted. When I recovered a little I found some black people about me, who I believed were some of those who brought me on board, and had been receiving their pay; they talked to me in order to cheer me, but all in vain. I asked them if we were not to be eaten by those white men with horrible looks, red faces, and loose hair. They told me I was not; and one of the crew brought me a small portion of spirituous liquor in a wine glass; but, being afraid of him, I would not take it out of his hand. One of the blacks therefore took it from him and gave it to me, and I took a little down my palate, which, instead of reviving me, as they thought it would, threw me into the greatest consternation at the strange feeling it produced, having never tasted any such liquor before. Soon after this the blacks who brought me on board went off, and left me abandoned to despair. I now saw myself deprived of all chance of returning to my native country, or even the least glimpse of hope of gaining the shore, which I now considered as friendly; and I even wished for my former slavery in preference to my present situation, which was filled with horrors of every kind, still heightened by my ignorance of what I was to undergo. I was not long suffered to indulge my grief; I was soon put down under the decks, and there I received such a salutation in my nostrils as I had never experienced in my life: so that, with the loathsomeness of the stench, and crying together, I became so sick and low that I was not able to eat, nor had I the least desire to taste any thing. I now wished for the last friend, death, to relieve me; but soon, to my grief, two of the white men offered me eatables; and, on my refusing to eat, one of them held me fast by the hands, and laid me across I think the windlass, and tied my feet, while the other flogged me severely. I had never experienced any thing of this kind before; and although, not being used to the water, I naturally feared that element the first time I saw it, yet nevertheless, could I have got over the nettings, I would have jumped over the side, but I could not; and, besides, the crew used to watch us very closely who were not chained down to the decks, lest we should leap into the water: and I have seen some of these poor African prisoners most severely cut for attempting to do so, and hourly whipped for not eating. This indeed was often the case with myself. In a little time after, amongst the poor chained men, I found some of my own nation, which in a small degree gave ease to my mind. I inquired of these what was to be done with us; they gave me to understand we were to be carried to these white people's country to work for them. I then was a little revived, and thought, if it were no worse than working, my situation was not so desperate: but still I feared I should be put to death, the white people looked and acted, as I thought, in so savage a manner; for I had never seen among any people such instances of brutal cruelty; and this not only shewn towards us blacks, but also to some of the whites themselves. One white man in particular I saw, when we were permitted to be on deck, flogged so unmercifully with a large rope near the foremast, that he died in consequence of it; and they tossed him over the side as they would have done a brute. This made me fear these people the more; and I expected nothing less than to be treated in the same manner. I could not help expressing my fears and apprehensions to some of my countrymen: I asked them if these people had no country, but lived in this hollow place (the ship): they told me they did not, but came from a distant one. 'Then,' said I, 'how comes it in all our country we never heard of them?' They told me because they lived so very far off. I then asked where were their women? had they any like themselves? I was told they had: 'and why,' said I, 'do we not see them?' they answered, because they were left behind. I asked how the vessel could go? they told me they could not tell; but that there were cloths put upon the masts by the help of the ropes I saw, and then the vessel went on; and the white men had some spell or magic they put in the water when they liked in order to stop the vessel. I was exceedingly amazed at this account, and really thought they were spirits. I therefore wished much to be from amongst them, for I expected they would sacrifice me: but my wishes were vain; for we were so quartered that it was impossible for any of us to make our escape. While we stayed on the coast I was mostly on deck; and one day, to my great astonishment, I saw one of these vessels coming in with the sails up. As soon as the whites saw it, they gave a great shout, at which we were amazed; and the more so as the vessel appeared larger by approaching nearer. At last she came to an anchor in my sight, and when the anchor was let go I and my countrymen who saw it were lost in astonishment to observe the vessel stop; and were not convinced it was done by magic. Soon after this the other ship got her boats out, and they came on board of us, and the people of both ships seemed very glad to see each other. Several of the strangers also shook hands with us black people, and made motions with their hands, signifying I suppose we were to go to their country; but we did not understand them. At last, when the ship we were in had got in all her cargo, they made ready with many fearful noises, and we were all put under deck, so that we could not see how they managed the vessel. But this disappointment was the least of my sorrow. The stench of the hold while we were on the coast was so intolerably loathsome, that it was dangerous to remain there for any time, and some of us had been permitted to stay on the deck for the fresh air; but now that the whole ship's cargo were confined together, it became absolutely pestilential. The closeness of the place, and the heat of the climate, added to the number in the ship, which was so crowded that each had scarcely room to turn himself, almost suffocated us. This produced copious perspirations, so that the air soon became unfit for respiration, from a variety of loathsome smells, and brought on a sickness among the slaves, of which many died, thus falling victims to the improvident avarice, as I may call it, of their purchasers. This wretched situation was again aggravated by the galling of the chains, now become insupportable; and the filth of the necessary tubs, into which the children often fell, and were almost suffocated. The shrieks of the women, and the groans of the dying, rendered the whole a scene of horror almost inconceivable. Happily perhaps for myself I was soon reduced so low here that it was thought necessary to keep me almost always on deck; and from my extreme youth I was not put in fetters. In this situation I expected every hour to share the fate of my companions, some of whom were almost daily brought upon deck at the point of death, which I began to hope would soon put an end to my miseries. Often did I think many of the inhabitants of the deep much more happy than myself. I envied them the freedom they enjoyed, and as often wished I could change my condition for theirs. Every circumstance I met with served only to render my state more painful, and heighten my apprehensions, and my opinion of the cruelty of the whites. One day they had taken a number of fishes; and when they had killed and satisfied themselves with as many as they thought fit, to our astonishment who were on the deck, rather than give any of them to us to eat as we expected, they tossed the remaining fish into the sea again, although we begged and prayed for some as well as we could, but in vain; and some of my countrymen, being pressed by hunger, took an opportunity, when they thought no one saw them, of trying to get a little privately; but they were discovered, and the attempt procured them some very severe floggings. One day, when we had a smooth sea and moderate wind, two of my wearied countrymen who were chained together (I was near them at the time), preferring death to such a life of misery, somehow made through the nettings and jumped into the sea: immediately another quite dejected fellow, who, on account of his illness, was suffered to be out of irons, also followed their example; and I believe many more would very soon have done the same if they had not been prevented by the ship's crew, who were instantly alarmed. Those of us that were the most active were in a moment put down under the deck, and there was such a noise and confusion amongst the people of the ship as I never heard before, to stop her, and get the boat out to go after the slaves. However two of the wretches were drowned, but they got the other, and afterwards flogged him unmercifully for thus attempting to prefer death to slavery. In this manner we continued to undergo more hardships than I can now relate, hardships which are inseparable from this accursed trade. Many a time we were near suffocation from the want of fresh air, which we were often without for whole days together. This, and the stench of the necessary tubs, carried off many. During our passage I first saw flying fishes, which surprised me very much: they used frequently to fly across the ship, and many of them fell on the deck. I also now first saw the use of the quadrant; I had often with astonishment seen the mariners make observations with it, and I could not think what it meant. They at last took notice of my surprise; and one of them, willing to increase it, as well as to gratify my curiosity, made me one day look through it. The clouds appeared to me to be land, which disappeared as they passed along. This heightened my wonder; and I was now more persuaded than ever that I was in another world, and that every thing about me was magic. At last we came in sight of the island of Barbadoes, at which the whites on board gave a great shout, and made many signs of joy to us. We did not know what to think of this; but as the vessel drew nearer we plainly saw the harbour, and other ships of different kinds and sizes; and we soon anchored amongst them off Bridge Town. Many merchants and planters now came on board, though it was in the evening. They put us in separate parcels, and examined us attentively. They also made us jump, and pointed to the land, signifying we were to go there. We thought by this we should be eaten by these ugly men, as they appeared to us; and, when soon after we were all put down under the deck again, there was much dread and trembling among us, and nothing but bitter cries to be heard all the night from these apprehensions, insomuch that at last the white people got some old slaves from the land to pacify us. They told us we were not to be eaten, but to work, and were soon to go on land, where we should see many of our country people. This report eased us much; and sure enough, soon after we were landed, there came to us Africans of all languages . . .

We were not many days in the merchant's custody before we were sold after their usual manner, which is this:—On a signal given, (as the beat of a drum) the buyers rush at once into the yard where the slaves are confined, and make choice of that parcel they like best. The noise and clamour with which this is attended, and the eagerness visible in the countenances of the buyers, serve not a little to increase the apprehensions of the terrified Africans, who may well be supposed to consider them as the ministers of that destruction to which they think themselves devoted. In this manner, without scruple, are relations and friends separated, most of them never to see each other again. I remember in the vessel in which I was brought over, in the men's apartment, there were several brothers, who, in the sale, were sold in different lots; and it was very moving on this occasion to see and hear their cries at parting. O, ye nominal Christians! might not an African ask you, learned you this from your God, who says unto you, Do unto all men as you would men should do unto you? Is it not enough that we are torn from our country and friends to toil for your luxury and lust of gain? Must every tender feeling be likewise sacrificed to your avarice? Are the dearest friends and relations, now rendered more dear by their separation from their kindred, still to be parted from each other, and thus prevented from cheering the gloom of slavery with the small comfort of being together and mingling their sufferings and sorrows? Why are parents to lose their children, brothers their sisters, or husbands their wives? Surely this is a new refinement in cruelty, which, while it has no advantage to atone for it, thus aggravates distress, and adds fresh horrors even to the wretchedness of slavery.

M. NOURBESE PHILIP

ZONG! #5

There is no telling this story; it must be told:
In 1781 a fully provisioned ship, the *Zong*,[1] captained by one
Luke Collingwood, leaves from the West Coast[2] of Africa with
a cargo of 470 slaves and sets sail for Jamaica. As is the cus-
tom, the cargo is fully insured. Instead of the customary six to
nine weeks, this fateful trip will take some four months on ac-
count of navigational errors on the part of the captain. Some of
the *Zong*'s cargo is lost through illness and lack of water; many
others, by order of the captain are destroyed: "Sixty negroes
died for want of water . . . and forty others . . . through thirst
and frenzy . . . threw themselves into the sea and were drowned;
and the master and mariners . . . were obliged to throw over-
board 150 other negroes."[3]
Captain Luke Collingwood is of the belief that if the African
slaves on board die a natural death, the owners of the ship will
have to bear the cost, but if they were "thrown alive into the
sea, it would be the loss of the underwriters."[4] In other words,
the massacre of the African slaves would prove to be more

1. The name of the ship was the *Zorg*, meaning "care" in Dutch. An error
was made when the name was repainted.

2. The ship left from the island of São Tomé off the coast of Gabon.

3. Gregson vs. Gilbert, 3 Dougl. 233. The case mentions 150 slaves killed.
James Walvin in *Black Ivory*, 131, others 130 and 132. The exact number of
African slaves murdered remains a slippery signifier of what was undoubt-
edly a massacre.

4. *Substance of the Debate on a Resolution for Abolishing the Slave Trade*,
London, 1806, pp. 178–9.

financially advantageous to the owners of the ship and its cargo than if the slaves were allowed to die of "natural causes."

Upon the ship's return to Liverpool, the ship's owners, the Messrs Gregson, make a claim under maritime insurance for the destroyed cargo, which the insurers, the Messrs Gilbert, refuse to pay. The ship's owners begin legal action against their insurers to recover their loss. A jury finds the insurers liable and orders them to compensate the ship's owners for their losses— their murdered slaves. The insurers, in turn, appeal the jury's decision . . . The three justices, Willes, Butler, and Mansfield, agree that a new trial should be held. The report of that decision, *Gregson v. Gilbert*, the formal name of the case more colloquially known as the *Zong* case, is the text I rely on to create the poems of *Zong!* To not tell the story that must be told.

ZONG! #5

     of

water

rains &

dead

        the more

     of

        the more

     of

negroes

             of

          water

          &

          weeks

            (three less than)

       rains

&

water

(three butts good)

of

sea and

perils

of water

(one day)

water—

day one . . .

of months

of

weeks

of

days

of

sustenance

lying

dead

  of

                                                        days

                                                of

                                        sour water

                                        enemies &

                want

        of

                died

                (seven out of seventeen)

                of

                                good

                        (the more of)

                of

        (eighteen instead of six)

                                dead

                                of rains

                                        (eleven days)

        of

        weeks

                (thirty not three)

                    of

                                        water

                                            day one . . .

for sustenance

                                            water

                                                day

one . . .
one day's

                                            water

                                                day

one . . .
sour

                                            water

                                                day

one . . .
three butts good

                            of voyage

                        (a month's)

of necessity

sufficient

and

last

the more

of

exist

want &

less than

of did not

&

the more of

of suffered

did not

exist

sustenance

water &

want

of

        dead

           the more of

of negroes

                      the more

           of

              instead

           of

JULIE OTSUKA

COME, JAPANESE!

On the boat we were mostly virgins. We had long black hair and flat wide feet and we were not very tall. Some of us had eaten nothing but rice gruel as young girls and had slightly bowed legs, and some of us were only fourteen years old and were still young girls ourselves. Some of us came from the city, and wore stylish city clothes, but many more of us came from the country and on the boat we wore the same old kimonos we'd been wearing for years—faded hand-me-downs from our sisters that had been patched and redyed many times. Some of us came from the mountains, and had never before seen the sea, except for in pictures, and some of us were the daughters of fishermen who had been around the sea all our lives. Perhaps we had lost a brother or father to the sea, or a fiancé, or perhaps someone we loved had jumped into the water one unhappy morning and simply swam away, and now it was time for us, too, to move on.

On the boat the first thing we did—before deciding who we liked and didn't like, before telling each other which one of the islands we were from, and why we were leaving, before even bothering to learn each other's names—was compare photographs of our husbands. They were handsome young men with dark eyes and full heads of hair and skin that was smooth and unblemished. Their chins were strong. Their posture, good. Their noses were straight and high. They looked like our brothers and fathers back home, only better dressed, in gray frock coats and fine Western three-piece suits. Some of them were standing on sidewalks in front of wooden A-frame houses with white picket fences and neatly mowed lawns, and some were leaning in driveways against Model T Fords. Some were sitting in studios on stiff high-backed chairs with their hands neatly folded and staring straight into the camera, as though they were ready to take on the world. All of them had promised to be there, waiting for us, in San Francisco, when we sailed into port.

On the boat, we often wondered: Would we like them? Would we love them? Would we recognize them from their pictures when we first saw them on the dock?

On the boat we slept down below, in steerage, where it was filthy and dim. Our beds were narrow metal racks stacked one on top of the other and our mattresses were hard and thin and darkened with the stains of other journeys, other lives. Our pillows were stuffed with dried wheat hulls. Scraps of food littered the passageways between berths and the floors were wet and slick. There was one porthole, and in the evening, after the hatch was closed, the darkness filled with whispers. Will it hurt? Bodies tossed and turned beneath the blankets. The sea rose and fell. The damp air stifled. At night we dreamed of our husbands. We dreamed of new wooden sandals and endless bolts of indigo silk and of living, one day, in a house with a chimney. We dreamed we were lovely and tall. We dreamed we were back in the rice paddies, which we had so desperately wanted to escape. The rice paddy dreams were always nightmares. We dreamed of our older and prettier sisters who had been sold to the geisha houses by our fathers so that the rest of us might eat, and when we woke we were gasping for air. For a second I thought I was her.

Our first few days on the boat we were seasick, and could not keep down our food, and had to make repeated trips to the railing. Some of us were so dizzy we could not even walk, and lay in our berths in a dull stupor, unable to remember our own names, not to mention those of our new husbands. Remind me one more time, I'm Mrs. Who? Some of us clutched our stomachs and prayed out loud to Kannon, the goddess of mercy— Where are you?—while others of us preferred to turn silently green. And often, in the middle of the night, we were jolted awake by a violent swell and for a brief moment we had no idea where we were, or why our beds would not stop moving, or why our hearts were pounding with such dread. Earthquake was the first thought that usually came to our minds. We reached out for our mothers then, in whose arms we had slept until the morning we left home. Were they sleeping now? Were they dreaming? Were they thinking of us night and day? Were they still walking three steps behind our fathers on the streets with their arms full of packages while our fathers carried nothing at all? Were they secretly envious of us for sailing away? Didn't I give you everything? Had they remembered to air out our old kimonos? Had they remembered to feed the cats? Had they made sure to tell us everything we needed to know? Hold your teacup with both hands, stay out of the sun, never say more than you have to.

Most of us on the boat were accomplished, and were sure we would make good wives. We knew how to cook and sew. We knew how to serve tea and arrange flowers and sit quietly on our flat wide feet for hours, saying absolutely nothing of substance at all. A girl must blend into a room: she must be present without appearing to exist. We knew how to behave at funerals, and how to write short, melancholy poems about the passing of autumn that were exactly seventeen syllables long. We knew how to pull weeds and chop kindling and haul water, and one of us—the rice miller's daughter—knew how to walk two miles into town with an eighty-pound sack of rice on her back without once breaking into a sweat. It's all in the way you breathe. Most of us had good manners, and were extremely polite, except for when we got mad and cursed like sailors. Most of us spoke like ladies most of the time, with our voices pitched high, and pretended to know much less than we did, and whenever we walked past the deckhands we made sure to take small, mincing steps with our toes turned properly in. Because how many times had our mothers told us: Walk like the city, not like the farm!

On the boat we crowded into each other's bunks every night and stayed up for hours discussing the unknown continent ahead of us. The people there were said to eat nothing but meat and their bodies were covered with hair (we were mostly Buddhist, and did not eat meat, and only had hair in the appropriate places). The trees were enormous. The plains were vast. The women were loud and tall—a full head taller, we had heard, than the tallest of our men. The language was ten times as difficult as our own and the customs were unfathomably strange. Books were read from back to front and soap was used in the bath. Noses were blown on dirty cloths that were stuffed back into pockets only to be taken out later and used again and again. The opposite of white was not red, but black. What would become of us, we wondered, in such an alien land? We imagined ourselves—an unusually small people armed only with our guidebooks—entering a country of giants. Would we be laughed at? Spat on? Or, worse yet, would we not be taken seriously at all? But even the most reluctant of us had to admit that it was better to marry a stranger in America than grow old with a farmer from the village. Because in America the women did not have to work in the fields and there was plenty of rice and firewood for all. And wherever you went the men held open the doors and tipped their hats and called out, "Ladies first" and "After you."

Some of us on the boat were from Kyoto, and were delicate and fair, and had lived our entire lives in darkened rooms at the back of the house. Some of us were from Nara, and prayed to our ancestors three times a day, and swore we could still hear the temple bells ringing. Some of us were farmers' daughters from Yamaguchi with thick wrists and broad shoulders who had never gone to bed after nine. Some of us were from a small mountain hamlet in Yamanashi and had only recently seen our first train. Some of us were from Tokyo, and had seen everything, and spoke beautiful Japanese, and did not mix much with any of the others. Many more of us were from Kagoshima and spoke in a thick southern dialect that those of us from Tokyo pretended we could not understand. Some of us were from Hokkaido, where it was snowy and cold, and would dream of that white landscape for years. Some of us were from Hiroshima, which would later explode, and were lucky to be on the boat at all though of course we did not then know it. The youngest of us was twelve, and from the eastern shore of Lake Biwa, and had not yet begun to bleed. My parents married me off for the betrothal money. The oldest of us was thirty-seven, and from Niigata, and had spent her entire life taking care of her invalid father, whose recent death made her both happy and sad. I knew I could only marry if he died. One of us was from Kumamoto, where there were no more eligible men—all of the eligible men had left the year before to find work in Manchuria—and felt fortunate to have found any kind of husband at all. I took one look at his photograph and told the matchmaker, "He'll do." One of us was from a silk-weaving village in Fukushima, and had lost her first husband to the flu, and her second to a younger and prettier woman who lived on the other side of the hill, and now she was sailing to America to marry her third. He's healthy, he doesn't drink, he doesn't gamble, that's all I needed to know. One of us was a former dancing girl from Nagoya who dressed beautifully, and had translucent white skin, and knew everything there was to know about men, and it was to her we turned every night with our questions. How long will it last? With the lamp lit or in the dark? Legs up or down? Eyes open or closed? What if I can't breathe? What if I get thirsty? What if he is too heavy? What if he is too big? What if he does not want me at all? "Men are really quite simple," she told us. And then she began to explain.

On the boat we sometimes lay awake for hours in the swaying damp darkness of the hold, filled with longing and dread, and wondered how we would last another three weeks.

On the boat we carried with us in our trunks all the things we would need for our new lives: white silk kimonos for our wedding night, colorful cotton kimonos for everyday wear, plain cotton kimonos for when we grew old, calligraphy brushes, thick black sticks of ink, thin sheets of rice paper on which to write long letters home, tiny brass Buddhas, ivory statues of the fox god, dolls we had slept with since we were five, bags of brown sugar with which to buy favors, bright cloth quilts, paper fans, English phrase books, flowered silk sashes, smooth black stones from the river that ran behind our house, a lock of hair from a boy we had once touched, and loved, and promised to write, even though we knew we never would, silver mirrors given to us by our mothers, whose last words still rang in our ears. You will see: women are weak, but mothers are strong.

On the boat we complained about everything. Bedbugs. Lice. Insomnia. The constant dull throb of the engine, which worked its way even into our dreams. We complained about the stench from the latrines—huge, gaping holes that opened out onto the sea—and our own slowly ripening odor, which seemed to grow more pungent by the day. We complained about Kazuko's aloofness, Chiyo's throat clearing, Fusayo's incessant humming of the "Teapicker's Song," which was driving us all slowly crazy. We complained about our disappearing hairpins—who among us was the thief?—and how the girls from first class had never once said hello from beneath their violet silk parasols in all the times they had walked past us up above on the deck. Just who do they think they are? We complained about the heat. The cold. The scratchy wool blankets. We complained about our own complaining. Deep down, though, most of us were really very happy, for soon we would be in America with our new husbands, who had written to us many times over the months. I have bought a beautiful house. You can plant tulips in the garden. Daffodils. Whatever you like. I own a farm. I operate a hotel. I am the president of a large bank. I left Japan several years ago to start my own business and can provide for you well. I am 179 centimeters tall and do not suffer from leprosy or lung disease and there is no history of madness in my family. I am a native of Okayama. Of Hyogo. Of Miyagi. Of Shizuoka. I grew up in the village next to yours and saw you once years ago at a fair. I will send you the money for your passage as soon as I can.

On the boat we carried our husbands' pictures in tiny oval lockets that hung on long chains from our necks. We carried them in silk purses and old tea tins and red lacquer boxes and in the thick brown envelopes from America in which they had originally been sent. We carried them in the sleeves of our kimonos, which we touched often, just to make sure they were still there. We carried them pressed flat between the pages of *Come, Japanese!* and *Guidance for Going to America* and *Ten Ways to Please a Man* and old, well-worn volumes of the Buddhist sutras, and one of us, who was Christian, and ate meat, and prayed to a different and longer-haired god, carried hers between the pages of a King James Bible. And when we asked her which man she liked better—the man in the photograph or the Lord Jesus Himself—she smiled mysteriously and replied, "Him, of course."

Several of us on the boat had secrets, which we swore we would keep from our husbands for the rest of our lives. Perhaps the real reason we were sailing to America was to track down a long-lost father who had left the family years before. He went to Wyoming to work in the coal mines and we never heard from him again. Or perhaps we were leaving behind a young daughter who had been born to a man whose face we could now barely recall—a traveling storyteller who had spent a week in the village, or a wandering Buddhist priest who had stopped by the house late one night on his way to Mt. Fuji.

On the boat we had no idea we would dream of our daughter every night until the day that we died, and that in our dreams she would always be three and as she was when we last saw her: a tiny figure in a dark red kimono squatting at the edge of a puddle, utterly entranced by the sight of a dead floating bee.

On the boat we ate the same food every day and every day we breathed the same stale air. We sang the same songs and laughed at the same jokes and in the morning, when the weather was mild, we climbed up out of the cramped quarters of the hold and strolled the deck in our wooden sandals and light summer kimonos, stopping, every now and then, to gaze out at the same endless blue sea. Sometimes a flying fish would land at our feet, flopping and out of breath, and one of us— usually it was one of the fishermen's daughters—would pick it up and toss it back into the water. Or a school of dolphins would appear out of nowhere and leap alongside the boat for

hours. One calm, windless morning when the sea was flat as
glass and the sky a brilliant shade of blue, the smooth black
flank of a whale suddenly rose up out of the water and then
disappeared and for a moment we forgot to breathe. *It was
like looking into the eye of the Buddha.*

On the boat we often stood on the deck for hours with the
wind in our hair, watching the other passengers go by. We saw
turbaned Sikhs from the Punjab who were fleeing to Panama
from their native land. We saw wealthy White Russians who
were fleeing from the revolution. We saw Chinese laborers
from Hong Kong who were going to work in the cotton fields of
Peru. We saw King Lee Uwanowich and his famous band of
gypsies, who owned a large cattle ranch in Mexico and were ru-
mored to be the richest band of gypsies in the world. We saw a
trio of sunburned German tourists and a handsome Spanish
priest and a tall, ruddy Englishman named Charles, who ap-
peared at the railing every afternoon at quarter past three and
walked several brisk lengths of the deck. Charles was traveling
in first class, and had dark green eyes and a sharp, pointy nose,
and spoke perfect Japanese, and was the first white person
many of us had ever seen. He was a professor of foreign lan-
guages at the university in Osaka, and had a Japanese wife, and
a child, and had been to America many times, and was end-
lessly patient with our questions. Was it true that Americans
had a strong animal odor? (Charles laughed and said, "Well,
do *I*?" and let us lean in close for a sniff.) And just how hairy
were they? ("About as hairy as I am," Charles replied, and then
he rolled up his sleeve to show us his arms, which were covered
with dark brown hairs that made us shiver.) And did they really
grow hair on their chests? (Charles blushed, and said he could
not show us his chest, and we blushed and explained that we
had not asked him to.) And were there still savage tribes of Red
Indians wandering all over the prairies? (Charles told us that all
the Red Indians had been taken away, and we breathed a sigh of
relief.) And was it true that the women in America did not have
to kneel down before their husbands or cover their mouths
when they laughed? (Charles stared at a passing ship on the ho-
rizon and then sighed and said, "Sadly, yes.") And did the men

and women there really dance cheek to cheek all night long? (Only on Saturdays, Charles explained.) And were the dance steps very difficult? (Charles said they were easy, and gave us a moonlit lesson in the foxtrot the following evening on the deck. *Slow, slow, quick, quick.*) And was downtown San Francisco truly bigger than the Ginza? (Why, of course.) And were the houses in America really three times the size of our own? (Indeed they were.) And did each house have a piano in the front parlor? (Charles said it was more like every other house.) And did he think we would be happy there? (Charles took off his glasses and looked down at us with his lovely green eyes and said, "Oh, yes, very.")

Some of us on the boat could not resist becoming friendly with the deckhands, who came from the same villages as we did, and knew all the words to our songs, and were constantly asking us to marry them. We already *are* married, we would explain, but a few of us fell in love with them anyway. And when they asked if they could see us alone—that very same evening, say, on the 'tween deck, at quarter past ten—we stared down at our feet for a moment and then took a deep breath and said, "Yes," and this was another thing we would never tell our husbands. *It was the way he looked at me*, we would think to ourselves later. Or, *He had a nice smile.*

One of us on the boat became pregnant but did not know it and when the baby was born nine months later the first thing she would notice was how much it resembled her new husband. *He's got your eyes.* One of us jumped overboard after spending the night with a sailor and leaving behind a short note on her pillow: *After him, there can be no other.* Another of us fell in love with a returning Methodist missionary she had met on the deck and even though he begged her to leave her husband for him when they got to America she told him that she could not. "I must remain true to my fate," she said to him. But for the rest of her life she would wonder about the life that could have been.

Some of us on the boat were brooders by nature, and preferred to stay to ourselves, and spent most of the voyage lying facedown in our berths, thinking of all the men we had left behind. The fruit seller's son, who always pretended not to notice us, but gave us an extra tangerine whenever his mother was not minding the store. Or the married man for whom we had once waited, on a bridge, in the rain, late at night, for two hours. And for what? A kiss and a promise. "I'll come again tomorrow," he had said. And even though we never saw him again we knew we would do it all over in an instant, because being with him was like being alive for the very first time, only better. And often, as we were falling asleep, we found ourselves thinking of the peasant boy we had talked to every afternoon on our way home from school—the beautiful young boy in the next village whose hands could coax up even the most stubborn of seedlings from the soil—and how our mother, who knew everything, and could often read our mind, had looked at us as though we were crazy. *Do you want to spend the rest of your life crouched over a field?* (We had hesitated and almost said yes, for hadn't we always dreamed of becoming our mother? Wasn't that all we had ever once wanted to be?)

On the boat we each had to make choices. Where to sleep and who to trust and who to befriend and how to befriend her. Whether or not to say something to the neighbor who snored, or talked in her sleep, or to the neighbor whose feet smelled even worse than our own, and whose dirty clothes were strewn all over the floor. And if somebody asked us if she looked good when she wore her hair in a certain way—in the "eaves" style, say, which seemed to be taking the boat by storm—and she did not, it made her head look too big, did we tell her the truth, or did we tell her she had never looked better? And was it all right to complain about the cook, who came from China, and only knew how to make one dish—rice curry—which he served to us day after day? But if we said something and he was sent back to China, where on many days you might not get any kind of rice at all, would it then be our fault? And was anybody listening to us anyway? Did anybody care?

Somewhere on the boat there was a captain, from whose cabin a beautiful young girl was said to emerge every morning at dawn. And of course we were all dying to know: Was she one of us, or one of the girls from first class?

On the boat we sometimes crept into each other's berths late at night and lay quietly side by side, talking about all the things we remembered from home: the smell of roasted sweet potatoes in early autumn, picnics in the bamboo grove, playing shadows and demons in the crumbling temple courtyard, the day our father went out to fetch a bucket of water from the well and did not return, and how our mother never mentioned him even once after that. *It was as though he never even existed. I stared down into that well for years.* We discussed favorite face creams, the benefits of leaden powder, the first time we saw our husband's photograph. *He looked like an earnest person, so I figured he was good enough for me.* Sometimes we found ourselves saying things we had never said to anyone, and once we got started it was impossible to stop, and sometimes we grew suddenly silent and lay tangled in each other's arms until dawn, when one of us would pull away from the other and ask, "But will it last?" And that was another choice we had to make. If we said yes, it would last, and went back to her—if not that night, then the next, or the night after that—then we told ourselves that whatever we did would be forgotten the minute we got off the boat. And it was all good practice for our husbands anyway.

A few of us on the boat never did get used to being with a man, and if there had been a way of going to America without marrying one, we would have figured it out.

On the boat we could not have known that when we first saw our husbands we would have no idea who they were. That the crowd of men in knit caps and shabby black coats waiting for us down below on the dock would bear no resemblance to the handsome young men in the photographs. That the photographs we had been sent were twenty years old. That the letters we had been written had been written to us by people other than our husbands, professional people with beautiful handwriting whose job it was to tell lies and win hearts. That when we first heard our names being called out across the water one of us would cover her eyes and turn away—*I want to go home*—but the rest of us would lift our heads and smooth down the skirts of our kimonos and walk down the gangplank and step out into the still warm day. *This is America*, we would say to ourselves, *there is no need to worry*. And we would be wrong.

FRANCISCO JIMÉNEZ

UNDER THE WIRE

"*La frontera*" is a word I often heard when I was a child living in *El Rancho Blanco*, a small village nestled on barren, dry hills several miles north of Guadalajara, Mexico. I heard it for the first time back in the late 1940s when Papá and Mamá told me and Roberto, my older brother, that someday we would take a long trip north, cross *la frontera*, enter California, and leave our poverty behind.

I did not know exactly what California was either, but Papá's eyes sparkled whenever he talked about it with Mamá and his friends. "Once we cross *la frontera*, we'll make a good living in California," he would say, standing up straight and sticking out his chest.

Roberto, who is four years older than I, became excited every time Papá talked about the trip to California. He didn't like living in *El Rancho Blanco*, especially after visiting our older cousin, Fito, in Guadalajara.

Fito had left *El Rancho Blanco*. He was working in a tequila factory and living in a two-bedroom house that had electricity and a water well. He told Roberto that he, Fito, didn't have to get up at four in the morning anymore, like my brother, to milk the five cows by hand and carry the milk in a large aluminum can on horse for several miles to the nearest road, where a truck would transport it to town to sell. He didn't have to go to the river for water, sleep on dirt floors, or use candles for light.

From then on, about the only thing Roberto liked about living in *El Rancho Blanco* was hunting for chicken eggs and attending church on Sundays.

I liked looking for eggs and going to Mass too. But what I enjoyed most was listening to stories. In the evenings, after supper, Papá's brother, *tío* Mauricio, and his family came over to visit. We sat around a fire built with dry cow chips and told stories while shaking out grain from ears of corn.

On one such evening Papá made the announcement: We were going to make the long-awaited trip across *la frontera* to California. Days later we packed our belongings in a suitcase and took the bus to Guadalajara to catch the train. Papá bought tickets on a second-class train, *Ferrocarriles Nacionales de México*. I had never seen a train before. It looked like metal huts on wheels strung together. We climbed in and took our seats. I stood to look out the window. As the train started to move, it jerked and made a loud clattering sound, like hundreds of milk cans crashing. I got scared and lost my balance. Papá caught me and told me to sit. I swung my legs, following the rhythm of the train. Roberto sat across from me, next to Mamá. He had a big grin on his face.

We traveled for two days and nights. During the night, we didn't get much sleep. The wooden seats were hard, and the train made loud noises, blowing its whistle and grinding its brakes. At the first train stop I asked Papá, "Is this California?"

"No *mi'jo*, we're not there yet," he answered patiently. "We have many more hours to go."

Noting that Papá had closed his eyes, I turned to Roberto and asked, "What's California like?"

"I don't know," he answered, "but Fito told me that people there sweep money off the streets."

"Where did Fito get that idea?" Papá said, opening his eyes and laughing.

"From Cantinflas," Roberto said assuredly. "He said Cantinflas said it in a movie."

"Cantinflas was joking," Papá responded, chuckling. "But it's true that life is better there."

"I hope so," Mamá said. Then, putting her arm around Roberto, she added softly, "*Dios lo quiera.*"

The train slowed down. I looked out the window and saw we were entering another town. "Is this it?" I asked.

"*¡Otra vez la burra al trigo!*" Papá said, frowning and rolling his eyes. "I'll tell you when we get there!"

"Be patient, Panchito," Mamá said, smiling. "We'll get there soon."

When the train stopped in Mexicali, Papá told us to get off. "We're almost there," he said, looking at me. We left the station. Papá carried our dark brown suitcase. We followed behind him until we reached a barbed wire fence. According to Papá, this was *la frontera*. He pointed out that across the gray wire barricade was California, that famous place I had heard so much about. On both sides of the fence were armed guards dressed in green uniforms. Papá called them *la migra*, and explained that we had to cross the fence to the other side without being seen by them.

Late that night, we walked for several miles away from town. Papá, who led the way, paused, looked all around to make sure no one could see us, and headed toward the fence. We walked along the wire wall until Papá spotted a small hole underneath the fence. Papá got on his knees and, with his hands, made the opening larger. We all crawled through like snakes. A few minutes later, we were picked up by a woman whom Papá had contacted in Mexicali. She had promised to pick us up in her car and drive us, for a fee, to a place where we would find work.

The woman drove all night, and at dawn we reached a tent labor camp on the outskirts of Guadalupe, a small town on the coast. She stopped the car by the side of a narrow road, near the camp.

"This is the place I told you about," she said wearily. "Here you'll find work picking strawberries."

Papá unloaded the suitcase from the trunk, took out his wallet, and paid the woman. "We have only seven dollars left," he said, biting his lower lip. After the woman drove away, we walked to the camp, following a dirt path lined on both sides by eucalyptus trees. Mamá held me by the hand very tightly. At the camp, Mamá and Papá were told that the foreman had left for the day.

We spent that night underneath the eucalyptus trees. We gathered leaves from the trees, which smelled like sweet gum, and piled them to lie on. Roberto and I slept between Papá and Mamá.

The following morning, I woke to the sound of a train whistle. For a split second I thought we were still on the train on our way to California. Spewing black smoke, it passed behind the camp, traveling much faster than the train we had taken from Guadalajara. As I followed it with my eyes, I heard a stranger's voice behind me. It was that of a woman who had stopped by to help. Her name was Lupe Gordillo; she was from the nearby camp. She brought us a few groceries and introduced us to the camp foreman, who spoke Spanish. He loaned us an army tent, which we pitched with his help. "You're lucky," he said. "This is the last tent we have."

"When can we start work?" Papá asked, rubbing his hands.

"In two weeks," the foreman answered.

"That can't be!" Papá exclaimed, shaking his head. "We were told we'd find work right away."

"I am sorry, the strawberries won't be ready to pick until then," the foreman responded, shrugging his shoulders and walking away.

After a long silence, Mamá said, "We'll manage, *viejo*. Once work starts, we'll be fine."

Roberto was quiet. He had a sad look in his eyes.

During the next two weeks, Mamá cooked outside on a makeshift stove using rocks and a *comal* Doña Lupe had given her. We ate wild *verdolagas* and rabbit and birds, which Papá hunted with a rifle he borrowed from a neighbor.

To pass the time, Roberto and I watched the trains go by behind the labor camp. We crawled underneath a barbed wire fence to get a closer look at them as they passed by several times a day.

Our favorite train came by every day at noon. It had a distinct whistle. We heard it coming from miles away. Roberto and I called it the Noon Train. Often, we would get there early and play on the railroad tracks while we waited for it. We ran straddling the rails or walked on them as fast as we could to see how far we could go without falling off. We also sat on the rails to feel them vibrate as the train approached. As days went by, we could recognize the conductor from afar. He slowed the train every time it went by and waved at us with his gray-and-white striped cap. We waved back.

One Sunday, Roberto and I crossed the fence earlier than usual to wait for the Noon Train. Roberto didn't feel like playing, so we sat on one of the rails, arms wrapped around our legs, foreheads on our knees. "I wonder where the train comes from," I said. "Do you know, Roberto?"

"I have been wondering too," he answered, slowly lifting his head. "I think it comes from California."

"California!" I exclaimed. "This is California!"

"I am not so sure," he said. "Remember what—"

The familiar Noon Train whistle interrupted him. We stepped off the rail and moved a few feet away from the tracks. The conductor slowed the train to a crawl, waved, and gently dropped a large brown bag in front of us as he went by. We picked it up and looked inside. It was full of oranges, apples, and candy.

"See, it does come from California!" Roberto exclaimed. We ran alongside the train, waving at the conductor. The train sped up and soon left us behind. We followed the rear of the train with our eyes until it got smaller and smaller and disappeared.

EVA HOFFMAN

From
LOST IN TRANSLATION

It is April 1959, I'm standing at the railing of the *Batory*'s upper deck, and I feel that my life is ending. I'm looking out at the crowd that has gathered on the shore to see the ship's departure from Gdynia—a crowd that, all of a sudden, is irrevocably on the other side—and I want to break out, run back, run toward the familiar excitement, the waving hands, the exclamations. We can't be leaving all this behind—but we are. I am thirteen years old, and we are emigrating. It's a notion of such crushing, definitive finality that to me it might as well mean the end of the world.

My sister, four years younger than I, is clutching my hand wordlessly; she hardly understands where we are, or what is happening to us. My parents are highly agitated; they had just been put through a body search by the customs police, probably as the farewell gesture of anti-Jewish harassment. Still, the officials weren't clever enough, or suspicious enough, to check my sister and me—lucky for us, since we are both carrying some silverware we were not allowed to take out of Poland in large pockets sewn onto our skirts especially for this purpose, and hidden under capacious sweaters.

When the brass band on the shore strikes up the jaunty mazurka rhythms of the Polish anthem, I am pierced by a youthful sorrow so powerful that I suddenly stop crying and try to hold still against the pain. I desperately want time to stop, to hold the ship still with the force of my will. I am suffering my first, severe attack of nostalgia, or *tęsknota*—a word that adds to nostalgia the tonalities of sadness and longing. It is a feeling whose shades and degrees I'm destined to know intimately, but at this hovering moment, it comes upon me like a visitation from a whole new geography of emotions, an annunciation of how much an absence can hurt. Or a premonition of absence, because at this divide, I'm filled to the brim with what I'm about to lose—images of Cracow, which I loved as one loves a person, of the sun-baked villages where we had taken summer vacations, of the hours I spent poring over passages of music with my piano teacher, of conversations and escapades with friends. Looking ahead, I come across an enormous, cold blankness—a darkening, an erasure, of the imagination, as if a camera eye has snapped shut, or as if a heavy curtain has been pulled over the future. Of the place where we're going—Canada—I know nothing. There are vague outlines of half a continent, a sense of vast spaces and little habitation. When my parents were hiding in a branch-covered forest bunker during the war, my father had a book with him called *Canada Fragrant with Resin* which, in his horrible confinement, spoke to him of majestic wilderness, of animals roaming without being pursued, of freedom. That is partly why we are going there, rather than to Israel, where most of our Jewish friends have gone. But to me, the word "Canada" has ominous echoes of the "Sahara." No, my mind rejects the idea of being taken there, I don't want to be pried out of my childhood, my pleasures, my safety, my hopes for becoming a pianist. The *Batory* pulls away, the foghorn emits its lowing, shofar sound, but my being is engaged in a stubborn refusal to move. My parents put their hands on my shoulders consolingly; for a moment, they allow themselves to acknowledge that there's pain in this departure, much as they wanted it.

Many years later, at a stylish party in New York, I met a woman who told me that she had had an enchanted childhood. Her father was a highly positioned diplomat in an Asian country, and she had lived surrounded by sumptuous elegance, the courtesy of servants, and the delicate advances of older men. No wonder, she said, that when this part of her life came to an end, at age thirteen, she felt she had been exiled from paradise, and had been searching for it ever since.

No wonder. But the wonder is what you can make a paradise out of. I told her that I grew up in a lumpen apartment in Cracow, squeezed into three rudimentary rooms with four other people, surrounded by squabbles, dark political rumblings, memories of wartime suffering, and daily struggle for existence. And yet, when it came time to leave, I, too, felt I was being pushed out of the happy, safe enclosures of Eden.

MOHSIN HAMID

From
HOW TO GET FILTHY RICH
IN RISING ASIA

One cold, dewy morning, you are huddled, shivering, on the packed earth under your mother's cot. Your anguish is the anguish of a boy whose chocolate has been thrown away, whose remote controls are out of batteries, whose scooter is busted, whose new sneakers have been stolen. This is all the more remarkable since you've never in your life seen any of these things.

The whites of your eyes are yellow, a consequence of spiking bilirubin levels in your blood. The virus afflicting you is called hepatitis E. Its typical mode of transmission is fecal-oral. Yum. It kills only about one in fifty, so you're likely to recover. But right now you feel like you're going to die.

Your mother has encountered this condition many times, or conditions like it anyway. So maybe she doesn't think you're going to die. Then again, maybe she does. Maybe she fears it. Everyone is going to die, and when a mother like yours sees in a third-born child like you the pain that makes you whimper under her cot the way you do, maybe she feels your death push forward a few decades, take off its dark, dusty headscarf, and settle with open-haired familiarity and a lascivious smile into this, the single mud-walled room she shares with all of her surviving offspring.

What she says is, "Don't leave us here."

Your father has heard this request of hers before. This does not make him completely unsusceptible to it, however. He is a man of voracious sexual appetite, and he often thinks while he is away of your mother's heavy breasts and solid, ample thighs, and he still longs to thrust himself inside her nightly rather than on just three or four visits per year. He also enjoys her unusually rude sense of humor, and sometimes her companionship as well. And although he is not given to displays of affection towards their young, he would like to watch you and your siblings grow. His own father derived considerable pleasure from the daily progress of crops in the fields, and in this, at least insofar as it is analogous to the development of children, the two men are similar.

He says, "I can't afford to bring you to the city."

"We could stay with you in the quarters."

"I share my room with the driver. He's a masturbating, chain-smoking, flatulent sisterfucker. There are no families in the quarters."

"You earn ten thousand now. You're not a poor man."

"In the city ten thousand makes you a poor man."

He gets up and walks outside. Your eyes follow him, his leather sandals unslung at the rear, their straps flapping free, his chapped heels callused, hard, crustacean-like. He steps through the doorway into the open-air courtyard located at the center of your extended family's compound. He is unlikely to linger there in contemplation of the single, shade-giving tree, comforting in summer, but now, in spring, still tough and scraggly. Possibly he exits the compound and makes his way to the ridge behind which he prefers to defecate, squatting low and squeezing forcefully to expel the contents of his colon. Possibly he is alone, or possibly he is not.

Beside the ridge is a meaty gully as deep as a man is tall, and at the bottom of that gully is a slender trickle of water. In this season the two are incongruous, the skeletal inmate of a concentration camp dressed in the tunic of an obese pastry chef. Only briefly, during the monsoon, does the gully fill to anything near capacity, and that too is an occurrence less regular than in the past, dependent on increasingly fickle atmospheric currents.

The people of your village relieve themselves downstream of where they wash their clothes, a place in turn downstream of where they drink. Farther upstream, the village before yours does the same. Farther still, where the water emerges from the hills as a sometimes-gushing brook, it is partly employed in the industrial processes of an old, rusting, and subscale textile plant, and partly used as drainage for the fart-smelling gray effluent that results.

Your father is a cook, but despite being reasonably good at his job and originating in the countryside, he is not a man obsessed with the freshness or quality of his ingredients. Cooking for him is a craft of spice and oil. His food burns the tongue and clogs the arteries. When he looks around him here, he does not see prickly leaves and hairy little berries for an effervescent salad, tan stalks of wheat for a heavenly balloon of stone-ground, stove-top-baked flatbread. He sees instead units of backbreaking toil. He sees hours and days and weeks and years. He sees the labor by which a farmer exchanges his allocation of time in this world for an allocation of time in this world. Here, in the heady bouquet of nature's pantry, your father sniffs mortality.

Most of the men of the village who now work in the city do return for the wheat harvest. But it is still too early in the year for that. Your father is here on leave. Nonetheless he likely accompanies his brothers to spend his morning cutting grass and clover for fodder. He will squat, again, but this time sickle in hand, and his movements of gather-cut-release-waddle will be repeated over and over and over as the sun too retraces its own incremental path in the sky.

Beside him, a single dirt road passes through the fields. Should the landlord or his sons drive by in their SUV, your father and his brothers will bring their hands to their foreheads, bend low, and avert their eyes. Meeting the gaze of a landlord has been a risky business in these parts for centuries, perhaps since the beginning of history. Recently some men have begun to do it. But they have beards and earn their keep in the seminaries. They walk tall, with chests out. Your father is not one of them. In fact he dislikes them almost as much as he does the landlords, and for the same reasons. They strike him as domineering and lazy.

Lying on your side with one ear on the packed earth, from your erect-worm's-height perspective you watch your mother follow your father into the courtyard. She feeds the water buffalo tethered there, tossing fodder cut yesterday and mixed with straw into a wooden trough, and milks the animal as it eats, jets of liquid smacking hard into her tin pail. When she is done, the children of the compound, your siblings and cousins, lead the buffalo, its calf, and the goats out to forage. You hear the swishing of the peeled branches they hold and then they are gone.

Your aunts next leave the compound, bearing clay pots on their heads for water and carrying clothes and soap for cleaning. These are social tasks. Your mother's responsibility is solitary. Her alone, them together. It is not a coincidence. She squats as your father is likely squatting, handle-less broom in her hand instead of a sickle, her sweep-sweep-waddle approximating his own movements. Squatting is energy efficient, better for the back and hence ergonomic, and it is not painful. But done for hours and days and weeks and years its mild discomfort echoes in the mind like muffled screams from a subterranean torture chamber. It can be borne endlessly, provided it is never acknowledged.

Your mother cleans the courtyard under the gaze of her mother-in-law. The old woman sits in shadow, the edge of her shawl held in her mouth to conceal not her attributes of temptation but rather her lack of teeth, and looks on in unquenchable disapproval. Your mother is regarded in the compound as vain and arrogant and headstrong, and these accusations have bite, for they are all true. Your grandmother tells your mother she has missed a spot. Because she is toothless and holds the cloth between her lips, her words sound like she is spitting.

Your mother and grandmother play a waiting game. The older woman waits for the younger woman to age, the younger woman waits for the older woman to die. It is a game both will inevitably win. In the meantime, your grandmother flaunts her authority when she can, and your mother flaunts her physical strength. The other women of the compound would be frightened of your mother were it not for the reassuring existence of the men. In an all-female society your mother would likely rise to be queen, a bloody staff in her hand and crushed skulls beneath her feet. Here the best she has been able to manage is for the most part to be spared severe provocation. Even this, cut off as she is from her own village, is no small victory.

Unsaid between your mother and your father is that on ten thousand a month he could, just barely, afford to bring your mother and you children to the city. It would be tight but not impossible. At the moment he is able to send most of his salary back to the village, where it is split between your mother and the rest of the clan. If she and you children were to move in with him, the flow of his money to this place would slow to a trickle, swelling like the water in the gully only in the two festival months when he could perhaps expect a bonus and hopefully would not have debts to clear.

You watch your mother slice up a lengthy white radish and boil it over an open fire. The sun has banished the dew, and even unwell as you are, you no longer feel cold. You feel weak, though, and the pain in your gut is as if a parasite is eating you alive from within. So you do not resist as your mother lifts your head off the earth and ladles her elixir into your mouth. It smells like a burp, like the gasses from a man's belly. It makes your gorge rise. But you have nothing inside that you can vomit, and you drink it without incident.

As you lie motionless afterwards, a young jaundiced village boy, radish juice dribbling from the corner of your lips and forming a small patch of mud on the ground, it must seem that getting filthy rich is beyond your reach. But have faith. You are not as powerless as you appear. Your moment is about to come. Yes, this book is going to offer you a choice.

Decision time arrives a few hours later. The sun has set and your mother has shifted you onto the cot, where you lie swaddled in a blanket even though the evening is warm. The men have returned from the fields, and the family, all except you, have eaten together in the courtyard. Through your doorway you can hear the gurgle of a water pipe and see the flare of its coals as one of your uncles inhales.

Your parents stand over you, looking down. Tomorrow your father will return to the city. He is thinking.

"Will you be all right?" he asks you.

It is the first question he has asked you on this visit, perhaps the first sentence he has uttered to you directly in months. You are in pain and frightened. So the answer is obviously no.

Yet you say, "Yes."

And take your destiny into your own hands.

Your father absorbs your croak and nods. He says to your mother, "He's a strong child. This one."

She says, "He's very strong."

You'll never know if it is your answer that makes your father change his answer. But that night he tells your mother that he has decided she and you children will join him in the city.

They seal the deal with sex. Intercourse in the village is a private act only when it takes place in the fields. Indoors, no couple has a room to themselves. Your parents share theirs with all three of their surviving children. But it is dark, so little is visible. Moreover, your mother and father remain almost entirely clothed. They have never in their lives stripped naked to copulate.

Kneeling, your father loosens the drawstring of his baggy trousers. Lying with her stomach on the floor, your mother pivots her pelvis and does the same. She reaches behind to tug on him with her hand, a firm and direct gesture not unlike her milking of the water buffalo this morning, but she finds him already ready. She rises onto all fours. He enters her, propping himself up with one hand and using the other on her breast, alternately to fondle and for purchase as he pulls himself forward. They engage in a degree of sound suppression, but muscular grunting, fleshy impact, traumatized respiration, and hydraulic suction nonetheless remain audible. You and your siblings sleep or pretend to sleep until they are done. Then they join you on your mother's cot, exhausted, and are within moments lost in their dreams. Your mother snores.

A month later you are well enough to ride with your brother and sister on the roof of the overloaded bus that bears your family and threescore cramped others to the city. If it tips over as it careens down the road, swerving in mad competition with other equally crowded rivals as they seek to pick up the next and next groups of prospective passengers on this route, your likelihood of death or at least dismemberment will be extremely high. Such things happen often, although not nearly as often as they don't happen. But today is your lucky day.

Gripping ropes that mostly succeed in binding luggage to this vehicle, you witness a passage of time that outstrips its chronological equivalent. Just as when headed into the mountains a quick shift in altitude can vault one from subtropical jungle to semi-arctic tundra, so too can a few hours on a bus from rural remoteness to urban centrality appear to span millennia.

Atop your inky-smoke-spewing, starboard-listing conveyance you survey the changes with awe. Dirt streets give way to paved ones, potholes grow less frequent and soon all but disappear, and the kamikaze rush of oncoming traffic vanishes, to be replaced by the enforced peace of the dual carriageway. Electricity makes its appearance, first in passing as you slip below a steel parade of high-voltage giants, then later in the form of wires running at bus-top eye level on either side of the road, and finally in streetlights and shop signs and glorious, magnificent billboards. Buildings go from mud to brick to concrete, then shoot up to an unimaginable four stories, even five.

At each subsequent wonder you think you have arrived, that surely nothing could belong more to your destination than this, and each time you are proven wrong until you cease thinking and simply surrender to the layers of marvels and visions washing over you like the walls of rain that follow one another seemingly endlessly in the monsoon, endlessly that is until they end, without warning, and then the bus shudders to a stop and you are finally, irrevocably there.

As you and your parents and siblings dismount, you embody one of the great changes of your time. Where once your clan was innumerable, not infinite but of a large number not readily known, now there are five of you. Five. The fingers on one hand, the toes on one foot, a minuscule aggregation when compared with shoals of fish or flocks of birds or indeed tribes of humans. In the history of the evolution of the family, you and the millions of other migrants like you represent an ongoing proliferation of the nuclear. It is an explosive transformation, the supportive, stifling, stabilizing bonds of extended relationships weakening and giving way, leaving in their wake insecurity, anxiety, productivity, and potential.

Moving to the city is the first step to getting filthy rich in rising Asia. And you have now taken it. Congratulations. Your sister turns to look at you. Her left hand steadies the enormous bundle of clothing and possessions balanced on her head. Her right hand grips the handle of a cracked and battered suitcase likely discarded by its original owner around the time your father was born. She smiles and you smile in return, your faces small ovals of the familiar in an otherwise unrecognizable world. You think your sister is trying to reassure you. It does not occur to you, young as you are, that it is she who needs reassurance, that she seeks you out not to comfort you, but rather for the comfort that you, her only recently recovered little brother, have in this moment of fragile vulnerability the capacity to offer her.

EDWIDGE DANTICAT

CHILDREN OF THE SEA

They say behind the mountains are more mountains. Now I know it's true. I also know there are timeless waters, endless seas, and lots of people in this world whose names don't matter to anyone but themselves. I look up at the sky and I see you there. I see you crying like a crushed snail, the way you cried when I helped you pull out your first loose tooth. Yes, I did love you then. Somehow when I looked at you, I thought of fiery red ants. I wanted you to dig your fingernails into my skin and drain out all my blood.

I don't know how long we'll be at sea. There are thirty-six other deserting souls on this little boat with me. White sheets with bright red spots float as our sail.

When I got on board I thought I could still smell the semen and the innocence lost to those sheets. I look up there and I think of you and all those times you resisted. Sometimes I felt like you wanted to, but I knew you wanted me to respect you. You thought I was testing your will, but all I wanted was to be near you. Maybe it's like you've always said. I imagine too much. I am afraid I am going to start having nightmares once we get deep at sea. I really hate having the sun in my face all day long. If you see me again, I'll be so dark.

Your father will probably marry you off now, since I am gone. Whatever you do, please don't marry a soldier. They're almost not human.

***

haiti est comme tu l'as laissé. yes, just the way you left it. bullets day and night. same hole. same everything. i'm tired of the whole mess. i get so cross and irritable. i pass the time by chasing roaches around the house. i pound my heel on their heads. they make me so mad. everything makes me mad. i am cramped inside all day. they've closed the schools since the army took over. no one is mentioning the old president's name. papa burnt all his campaign posters and old buttons. manman buried her buttons in a hole behind the house. she thinks he might come back. she says she will unearth them when he does. no one comes out of their house. not a single person. papa wants me to throw out those tapes of your radio shows. i destroyed some music tapes. but i still have your voice. i thank god you got out when you did. all the other youth federation members have disappeared. no one has heard from them. i think they might all be in prison. maybe they're all dead. papa worries a little about you. he doesn't hate you as much as you think. the other day i heard him asking manman, do you think the boy is dead? manman said she didn't know. i think he regrets being so mean to you. i don't sketch my butterflies anymore because i don't even like seeing the sun. besides, manman says that butterflies can bring news. the bright ones bring happy news and the black ones warn us of deaths. we have our whole lives ahead of us. you used to say that, remember? but then again things were so very different then.

***

There is a pregnant girl on board. She looks like she might be our age. Nineteen or twenty. Her face is covered with scars that look like razor marks. She is short and speaks in a singsong that reminds me of the villagers in the north. Most of the other people on the boat are much older than I am. I have heard that a lot of these boats have young children on board. I am glad this one does not. I think it would break my heart watching some little boy or girl every single day on this sea, looking into their empty faces to remind me of the hopelessness of the future in our country. It's hard enough with the adults. It's hard enough with me.

I used to read a lot about America before I had to study so

much for the university exams. I am trying to think, to see if I
read anything more about Miami. It is sunny. It doesn't snow
there like it does in other parts of America. I can't tell exactly
how far we are from there. We might be barely out of our own
shores. There are no borderlines on the sea. The whole thing
looks like one. I cannot even tell if we are about to drop off the
face of the earth. Maybe the world is flat and we are going to find
out, like the navigators of old. As you know, I am not very reli-
gious. Still I pray every night that we won't hit a storm. When I
do manage to sleep, I dream that we are caught in one hurricane
after another. I dream that the winds come of the sky and claim
us for the sea. We go under and no one hears from us again.

I am more comfortable now with the idea of dying. Not that
I have completely accepted it, but I know that it might happen.
Don't be mistaken. I really do not want to be a martyr. I know
I am no good to anybody dead, but if that is what's coming, I
know I cannot just scream at it and tell it to go away.

I hope another group of young people can do the radio show.
For a long time that radio show was my whole life. It was nice
to have radio like that for a while, where we could talk about
what we wanted from government, what we wanted for the fu-
ture of our country.

There are a lot of Protestants on this boat. A lot of them see
themselves as Job or the Children of Israel. I think some of
them are hoping something will plunge down from the sky and
part the sea for us. They say the Lord gives and the Lord takes
away. I have never been given very much. What was there to
take away?

**

if only i could kill. if i knew some good *wanga* magic. i would
wipe them off the face of the earth. a group of students got
shot in front of fort dimanche prison today. they were demon-
strating for the bodies of the radio six. that is what they are
calling you all. the radio six. you have a name. you have a rep-
utation. a lot of people think you are dead like the others. they
want the bodies turned over to the families. this afternoon,

the army finally did give some bodies back. they told the families to go collect them at the rooms for indigents at the morgue. our neighbor madan roger came home with her son's head and not much else. honest to god, it was just his head. at the morgue, they say a car ran over him and took the head off his body. when madan roger went to the morgue, they gave her the head. by the time we saw her, she had been carrying the head all over port-au-prince. just to show what's been done to her son. the macoutes by the house were laughing at her. they asked her if that was her dinner. it took ten people to hold her back from jumping on them. they would have killed her, the dogs. i will never go outside again. not even in the yard to breathe the air. they are always watching you, like vultures. at night i can't sleep. i count the bullets in the dark. i keep wondering if it is true. did you really get out? i wish there was some way i could be sure that you really went away. yes, i will. i will keep writing like we promised to do. i hate it, but i will keep writing. you keep writing too, okay? and when we see each other again, it will seem like we lost no time.

***

Today was our first real day at sea. Everyone was vomiting with each small rocking of the boat. The faces around me are showing their first charcoal layer of sunburn. "Now we will never be mistaken for Cubans," one man said. Even though some of the Cubans are black too. The man said he was once on a boat with a group of Cubans. His boat had stopped to pick up the Cubans on an island off the Bahamas. When the Coast Guard came for them, they took the Cubans to Miami and sent him back to Haiti. Now he was back on the boat with some papers and documents to show that the police in Haiti were after him. He had a broken leg too, in case there was any doubt.

One old lady fainted from sunstroke. I helped revive her by rubbing some of the salt water on her lips. During the day it can be so hot. At night, it is so cold. Since there are no mirrors, we look at each others faces to see just how frail and sick we are starting to look.

Some of the women sing and tell stories to each other to appease the vomiting. Still, I watch the sea. At night, the sky and the sea are one. The stars look so huge and so close. They make for very bright reflections in the sea. At times I feel like I can just reach out and pull a star down from the sky as though it is a breadfruit or a calabash or something that could be of use to us on this journey.

When we sing, *Beloved Haiti, there is no place like you. I had to leave you before I could understand you,* some of the women start crying. At times, I just want to stop in the middle of the song and cry myself. To hide my tears. I pretend like I am getting another attack of nausea, from the sea smell. I no longer join in the singing.

You probably do not know much about this, because you have always been so closely watched by your father in that well-guarded house with your genteel mother. No, I am not making fun of you for this. If anything, I am jealous. If I was a girl, maybe I would have been at home and not out politicking and getting myself into something like this. Once you have been at sea for a couple of days, it smells like every fish you have ever eaten, every crab you have ever caught, every jellyfish that has ever bitten your leg. I am so tired of the smell. I am also tired of the way the people on this boat are starting to stink. The pregnant girl, Célianne, I don't know how she takes it. She stares into space all the time and rubs her stomach.

I have never seen her eat. Sometimes the other women offer her a piece of bread and she takes it, but she has no food of her own. I cannot help feeling like she will have this child as soon as she gets hungry enough.

She woke up screaming the other night. I thought she had a stomach ache. Some water started coming into the boat in the spot where she was sleeping. There is a crack at the bottom of the boat that looks as though, if it gets any bigger, it will split the boat in two. The captain cleared us aside and used some tar to clog up the hole. Everyone started asking him if it was okay, if they were going to be okay. He said he hoped the Coast Guard would find us soon.

You can't really go to sleep after that. So we all stared at the

tar by the moonlight. We did this until dawn. I cannot help
but wonder how long this tar will hold out.

***

papa found your tapes. he started yelling at me, asking if I was
crazy keeping them. he is just waiting for the gasoline ban to be
lifted so we can get out of the city. he is always pestering me
these days because he cannot go out driving his van. all the
american factories are closed. he kept yelling at me about the
tapes. he called me selfish, and he asked if i hadn't seen or heard
what was happening to man-crazy whores like me. i shouted
that i wasn't a whore. he had no business calling me that. he
pushed me against the wall for disrespecting him. he spat in my
face. i wish those macoutes would kill him. i wish he would
catch a bullet so we could see how scared he really is. he said to
me. i didn't send your stupid trouble maker away. i started yell-
ing at him. yes, you did. yes, you did. yes, you did, you pig peas-
ant. i don't know why i said that. he slapped me and kept
slapping me really hard until manman came and grabbed me
away from him. i wish one of those bullets would hit me.

***

The tar is holding up so far. Two days and no more leaks. Yes, I
am finally an African. I am even darker than your father. I
wanted to buy a straw hat from one of the ladies, but she would
not sell it to me for the last two gourdes I have left in change. Do
you think your money is worth anything to me here? she asked
me. Sometimes, I forget where I am. If I keep daydreaming like I
have been doing, I will walk off the boat to go for a scroll.

The other night I dreamt that I died and went to heaven. This
heaven was nothing like I expected. It was at the bottom of the
sea. There were starfishes and mermaids all around me. The
mermaids were dancing and singing in Latin like the priests do
at the cathedral during Mass. You were there with me too, at
the bottom of the sea. You were with your family, off to the
side. Your father was acting like he was better than everyone

else and he was standing in front of a sea cave blocking you from my view. I tried to talk to you. but every time I opened my mouth, water bubbles came out. No sounds.

**

they have this thing now that they do. if they come into a house and there is a son and mother there, they hold a gun to their heads. they make the son sleep with his mother. if it is a daughter and father, they do the same thing. some nights papa sleeps at his brother's, uncle pressoir's house. uncle pressoir sleeps at our house. just in case they come. that way papa will never be forced to lie down in bed with me. instead, uncle pressoir would be forced to, but that would not be so bad. we know a girl who had a child by her father that way. that is what papa does not want to happen, even if he is killed. there is still no gasoline to buy. otherwise we would be in ville rose already. papa has a friend who is going to get him some gasoline from a soldier. as soon as we get the gasoline, we are going to drive quick and fast until we find civilization. that's how papa puts it, civilization. he says things are not as bad in the provinces. i am still not talking to him. i don't think i ever will. manman says it is not his fault. he is trying to protect us. he cannot protect us. only god can protect us. the soldiers can come and do with us what they want. that makes papa feel weak, she says. he gets angry when he feels weak. why should he be angry with me? i am not one of the pigs with the machine guns. she asked me what really happened to you. she said she saw your parents before they left for the provinces. they did not want to tell her anything. i told her you took a boat after they raided the radio station. you escaped and took a boat to heaven knows where. she said, he was going to make a good man, that boy. sharp, like a needle point, that boy, he took the university exams a year before everyone else in this area. manman has respect for people with ambitions. she said papa did not want you for me because it did not seem as though you were going to do any better for me than he and manman could. he wants me to find a man who will do me

some good. someone who will make sure that i have more
than i have now. it is not enough for a girl to be just pretty
anymore. we are not that well connected in society. the kind
of man that papa wants for me would never have anything to
do with me. all anyone can hope for is just a tiny bit of love,
manman says, like a drop in a cup if you can get it, or a water-
fall, a flood, if you can get that too. we do not have all that
many high-up connections, she says, but you are an educated
girl. what she counts for educated is not much to anyone but
us anyway. they should be announcing the university exams
on the radio next week. then i will know if you passed. i will
listen for your name.

***

We spent most of yesterday telling stories. Someone says, Krik?
You answer, Krak! And they say, I have many stories I could
tell you, and then they go on and tell these stories to you, but
mostly to themselves. Sometimes it feels like we have been at
sea longer than the many years that I have been on this earth.
The sun comes up and goes down. That is how you know it has
been a whole day. I feel like we are sailing for Africa. Maybe
we will go to Guinin, to live with the spirits, to be with every-
one who has come and has died before us. They would proba-
bly turn us away from there too. Someone has a transistor and
sometimes we listen to radio from the Bahamas. They treat
Haitians like dogs in the Bahamas, a woman says. To them, we
are not human. Even though their music sounds like ours.
Their people look like ours. Even though we had the same Af-
rican fathers who probably crossed these same seas together.

  Do you want to know how people go to the bathroom on
the boat? Probably the same way they did on those slaves ships
years ago. They set aside a little corner for that. When I have
to pee, I just pull it, lean over the rail, and do it very quickly.
When I have to do the other thing, I rip a piece of something,
squat down and do it, and throw the waste in the sea. I am al-
ways embarrassed by the smell. It is so demeaning having to
squat in front of so many people. People turn away, but not

always. At times I wonder if there is really land on the other side of the sea. Maybe the sea is endless. Like my love for you.

***

last night they came to madan roger's house. papa hurried inside as soon as madan roger's screaming started. the soldiers were looking for her son. madan roger was screaming, you killed him already. we buried his head. you can't kill him twice. they were shouting at her, do you belong to the youth federation with those vagabonds who were on the radio? she was yelling, do i look like a youth to you? can you identify your son's other associates? they asked her. papa had us tiptoe from the house into the latrine out back. we could hear it all from there. i thought i was going to choke on the smell of rotting poupou. they kept shouting at madan roger, did your son belong to the youth federation? wasn't he on the radio talking about the police? did he say, down with tonton macoutes? did he say, down with the army? he said that the military had to go; didn't he write slogans? he had meetings, didn't he? he demonstrated on the streets. you should have advised him better. she cursed on their mothers' graves. she just came out and shouted it, i hope your mothers will never rest in their cursed graves! she was just shouting it out, you killed him once already! you want to kill me too? go ahead. i don't care anymore. i'm dead already. you have already done the worst to me that you can do. you have killed my soul. they kept at it, asking her questions at the top of their voices: was your son a traitor? tell me all the names of his friends who were traitors just like him. madan roger finally shouts, yes, he was one! he belonged to that group. he was on the radio. he was on the streets at these demonstrations. he hated you like i hate you criminals. you killed him. they start to pound at her. you can hear it. you can hear the guns coming down on her head. it sounds like they are cracking all the bones in her body. manman whispers to papa. you can't just let them kill her. go and give them some money like you gave them for your daughter. papa says, the only money i have left is to get us out of here tomorrow. manman whispers, we cannot just stay

here and let them kill her. manman starts moving like she is
going out the door. papa grabs her neck and pins her to the la-
trine wall. tomorrow we are going to ville rose, he says. you will
not spoil that for the family. you will not put us in that situa-
tion. you will not get us killed. going out there will be like try-
ing to raise the dead. she is not dead yet, manman says, maybe
we can help her. i will make you stay if i have to, he says to her.
my mother buries her face in the latrine wall. she starts to cry.
you can hear madan roger screaming. they are beating her,
pounding on her until you don't hear anything else. manman
tells papa. you cannot let them kill somebody just because you
are afraid. papa says, oh yes, you *can* let them kill somebody
because you are afraid. they are the law. it is their right. we are
just being good citizens, following the law of the land. it has
happened before all over this country and tonight it will hap-
pen again and there is nothing we can do.

***

Célianne spent the night groaning. She looks like she has been
ready for a while, but maybe the child is being stubborn. She
just screamed that she is bleeding. There is an older woman
here who looks like she has had a lot of children herself. She
says Célianne is not bleeding at all. Her water sack has broken.
     The only babies I have ever seen right after birth are baby
mice. Their skin looks veil thin. You can see all the blood ves-
sels and all their organs. I have always wanted to poke them to
see if my finger would go all the way through the skin.
     I have moved to the other side of the boat so I will not have
to look *inside* Célianne. People are just watching. The captain
asks the midwife to keep Célianne steady so she will not rock
any more holes into the boat. Now we have three cracks cov-
ered with tar. I am scared to think of what would happen if we
had to choose among ourselves who would stay on the boat
and who should die. Given the choice to make a decision like
that, we would all act like vultures, including me.
     The sun will set soon. Someone says that this child will be
just another pair of hungry lips. At least it will have its

mother's breasts, says an old man. Everyone will eat their last scraps of food today.

***

there is a rumor that the old president is coming back. there is a whole bunch of people going to the airport to meet him. papa says we are not going to stay in port-au-prince to find out if this is true or if it is a lie. they are selling gasoline at the market again. the carnival groups have taken to the streets. we are heading the other way, to ville rose. maybe there i will be able to sleep at night. it is not going to turn out well with the old president coming back, manman now says. people are just too hopeful, and sometimes hope is the biggest weapon of all to use against us. people will believe anything. they will claim to see the christ return and march on the cross backwards if there is enough hope. manman told papa that you took the boat. papa told me before we left this morning that he thought himself a bad father for everything that happened. he says a father should be able to speak to his children like a civilized man. all the craziness here has made him feel like he cannot do that anymore. all he wants to do is live. he and manman have not said a word to one another since we left the latrine. i know that papa does not hate us, not in the way that i hate those soldiers, those macoutes, and all those people here who shoot guns. on our way to ville rose, we saw dogs licking two dead faces. one of them was a little boy who was lying on the side of the road with the sun in his dead open eyes. we saw a soldier shoving a woman out of a hut, calling her a witch. he was shaving the woman's head, but of course we never stopped. papa didn't want to go in madan roger's house and check on her before we left. he thought the soldiers might still be there. papa was driving the van real fast. i thought he was going to kill us. we stopped at an open market on the way. manman got some black cloth for herself and for me. she cut the cloth in two pieces and we wrapped them around our heads to mourn madan roger. when i am used to ville rose, maybe i will sketch you some butterflies, depending on the news that they bring me.

***

Célianne had a girl baby. The woman acting as a midwife is holding the baby to the moon and whispering prayers. . . . *God, this child You bring into the world, please guide her as You please through all her days on this earth.* The baby has not cried.

We had to throw our extra things in the sea because the water is beginning to creep in slowly. The boat needs to be lighter. My two gourdes in change had to be thrown overboard as an offering to Agwé, the spirit of the water. I heard the captain whisper to someone yesterday that they might have to *do something* with some of the people who never recovered from seasickness. I am afraid that soon they may ask me to throw out this notebook. We might all have to strip down to the way we were born, to keep ourselves from drowning.

Célianne's child is a beautiful child. They are calling her Swiss, because the word *Swiss* was written on the small knife they used to cut her umbilical cord. If she was my daughter, I would call her soleil, sun, moon, or star, after the elements. She still hasn't cried. There is gossip circulating about how Célianne became pregnant. Some people are saying that she had an affair with a married man and her parents threw her out. Gossip spreads here like everywhere else.

Do you remember our silly dreams? Passing the university exams and then studying hard to go until the end, the farthest of all that we can go in school. I know your father might never approve of me. I was going to try to win him over. He would have to cut out my heart to keep me from loving you. I hope you are writing like you promised. Jésus, Marie, Joseph! Everyone smells so bad. They get into arguments and they say to one another, "It is only my misfortune that would lump me together with an indigent like you." Think of it. They are fighting about being superior when we all might drown like straw.

There is an old toothless man leaning over to see what I am writing. He is sucking on the end of an old wooden pipe that has not seen any fire for a very long time now. He looks like a painting. Seeing things simply, you could fill a museum with the sights you have here. I still feel like such a coward for running away. Have you heard anything about my parents? Last time I saw them on the beach, my mother had a *kriz*. She just fainted on the sand. I saw her coming to as we started sailing away. But of course I don't know if she is doing all right.

The water is really piling into the boat. We take turns pouring bowls of it out. I don't know what is keeping the boat from splitting in two. Swiss isn't crying. They keep slapping her behind, but she is not crying.

***

of course the old president didn't come. they arrested a lot of people at the airport, shot a whole bunch of them down. i heard it on the radio. while we were eating tonight, i told papa that i love you. i don't know if it will make a difference. i just want him to know that i have loved somebody in my life. in case something happens to one of us. i think he should know this about me, that i have loved someone besides only my mother and father in my life. i know you would understand. you are the one for large noble gestures. i just wanted him to know that i was capable of loving somebody. he looked me straight in the eye and said nothing to me. i love you until my hair shivers at the thought of anything happening to you. papa just turned his face away like he was rejecting my very birth. i am writing you from under the banyan tree in the yard in our new house. there are only two rooms and a tin roof that makes music when it rains, especially when there is hail, which falls like angry tears from heaven. there is a stream down the hill from the house, a stream that is too shallow for me to drown myself. manman and i spend a lot of time talking under the banyan tree. she told me today that sometimes you have to choose between your father and the man you love. her whole family did not want her to marry papa because he was a gardener from ville rose and her family was from the city and some of them had even gone to university. she whispered everything under the banyan tree in the yard so as not to hurt his feelings. i saw him looking at us hard from the house. i heard him clearing his throat like he

heard us anyway, like we hurt him very deeply somehow just
by being together.

**

Célianne is lying with her head against the side of the boat. The
baby still will not cry. They both look very peaceful in all this
chaos. Célianne is holding her baby tight against her chest. She
just cannot seem to let herself throw it in the ocean. I asked her
about the baby's father. She keeps repeating the story now with
her eyes closed, her lips barely moving.

She was home one night with her mother and brother Lionel
when some ten or twelve soldiers burst into the house. The sol-
diers held a gun to Lionel's head and ordered him to lie down
and become intimate with his mother. Lionel refused. Their
mother told him to go ahead and obey the soldiers because she
was afraid that they would kill Lionel on the spot if he put up
more of a fight. Lionel did as his mother told him, crying as
the soldiers laughed at him, pressing the gun barrels farther
and farther into his neck.

Afterwards, the soldiers tied up Lionel and their mother, then
they each took turns raping Célianne. When they were done,
they arrested Lionel, accusing him of moral crimes. After that
night, Célianne never heard from Lionel again.

The same night, Célianne cut her face with a razor so that no
one would know who she was. Then as facial scars were heal-
ing, she started throwing up and getting rashes. Next thing she
knew, she was getting big. She found out about the boat and got
on. She is fifteen.

**

manman told me the whole story today under the banyan tree.
the bastards were coming to get me. they were going to arrest
me. they were going to peg me as a member of the youth fed-
eration and then take me away. papa heard about it. he went
to the post and paid them money, all the money he had. our
house in port-au-prince and all the land his father had left

him, he gave it all away to save my life. this is why he was so mad. tonight manman told me this under the banyan tree. i have no words to thank him for this. i don't know how. you must love him for this, manman says, you must. it is something you can never forget, the sacrifice he has made. i cannot bring myself to say thank you, now he is more than my father. he is a man who gave everything he had to save my life. on the radio tonight, they read the list of names of people who passed the university exams. you passed.

***

We got some relief from the seawater coming in. The captain used the last of his tar, and most of the water is staying out for a while. Many people have volunteered to throw Célianne's baby overboard for her. She will not let them. They are waiting for her to go to sleep so they can do it, but she will not sleep. I never knew before that dead children looked purple. The lips are the most purple because the baby is so dark. Purple like the sea after the sun has set.

Célianne is slowly drifting off to sleep. She is very tired from the labor. I do not want to touch the child. If anybody is going to throw it in the ocean, I think it should be her. I keep thinking, they have thrown every piece of flesh that followed the child out of her body into the water. They are going to throw the dead baby in the water. Won't these things attract sharks?

Célianne's fingernails are buried deep in the child's naked back. The old man with the pipe just asked. "Kompè, what are you writing?" I told him. "My will."

***

I am getting used to ville rose. there are butterflies here, tons of butterflies. so far none has landed on my hand, which means they have no news for me. i cannot always bathe in the stream near the house because the water is freezing cold. the only time it feels just right is at noon, and then there are a dozen eyes who might see me bathing. i solved that by getting a bucket of water in the morning and leaving it in the sun and then bathing myself once it is night under the banyan tree. the banyan now is my most trusted friend. they say banyans can last hundreds of years. even the branches that lean down from them become like trees themselves. a banyan could become a forest, manman says, if it were given a chance. from the spot where i stand under the banyan, i see the mountains, and behind those are more mountains still. so many mountains that are bare like rocks. i feel like all those mountains are pushing me farther and farther away from you.

***

She threw it overboard. I watched her face knot up like a thread, and then she let go. It fell in a splash, floated for a while, and then sank. And quickly after that she jumped in too. And just as the baby's head sank, so did hers. They went together like two bottles beneath a waterfall. The shock lasts only so long. There was no time to even try and save her. There was no question of it. The sea in that spot is like the sharks that live there. It has no mercy.

They say I have to throw my notebook out. The old man has to throw out his hat and his pipe. The water is rising again and they are scooping it out. I asked for a few seconds to write this last page and then promised that I would let it go. I know you will probably never see this, but it was nice imagining that I had you here to talk to.

I hope my parents are alive. I asked the old man to tell them what happened to me, if he makes it anywhere. He asked me to write his name in "my book." I asked him for his full name. It is Justin Moïse André Nozius Joseph Frank Osnac Maximilien. He says it all with such an air that you would think him a king. The old man says, "I know a Coast Guard ship is coming. It came to me in my dream." He points to a spot far into the distance. I look where he is pointing. I see nothing. From here, ships must be like a mirage in the desert.

I must throw my book out now. It goes down to them,

Célianne and her daughter and all those children of the sea who might soon be claiming me.

I go to them now as though it was always meant to be, as though the very day that my mother birthed me, she had chosen me to live life eternal, among the children of the deep blue sea, those who have escaped the chains of slavery to form a world beneath the heavens and the blood-drenched earth where you live.

Perhaps I was chosen from the beginning of time to live there with Agwé at the bottom of the sea. Maybe this is why I dreamed of the starfish and the mermaids having the Catholic Mass under the sea. Maybe this was my invitation to go. In any case, I know that my memory of you will live even there as I too become a child of the sea.

***

today i said thank you. i said thank you, papa, because you saved my life. he groaned and just touched my shoulder, moving his hand quickly away like a butterfly. and then there it was, the black butterfly floating around us. i began to run and run so it wouldn't land on me, but it had already carried its news. i know what must have happened. tonight i listened to manman's transistor under the banyan tree. all i hear from the radio is more killing in port-au-prince. the pigs are refusing to let up. i don't know what's going to happen, but i cannot see staying here forever. i am writing to you from the bottom of the banyan tree. manman says that banyan trees are holy and sometimes if we call the gods from beneath them, they will hear our voices clearer. now there are always butterflies around me, black ones that i refuse to let find my hand. i throw big rocks at them, but they are always too fast. last night on the radio, i heard that another boat sank off the coast of the bahamas. i can't think about you being in there in the waves. my hair shivers. from here, i cannot even see the sea. behind these mountains are more mountains and more black butterflies still and a sea that is endless like my love for you.

PAULETTE RAMSAY

From
AUNT JEN

30 June 1971

Dear Aunt Jen,

Today I sat and thought about you for a long, long
time. I thought about how strange it is that you're my
mother and I am your daughter and you are there and I
am here and we don't know each other and if I came to
England or if you came to Jamaica we would pass each
other on the streets and you would not know me and I
would not know you . . . We would pass each other and
not know that we are flesh and blood. That is really
strange.

I tried to picture you sitting in your house in England.
I can barely see a body. Maybe it's a body like Ma's, only
a little younger. Maybe it's a body like mine, only older.
It's very hard to see a picture of you in my mind. I can't
see a face. I tried to imagine the face of a lady who looks
like Uncle Roy and Uncle Johnny but it's not working. I
tried to picture a lady who looks like me, as Uncle Eddy
said, but that does not work either. It's like trying to see
my own face in a dirty mirror. I'm still hoping you will
send me a photograph of yourself.

Your daughter
Your dau
Sunshine

DINAW MENGESTU

AN HONEST EXIT

Thirty-five years after my father left Ethiopia, he died in a room in a boarding house in Peoria, Illinois, that came with a partial view of the river. We had never spoken much during his lifetime, but, on a warm October morning in New York shortly after he died, I found myself having a conversation with him as I walked north on Amsterdam Avenue, toward the high school where for the past three years I had been teaching a course in Early American literature to privileged freshmen.

"That's the Academy right there," I told him. "You can see the top of the bell tower through the trees. I'm the only one who calls it the Academy. That's not its real name. I stole it from a short story by Kafka that I read in college—a monkey who's been trained to talk gives a speech to an academy. I used to wonder if that was how my students and the other teachers, even with all their liberal, cultured learning, saw me—as a monkey trying to teach their language back to them. Do you remember how you spoke? I hated it. You used those short, broken sentences that sounded as if you were spitting out the words, as if you had just learned them but already despised them, even the simplest ones. 'Take this.' 'Don't touch.' 'Leave now.'"

I arrived in my classroom ten minutes before the bell rang, just as the first of my students trickled in. They were the smartest, and took their seats near the center. The rest arrived in no discernible order, but I noticed that all of them, smart and stupid alike, seemed hardly to talk, or, if they talked, it was only in whispers. Most said hello as they entered, but their voices were more hesitant than usual, as if they weren't sure that it was really me they were addressing.

"I'm sorry for having missed class the other day," I began, and because I felt obliged to explain my absence I told them the truth. "My father passed away recently. I had to attend to his affairs."

And yet, because I had just finished talking to him, I felt that I hadn't said enough. So I continued. "He was sixty-seven years old when he died. He was born in a small village in northern Ethiopia. He was thirty-two when he left his home for a port town in Sudan in order to come here."

And while I could have ended there I had no desire to. I needed a history more complete than the strangled bits that he had owned and passed on to me—a short, brutal tale of having been trapped as a stowaway on a ship. So I continued with my father's story, knowing that I could make up the missing details as I went.

He was an engineer before he left Ethiopia, I told my students, but after spending several months in prison for attending a political rally banned by the government he was reduced to nothing. He knew that if he returned home he would eventually be arrested again, and that this time he wouldn't survive, so he took what little he had left and followed a group of men who told him that they were heading to Sudan, because it was the only way out.

For one week he walked west. He had never been in this part of the country before. Everything was flat, from the land to the horizon, one uninterrupted stream that not even a cloud dared to break. The fields were thick with wild green grass and bursts of yellow flowers. Eventually he found a ride on the back of a pickup truck already crowded with refugees heading toward the border. Every few hours, they passed a village, each one a cluster of thatch-roofed huts with a dirt road carved down the middle, where children eagerly waved as the refugees passed, as if the simple fact that they were travelling in a truck meant they were off to someplace better.

When he finally arrived at the port town in Sudan, he had already lost a dozen pounds. His slightly bulbous nose stood in stark contrast to the sunken cheeks and wide eyes that seemed to have been buried deep above them. His clothes fit him poorly. His hands looked larger; the bones were more visible. He thought his fingers were growing.

This was the farthest from home he had ever travelled, but he knew that he couldn't stay there. He wanted to leave the entire continent far behind, for Europe or America, where life was rumored to be better.

It was the oldest port in Sudan and one of the oldest cities in the country. At its peak, fifty thousand people had lived there, but now only a fraction of the population was left. Several wars had been fought nearby, the last one in 1970, between a small group of rebels and the government. There were burned-out tanks on the edge of town and dozens of half-destroyed, abandoned houses. There was sand and dust everywhere, and on most days the temperature came close to a hundred degrees. The people who lived there were desperately poor. Some worked as fishermen but most spent their days by the dock, looking for work unloading crates from the dozens of small freight ships in the harbor. My father was told that he could find a job there, and that if he was patient and earned enough money he could even buy his way out of the country on one of the boats.

The bell for the end of first period rang then. My students waited a moment before gathering their bags and leaving; they were either compelled or baffled by what I had told them. I tried to see them all in one long glance before they were gone. They had always been just bodies to me, a prescribed number that came and went each day of the semester until they were replaced by others, who would do the same. For a few seconds, though, I saw them clearly—the deliberately rumpled hair of the boys and the neat, tidy composure of the girls in opposition. They were still in the making, each and every one of them. Somehow I had missed that. None of them looked away or averted their gaze from mine, which I took as confirmation that I could continue.

As I walked home that night I was aware of a growing vortex of e-mails and text messages being passed among my students. Millions of invisible bits of data were being transmitted through underground cable wires and satellite networks, and I was their sole subject and object of concern. I don't know why I found so much comfort in that thought, but it nearly lifted me off the ground, and suddenly, everywhere, I felt embraced. As I walked down Riverside Drive, with the Hudson River and the rush of traffic pouring up and down the West Side Highway to my right, the tightly controlled neighborhood borders and divisions hardly mattered.

The next day at the Academy I told my students at the start of class that they could put their anthologies and worksheets away. "We won't be needing them for now," I said.

My father's first job at the port was bringing tea to the dockworkers, a job for which he was paid only in tips—a few cents here and there that gradually added up. On an average day, he would serve anywhere between three and five hundred cups of tea. He could carry as many as ten at a time on a large wooden platter that he learned to balance on his forearm. As a child he had been clumsy; his father would often yell at him for breaking a glass or for being unable to bring him a cup of coffee without spilling it. So as soon as he got the job he began practicing at night with a tray full of stones that were as light as the cups of tea. If the stones moved he knew he had failed and would try again, until eventually he probably could have walked several miles without spilling a drop of tea or shifting a single stone.

He hid his earnings in a pocket sewn into the inside of his pants. The one friend he had in town, a man by the name of Abrahim, had told him never to let anyone know how much money he had: "If someone sees you have two dollars, he will think you have twenty. It's always better to make people think you have nothing at all."

Abrahim was the one who found him the job carrying tea. He met my father on his third day in town and knew immediately that he was a foreigner. He went up to him and said, in perfect English, "Hello. My name is Abrahim, like the prophet. Let me help you while you're in this town."

He was several inches shorter and better dressed than most of the other men that my father had seen there. His head was bald, with the exception of two graying tufts of hair that arced behind his ears. The last two fingers on his right hand looked as if they had been crushed and then tied together. He bowed slightly when he introduced himself and walked with what might have been a small limp, which in my father's mind made trusting him easier.

At first, my father slept outside, near the harbor, where hundreds of other men also camped out, most of them refugees like him. Abrahim had told him that it was dangerous to sleep alone, but he had also said that if he slept in the town he was certain to be beaten and arrested by the police.

After a week out there, he heard footsteps near his head just as he was falling asleep. When he opened his eyes and looked up he saw three men standing nearby, their backs all slightly turned to him, so that he could see only their long white djellabahs, dirty but not nearly as filthy as some of the others that he had recently seen. As he watched, one of the men lifted his hands into the air slowly, as if he were struggling to pass something over his head. He recited a prayer that my father had heard several times on his way to Sudan and on multiple occasions in Ethiopia at the homes of Muslim friends. The man repeated the prayer a second and then a third time, and when he was finished the two other men bent down and picked up what at first appeared to be a sack of grain but which, he realized a second later, was clearly a body. The man had been lying there when my father went to sleep. There had been nothing to indicate that he was dead or even injured. When my father told Abrahim the next day, his response was simple: "Don't think about it too much. It's easy to die around here and have no one notice."

He promised to find my father a better place to sleep, and he did. Later that same day, he found my father preparing his mat near the harbor, and told him to follow him. "I have a surprise for you," he said.

The owner of the boarding house where he was going to stay from now on was a business associate of Abrahim's. "We've worked together many times over the years," Abrahim told my father, although he never explained what they did. When my father asked him how he could repay his kindness, he waved the question away. "Don't worry," Abrahim told him. "You can do something for me later."

Unlike most of what I had told my students so far, Abrahim had a real history that I could draw on. My father had mentioned him regularly, not as a part of normal conversation but as a casual aside that could come up at any time without warning. Unbidden, my father had often said that Abrahim was the only real friend he had ever had, and on several occasions he had credited him with saving his life. At other times, my father had claimed that the world was full of crooks, and that after his experiences with a man named Abrahim in Sudan he would never trust a Sudanese, Muslim, or African again.

The Abrahim who came to life in my classroom was a far nobler man than the one I had previously imagined. This Abrahim had a flair for blunt but poetic statements, like the time he told my father that even the sand in the port town was of an inferior quality to the kind he had known in his home village, hundreds of kilometres west of there. "Everything here is shit," he said. "Even the sand."

Eventually he got my father a better-paying second job, as a porter on the docks. He told him, "You're going to be my best investment yet. Everything I give to you I will get back tenfold." Abrahim came by almost every day to share a cup of tea shortly after evening prayers, when hundreds of individual trails of smoke from the campfires wound their way up into the sky. He would pinch and pull at my father's waist as if he were a goat or a sheep and then say, "What do you expect? I have to check on the health of my investment." Afterward, as he was leaving, he always offered the same simple piece of advice:

"Stretch, Yosef!" he would yell out. "Stretch all the time, until your body becomes as loose as a monkey's."

At the docks, my father carried boxes from dawn until midday, when it got too hot to work. Before his shift at the teahouse, he would take a nap under a tree and look at the sea and think about the water in front of him. Like most of the men, he was thirsty all the time and convinced that there was something irreparably cruel about a place that put water that could not be drunk in front of you. He imagined building a boat of his own, something simple but sturdy that could at the very least make its way across the gulf to Saudi Arabia. And, if that were to fail, then he'd stuff himself into a box and drift until he reached a foreign shore or died trying.

At least once or twice a week, Abrahim would pick my father up from his room in the evening and walk him down to the docks in order to explain to him how the port town really worked. The only lights they saw came from the scattered fires around which groups of men were huddled. Despite the darkness, people moved about freely and in greater numbers than during the day. It was as if a second city were buried underneath the first, and excavated each night. Women without veils could be spotted along some of the narrow back streets, and my father could smell roasting meat and strong liquor.

"The ships that you see at the far end of the port are all government-controlled," Abrahim told my father. "They carry one of two things: food or weapons. We don't make either in Sudan. You may have noticed this. That doesn't mean we don't love them equally. Maybe the weapons more. Have you ever seen a hungry man with a gun? Of course not. Always stay away from that part of the dock. It's run by a couple of generals and a colonel who report straight to the President. They are like gods in this little town, but with better cars. If a soldier sees you there's nothing I can do to help. Not even God will save a fool.

"The food is supposed to go to the south. It comes from all over the world in great big sacks that say 'U.S.A.' Instead, it goes straight to Khartoum with the weapons. And do you know why? Because it's easier and cheaper to starve people to death than to shoot them. Bullets cost money. Soldiers cost money. Keeping all the food in a warehouse costs nothing."

In the course of several evenings, Abrahim worked his way down the line of boats docked in the harbor. His favorite ones, he said, were those near the end.

"Those ships over there—all the way at the other end. Those

are the ones you need to think about. Those are the ones that
go to Europe. You know how you can tell? Look at the flags.
You see that one there—with the black and gold? It goes all the
way to Italy or Spain. Maybe even France. Some of the men
who work on it are friends of mine. Business associates. You
can trust them. They're not like the rest of the people here, who
will disappear with your money."

After that night, my father began to take seriously Abrahim's
advice about stretching. He worked his body into various posi-
tions that he would hold for ten or fifteen minutes, and then for
as long as an hour. At night before he went to bed he practiced
sitting with his legs crossed, and then he stretched his back by
curling himself into a ball. After four months he could hold
that position for hours, which was precisely what Abrahim told
him he would need to do.

"The first few hours will be the hardest," he said. "You'll
have to be on the ship before it's fully loaded, and then you
will have to stay completely hidden. Only once it's far out to
sea will you be able to move."

My father thought about writing a letter to his family, but
he didn't know what to say. No one knew for certain if he was
alive, and, until he was confident that he would remain so, he
preferred to keep it that way. It was better than writing home
and saying, "Hello. I miss you. I'm alive and well," when only
the first half of that statement was certain still to be true by
the time the letter arrived.

Four months and three weeks after my father arrived in the
port town, war broke out in the east. A garrison of soldiers sta-
tioned in a village five hundred miles away revolted, and with
the help of the villagers began to take over vast swaths of terri-
tory in the name of forming an independent state for all the
black tribes of the country. There were rumors of massacres on
both sides. Who was responsible for the killing always de-
pended on who was talking. It was said that in one village all
the young boys had been forced to dig graves for their parents
and siblings before watching their executions. Afterward they
were forced to join the rebellion that still didn't have a name.

Factions began to erupt all over the town. Older men who

remembered the last war tended to favor the government, since they had once been soldiers as well. Anyone who was born in the south of the country was ardently in favor of the rebels, and many vowed to join them if they ever came close.

Abrahim and my father stopped going to the port at night. "When the fighting breaks out here," Abrahim told him, "they'll attack the port first. They'll burn the local ships and try to take control of the government ones."

Every day more soldiers arrived. There had always been soldiers in town, but these new ones were different. They came from the opposite corner of the country and spoke none of the local languages; what Arabic they spoke was often almost impossible to understand. The senior commanders, who rode standing up in their jeeps, all wore bright-gold sunglasses that covered half their face, but it was clear regardless that they were foreigners, and had been brought here because they had no attachment to the town or to its people.

At night my father often heard gunfire mixed in with the sound of dogs howling. Every day he pleaded with Abrahim to help him find a way out.

"I have plenty of money saved now," he said, even though it was a lie. If there was an honest exit, he would find a way to pay for it. Abrahim's response was always the same: "A man who has no patience here is better off in Hell."

Two weeks after the first stories of the rebellion appeared, there was talk in the market of a mile-long convoy of jeeps heading toward the town. The foreign ships had begun to leave the port that morning. The rebels were advancing, and would be there by the end of the afternoon. Within hours the rumors had circled the town. They would spare no one. They would attack only the soldiers. They would be greeted as liberators. They were like animals and should be treated as such. My father watched as the women who lived nearby folded their belongings into bags and made for the road with their children at their side or strapped to their backs. Where are they going? he wondered. They have the sea on one side and a desert on the other.

Abrahim found him after lunch. There was no one to serve tea to that day.

"I see you're very busy," he said. "You want me to come back when it's less crowded?"

"Are you leaving?" my father asked him.

"I already have," Abrahim said. "A long time ago. My entire family is already in Khartoum. I'm just waiting for my body to join them."

By late in the afternoon they could hear distant mortar shells slamming into the desert. "They're like children with toys," Abrahim said, pointing out to the desert from the roof of the boarding house, where they were standing. "They don't even know yet how far they can shoot with their big guns. There's nothing out there—or maybe they'll get lucky and kill a camel. They'll keep doing that until eventually they run out of shells, or camels.

"It's going to be terrible what happens to them," Abrahim continued. "They think they can scare away the soldiers because they have a couple of big guns. They think it's 1898 and the Battle of Omdurman again, except now they're the British."

My father never thought that war could look simple or pathetic, but from that rooftop it did. The rebels were loudly announcing their approach, and, from what my father could see, the soldiers in the town had disappeared. He began to think that Abrahim was wrong, and that the rebels, despite their foolishness, would sweep into town with barely a struggle. He was thinking whether or not to say this to Abrahim when he heard the first distant rumbling over his head. Abrahim and my father turned and looked out toward the sea, where a plane was approaching, flying far too low. Within a minute, it was above them.

"This will be over soon," Abrahim said. They both waited to hear the sound of a bomb dropping, but nothing happened. The plane had pulled up at the last minute. Shots were harmlessly fired in its direction and the convoy kept approaching—a long, jagged line of old pickup trucks trying to escape the horizon.

When the same plane returned twenty minutes later, three slimmer and clearly foreign-made jets were flying close to it.

"The first was just a warning," Abrahim said. "To give them

a chance to at least try to run away. They were too stupid to understand that. They thought they had won."

The planes passed. My father and Abrahim counted the seconds. Even from a distance they made a spectacular roar—at least seven bombs were dropped directly onto the rebels, whose convoy disappeared into a cloud of smoke and sand. From some of the neighboring rooftops there were shouts of joy. Soldiers were soon spilling back out into the street singing their victory.

"They should never have tried to take the port," Abrahim said. "They could have spent years fighting in the desert for their little villages and no one would have really bothered them. But do you think any of those big countries were going to risk losing this beautiful port? By the end of tonight all the foreign ships will be back. Their governments will tell them that it's safe. They've taken care of the problem, and soon, maybe in a day or two, you'll be able to leave."

A week later, during my father's mid-afternoon break, Abrahim found him resting in his usual spot in the shade, staring out at the water. The two of them walked to a nearby café, and for the first time since my father had come to Sudan someone brought him a cup of tea and lunch.

"This is your going-away meal. Enjoy it," Abrahim said. "You're leaving tonight."

Abrahim ordered a large plate of grilled meats—sheep intestines and what looked to be the neck of a goat—cooked in a brown stew, a feast unlike anything my father had eaten in months. When the food came, he wanted to cry and was briefly afraid to eat it. Abrahim had always told him never to trust anyone, and of course my father had extended that advice to Abrahim himself. Perhaps this was Abrahim's final trick on him: perhaps the food would disappear just as he leaned over to touch it, or perhaps it was poisoned with something that would send him off into a deep sleep from which he would awake in shackles. My father reached into his pants and untied the pouch in which he carried all his money. He placed it on the table.

"That's everything I have," he said. "I don't know if it's enough."

Abrahim ignored the money and dipped into the food with a piece of bread.

"After where your hand has just been I suggest you wash it before eating," he said. "And take your purse with you."

When they were finished, Abrahim walked my father to a part of the town he had never seen before—a wide dusty street that grew increasingly narrow, until the tin-roofed shacks that lined it were almost touching one another. Abrahim and my father stopped in front of one of the houses, and Abrahim pulled back the curtain that served as the door. Inside, a heavyset older woman, head partly veiled, sat behind a wooden counter on top of which rested a row of variously sized glass bottles. Abrahim grabbed one and told my father to take a seat in the corner of the room where a group of pillows had been laid. He negotiated and argued with the woman for several minutes until, finally, he pulled a bundle of Sudanese notes from his breast pocket. He sat down next to my father and handed the bottle to him.

"A drink for the road," he said. "Take it slow."

If Abrahim's intention was to harm him, then so be it, my father thought. A decent meal and a drink afterward were not the worst way to go. If such things had been offered to every dying man in this town, then the line of men waiting to die would have stretched for miles.

"Give me your little purse now," Abrahim said. My father handed him the pouch and Abrahim flipped through the bills. He took a few notes from his own pile and added it to the collection.

"This will buy you water, maybe a little food, and the silence of a few people on board. Don't expect anything else from them. Don't ask for food or for anything that they don't give you. Don't look them in the eyes, and don't try to talk to them. They will act as if you don't exist, which is the best thing. If you do exist then they will throw you overboard at night. Men get on board and they begin to complain. They say their backs hurt or their legs hurt. They say they're thirsty or hungry. When that happens they're gagged and thrown into the sea, where they can have all the space and water they want."

My father took a sip of the liquor, whose harsh, acrid smell had filled the air the moment Abrahim popped the lid.

"When you get to Europe, this is what you are going to do. You are going to be arrested. You will tell them that you want political asylum and they will take you to a jail that looks like Heaven. They will give you food and clothes and even a bed to sleep in. You may never want to leave—that's how good it will feel. Tell them you were fighting against the Communists and they will love you. They will give you your pick of countries, and you will tell them that you want to go to England. You will tell them that you have left behind your wife in Sudan, and that her life is now in danger and you want her to come as well. You will show them this picture."

Abrahim pulled from his wallet a photograph of a young girl, no older than fifteen or sixteen, dressed in a bizarre array of Western clothes—a pleated black-and-white polka-dot dress that was several sizes too large, a pair of high-top sneakers, and makeup that had been painted on to make her look older.

"This is my daughter. She lives in Khartoum right now with her mother and aunts. She's very bright. The best student in her class. When you get to England you're going to say that she's your wife. This is how you're going to repay me. Do you understand?"

My father nodded.

"This is proof of your marriage," Abrahim said. "I had to spend a lot of money to get that made."

Abrahim handed him a slip of paper that had been folded only twice in its life, since such paper didn't last long in environments like this. The words spelled it out clearly. My father had been married for almost two years to a person he had never met.

"You will give this to someone at the British Embassy," Abrahim said, laying his hands on top of my father's, as if the two were entering into a secret pact simply by touching the same piece of paper. "It may take some weeks, but eventually they will give her the visa. You will then call me from London, and I will take care of the rest. We have the money for the ticket, and some more for both of you when she arrives. Maybe after one or two years her mother and I will join you in London. We will buy a home. Start a business together. My daughter will continue her studies."

Even for a skeptical man like my father, who had little faith in governments, the story was seductive: a tale that began with heavenly prisons and ended with a pre-made family living in a home in London. He didn't want to see how much Abrahim believed in it himself, and so he kept his head slightly turned away. When it came to Europe or America, even people supposedly hardened by time and experience were susceptible to almost childish fantasies.

My father took the photograph from Abrahim and placed it in his pocket. He didn't say, "Of course I will do this," or even a simple "Yes," because such confirmation would have meant that there was an option to refuse, and no such thing existed between them. Abrahim told him to finish his drink. "Your ship is waiting," he said.

Soon, stories about my father were circulating freely around the Academy. I heard snippets of my own narrative played back to me in a slightly distorted form—in these versions, the story might take place in the Congo, amid famine. One version I heard said that my father had been in multiple wars across Africa. Another claimed that he had lived through a forgotten genocide, one in which tens of thousands were killed in a single day. Some wondered whether he had also been in Rwanda—or in Darfur, where such things were commonly known to occur.

Huge tides of sympathy were mounting for my dead father and me. Students I had never spoken to now said hello to me when they saw me in the hallway. There were smiles for me everywhere I went, all because I had brought directly to their door a tragedy that outstripped anything they could personally have hoped to experience.

I knew that it was only a matter of time before I was called to account for what I had been teaching my students. On a Friday, the dean caught me in the hall just as I was preparing to enter my classroom. There was nothing threatening or angry in his voice. He simply said, "Come and see me in my office when your class is over."

That day I decided to skip the story and return to my usual syllabus. I said to my students, "We have some work to catch up on today. Here are the assignments from last week. I want you to work on them quietly." If they groaned or mumbled something, I didn't hear it, and hardly cared. When class was over, I walked slowly up the three flights of stairs that led to the dean's office. He was waiting for me with the door open. His wide and slightly awkward body was pitched over the large wooden desk far enough so that it might have made it difficult for him to breathe. As soon as I sat down, he leaned back and exhaled.

"How was class today?" he asked me.

"Fine," I told him. "Nothing exceptional."

"I've heard some of the stories about your father that you've been telling your students," he said. At that point I expected him to reveal at least a hint of anger at what I had done, but there wasn't even a dramatic folding of the arms.

"It's very interesting what they're saying," he said. "Awful, of course, as well. No one should have to live through anything even remotely like that, which leads me to ask: How much of what they're saying is true?"

"Almost none of it," I told him. I was ready to admit that I had made up most of what I had told my students—the late nights at the port, the story of an invading rebel army storming across the desert. But before I could say anything further he gave me a sly, almost sarcastic smile.

"Well, regardless of that," he said, "it's good to hear them talking about important things. So much of what I hear from them is shallow, silly rumors. They can sort out what's true for themselves later."

And that was all it came down to: I had given my students something to think about, and whether what they heard from me had any relationship to reality hardly mattered; real or not, it was all imaginary for them. That death was involved only made the story more compelling.

I began my final lesson with my father and Abrahim walking down to the pier on their last morning together. They didn't say much along the way, but on occasion a few words slipped out. Abrahim had important ideas that he wanted to express, but he had never known the exact words for them in any language. If he could have, he would have grabbed my father firmly by the wrist and held him until he was certain that he understood just how much he depended on him and how much he had begun almost to hate him for that. My father, meanwhile, was desperate to get away. He was terrified of boarding the ship, but he was more frightened of Abrahim's desire.

When they reached the pier, Abrahim pointed to the last of three boats docked in the harbor. "It's that one," he said. "The one with the blue hull."

My father stared at the boat for a long time and tried to imagine what it would be like to be buried inside it, first for an hour and then for a day. He didn't have the courage to imagine anything longer. The boat was old, but almost everything in the town was old.

There was a tall, light-skinned man waiting at the end of the docks. He was from one of the Arab tribes in the north. Such men were common in town. They controlled most of its business and politics and had done so for centuries. They were traders, merchants, and sold anything or anyone. They held themselves at a slight remove from other men, gowned in spotless white or, on occasion, pastel-colored robes that somehow proved immune to the dust that covered every inch of the town.

"He's arranged everything," Abrahim said. "That man over there."

My father tried to make out his face from where they were standing, but the man seemed to understand that they were talking about him and kept his head turned slightly away. The only feature that my father could make out was an abnormally long and narrow nose, a feature that seemed almost predatory.

Abrahim handed my father a slip of yellow legal paper on which he had written something in Arabic. He would have liked Abrahim to say something kind and reassuring to him. He wanted him to say, "Have a safe journey" or "Don't worry. You're going to be fine," but he knew that he could stand there for years and no such reassurances would come. "Don't keep him waiting," Abrahim said. "Give him the note and your money. And do whatever he tells you." When my father was halfway between Abrahim and the man, Abrahim called out to him, "I'll be waiting to hear from you soon," and my father knew that was the last time he would ever hear Abrahim's voice.

My father handed over the slip of paper Abrahim had given him. He couldn't read what was written on it and was worried that it might say any of a thousand different things, from "Treat this man well" to "Take his money and do whatever you want with him."

The man pointed to a group of small storage slots at the stern of the boat that were used for holding the more delicate cargo. These crates were usually unloaded last, and he had often seen people waiting at the docks for hours to receive them. They always bore the stamp of a Western country and carried their instructions in a foreign language—"*Cuidado*," "Fragile." He had unloaded several such crates himself recently, and while he had never known their actual contents he had tried to guess what was inside: cartons of powdered milk, a television or stereo, vodka, Scotch, Ethiopian coffee, soft blankets, clean water, hundreds of new shoes and shirts and underwear. Anything that he was missing or knew he would never have he imagined arriving in those boxes.

There was a square hole just large enough for my father to fit into if he pulled his knees up to his chest. He understood that this was where he was supposed to go and yet naturally he hesitated, sizing up the dimensions just as he had once sized up the crates he had helped unload.

My father felt the man's hand around the back of his neck, pushing him toward the ground. He wanted to tell the man that he was prepared to enter on his own, and had in fact been preparing to do so for months now, but he wouldn't have been understood, so my father let himself be led. He crawled into the space on his knees, which was not how he would have liked to enter. Head first was the way to go, but it was too late now. In a final humiliating gesture, the man shoved him with his foot, stuffing him inside so quickly that his legs and arms collapsed around him. He had just enough time to arrange himself before the man sealed the entrance with a wooden door that was resting nearby.

Before getting on the boat, my father had made a list of things to think about in order to get through the journey. They were filed away under topic headings such as The Place Where I Was Born, Plans for the Future, and Important Words in English. He wasn't sure if he should turn to them now or wait until the boat was out of the harbor. The darkness inside the box was alarming, but it wasn't yet complete. Light still filtered in through the entrance, and continued to do so until the hull was closed and the boat began to pull away from the shore. He remembered that as a child he had often been afraid of the dark, a foolish, almost impossible thing for a country boy, but there it was. Of the vast extended family that lived around him, his mother was the only one who never mocked him for this, and even though he would have liked to save her image for later in the journey, at a point when he was far off at sea, he let himself think about her now. He saw her as she looked shortly before she died. She had been a large woman, but at that point there wasn't much left of her. Her hair hadn't gone gray yet, but it had been cut short on the advice of a cousin who had dreamed that the illness attacking her body was buried somewhere in her head and needed a way out. Desperate, she had had almost all her hair cut off, which had made her look even younger than her thirty-something years. This was the image he had, of his mother in an almost doll-like state, just two months before she died, and while he would have liked to have a better memory of her, he settled for the one he'd been given and closed his eyes to concentrate on it. It would be some minutes before he noticed the engine churning as the ship pulled up its anchors and slowly headed out to sea.

When I reached this point, I knew that it was the last thing I was going to say to my class. Soon, the dean would call me back to his office to tell me that, as interesting as my father's story was, it had gone on long enough, and it was time to return my class to normal, or risk my place at the Academy. The bell rang, and, as when I had begun this story, there were a good ten to fifteen seconds when no one in the classroom moved. My students, for all their considerable wealth and privilege, were still at an age where they believed that the world was a fascinating, remarkable place, worthy of curious inquiry and close scrutiny, and I'd like to think that I had reminded them of that. Soon enough they would grow out of that and concern themselves with the things that were most immediately relevant to their own lives. Eventually one bag was picked up off the floor, and then twenty-eight others joined it. Most of my students waved or nodded their heads as they left the room, and there was a part of me that wanted to call them back to their seats and tell them that the story wasn't quite finished yet. Getting out of Sudan was only the beginning; there was still much more ahead. Sometimes, in my imagination, that is exactly what I tell them. I pick up where I left off, and go on to describe to them how, despite all appearances, my father did not actually make it off that boat alive. He arrived in Europe just as Abrahim had promised he would, but an important part of him had died during the journey, somewhere in the final three days, when he was reduced to drinking his urine for water and could no longer feel his hands or feet.

He spent six months in a detention camp on an island off the coast of Italy. He was surprised to find that there were plenty of other men like him there, from every possible corner of Africa, and that many had fared worse than he had. He heard stories of men who had died trying to make a similar voyage, who had suffocated or been thrown overboard alive. My father couldn't even bring himself to pity them. Contrary to what Abrahim had told him, there was nothing even remotely heavenly about where he was held: one large whitewashed room with cots every ten inches and bars over the windows. The guards often yelled at him and the other prisoners. He learned a few words in Italian and was mocked viciously the first time he used them. He was once forced to repeat a single phrase over and over to each new guard who arrived. When he tried to refuse, his first meal of the day, a plate of cold, dry meat and stale bread, was taken away from him. "Speak," the guards commanded, and he did so dozens of times in the course of several days, even though there was no humor left in it for anyone.

"You speak Italian?" the guards asked.

"No."

Speak. Talk. Or, more rarely, Say something.

In Italy he was given asylum and set free. From there he worked his way north and then west across Europe. He met dozens of other Abrahims, men who promised him that when they made it to London the rest of their lives would finally resolve into the picture they had imagined. "It's different there," they always said. There had to be at least one place in this world where life could be lived in accordance with the plans and dreams they had concocted for themselves. For most, that place was London; for some it was Paris, and for a smaller but bolder few it was America. That faith had carried them this far, and even though it was weakening, and needed constant readjustment ("Rome is not what I thought it would be. France will surely be better"), it persisted out of sheer necessity. By the time my father finally made it to London, eighteen months later, he had begun to think of all the men he met as variations of Abrahim, all of them crippled and deformed by their dreams.

Abrahim had followed him all the way to London to test him, and my father was determined to settle that debt now that he was there. On his first day in the city he found a quiet corner of Hampstead Heath. An American guidebook that he had picked up in France had said that he would be afforded a wide, sweeping view of the city from there. At the edge of the park, with London at his feet, he set fire to all the documents that he had brought with him from Sudan. The fake marriage license turned to ashes in seconds. The picture of Abrahim's daughter melted away near a large green hedge with ripe, inedible red

berries hanging from it. For many nights afterward, he refused
to think about her or her father. There were no rewards in life
for such stupidity, and he promised himself never to fall victim
to that kind of blind, wishful thinking. Anyone who did de-
served whatever suffering he was bound to meet.

SALMAN RUSHDIE

GOOD ADVICE IS RARER THAN RUBIES

On the last Tuesday of the month, the dawn bus, its headlamps still shining, brought Miss Rehana to the gates of the British Consulate. It arrived pushing a cloud of dust, veiling her beauty from the eyes of strangers until she descended. The bus was brightly painted in multicoloured arabesques, and on the front it said 'MOVE OVER DARLING' in green and gold letters; on the back it added 'TATA-BATA' and also 'O.K. GOOD-LIFE'. Miss Rehana told the driver it was a beautiful bus, and he jumped down and held the door open for her, bowing theatrically as she descended.

Miss Rehana's eyes were large and black and bright enough not to need the help of antimony, and when the advice expert Muhammad Ali saw them he felt himself becoming young again. He watched her approaching the Consulate gates as the light strengthened, and asking the bearded lala who guarded them in a gold-buttoned khaki uniform with a cockaded turban when they would open. The lala, usually so rude to the Consulate's Tuesday women, answered Miss Rehana with something like courtesy.

'Half an hour,' he said gruffly. 'Maybe two hours. Who knows? The sahibs are eating their breakfast.'

The dusty compound between the bus stop and the Consulate was already full of Tuesday women, some veiled, a few bare-faced like Miss Rehana. They all looked frightened, and leaned heavily on the arms of uncles or brothers, who were trying to look confident. But Miss Rehana had come on her own, and did not seem at all alarmed.

Muhammad Ali, who specialised in advising the most vulnerable-looking of these weekly supplicants, found his feet leading him towards the strange, big-eyed, independent girl.

'Miss,' he began. 'You have come for permit to London, I think so?'

She was standing at a hot-snack stall in the little shanty-town by the edge of the compound, munching chilli-pakoras contentedly. She turned to look at him, and at close range those eyes did bad things to his digestive tract.

'Yes, I have.'

'Then, please, you allow me to give some advice? Small cost only.'

Miss Rehana smiled. 'Good advice is rarer than rubies,' she said. 'But alas, I cannot pay. I am an orphan, not one of your wealthy ladies.'

'Trust my grey hairs,' Muhammad Ali urged her. 'My advice is well tempered by experience. You will certainly find it good.'

She shook her head. 'I tell you I am a poor potato. There are women here with male family members, all earning good wages. Go to them. Good advice should find good money.'

I am going crazy, Muhammad Ali thought, because he heard his voice telling her of its own volition, 'Miss, I have been drawn to you by Fate. What to do? Our meeting was written. I also am a poor man only, but for you my advice comes free.'

She smiled again. 'Then I must surely listen. When Fate sends a gift, one receives good fortune.'

He led her to the low wooden desk in his own special corner of the shanty-town. She followed, continuing to eat pakoras from a little newspaper packet. She did not offer him any.

Muhammad Ali put a cushion on the dusty ground. 'Please to sit.' She did as he asked. He sat cross-legged across the desk from her, conscious that two or three dozen pairs of male eyes were watching him enviously, that all the other shanty-town men were ogling the latest young lovely to be charmed by the old grey-hair fraud. He took a deep breath to settle himself.

'Name, please.'

'Miss Rehana,' she told him. 'Fiancée of Mustafa Dar of Bradford, London.'

'Bradford, England,' he corrected her gently. 'London is a town only, like Multan or Bahawalpur. England is a great nation full of the coldest fish in the world.'

'I see. Thank you,' she responded gravely, so that he was unsure if she was making fun of him.

'You have filled application form? Then let me see, please.'

She passed him a neatly folded document in a brown envelope.

'Is it OK?' For the first time there was a note of anxiety in her voice.

He patted the desk quite near the place where her hand rested. 'I am certain,' he said. 'Wait on and I will check.'

She finished the pakoras while he scanned her papers.

'Tip-top,' he pronounced at length. 'All in order.'

'Thank you for your advice,' she said, making as if to rise. 'I'll go now and wait by the gate.'

'What are you thinking?' he cried loudly, smiting his forehead. 'You consider this is easy business? Just give the form and poof, with a big smile they hand over the permit? Miss Rehana, I tell you, you are entering a worse place than any police station.'

'Is it so, truly?' His oratory had done the trick. She was a captive audience now, and he would be able to look at her for a few moments longer.

Drawing another calming breath, he launched into his set speech. He told her that the sahibs thought that all the women who came on Tuesdays, claiming to be dependents of bus drivers in Luton or chartered accountants in Manchester, were crooks and liars and cheats.

She protested, 'But then I will simply tell them that I, for one, am no such thing!'

Her innocence made him shiver with fear for her. She was a sparrow, he told her, and they were men with hooded eyes, like hawks. He explained that they would ask her questions, personal questions, questions such as a lady's own brother would be too shy to ask. They would ask if she was virgin, and, if not, what her fiancé's love-making habits were, and what secret nicknames they had invented for one another.

Muhammad Ali spoke brutally, on purpose, to lessen the shock she would feel when it, or something like it, actually happened. Her eyes remained steady, but her hands began to flutter at the edges of the desk.

He went on:

'They will ask you how many rooms are in your family home, and what colour are the walls, and what days do you empty the rubbish. They will ask your man's mother's third cousin's aunt's step-daughter's middle name. And all these things they have already asked your Mustafa Dar in his Bradford. And if you make one mistake, you are finished.'

'Yes,' she said, and he could hear her disciplining her voice. 'And what is your advice, old man?'

It was at this point that Muhammad Ali usually began to whisper urgently, to mention that he knew a man, a very good type, who worked in the Consulate, and through him, for a fee, the necessary papers could be delivered, with all the proper authenticating seals. Business was good, because the women would often pay him five hundred rupees or give him a gold bracelet for his pains, and go away happy.

They came from hundreds of miles away—he normally made sure of this before beginning to trick them—so even when they discovered they had been swindled they were unlikely to return. They went away to Sargodha or Lalukhet and began to pack, and who knows at what point they found out they had been gulled, but it was at a too-late point, anyway.

Life is hard, and an old man must live by his wits. It was not up to Muhammad Ali to have compassion for these Tuesday women.

But once again his voice betrayed him, and instead of starting his customary speech it began to reveal to her his greatest secret.

'Miss Rehana,' his voice said, and he listened to it in amazement, 'you are a rare person, a jewel, and for you I will do what I would not do for my own daughter, perhaps. One document has come into my possession that can solve all your worries at one stroke.'

'And what is this sorcerer's paper?' she asked, her eyes unquestionably laughing at him now.

His voice fell low-as-low.

'Miss Rehana, it is a British passport. Completely genuine and pukka goods. I have a good friend who will put your name and photo, and then, hey-presto, England there you come!'

He had said it!

Anything was possible now, on this day of his insanity. Probably he would give her the thing free-gratis, and then kick himself for a year afterwards.

Old fool, he berated himself. *The oldest fools are bewitched by the youngest girls.*

'Let me understand you,' she was saying. 'You are proposing I should commit a crime . . .'

'Not crime,' he interposed. 'Facilitation.'

'. . . and go to Bradford, London, illegally, and therefore justify the low opinion the Consulate sahibs have of us all. Old babuji, this is not good advice.'

'Bradford, *England*,' he corrected her mournfully. 'You should not take my gift in such a spirit.'

'Then how?'

'Bibi, I am a poor fellow, and I have offered this prize because you are so beautiful. Do not spit on my generosity. Take the thing. Or else don't take, go home, forget England, only do not go into that building and lose your dignity.'

But she was on her feet, turning away from him, walking towards the gates, where the women had begun to cluster and the lala was swearing at them to be patient or none of them would be admitted at all.

'So be a fool,' Muhammad Ali shouted after her. 'What goes of my father's if you are?' (Meaning, what was it to him.)

She did not turn.

'It is the curse of our people,' he yelled. 'We are poor, we are ignorant, and we completely refuse to learn.'

'Hey, Muhammad Ali,' the woman at the betel-nut stall called across to him. 'Too bad, she likes them young.'

That day Muhammad Ali did nothing but stand around near the Consulate gates. Many times he scolded himself, *Go from here, old goof, lady does not desire to speak with you any further.* But when she came out, she found him waiting.

'Salaam, advice wallah,' she greeted him.

She seemed calm, and at peace with him again, and he thought, *My God, ya Allah, she has pulled it off. The British sahibs also have been drowning in her eyes and she has got her passage to England.*

He smiled at her hopefully. She smiled back with no trouble at all.

'Miss Rehana Begum,' he said, 'felicitations, daughter, on what is obviously your hour of triumph.'

Impulsively, she took his forearm in her hand.

'Come,' she said. 'Let me buy you a pakora to thank you for your advice and to apologise for my rudeness, too.'

They stood in the dust of the afternoon compound near the bus, which was getting ready to leave. Coolies were tying bedding rolls to the roof. A hawker shouted at the passengers, trying to sell them love stories and green medicines, both of which cured unhappiness. Miss Rehana and a happy Muhammad Ali ate their pakoras sitting on the bus's 'front mudguard', that is, the bumper. The old advice expert began softly to hum a tune from a movie soundtrack. The day's heat was gone.

'It was an arranged engagement,' Miss Rehana said all at once. 'I was nine years old when my parents fixed it. Mustafa Dar was already thirty at that time, but my father wanted someone who could look after me as he had done himself and Mustafa was a man known to Daddyji as a solid type. Then my parents died and Mustafa Dar went to England and said he would send for me. That was many years ago. I have his photo, but he is like a stranger to me. Even his voice, I do not recognise it on the phone.'

The confession took Muhammad Ali by surprise, but he nodded with what he hoped looked like wisdom.

'Still and after all,' he said, 'one's parents act in one's best interests. They found you a good and honest man who has kept his word and sent for you. And now you have a lifetime to get to know him, and to love.'

He was puzzled, now, by the bitterness that had infected her smile.

'But, old man,' she asked him, 'why have you already packed me and posted me off to England?'

He stood up, shocked.

'You looked happy—so I just assumed . . . excuse me, but they turned you down or what?'

'I got all their questions wrong,' she replied. 'Distinguishing marks I put on the wrong cheeks, bathroom decor I completely redecorated, all absolutely topsy-turvy, you see.'

'But what to do? How will you go?'

'Now I will go back to Lahore and my job. I work in a great house, as ayah to three good boys. They would have been sad to see me leave.'

'But this is tragedy!' Muhammad Ali lamented. 'Oh, how I pray that you had taken up my offer! Now, but, it is not possible, I regret to inform. Now they have your form on file, cross-check can be made, even the passport will not suffice.

'It is spoilt, all spoilt, and it could have been so easy if advice had been accepted in good time.'

'I do not think,' she told him, 'I truly do not think you should be sad.'

Her last smile, which he watched from the compound until the bus concealed it in a dust-cloud, was the happiest thing he had ever seen in his long, hot, hard, unloving life.

WARSAN SHIRE

CONVERSATIONS ABOUT HOME (AT THE DEPORTATION CENTRE)

Well, I think home spat me out, the blackouts and curfews like tongue against loose tooth. God, do you know how difficult it is, to talk about the day your own city dragged you by the hair, past the old prison, past the school gates, past the burning torsos erected on poles like flags? When I meet others like me I recognise the longing, the missing, the memory of ash on their faces. No one leaves home unless home is the mouth of a shark. I've been carrying the old anthem in my mouth for so long that there's no space for another song, another tongue or another language. I know a shame that shrouds, totally engulfs. I tore up and ate my own passport in an airport hotel. I'm bloated with language I can't afford to forget.

***

They ask me how did you get here? Can't you see it on my body? The Libyan desert red with immigrant bodies, the Gulf of Aden bloated, the city of Rome with no jacket. I hope the journey meant more than miles because all of my children are in the water. I thought the sea was safer than the land. I want to make love but my hair smells of war and running and running. I want to lay down, but these countries are like uncles who touch you when you're young and asleep. Look at all these borders, foaming at the mouth with bodies broken and desperate. I'm the colour of hot sun on my face, my mother's remains were never buried. I spent days and nights in the stomach of the truck, I did not come out the same. Sometimes it feels like someone else is wearing my body.

* * *

I know a few things to be true. I do not know where I am going, where I have come from is disappearing, I am unwelcome and my beauty is not beauty here. My body is burning with the shame of not belonging, my body is longing. I am the sin of memory and the absence of memory. I watch the news and my mouth becomes a sink full of blood. The lines, the forms, the people at the desks, the calling cards, the immigration officer, the looks on the street, the cold settling deep into my bones, the English classes at night, the distance I am from home. But Al-hamdulilah all of this is better than the scent of a woman completely on fire, or a truckload of men who look like my father, pulling out my teeth and nails, or fourteen men between my legs, or a gun, or a promise, or a lie, or his name, or his manhood in my mouth.

* * *

I hear them say, go home, I hear them say, fucking immigrants, fucking refugees. Are they really this arrogant? Do they not know that stability is like a lover with a sweet mouth upon your body one second and the next you are a tremor lying on the floor covered in rubble and old currency waiting for its return. All I can say is, I was once like you, the apathy, the pity, the ungrateful placement and now my home is the mouth of a shark, now my home is the barrel of a gun. I'll see you on the other side.

DUNYA MIKHAIL

ANOTHER PLANET

I have a special ticket
to another planet
beyond this Earth.
A comfortable world, and beautiful:
a world without much smoke,
not too hot
and not too cold.
The creatures
are gentler there,
and the governments
have no secrets.
The police are nonexistent:
there are no problems
and no fights.
And the schools
don't exhaust their students
with too much work
for history has yet to start
and there's no geography
and no other languages.
And even better:
the war
has left its "r" behind
and turned into love,
so the weapons sleep
beneath the dust,
and the planes pass by
without shelling the cities,

and the boats
look like smiles
on the water.
All things
are peaceful
and kind
on the other planet
beyond this Earth.
But still I hesitate
to go alone.

(TRANSLATED FROM THE ARABIC
BY KAREEM JAMES ABU-ZEID)

ARRIVALS

And, hungry for the old, familiar ways,
I turned aside and bowed my head and wept.
—CLAUDE McKAY, "THE TROPICS IN NEW YORK"

PHILLIS WHEATLEY

ON BEING BROUGHT FROM AFRICA TO AMERICA

'Twas mercy brought me from my Pagan land,
Taught my benighted soul to understand
That there's a God, that there's a Saviour too:
Once I redemption neither sought nor knew.
Some view our sable race with scornful eye,
"Their colour is a diabolic die."
Remember, Christians, Negros, black as Cain,
May be refin'd and join th'angelic train.

CLAUDE McKAY

THE TROPICS IN NEW YORK

Bananas ripe and green, and ginger-root,
Cocoa in pods and alligator pears,
And tangerines and mangoes and grape fruit,
Fit for the highest prize at parish fairs,

Set in the window, bringing memories
Of fruit-trees laden by low-singing rills,
And dewy dawns, and mystical blue skies
In benediction over nun-like hills.

My eyes grew dim, and I could no more gaze;
A wave of longing through my body swept,
And, hungry for the old, familiar ways,
I turned aside and bowed my head and wept.

E. R. BRAITHWAITE

From
TO SIR, WITH LOVE

I did not become a teacher out of any sense of vocation; mine was no considered decision in the interests of youthful humanity or the spread of planned education. It was a decision forced on me by the very urgent need to eat; it was a decision brought about by a chain of unhappy experiences which began about a week after my demobilization from the Royal Air Force in 1945.

* * *

At the Demobilization Center, after the usual round of Medical inspection, return of Service equipment, and issue of allowances and civilian clothing, I had been interviewed by an officer whose job it was to advise on careers. On learning that I had a science degree and varied experience in engineering technology, he expressed the opinion that I would have no difficulty in finding a good civilian job. Industry was re-organizing itself for post-war production and there was already an urgent demand for qualified technologists, especially in the field of electronics, which was my special interest. I had been very much encouraged by this, as I had made a point of keeping up with new trends and developments by borrowing books through the Central Library System, and by subscribing to various technical journals and magazines, so I felt quite confident of my ability to hold down a good job. He had given me a letter of introduction to the Higher Appointments Office in Tavistock

Square, London, and suggested that I call on them as soon as I had settled myself in "digs" and had enjoyed a short holiday.

While operating from the R.A.F. Station at Hornchurch in Essex during the war, I had met and been frequently entertained by an elderly couple who lived not far away at Brentwood; I had kept in touch with them ever since and had promised to stay with them after demobilization. I now went to live with them, and soon felt completely at home and at peace. They both professed to be atheists, but, judging by their conduct, they exhibited in their daily lives all those attributes which are fundamental to real, active Christianity. They were thoughtful for my comfort in every way, and shared many of my interests and pursuits with a zest which might well have been envied by much younger people. Together we went down to Torquay for a two-week holiday and returned to Brentwood completely refreshed.

Shortly after our return, I visited the Appointments Office, where I was interviewed by two courteous, impersonal men who questioned me closely on my academic background, service career and experience in industry. I explained that after graduating I had worked for two years as a Communications Engineer for the Standard Oil Company at their Aruba Refinery, earning enough to pay for post-graduate study in England. At the end of the interview they told me that I would be notified of any vacancies suitable to my experience and qualifications. Two weeks later I received a letter from the Appointments Office, together with a list of three firms, each of which had vacancies for qualified Communications Engineers. I promptly wrote to each one, stating my qualifications and experience, and soon received very encouraging replies, each with an invitation to an interview. Everything was working very smoothly and I felt on top of the world.

I was nervous as I stood in front of the Head Office in Mayfair; this firm had a high international reputation and the thought of being associated with it added to my excitement. Anyway, I reasoned, this was the first of the interviews, and if I boobed here there were still two chances remaining. The uniformed commissionaire courteously opened the large doors for me, and as I approached the receptionist's desk she smiled quite pleasantly.

"Good morning." Her brows were raised in polite inquiry.

"Good morning," I replied. "My name is Braithwaite. I am here for an interview with Mr. Symonds."

I had taken a great deal of care with my appearance that morning. I was wearing my best suit with the right shirt and tie and pocket handkerchief; my shoes were smartly polished, my teeth were well brushed and I was wearing my best smile—all this had passed the very critical inspection of Mr. and Mrs. Belmont with whom I lived. Yet the receptionist's smile suddenly wavered and disappeared. She reached for a large diary and consulted it as if to verify my statement, then she picked up the telephone and, cupping her hand around the mouthpiece as if for greater privacy, spoke rapidly into it, watching me furtively the while.

"Will you come this way?" She set off down a wide corridor, her back straight and stiff with a disapproval which was echoed in the tap-tap of her high heels. As I walked behind her I thought: normally she'd be swinging it from side to side; now it's stiff with anger.

At the end of the corridor we entered an automatic lift: the girl maintained a silent hostility and avoided looking at me. At the second floor we stepped out into a passage on to which several rooms opened; pausing briefly outside one of them she said "In there", and quickly retreated to the lift. I knocked on the door and entered a spacious room where four men were seated at a large table.

One of them rose, walked around to shake hands with me and introduce his colleagues, and then indicated a chair in which I seated myself. After a brief inquiry into my place of birth and R.A.F. service experience, they began to question me closely on telecommunications and the development of electronics in that field. The questions were studied, deliberate, and suddenly the nervousness which had plagued me all the morning disappeared; now I was confident, at ease with a familiar subject. They questioned me on theory, equipment, circuits, operation; on my training in the U.S.A., and on my experience there and in South America. They were thorough, but I was re-laxed now; the years of study, field work and post-graduate research were about to pay off, and I knew that I was holding my own, and even enjoying it.

And then it was all over. Mr. Symonds, the gentleman who had welcomed me, leaned back in his chair and looked from one to another of his associates. They nodded to him, and he said:

"Mr. Braithwaite, my associates and I are completely satisfied with your replies and feel sure that in terms of qualification, ability and experience, you are abundantly suited to the post we have in mind. But we are faced with a certain difficulty. Employing you would mean placing you in a position of authority over a number of our English employees, many of whom have been with us a very long time, and we feel that such an appointment would adversely affect the balance of good relationship which has always obtained in this firm. We could not offer you that post without the responsibility, neither would we ask you to accept the one or two other vacancies of a different type which do exist, for they are unsuitable for someone with your high standard of education and ability. So, I'm afraid, we will not be able to use you." At this he rose, extending his hand in the courtesy of dismissal.

I felt drained of strength and thought; yet somehow I managed to leave that office, navigate the passage, lift and corridor, and walk out of the building into the busy sunlit street. I had just been brought face to face with something I had either forgotten or completely ignored for more than six exciting years—my black skin. It had not mattered when I volunteered for aircrew service in 1940, it had not mattered during the period of flying training or when I received my wings and I was posted to a squadron; it had not mattered in the hectic uncertainties of operational flying, of living and loving from day to day, brothered to men who like myself had no tomorrow and could not afford to fritter away today on the absurdities of prejudice; it had not mattered when, uniformed and winged, I visited theaters and dance-halls, pubs and private houses.

I had forgotten about my black face during those years. I saw it daily yet never noticed its color. I was an airman in flying kit while on His Majesty's business, smiled at, encouraged, welcomed by grateful civilians in bars or on the street, who saw not me, but the uniform and its relationship to the glorious, undying "Few." Yes, I had forgotten about my skin when I had so eagerly discussed my post-war prospects with the Careers Officer and the Appointments people; I had quite forgotten about it as I jauntily entered that grand, imposing building. . . .

Now, as I walked sadly away, I consciously averted my eyes from the sight of my face reflected fleetingly in the large plate glass shop windows. Disappointment and resentment were a solid bitter rising lump inside me; I hurried into the nearest public lavatory and was violently sick.

Relieved, I walked about, somewhat aimlessly, and tried to pull myself together. The more I thought of it the more I realized that the whole interview had been a waste of time. They had agreed on their decision before I had walked into that office; the receptionist had told them about my black face, and all that followed, had been a cruel, meaningless charade. I stopped suddenly, struck by a new realization. Those folk must have looked at my name on the application forms and immediately assumed that I was white; there was nothing about the name Braithwaite to indicate my color, so the flowery letters and pleasant invitation to interview were really intended for the white applicant they imagined me to be. God, how they must have hated me for the trick I had so unwittingly played on them!

Acting on a sudden impulse, I went into a telephone booth and in turn called the two remaining firms. I explained that I wanted to let them know that I was a Negro, but would be very happy to attend for the interview if my color was no barrier to possible employment. In each case I was thanked for telephoning, but informed that the post had already been filled and it had been their intention to write me to that effect. So that was that. Angered and disgusted, I caught a train to take me as quickly as possible to the only place in all Britain where I knew I would feel safe and wanted—the Belmont home in Brentwood.

Belief in an ideal dies hard. I had believed in an ideal for all the twenty-eight years of my life—the ideal of the British Way of Life.

It had sustained me when as a youth in a high school of nearly all white students I had had to work harder or run faster than they needed to do in order to make the grade. It had inspired me in my College and University years when ideals were dragged in the dust of disillusionment following the Spanish Civil War. Because of it I had never sought to acquire American citizenship, and when, after graduation and two years of field work in Venezuela, I came to England for post-graduate study in 1939, I felt that at long last I was personally identified with the hub of fairness, tolerance and all the freedoms. It was therefore without any hesitation that I volunteered for service with the Royal Air Force in 1940, willing and ready to lay down my life for the preservation of the ideal which had been my lode-star. But now that self-same ideal was gall and wormwood in my mouth.

The majority of Britons at home have very little appreciation of what that intangible yet amazingly real and invaluable export—the British Way of Life—means to colonial people; and they seem to give little thought to the fantastic phenomenon of races so very different from themselves in pigmentation, and widely scattered geographically, assiduously identifying themselves with British loyalties, beliefs and traditions. This attitude can easily be observed in the way in which the colored Colonial will quote the British systems of Law, Education and Government, and will adopt fashions in dress and social codes, even though his knowledge of these things has depended largely on secondhand information. All this is especially true of the West Indian Colonials, who are predominantly the descendants of slaves who were forever removed from the cultural influence of their forefathers, and who lived, worked, and reared their children through the rigors of slavery and the growing pains of gradual enfranchisement, according to the only example they knew—the British Way.

The ties which bind them to Britain are strong, and this is very apparent on each occasion of a Royal visit, when all of them young and old, rich and poor, join happily together in unrestrained and joyful demonstrations of welcome. Yes, it is wonderful to be British—until one comes to Britain. By dint of careful saving or through hard-won scholarships many of them arrive in Britain to be educated in the Arts and Sciences and in the varied processes of legislative and administrative government. They come, bolstered by a firm, conditioned belief that Britain and the British stand for all that is best in both Christian and Democratic terms; in their naiveté they ascribe these high principles to all Britons, without exception.

I had grown up British in every way. Myself, my parents and my parents' parents, none of us knew or could know any other way of living, of thinking, of being; we knew no other cultural pattern, and I had never heard any of my forebears complain about being British. As a boy I was taught to appreciate English literature, poetry and prose, classical and contemporary, and it was absolutely natural for me to identify myself with the British heroes of the adventure stories against the villains of the piece who were invariably non-British and so, to my boyish mind, more easily capable of villainous conduct. The more selective reading of my college and university life was marked by the same predilection for English literature, and I did not hesitate to defend my preferences to my American colleagues. In fact, all the while in America, I vigorously resisted any criticism of Britain or British policy, even when in the privacy of my own room, closer examination clearly proved the reasonableness of such criticism.

It is possible to measure with considerable accuracy the rise and fall of the tides, or the behavior in space of objects invisible to the naked eye. But who can measure the depths of disillusionment? Within the somewhat restricted sphere of an academic institution, the Colonial student learns to heal, debate, to paint and to think; outside that sphere he has to meet the indignities and rebuffs of intolerance, prejudice and hate. After qualification and establishment in practice or position, the trials and successes of academic life are half forgotten in the hurly-burly of living, but the hurts are not so easily forgotten. Who can predict the end result of a landlady's coldness, a waiter's discourtesy, or the refusal of a young woman to dance?

The student of today may be the Prime Minister of tomorrow. Might not some future important political decision be influenced by a remembered slight or festering resentment? Is it reasonable to expect that those sons of Nigeria, the West Indies, British Guiana, Honduras, Malaya, Ceylon, Hong Kong and others who are constitutionally agitating for self-government, are completely unaffected by experiences of intolerance suffered in Britain and elsewhere?

To many in Britain a Negro is a "darky" or a "nigger" or a "black"; he is identified, in their minds, with inexhaustible brute strength; and often I would hear the remark "working like a nigger" or "laboring like a black" used to emphasize some occasion of sustained effort. They expect of him a courteous subservience and contentment with a lowly state of menial employment and slum accommodation. It is true that here and there one sees Negroes as doctors, lawyers or talented entertainers, but they are somehow considered "different" and not to be confused with the mass.

I am a Negro, and what had happened to me at that interview constituted, to my mind, a betrayal of faith. I had believed in freedom, in the freedom to live in the kind of dwelling I wanted, providing I was able and willing to pay the price; and in the freedom to work at the kind of profession for which I was qualified, without reference to my racial or religious origins. All the big talk of Democracy and Human Rights seemed as spurious as the glib guarantees with which some manufacturers underwrite their products in the confident hope that they will never be challenged. The Briton at home takes no responsibility for the protestations and promises made in his name by British officials overseas.

I reflected on my life in the U.S.A. There, when prejudice is felt, it is open, obvious, blatant; the white man makes his position very clear, and the black man fights those prejudices with equal openness and fervor, using every constitutional device available to him. The rest of the world in general and Britain in particular are prone to point an angrily critical finger at American intolerance, forgetting that in its short history as a nation it has granted to its Negro citizens more opportunities for advancement and betterment, *per capita*, than any other nation in the world with an indigenous Negro population. Each violent episode, though greatly to be deplored, has invariably preceded some change, some improvement in the American Negro's position. The things they have wanted were important enough for them to fight and die for, and those who died did not give their lives in vain. Furthermore, American Negroes have been generally established in communities in which their abilities as laborer, artisan, doctor, lawyer, scientist, educator and entertainer have been directly or indirectly of benefit to that community; in terms of social and religious intercourse they have been largely independent of white people.

In Britain I found things to be very different. I have yet to meet a single English person who has actually admitted to anti-Negro prejudice; it is even generally believed that no such thing exists here. A Negro is free to board any bus or train and sit anywhere, provided he has paid the appropriate fare; the fact that many people might pointedly avoid sitting near him is casually overlooked. He is free to seek accommodation in any licensed hotel or boarding house—the courteous refusal which frequently follows is never ascribed to prejudice. The betrayal I now felt was greater because it had been perpetrated with the greatest of charm and courtesy.

I realized at that moment that I was British, but evidently not a Briton, and that fine differentiation was now very important; I would need to re-examine myself and my whole future in terms of this new appraisal.

SAM SELVON

COME BACK TO GRENADA

Every time when winter come round, George so cold that he have to give up trying to get warm, and he used to sit down by the gas fire in the basement room he had in Bayswater, and think back 'bout them days in Grenada before the war.

Is so it was with him every winter—when the cold hit him so, he long to go back home, but in the summer, when all them white girls have on pretty clothes and coasting in the park, you mad to tell him then 'bout going back home, he want to kill you, he would say that you talking damn foolishness, that Brit'n is he country, and that he never going back to no small island life.

Well sometimes some of the boys used to drop round to have an old talk, especially on a Sunday morning, because George working night in a factory where they making things to clean pot and pan, and any other time but on a Sunday morning he does be sleeping sound, and if anybody mad enough to come and see him during the week, he play as if he didn't hear the bell when they ring it. If they ask him 'bout it afterwards, he say, 'Man, the bell not working properly, I tell the damn landlord 'bout it, but up to now he ain't fix it.'

Well Sunday morning is big old talk, George still lying down in bed under the blankets, and the boys making themself at home, some on the ground, some sitting down on the edge of the bed, some standing up. The fellars used to mop George coffee and bread good, so George begin to get up early and make breakfast and put away everything before they come, because some of them real hard, if even they ain't hungry they storing away something for when they go back outside.

So it turn out like a joke—the boys saying, 'But a-a, George, you living bad, man. No bread? No coffee?'

And George warm under the blankets and he belly full up with food, would laugh kiff-kiff as if is a joke in truth, and say, 'No man, I didn't have time to buy my rations yesterday.'

As for the gas fire, when old talk going hot and the gas burning low, George used to sit up and reach for he trousers from off the chair where they hanging and fumble in the pocket and say, 'I did forget to get some shillings for the meter. Any of you-all have a shilling?'

Then all the boys would begin to put they hand in they pocket and look all about, saying, no, they sorry man, but they ain't have a shilling, they only have two-shilling and sixty-cent piece, what ain't no use as the slot in the meter could only hold shilling. But in the end one of them does always have to shell up one, because George laying down there and he wouldn't budge until one of them find a shilling somewhere: 'Aps! Look I have one, it was right down in the corner of my pocket, I didn't feel it the first time.'

And the old talk does always be about home in the West Indies, in Trinidad and Jamaica and Barbados and Grenada, what they used to do, how they used to catch cascadoo in the river with pin and twine, and fly mad bull and play zwill, and pitch marble with byayr and buicken and buttards one, and talaline farts, and how rum so cheap back home, but over here everybody only drinking tea and ale. The old talk coming and going, they talking about all kind of thing, but in the end is always about home in the West Indies, how life was so good. But even though they saying that none of them making the suggestion to go back, as if they shame to say they miss home though they talking about good calaloo and pound plantain lunch on a Sunday, or a breadfruit roast with saltfish, and how down there the sun does be shining all the time.

Is some real characters does come round by George. You might think that when they come England they go change a little bit when they mix up with the English people and them, but is just as if they in a backyard in George Street in Port of Spain, all kind of common laugh and bacchanal talk going on brisk. They does treat Piccadilly Circus like Green Corner, and walked down Oxford Street is if they breezing down Frederick Street, and if they meet you in the road or in a bus or in the tube, is a big shout, 'What happening there, papa?'

And as for how they dress, nobody does mind your business in this London, so the boys cool, no fuss, all kind of second hand jacket and mildew overcoat and old hat with the brim turn up.

It had a fellar name Fatman. Well nobody know how he living, he is a man of mystery, because he ain't have no work, and the way he does get on, the small raise from the National Assistance is not the cause. One day the boys surprise to see Fatman driving motor car. 'Which part you get that, old man?' they ask him.

'I pick it up cheap down by Kensal Rise, man,' he answer them.

Well the second day Fatman get this car he meet up in an accident with a bus and he had to go to court. He come round by George mourning, with a lot of forms he had to full up. Fatman always confuse when he have forms to full up, and in this country you have bags of that to do. He and he wife always arguing, is not that way, no, you put the date in the wrong place, man, why you so stupid, you can't see where it say date of birth in the next line? So Fatman take up the forms and go round by George to full them up.

Then it have another fellar name Gogee, who from Trinidad. Gogee is really a nice fellar, but he like to get on ignorant sometimes. It have a thing with he and another Trinidadian fellar name Scottie what does always make George laugh for so. Scottie is a fellar with a little education, and he well like the English customs and thing, he does be polite and say thanks and he does get up in the bus and the tube to let them women sit down, which is a thing even them Englishmen don't do. And when he dress, you think is some Englishman going to work in the city, with bowler hat and umbrella and brief case. Only thing Scottie face black.

Well Scottie used to organise little fêtes here and there, like dance and party and so on. And everytime he worried if Gogee would turn up, because Gogee like to play rab and make Scottie feel small, though it does only be fun he making. Like one time, Scottie standing up near the door of the dancehall, dressup in black suit and bow tie, saying good evening and how do you do to all the people that coming to the dance. Well you could imagine Gogee bursting through the door in a hot jitterbug suit and bawling out, 'Scottie, you old reprobate! What happening?'

Naturally Scottie feel bad that in front of all these English people Gogee getting on so. 'Listen man,' he plead with Gogee, 'Why don't you behave and comport yourself properly in front of people and stop behaving like a ruffian?'

That put Gogee in a real worthless mood, and the more Scottie try to be gentleman, the more Gogee getting on like if he back in Trinidad, and he meet up with a good friend unexpected at a freeness.

'But how Scottie man, you looking prosperous, things going good with you. I hear you did make bags of money out of that fête you had by King's Cross last Saturday night. You think you will make a lot tonight? You got a good band playing tonight?'

And with that Gogee push past Scottie and barge into the dancehall, ignoring the fellar that collecting tickets as if is he self what giving the dance.

And during the fête, whenever Gogee catch Scottie watching him out of the corner of he eye, he starting to jock waist for so, and fanning with he jacket, and jumping up as if he at a Carnival slackness in the Queen's Park Building, only to make Scottie get vex.

Scottie shaking he head and saying he don't know why the boys don't behave like gentlemen for a change, that the English people would say how they don't know how to get on civilise. But Gogee and the boys high, they having a royal time, they only getting the band to play calypso and they dancing left and right.

Whenever Scottie have a fête, he too frighten that the boys rob and cause fight and disgrace, but it never have anything serious, except the time when a Jamaican fellar bust a coca-cola bottle on Fatman head because Fatman did dancing too close with he girl.

Poor Scottie, he not a bad sort of fellar really, but the boys like to pick on him so much, because they feel he playing stuckup and talking like Englishman. And now from the time Scottie see them coming through the door at any fête he giving, he know they not going to pay, and he does tell them to pass in quick and don't stand up and jam the door. It get so that all them West Indian hear how Scottie is a gentleman, and you should know that none of them ever pay at any of Scottie fête.

Then again, the boys might start to give Frederick picong when Scottie beg them to ease up. If Fatman is man of mystery, well Frederick is mystery father, because he is one Jamaican that you could never contact at all, he don't stay in one place for long. It must be ain't have nobody who know this London like he, it ain't have a part that he ain't live in already, and why you think? Because he don't pay rent no place where he got to live. Is test like him who muddy the water for a lot of other fellars. When Frederick get a place what taking coloured people, he tell the landlord that he is student, and that he does get money from home every two weeks. And he move in with everything, including an old banjo that he does play when he walking in the road, or standing up in a queue. Then when the Saturday come and the landlord come round to collect the rent, no mister Frederick there at all, he out off long time, in the night when it dark and nobody could see.

Next time you hear 'bout Frederick, is because he gone the other side of London to live. One day you hear he living Notting Hill Gate, the next day you hear he move and gone Clapham, a week after that you might bounce him up in Highgate. So he moving from landlord to landlord, owing them one two three weeks rent. Is a good thing London such a big place—by the time Frederick go round by all the places, he go be an old man and still doing the same thing, and still he would have plenty new places to go.

And the truth is, he really start up like a student, but he get in a mooch with an English girl, and since that time he forget all about studying and he start to hustle.

Well all these episodes coming up in the old talk in George

room. Until if George get in a good mood, he might get up and make some tea for the boys, and take a bread and some butter out of the cupboard.

They always giving George tone about going back to the West Indies, because George leave an old grandmother back home and she always writing and saying why you don't come back to Grenada, and telling him she would dead soon, that he better come quick. And he have a girlfriend too that he leave behind, the poor girl writing nearly every week, darling dou-dou why you don't come back Grenada and let we married?

But is as if London get in George blood, all the big building, all the big light and the big celebration, the trains that does go under the ground, and how nobody minding you business like in a small island. He used to stand up by the Circus and watch all them big advertising light going on and going off, like if is Carnival all the time, and people moving all about in the big life in London, all kind of Rolls-Royce in the road, and them rich people going theatre and ballet. One time Scottie did even encourage him to go to the Royal Albert Hall to hear a fellar play violin, and George put on a clean suit and he went and sit down, but when it was halfway he tell Scottie to come and go.

So even though it have times when things hard with him, still he feel as if he can't leave London at all. In the winter, when snow come and it so cold that he have to wear two three pull-over even when he sleeping, he does get a feeling to leave, because life hard in the winter, not even a shilling to put in the gas. Them times, he does think a lot 'bout Grenada, how down there the sun shining all the time, you could bathe in the sea everyday. Here it so cold that George does only bathe 'bout once a month, and not only because the weather grim, but it have so much confusion when you want to bathe, you have to clean out this big basin thing that just like a coffin, then you have to put money in the gas to get hot water, and let the water full up in the basin. You does have to sit down in it. You know how some-times them people in the country back home bathing the chil-dren, putting them in a bucket of water? Well is just like that.

Well, he have enough money save up, so when is winter the thought does come to him.

But after when the winter gone and birds sing and all the trees begin to put on leaves again, and flowers come and now and then the old sun shining, George would say he go stay until after the summer.

Every year is the same story, that's why he still in this country. In the beginning George used to shape up by the National Assistance people every week, but since he get this nightwork he working steady. Them English people think the boys lazy and goodfornothing and always on the dole, but George know is only because the white people don't want to give them work.

One time when he did new in England George get a work in a factory, and all the people in the place say they go strike unless the boss fire George. It was a big ballad in all the papers, they put it under a big headline, saying how the colour bar was causing trouble again, and a fellar come with a camera and wanted to take George photo, but George say no. Anyway a few days after that the boss call George and tell him that he worry, but as they cutting down the staff he would have to go. He put it in a real diplomatic way, so as not to make George feel bad, but he did well know is only because they didn't want him in the place.

So it not really as easy for the boys as some people think. True, it have some of them what only want to ants on the government, and don't do no work, only playing billiards and rummy all the time, but the majority of the boys willing to work if they could hustle a job somewhere.

Them was grim days when George wasn't working. He had to hustle all about, and sometimes nothing but a cup of weak tea to face the cold. He see real hell to get a place to live, all about landlords and landladies saying that they sorry, the rooms full up, but in truth is because they don't like black people.

Sometimes when George did walking down the road minding he own business, some little white child bawl out, 'Mummy, look at that black man!' And poor George don't know what to do. The child mother scold it and say, 'You mustn't say that, dear.'

But thing like that happen so much time that George skin come like rubber, and he bounce like a ball from house to house until he feel like if the vengeance of Moco on him. Then he get the basement room in Bayswater. Is a Pole who own the house, too besides, that's why he get the room.

Right after that he start up the nightwork and things brighten up a little bit. He eating regular meals and now and then he going to the tailor in Charing Cross Road and getting fit for a sharp suit, because now he have money is no more readymade or secondhand for him.

Every Saturday morning, he does go by a continental shop which part have a lot of food to see, like what he accustom to, like red beans and blackeye peas and rice and saltfish. It even have dasheen and green fig sometimes. It have a lot of spades docs go in that shop to buy, bags of them, and is joke to see how they does get on just as if they in a Chinaman shop back home. Couple Jamaica woman does stand up and talk while they waiting for message, 'But girl, if I tell you! She did lose the baby, yes . . . halfpound saltfish, please, the dry codfish. Yes, as I was telling you. . . . and two pound rice, and halfpound red beans, no, not that one, that one in the bag in the corner . . .'

This time so, they ain't bothering they head about the other people in the queue at all, they mauvalanging and bursting out in some loud kya-kya laugh like them macoumere in the market in George Street back home.

And George can't help thinking how things change a lot since he first come England, how now it have so many spades that you bouncing up with one every corner you turn. All them ships that coming bringing more and more, and all the newspapers writing about how these West Indians coming and like nothing could stop them, and how the Government best hads do something or else plenty trouble would cause in London.

And again long time thing like saltfish hard like gold to get. George had was to go in a small shop in Soho what was the only place in London you could get that, but now it have 'bout ten shop with it, because the English shopkeepers like they know the spades like they little fish.

Another thing is, George don't know how so many people know him, but every time a shipload of fellars land up in Paddington from the boat train, plenty of them coming round by George, saying that so and so did tell them that George would help them out when they reach in London. He come like godfather, he don't know how to refuse them, all these fellars coming and putting they worries on he shoulders, how they can't find a work, how it so cold, how place hard to get. Well George do what he could to ease the situation for them—he get about four work for some Jamaican in the factory where he is, and in the evening when he get time off, if he in a good mood he go round with them now and then to look for place to live, because by this time George know all them landlord and landlady who don't want no black people in they house.

He did have good fun with them Jamaican, they used to come and tell him how they get lose on the tube, how they wanted to go Piccadilly but they find theyself in Shepherd Bush. And George say that they 'fraid to put they money in the bank, that they does keep it in a suitcase under the bed, and count it up every week, and when it have enough they sending for they brother and sister and cousin.

Long time George used to feel lonely little bit, but all that finish with since so much West Indian come London. All kind of steel band fête all about in the city, in St. Pancras Hall, down Wimbledon, all down by Pentonville. The boys beating pan in Piccadilly Circus and even jumping up in the road when the Lord Mayor did riding in he coach.

So now all those things George does be studying when the idea come in he head to go back Grenada. He study what he would do if he go back in that small island, and he feel that he would never get on if he go back. It have so many things in London that he don't agree with, so much prejudice about the place, so much hustling, things so expensive. And yet every year when the spring round the corner, is as if it give him a new spirit to stay.

Then in the summer he putting on jitterbug shirt and walking about, coasting all by Hyde Park in the night, standing up by the corner near Marble Arch listening to them fellars who does stand up on box and say what they like and no policeman don't interfere with them, and eyeing any sharp craft that standing up near, waiting to ask if she would come in the yard for a cup of tea. He done with English girls now, is only continental he looking for, French and Norwegian in front.

When he have a night off, is because he dressing up and walking from the Water to Trafalgar Square, watching the night life, thinking how he in this big country walking about, instead of sitting down on some concrete bridge over a canal in the West Indies old talking with the boys. Is how you want him to leave this big life?

Is true sometimes when he think serious he could see that he ain't getting no place in a hurry, that is the same thing he doing everyday. But still, it don't matter what you do, as long as you living in London, that is a big thing in itself, that alone have big prestige, he could imagine how the people back home when they talk about him how they does say that he is a big shot, that he living in the same place as the Queen. They don't know how he catching he royal to make a living.

But that was another thing, how London so full up of people that it don't matter what you do, nobody does mind your business. One time a fellar in a room next to George did dead and nobody know nothing for 'bout a week. The tess stay here all this time, dead, and nobody don't know nothing even though they living in the same house. That was the one thing used to frighten George sometimes. . . . how he ain't have no family to watch over him if he sick, and nobody to turn to in hard times. But that thought like a drop in the ocean.

And so year after year the same thing happening again and again. He telling he grandmother and this girl in Grenada that yes, he would come next year, but when next year came he still doing the nightwork in the factory, he still old talking with the boys on a Sunday morning, he still coasting all about the streets of London, with no definite place to go, no definite aim in life.

And it reach a stage now where he get so accustom to the pattern that he can't do anything about it. All he know is that he living in London, and that he will dead there one day. And that is all. He not worrying he head about anything else. He not even bothering with the colour bar question any more. At first he used to get on ignorant when anybody tell him anything, but now he just smiling like a philosopher when they call him a black man. He can't even sympathise with them fellars who new and feel the lash for the first time and come round by him to mourn, like when landlord slam door in they face, or people leave them standing up in the queue to attend to somebody else. All them things happen to him already, and he pass through all them stages, so now he does only smile when the boys in sorrow.

Even the winter come like nothing now, he laughing to see Englishman stamping foot in the bus queue to keep warm, while he just have he hand in he pocket standing up cool. And he get a lot of English habit now, like talking about the weather, and if anybody say how it cold he used to talk like an old veteran 'bout the winter this country had some years ago. He drinking tea all the time, and reading newspaper in the tube and bus.

In fact, he and Scottie is good friend now, and the other day he buy a bowler hat and an umbrella and they went for a walk in the park, the two of them talking and nodding they head, and saying good evening to all the sharp girls that pass. He even reading *The Times* now . . . whenever he going out, he folding *The Times* so that the name would show and putting it under he arm.

And so as far as he could see, is no more Grenada for him at all. Especially now how so much West Indians hustling up to the old Brit'n, as if things really brown in the islands. And the way he have it figure out, if he stay in the work he have now, he go be able to peel off and spend the summer on the continent. It have a sharp Austrian girl does visit him in the yard . . . she come over here to work as a maidservant for some rich people, and George make contact one night in Baker Street, where she was standing waiting for a bus. Well, she tell him she going back in the summer, and that he must too.

And that is the case. When he think 'bout home it does look so far away that he feel as if he don't belong there no more.

And though he does really miss the sun, he make up he mind to write to grandmother and this girl and tell them that they best hads forget all about him, because he staying in this big country until he dead, and he ain't coming back to Grenada unless he win a big football pool, and even then, it would only be for a holiday.

SHAUNA SINGH BALDWIN

MONTREAL 1962

In the dark at night you came close and your voice was a whisper though there is no one here to wake. "They said I could have the job if I take off my turban and cut my hair short." You did not have to say it. I saw it in your face as you took off your new coat and galoshes. I heard their voices in my head as I looked at the small white envelopes I have left in the drawer, each full of one more day's precious dollars—the last of your savings and my dowry. Mentally, I converted dollars to rupees and thought how many people in India each envelope could feed for a month.

This was not how they described emigrating to Canada. I still remember them saying to you, "You're a well-qualified man. We need professional people." And they talked about freedom and opportunity for those lucky enough to already speak English. No one said then, "You must be reborn white-skinned—and clean-shaven to show it—to survive." Just a few months ago, they called us exotic new Canadians, new blood to build a new country.

Today I took one of my wedding saris to the neighbourhood dry cleaner and a woman with no eyebrows held it like a dishrag as she asked me, "Is it a bed sheet?"

"No," I said.

"Curtains?"

"No."

I took the silk back to our basement apartment, tied my hair in a tight bun, washed the heavy folds in the metal bathtub, and hung it, gold threads glinting, on a drip-dry hanger.

When I had finished, I spread a bed sheet on the floor of the bathroom, filled my arms with the turbans you'd worn last week, and knelt there surrounded by the empty soft hollows of scarlet, navy, earth brown, copper, saffron, mauve, and bright parrot green. As I waited for the bathtub to fill with warm soapy water I unravelled each turban, each precise spiral you had wound around your head, and soon the room was full of soft streams of muslin that had protected your long black hair.

I placed each turban in turn on the bubbly surface and watched them grow dark and heavy, sinking slowly, softly into the warmth. When there were no more left beside me, I leaned close and reached in, working each one in a rhythm bone-deep, as my mother and hers must have done before me, that their men might face the world proud. I drained the tub and new colours swelled—deep red, dark black mud, rust, orange, soft purple, and jade green.

I filled the enamel sink with clean water and starch and lifted them as someday I will lift children. When the milky bowl had fed them, my hands massaged them free of alien red-blue water. I placed them carefully in a basin and took them out into our grey two rooms to dry. I placed a chair by the window and climbed on it to tie the four corners of each turban length to the heavy curtain rod. Each one in turn, I drew out three yards till it was folded completely in two. I grasped it firmly at its sides and swung my hands inward. The turban furrowed before me. I arced my hands outward and it became a canopy. Again inward, again outward, hands close, hands apart, as though I was back in Delhi on a flat roof under a hot sun or perhaps near a green field of wheat stretching far to the banks of the Beas.

As the water left the turbans, I began to see the room through muslin screens. The pallid walls, the radiator you try every day to turn up hotter for me, the small windows, unnaturally high. When the turbans were lighter, I set the dining chairs with their half-moon backs in a row in the middle of the well-worn carpet and I draped the turbans over their tops the way Gidda dancers wear their chunnis pinned tight in the centre parting of their hair. Then I sat on the carpet before them, willing them: dance for me—dance for us. The chairs stood as stiff and wooden as ignorant Canadians, though I know maple is softer than chinar.

Soon the bands of cloth regained all their colour, filling the room with sheer lightness. Their splendour arched upwards, insisting upon notice, refusing the drabness, refusing obscurity, wielding the curtain rod like the strut of a defending champion.

From the windows over my head came the sounds of a Montreal afternoon, and the sure step of purposeful feet on the sidewalk. Somewhere on a street named in English where the workers speak joual I imagined your turban making its way in the crowds bringing you home to me.

Once again I climbed on a chair and I let your turbans loose. One by one, I held them to me, folding in their defiance, hushing their unruly indignation, gentling them into temporary submission. Finally, I faced them as they sat before me.

Then I chose my favourite, the red one you wear less and less, and I took it to the bedroom. I unfurled the gauzy scarlet on our bed and it seemed as though I'd poured a pool of the sainted blood of all the Sikh martyrs there. So I took a corner and tied it to the doorknob just as you do in the mornings instead of waking me to help you. I took the diagonal corner to the very far end of the room just as you do, and rolled the scarlet inward as best I could within the cramped four walls. I had to untie it from the doorknob again to roll the other half, as I used to every day for my father, then my brother, and now you. Soon the scarlet rope lay ready.

I placed it before the mirror and began to tie it as a Sardar would, one end clenched between my teeth to anchor it, arms raised to sweep it up to the forehead, down to the nape of the neck, around again, this time higher. I wound it swiftly, deftly, till it jutted haughtily forward, adding four inches to my stature. Only when I had pinned the free end to the peak did I let the end clenched between my teeth fall. I took the saliva-darkened cord, pulled it back where my hair bun rested low, and tucked it up over the turban, just as you do.

In the mirror I saw my father as he must have looked as a

boy, my teenage brother as I remember him, you as you face Canada, myself as I need to be.

The face beneath the jaunty turban began to smile.

I raised my hands to my turban's roundness, eased it from my head and brought it before me, setting it down lightly before the mirror. It asked nothing now but that I be worthy of it.

And so, my love, I will not let you cut your strong rope of hair and go without a turban into this land of strangers. The knot my father tied between my chunni and your turban is still strong between us, and it shall not fail you now. My hands will tie a turban every day upon your head and work so we can keep it there. One day our children will say, "My father came to this country with very little but his turban and my mother learned to work because no one would hire him."

Then we will have taught Canadians what it takes to wear a turban.

EMINE SEVGI ÖZDAMAR

From
THE BRIDGE OF THE
GOLDEN HORN

On Stresemannstrasse at that time, it was 1966, there was a baker's shop, an old woman sold bread there. Her head looked like a loaf of bread that a sleepy baker's apprentice had baked, big and lopsided. She bore it on her hunched-up shoulders as if it were on a coffee tray. It was nice going into this bread shop, because one didn't have to say the word bread, one could point at the bread.

If the bread was still warm, it was easier to learn by heart the headlines from the newspaper which was displayed in a glass case out on the street. I pressed the warm bread to my chest and my stomach and shifted from one leg to another on the cold street like a stork.

I couldn't speak a word of German and learned the sentences, just as, without speaking any English, one sings 'I can't get no satisfaction'. Like a chicken that goes clack clack clack. Clack clack clack could be the reply to a sentence one didn't want to hear. For example, someone asked 'Niye böyle gürültüyle yürü-yorsun?' (Why do you make so much noise when you walk?) and I answered with a German headline: 'When household goods become used goods.'

Perhaps I learned the headlines by heart, because before I had come to Berlin as a worker, I had been in a youth theatre group for six years. My mother, my father were always asking me: 'How can you learn so many sentences by heart, isn't it hard?' Our directors told us: 'You must learn your lines so well that you can even say them in your dreams.' I began to repeat my lines when I was dreaming; sometimes I forgot them, woke up very much afraid, immediately repeated the lines and fell asleep again. To forget one's lines—that was as if in mid-air a trapeze artist doesn't reach her partner's hand and falls down. But people loved those who carried out their professions between death and life. I got applause in the theatre, but not at home from my mother. Sometimes she had even lent me her beautiful hats and ball gowns for my parts, but when I stopped doing schoolwork because of the theatre, she said to me: 'Why don't you learn your school exercises as well as you do your parts? You'll have to repeat a year.' She was right, I learned only the lines of plays, even the lines of the others I was acting with. When I was sixteen, I played the part of Titania, Queen of the Fairies, in Shakespeare's *A Midsummer Night's Dream*.

> *Haydi, halka olun, bir peri şarkisi söyleyin*
> *(Come, now a roundel and a fairy song,)*
> *Then for the third part of a moment hence:*
> *Some to kill cankers in the muskrose buds . . .*

I couldn't keep up with school any more. My mother wept. 'Can Shakespeare or Molière help you now? Theatre has burned up your life.'—'Theatre is my life, how can my life burn itself? Jerry Lewis didn't have a leaving certificate either, but you love him, Mother. Harold Pinter left school for the theatre, too.'—'But their names are Jerry Lewis and Harold Pinter.'— 'I'm going to go to theatre school.'—'If you're not successful, you'll be unhappy. You'll starve. Finish school, otherwise your father won't give you any money. You could be a lawyer, you love speaking. Lawyers are like actors, but they don't starve, do they? Do your leaving certificate.' I replied:

'*Adi olmayan cinsten bir ruhum* (I am a spirit of no common rate).'

My mother replied: 'You want to make an ass of me and frighten me as if I were your mortal enemy, and you want to kill me with worry. Perhaps I'm partly to blame, but I'm your mother and I'm going to run out of patience soon.'

She wept. I replied: 'Scorn and derision never come in tears.'

'My daughter, you are so terribly wild and still so young.'

> *I will not trust you, I,*
> *Nor longer stay in your curst company.*
> *Your hands than mine are quicker for a fray.*
> *My legs are longer, though, to run away!*

I didn't laugh at home any more, because the rows between me and my mother never stopped. My father didn't know what to do and merely said, 'Don't either of you do anything you'll regret! Why do you force us to speak so harshly?' I replied:

> *My lord, fair Helen told me of their stealth,*
> *Of this their purpose hither to this wood.*

The sun shone in Istanbul and the newspapers hung outside the kiosks with the headlines: 'Germany wants even more Turkish workers', 'Germany takes Turks'.

I thought, I will go to Germany, work for a year, then I'll go to theatre school. I went to the Istanbul recruitment office. 'How old are you?'—'Eighteen.' I was healthy and after two weeks I got a passport and a one-year contract with Telefunken in Berlin.

My mother didn't say anything any more, but instead smoked non-stop. We sat in clouds of smoke. My father said: 'May Allah bring you to your senses in Germany. You can't even fry an egg. How are you going to make radio valves at Telefunken? Finish school. I don't want my daughter to be a worker. It's not a game.'

On the train from Istanbul to Germany I had walked backwards and forwards along the train corridor for a couple of nights and looked at all the women who were going there as workers. They had rolled down their stockings below the knee, the thick rubber straps left marks on their skin. It was easier for me to tell from their naked knees that we were still far from Germany than from the signs of the stations we passed and whose names we could not read. 'What a never-ending journey,' said one woman. All were silently in agreement, no one had thought of saying a word, the smokers just took out their cigarettes, looked at each other and smoked. Those who didn't smoke looked out of the window. One said: 'It's got dark again.' Another said: 'Yesterday it got dark like that too.' Each cigarette pushed the train on more quickly. No one looked at their watch, they looked at the cigarettes, which they constantly lit up. For three days, three nights, we hadn't taken our clothes off. Only a pair of shoes lay on the floor and vibrated along with the train. When one of the women wanted to go to the toilet, she quickly slipped on any pair of shoes, so the women went to the blocked toilets hopping comically in someone else's shoes. I realised that I was looking for women who looked like my mother. One had legs like my mother. I put on my sunglasses and quietly began to cry. On the floor of the train I didn't see any shoes that were my mother's. How nicely her and my shoes had stood side by side in Istanbul. How easily we slipped on our shoes together and went to the cinema to Liz Taylor or to the Opera.

Mama, Mama.

I thought, I shall arrive, get a bed, and then I shall always think about my mother, that will be my work. I began to cry even more and was cross, as if I hadn't left my mother, but my mother had left me. I hid my face behind the Shakespeare book.

When the night had come to an end, the train arrived in Munich. The women who had taken off their shoes days ago had swollen feet and sent those who had kept on their shoes to buy cigarettes and chocolate. *Çikolata—çikolata.*

I lived with lots of women in a women workers' hostel. We said hossel. We all worked in the radio factory, each one of us had to have a magnifying glass in our right eye while we were working. Even when we came back to the hossel in the evening, we looked at one another or the potatoes we were peeling with our right eye. A button came off, the women sewed the button on again with a wide-open right eye. The left eye always narrowed and remained half shut. We also slept with the left eye a little screwed up, and at five o'clock in the morning, when we were looking for our trousers or skirts in the semi-darkness, I saw that, like me, the other women were looking only with their right eye. Since starting work in the radio valve factory we believed our right eye more than our left eye. With the right eye behind the magnifying glass one could bend the thin wires of the little radio valves with tweezers. The wires were like the legs of a spider, very fine, almost invisible without the magnifying glass. The factory boss's name was Herr Schering. Sherin, said the women, they also said Sher. Then they stuck Herr to Sher, so that some women called him Herschering or Herscher.

We had been in Berlin for a week. The Herscher decided that on the tenth of November, the anniversary of Atatürk's death, we should stand up for Atatürk for a couple of minutes at five past nine precisely, just as in Turkey. At five past nine on 10 November we stood up at our machines on the factory floor, and once again our right eyes were bigger than the left. The women who wanted to weep, wept with their right eye, so that their tears ran down over their right breast on to their right shoe. So with our tears for Atatürk's death we made the Berlin factory floor wet. The neon lights on the ceilings and on the machines were strong and quickly dried the tears. Some women had forgotten the magnifying glass in their right eye when they stood up for Atatürk, their tears collected in the magnifying glass and fogged the lens.

We never saw the Herscher. The Turkish interpreter carried his German words to us as Turkish words: 'Herscher has said that you . . .' Because I never saw this Herscher, I looked for him in the face of the Turkish interpreter. She came, her shadow fell over the little radio valves in front of us.

While we were working we lived in a single picture: our fingers, the neon light, the tweezers, the little radio valves and their spider legs. The picture had its own voices, we detached ourselves from the voices of the world and from our own bodies.

The spine disappeared, the breasts disappeared, the hair on one's head disappeared. Sometimes I had to sniff up mucus, I put off sniffing up the mucus for longer and longer, as if doing it could break up the enlarged picture in which we lived. When the Turkish interpreter came and her shadow fell on this picture, the picture tore like a film, the sound disappeared and there was a hole. Then, when I looked at the interpreter's face, I again heard the voices of the aeroplanes, which were somewhere in the sky, or a metal thing fell on the factory floor and made an echo. I saw that at the very moment that the women interrupted their work, dandruff fell on to their shoulders. Like a postman who brings a registered letter and waits for a signature, so the interpreter, after she had translated Herschering's German sentences into Turkish for us, waited for the word okay.

If a woman, instead of the English okay, used the Turkish word *tamam,* the interpreter again asked: Okay?, until the woman said, 'Okay'. When a woman's okay was slow in coming, because she was just bending the little legs of a radio valve with her tweezers and didn't want to make a mistake or was inspecting the valve through her magnifying glass, then in her impatience the interpreter puffed her fringe up from her forehead until the English okay came.

When we went with her to the factory doctor, we said to her: 'Say to the doctor that I'm really ill, okay?'

The word okay also came into the hossel . . .

'You're cleaning the room tomorrow, okay?'

'Tamam.'

'Say okay.'

'Okay.'

In my first days in Berlin the city was like an endless building to me. Even between Munich and Berlin the country was like a single building. Out of the train door in Munich with the other women, through the door of the Travellers' Aid. Rolls—coffee—milk—nuns—neon lights, then out of the door of the Travellers' Aid, then through the door of the aeroplane, out of the plane door in Berlin, through the door of the bus, out of the door of the bus, through the door of the Turkish women's hossel, out of the hossel door, through the Hertie department store door at the Hallesches Tor (Halle Gate). From the hossel door we went to the Hertie door, we had to walk under an underground railway bridge. Groceries were on the top floor of Hertie. We were three girls, wanted to buy sugar, salt, eggs, toilet paper and toothpaste at Hertie. We didn't know the words. Sugar, salt. In order to describe sugar, we mimed coffee-drinking to a sales assistant, then we said shak shak. In order to describe salt, we spat on Hertie's floor and said: 'Eeeh.' In order to describe eggs, we turned our backs to the assistant, wiggled our backsides and said: 'Clack, clack, clack.' We got sugar, salt and eggs, but it didn't work with toothpaste. We got bathroom cleaning liquid. So my first German words were shak shak, eeeh, clack clack clack.

We got up at five in the morning. In each room there were six beds, in pairs one above the other.

Two sisters who weren't married slept in the first two beds of my room. They wanted to save money and fetch their brothers to Germany. They talked about their brothers as if they were part of a life they had already lived when they were in the world another time, so that I sometimes thought their brothers were dead. When one of the two wept or didn't finish her food or had caught a cold, the other said to her: 'Your brothers mustn't hear about that. If your brothers hear that!' After work they wore pale blue dressing gowns in the hossel, made of an electrically charged material. When they had their periods their hair was charged too, and their dressing gowns of electrically charged material gave off noises in the room. When one of the sisters came down from her bed and in the dark, damp early morning put on her shoes, she sometimes put on her sister's shoes, and her feet didn't notice, because the shoes were so alike.

In the evening after work the women went to their rooms and ate at their tables. But the evening didn't begin, the evening was gone. One ate because one wanted to quickly fetch the night into the room. We leapt over the evening into the night.

The two sisters sat at the table, leant a mirror against a sauce-
pan and put their hair in curlers. Both had rolled their stock-
ings below their knees. Their naked knees showed me that the
light would soon be put out in the room. The two talked as if
they were alone in the room:
  'Hurry up, we have to go to sleep.'
  'Who's turning the light off today, you or me?'
  One stood at the door, her hand on the light switch, and
waited until the other had lain down in bed. She laid her head
with the curlers on the pillow, as if she were carefully backing a
car into a parking space. When she had properly laid her head
down, she said: 'Turn it off!' Then her sister turned off the light.
  We, the other four girls, were still sitting at the table, some
were writing letters. The darkness cut us apart. We undressed
in the dark. Sometimes a pencil fell down. When everyone was
in bed and everything was quiet, we could hear the electrically
charged material of the two pale blue dressing gowns, which
hung on hooks.

Ever since I had been a child in Istanbul, I had been in the habit
of praying to the dead every night. I first of all recited the prayers,
then recited the names of dead people whom I had not known,
but whom I had heard of. When my mother and grandmother
told stories, they talked a great deal about people who had died.
I had learned their names by heart, listed them every night in
bed and gave prayers for their souls. That took an hour. My
mother said: 'If one forgets the souls of the dead, their souls will
be in pain.' In the first nights in Berlin I prayed for the dead, too,
but I quickly grew tired, because we had to get up so early. I fell
asleep before I had said all the names of my dead. So I slowly lost
my dead in Berlin. I thought, when I go back to Istanbul, I'll
start to count my dead again there. I had forgotten the dead, but
I had not forgotten my mother. I lay down in bed to think about
my mother. But I didn't know how one thinks about mothers. To
fall in love with a film actor and to think about him at night—
for example, how I would kiss him—that was easier.

But how does one think about a mother?

Some nights, like a film running backwards, I went from the hossel door to the train on which I had got here. I also had the train run backwards. The trees ran backwards past the window, but the journey was too long, I got only as far as Austria. The mountains had their tops in the mist, and it was hard to make a train run backwards in the mist. That's where I fell asleep. I also noticed that I thought about my mother when I didn't eat anything and remained hungry, or when I pulled out the skin on my fingers a bit and it hurt. Then I thought, this pain is my mother. So I went to bed hungry more often or with sore fingers.

Rezzan, who slept above me, didn't eat properly either. I thought, she's thinking about her mother, too. Rezzan stayed awake for a long time and turned in bed in the dark from left to right, then she took her pillow from one end of the bed and put it at the other end. After a while she again started to turn from left to right, from right to left. Below I thought with half my head about my mother, and with the other half I began to think about Rezzan's mother as well.

Two cousins from Istanbul slept in the other pair of bunk beds. They were working in the factory in order to go to university afterwards. One had two little braids and deep scars on her face, because as a teenager she hadn't left her pimples in peace, and she had bad breath. The other cousin was beautiful and sent the one who had bad breath to the post office or to Hertie. Once she came back from the post office, and the beautiful cousin forced her to lie down on the table, she rolled up her sleeves, then she pulled the belt out of her jeans and struck her cousin across the back with the belt. The two sisters in their pale blue dressing gowns, Rezzan and I said:

'What are you doing?'

She shouted: 'The whore went to the post office and came back late.'

We said: 'She hasn't got wings, is she supposed to fly? She didn't come back too late.'

'No, don't interfere.

'Don't interfere.

'Don't interfere.

'Don't interfere.'

And with every sentence she struck her cousin across the back, but looked us in the eyes as she did so. Her pupils spun like a light that had gone crazy, like all the other women her right eye was bigger than her left.

That night, as everyone lay in bed, the two sisters with their curlers one above the other in two beds, the two cousins one above the other in two beds, Rezzan and I one above the other in two beds, the cousin who had bad breath and had been beaten suddenly climbed up on to the bed of her cousin who was beautiful and had beaten. In the darkness they pulled the blanket out of the quilt cover, dropped it on the floor and crawled into the cover as into a sleeping bag, buttoned it up and then—buttoned up in this bag—they kissed each other slurp slurp and made love. And we, the other four, listened without moving.

Opposite the women's hossel was the Hebbel Theatre. The theatre was lit up and a neon sign was constantly going on and off. This light also fell into our room. When the sign went out, then from that day I heard kiss voices slurp slurp in the dark, when the sign was on I saw the curlers on the two sisters' heads gleaming on their pillows in the semi-darkness and the two pairs of shoes on the linoleum floor.

Rezzan, who slept above me, never took off her shoes at night. She always lay in bed in her clothes and shoes. When she slept she held her toothbrush in her hand, and the toothpaste was under her pillow. Like me Rezzan wanted to become an actress. Some nights, as the light of the Hebbel Theatre went on and off, we talked quietly from bed to bed about theatre. Rezzan asked: 'Which part do you want to play, Ophelia?'—'No, I'm too thin, too big for Ophelia. But maybe Hamlet.'—'Why?'—'I don't know. And you?'—'The woman in *Cat on a Hot Tin Roof* by Tennessee Williams.'—'I don't know Tennessee.'—'He was homosexual and left school for the theatre, like us.'—'Did you know that Harold Pinter left school, too?'—'Do you know *The Servant* by Harold Pinter?'—'No.'—'An aristocrat is looking for a servant. In the end the servant becomes the master and the master the servant. Goodnight.' Rezzan said nothing, the rollers of the two sisters gleamed in their beds as the light of the Hebbel Theatre went on and off.

When we got up at five in the morning, Rezzan was already finished. She brushed her teeth and made coffee, a full cup of coffee in one hand, her toothbrush in the other. Brushing her teeth shuff shuff she walked up and down the long corridors of the women's hossel. All the other women were still running around in their dressing gowns, with towels around their bodies or in their underpants. But Rezzan already had her jacket and skirt on. All the women looked at Rezzan as if she were their clock and then did things faster. Sometimes they even went to the bus stop too early, because Rezzan was already standing there. In the darkness Rezzan looked in the direction of the bus, and the women looked at Rezzan's face.

In the morning the Hebbel Theatre had no lights on. Only our women's shadows waiting for the bus lay on the snow. When the bus came and took us, only the marks of our shoes and splotches of coffee were left in the snow in front of our women's hossel, because some women came to the bus stop with their full cups of coffee, and when the bus came and the door opened tisspamp, they poured what was left on to the snow. The lights of the bread shop were on, in the newspaper case the headline of the day was: HE WAS NO ANGEL. Out of the bus window on my right I saw the newspaper, out of the bus window on my left I saw the ruin of the Anhalt railway station, which like the Hebbel Theatre was opposite our hossel. We called it the broken station. The Turkish word for 'broken' also means offended. So it was also called 'the offended station'.

Just before we reached the factory, the bus had to drive up a long, steep street. A bus full of women tipped backwards. Then came a bridge, there we tipped forward, and there, every wet, half-dark morning, I saw two women walking hand in hand. Their hair was cut short, they wore skirts and shoes with low heels, their knees were cold, behind them I saw the canal and dark factory buildings. The asphalt of the bridge was cracked, rain collected in the holes, in the lights of the bus the women's shadows were thrown on the rainwater and on the canal. The shadows of their knees trembled in the rainwater more than their real knees. They never looked at the bus, but never looked at each other either. One of the women was taller than the other, she had taken the hand of the smaller woman in hers. It looked as if at this time of the morning they were the only living people in this city. It was as if the morning through which they walked was sewn on to the night. Were they coming out of the night or were they coming out of the morning? I didn't know. Were they going to the factory or to the cemetery, or were they coming from a cemetery?

Outside the radio valve factory all the doors of the bus opened, the snow came into the bus with the wind and got out again with the women's hair, eyelashes and coats. The factory yard swallowed us in the darkness. It was snowing more heavily; the women crowded more closely together, walked through the bright snowflakes, as if someone was shaking out stars on to them. Their coats, skirts fluttered and made quiet noises amidst the factory hooters. The snow went with them as far as the time clock, with one wet hand tink tink tink they pushed the cards in, with the other they shook the snow from their coats. The snow made the cards and the floor in front of the porter's lodge wet. The porter rose a little from his chair, that was his job. I tried out my German sentence, which I had learned from today's newspaper headline, on him: 'Hewasnoangel'— 'Morningmorning,' he said.

On the factory floor there were only women. Each one sat alone at a green-painted iron table. Each face looked at another woman's back. While one was working, one forgot the faces of the other women. One saw nothing but hair, beautiful hair, tired hair, old hair, young hair, combed hair, falling-out hair. We saw only one woman's face, the face of the only woman who was standing, Frau Mischel. Forewoman. When the machines of the Greek women workers broke down, they called out to her: 'Frau Missel, comere.' Their tongues couldn't pronounce a 'sch'. When we, our magnifying glasses in our right eyes, looked at Frau Missel, we always saw one half of Frau Missel bigger than the other half. Just as she always saw our right eyes bigger than our left eyes. That's why Frau Missel always looked at our right eyes. All day her shadow fell on the green iron workbenches.

Only in the toilet room could I see the women's faces. There women stood against the white tiled walls under strip lights and smoked. They rested their right elbow in their left hand, and the right hand with the cigarette moved in the air in front of their mouths. Because the toilet had such strong strip lights, smoking looked like work, too. At the time one could buy a cigarette from German women workers for ten pfennigs. Stuyvesant—HB.

Sometimes Frau Missel came, opened the door and looked into the toilet room, said nothing, shut the door, went. Then, as if the lights had gone out, the last smokers dropped their cigarettes in the toilet bowls and flushed the toilet water down. On quiet feet we then went from the toilet room into the factory hall, but the toilet water noises followed us for a while. When we sat down our hair was always a little more nervous than the hair of the women who never left their green tables for a smoke.

For the first few weeks we lived between hossel door, Hertie door, bus door, radio valve factory door, factory toilet door, hossel room table and factory green iron table. Once all the women could find the things they were looking for in Hertie and had learned to say bread, once they had remembered the proper name of their bus stop—at first they had noted the name of the stop as 'stop'—the women one day switched on the television in the hossel lounge.

The TV had been there from the start. 'Let's see what's on,' said one woman. From that day many women watched figure skating on TV in the hossel lounge in the evening. There, too, I saw the women from behind again, as in the factory. When they returned to the hossel from the radio valve factory, they changed into their nightshirts, boiled potatoes, macaroni, fried potatoes, eggs in the kitchen. The sound of boiling water, hissing frying pans mixed with their thin, thick voices, and everything rose in the kitchen air, their words, their faces, their different dialects, the gleam of knives in their hands, the bodies waiting for the shared pots and pans, nervously running kitchen tap water, a stranger's spit on a plate.

It looked like the shadow plays in traditional Turkish theatre. In it figures came on to the stage, each speaking their own dialect—Turkish Greeks, Turkish Armenians, Turkish Jews, different Turks from different towns and classes and with different dialects—they all misunderstood each other, but kept on talking and playing, like the women in the hossel, they misunderstood each other in the kitchen, but handed each other the knives or pots, or one rolled up another's pullover sleeve, so that it didn't hang into the pot. Then the hossel warden came, the only one who could speak German, and checked that everything in the kitchen was clean. After the meal the women took off their nightdresses, put on their clothes, some also put on make-up, as if they were going to the cinema, and came into the hossel lounge, turned the light off and sat down in front of the figure skaters. While the older women sat like that in the cinema, we, the three youngest girls—we were all virgins and loved our mothers—went to the snack bar opposite the hossel. The man made meatballs out of horses—we didn't know that, because we couldn't speak any German. Meat balls were our mothers' favourite food. The horse meatballs in our hands, we went to our offended station, ate the horses and looked at the weakly illuminated Turkish women's hossel windows. The offended station was no more than a battered wall and a projecting front section with three gateways. If we made a noise in the night with the meatball paper bags, we held our breath and didn't know whether it was us or someone else. There on the ground of the offended station we lost sense of time. Every morning this dead station had woken up, people had been walking there who were no longer there. When the three of us walked there, it was as if my life had already been lived. We went through a hole, walked to the end of the plot of land without speaking. Then, without saying anything to one another, we walked backwards to the hole that once had perhaps been the door of the offended station. And as we walked backwards we loudly blew out our breath. It was cold, the night and the cold took our loud breath and turned it into thick smoke. Then we went back to the street again, I looked behind me to see the remainder of our breath still in the air behind the door space. It was as if the station was in a quite different time. In front of the offended station there was a phone booth. When the three of us walked past it, we talked loudly, as if our parents in Turkey could hear us.

(TRANSLATED FROM THE GERMAN
BY MARTIN CHALMERS)

MARJANE SATRAPI

From
PERSEPOLIS 2:
THE STORY OF A RETURN

THE HARDER I TRIED TO ASSIMILATE, THE MORE I HAD THE FEELING THAT I WAS DISTANCING MYSELF FROM MY CULTURE, BETRAYING MY PARENTS AND MY ORIGINS, THAT I WAS PLAYING A GAME BY SOMEBODY ELSE'S RULES.

EACH TELEPHONE CALL FROM MY PARENTS REMINDED ME OF MY COWARDICE AND MY BETRAYAL. I WAS AT ONCE HAPPY TO HEAR THEIR VOICES AND ASHAMED TO TALK TO THEM.

- YES, I'M DOING FINE. I'M GETTING GOOD GRADES.

- FRIENDS? OF COURSE, LOTS!

- DAD...

- DAD, I LOVE YOU!

- YOU HAVE SOME GOOD FRIENDS?

- THAT DOESN'T SURPRISE ME, YOU ALWAYS HAD A TALENT FOR COMMUNICATING WITH PEOPLE!

- EAT ORANGES. THEY'RE FULL OF VITAMIN C.

- US TOO, WE ADORE YOU. YOU'RE THE CHILD ALL PARENTS DREAM OF HAVING!

IF ONLY THEY KNEW... IF THEY KNEW THAT THEIR DAUGHTER WAS MADE UP LIKE A PUNK, THAT SHE SMOKED JOINTS TO MAKE A GOOD IMPRESSION, THAT SHE HAD SEEN MEN IN THEIR UNDERWEAR WHILE THEY WERE BEING BOMBED EVERY DAY, THEY WOULDN'T CALL ME THEIR DREAM CHILD.

I FELT SO GUILTY THAT WHENEVER THERE WAS NEWS ABOUT IRAN, I CHANGED THE CHANNEL.

IT WAS TOO UNBEARABLE.

DID YOU WATCH TV YESTERDAY? YOU MUST BE WORRIED.

NO, IT'S OKAY! I TALKED TO MY PARENTS. THEY'RE FINE.

I WAS LYING. I KNEW NOTHING AND I DIDN'T WANT TO KNOW MORE.

I WANTED TO FORGET EVERYTHING, TO MAKE MY PAST DISAPPEAR, BUT MY UNCONSCIOUS CAUGHT UP WITH ME.

(TRANSLATED FROM THE FRENCH
BY ANJALI SINGH)

MARINA LEWYCKA

From
STRAWBERRY FIELDS

"Irina, my baby, you can still change your mind! You don't have to go!"

Mother was wailing and dabbing at her pinky eyes with a tissue, causing an embarrassing scene at the Kiev bus station.

"Mother, please! I'm not a baby!"

You expect your mother to cry at a moment like this. But when my craggy old Papa turned up too, his shirt all crumpled and his silver hair sticking up like an old-age porcupine, okay, I admit it rattled me. I hadn't expected him to come to see me off.

"Irina, little one, take care."

"*Shcho ti,* Papa. What's all this about? Do you think I'm not coming back?"

"Just take care, my little one." Sniffle. Sigh.

"I'm not little, Papa. I'm nineteen. Do you think I can't look after myself?"

"Ah, my little pigeon." Sigh. Sniffle. Then Mother started up again. Then—I couldn't help myself—I started up too, sighing and sniffling and dabbing my eyes, until the bus driver told us to get a move on, and Mother shoved a bag of bread and salami and a poppy seed cake into my hands, and we were off. From Kiev to Kent in forty-two hours.

Okay, I admit, forty-two hours on a bus is not amusing. By the time we reached Lviv, the bread and salami were all gone. In Poland, I noticed that my ankles were starting to swell. When we stopped for fuel somewhere in Germany, I stuffed the last crumbs of the poppy-seed cake into my mouth and washed it down with nasty metallic-tasting water from a tap that was marked not for drinking. In Belgium my period started, but I didn't notice until the dark stain of blood seeped through my jeans onto the seat. In France I lost all sensation in my feet. On the ferry to Dover I found a toilet and cleaned myself up. Looking into the cloudy mirror above the washbasin I hardly recognized the wan dark-eyed face that stared back at me—was that me, that scruffy straggly-haired girl with bags under her eyes? I walked around to restore the circulation in my legs, and, standing on the deck at dawn, I watched the white cliffs of England materialize in the pale watery light, beautiful, mysterious, the land of my dreams.

In Dover I was met off the boat by Vulk, waving a bit of card with my name on it—Irina Blazkho. Typical—he'd gotten the spelling wrong. He was the type Mother would describe as a person of minimum culture, wearing a horrible black fake-leather jacket, like a comic-strip gangster—what a *koshmar!*—it creaked as he walked. All he needed was a gun.

He greeted me with a grunt. "Hrr. You heff passport? Peppers?"

His voice was deep and sludgy, with a nasty whiff of cigarette smoke and tooth decay on his breath.

This gangster-type should brush his teeth. I fumbled in my bag, and before I could say anything, he grabbed my passport and Seasonal Agricultural Worker papers and stowed them in the breast pocket of his *koshmar* jacket.

"I keep for you. Is many bed people in England. Can stealing from you."

He patted the pocket and winked. I could see straightaway that there was no point in arguing with a person of his type, so I hoisted my bag onto my shoulder and followed him across the car park to a huge shiny black vehicle that looked like a cross between a tank and a Zill, with darkened windows and gleaming chrome bars in the front—a typical mafia-machine. These high-status cars are popular with primitive types and social undesirables. In fact he looked quite a bit like his car: overweight, built like a tank, with a gleaming silver front tooth, a shiny black jacket, and a straggle of hair tied in a pony-tail hanging down his back like an exhaust pipe. Ha ha.

He gripped my elbow, which was quite unnecessary—stupid man, did he think I might try to escape?—and pushed me onto the backseat with a shove, which was also unnecessary. Inside, the mafia-machine stank of tobacco. I sat in silence looking nonchalantly out the window while he scrutinized me rudely through the rearview mirror. What did he think he was staring at? Then he lit up one of those thick vile-smelling cigars—Mother calls them New Russian cigarettes—what a stink! and started puffing away. Puff. Stink.

I didn't take in the scenery that flashed past through the black-tinted glass—I was too tired—but my body registered every twist in the lane, and the sudden jerks and jolts when he braked and turned. This gangster-type needs some driving lessons.

He had some potato chips wrapped in a paper bundle on the passenger seat beside him, and every now and then he would plunge his left fist in, grab a handful of chips, and cram them into his mouth. Grab. Cram. Chomp. Grab. Cram. Chomp. Not very refined. The chips smelled fantastic, though. The smell of the cigar, the lurching motion as he steered with one hand and stuffed his mouth with the other, the low, dragging pain from my period—it was all making me feel queasy and hungry at the same time. In the end, hunger won out. I wondered what language this gangster-type would talk. Belarusian? He looked too dark for a Belarus. Ukrainian? He didn't look Ukrainian. Maybe from somewhere out east? Chechnya? Georgia? What do Georgians look like? The Balkans? Taking a guess, I asked in Russian, "Please, Mr. Vulk, may I have something to eat?"

He looked up. Our eyes met in the rearview mirror. He had real gangster-type eyes—poisonous black berries in eyebrows as straggly as an overgrown hedge. He studied me in that offensive way, sliding his eyes all over me.

"Little flovver vants eating?" He spoke in English, though he must have understood my Russian. Probably he came from one of those newly independent nations of the former Soviet Union

where everyone can speak Russian but nobody does. Okay, so
he wanted to talk English? I'd show him.

"Yes indeed, Mr. Vulk. If you could oblige me, if it does not
inconvenience you, I would appreciate something to eat."

"No problema, little flovver!"

He helped himself to one more mouthful of chips—grab,
cram, chomp—then scrunched up the remnants in the oily
paper and passed them over the back of the seat. As I reached
forward to take them, I saw something else nestled down on the
seat beneath where the chips had been. Something small, black,
and scary. *Shcho to!* Was that a real gun?

My heart started hammering. What did he need a gun for?
Mama, Papa, help me! Okay, just pretend not to notice. Maybe
it's not loaded. Maybe it's just one of those cigar lighters. So I
unfolded the crumpled paper—it was like a snug, greasy nest.
The chips inside were fat, soft, and still warm. There were only
about six left, and some scraps. I savored them one at a time.
They were lightly salty, with a touch of vinegar, and they were
just—mmm!—indescribably delicious. The fat clung to the edges
of my lips and hardened on my fingers, so I had no choice but to
lick it off, but I tried to do it discreetly.

"Thank you," I said politely, for rudeness is a sign of mini-
mum culture.

"No problema. No problema." He waved his fist about as if
to show how generous he was. "Food for eat in transit. All vill
be add to your living expense."

Living expense? I didn't need any more nasty surprises. I
studied his back, the creaky stretched-at-the-seams jacket, the
ragged ponytail, the thick, yellowish neck, the flecks of dan-
druff on the fake-leather collar. I was starting to feel queasy
again.

"What is this, expense?"

"Expense. Expense. Foods. Transports. Accommodations."
He took both hands off the steering wheel and waved them in
the air. "Life in vest is too much expensive, little flovver. Who
you think vill be pay for all such luxury?"

Although his English was appalling, those words came rolling out like a prepared speech. "You think this vill be providing all for free?"

So Mother had been right. "Anybody can see this agency is run by crooks. Anybody but you, Irina." (See how Mother has this annoying habit of putting me down?) "And if you tell them lies, Irina, if you pretend to be student of agriculture when you are nothing of the sort, who will help you if something goes wrong?"

Then she went on in her hysterical way about all the things that go wrong for Ukrainian girls who go west—all those rumors and stories in the papers.

"But everyone knows these things only happened to stupid and uneducated girls, Mother. They're not going to happen to me."

"If you will please say me what are the expenses, I will try to meet them."

I kept my voice civilized and polite. The chrome-bar tooth gleamed.

"Little flovver, the expense vill be first to pay, and then you vill be pay. Nothing to be discuss. No problema."

"And you will give me back my passport?"

"Exact. You verk, you get passport. You no verk, you no passport. Someone mekka visit in you Mama in Kiev, say Irina no good verk, is mek big problem for her."

"I have heard that in England—"

"England is a change, little flovver. Now England is land of possibility. England is not like in you school book."

I thought of dashing Mr. Brown from *Let's Talk English*—if only he were here!

"You have an excellent command of English. And of Russian maybe?"

"English. Russian. Serbo-Croat. German. All languages."

So he sees himself as a linguist; okay, keep him talking.

"You are not a native of these shores, I think, Mr. Vulk?"

"Think everything vat you like, little flovver." He gave me a leering wink in the mirror, and a flash of silver tooth. Then he started tossing his head from side to side as if to shake out his dandruff.

"This, you like? Is voman attract?"

It took me a moment to realize he was referring to his pony-tail. Was this his idea of flirtation? On the scale of attractive-ness, I would give him a zero. For a person of minimum culture he certainly had some pretensions. What a pity Mother wasn't here to put him right.

"It is absolutely irresistible, Mr. Vulk."

"You like? Eh, little flovver? You vant touch?"

The ponytail jumped up and down. I held my breath.

"Go on. Hrr. You can touch him. Go on," he said with hor-rible oily enthusiasm.

I reached out my hand, which was still greasy and smelled of chips.

"Go on. Is pleasure for you."

I touched it—it felt like a rat's tail. Then he flicked his head, and it twitched beneath my fingers like a live rat.

"I heff hear that voman is cannot resisting such a hair it re-minding her of men's oggan."

What on earth was he talking about now?

"Oggan?"

He made a crude gesture with his fingers.

"Be not afraid, little flovver. It reminding you of boyfriend. Hah?"

"No, Mr. Vulk, because I do not have a boyfriend."

I knew straightaway it was the wrong thing to say, but it was too late. The words just slipped out, and I couldn't bring them back.

"Not boyfriend? How is this little flovver not boyfriend?" His voice was like warm chip fat. "Hrr. Maybe in this case is good possibility for me?"

That was a stupid mistake. He's got you now. You're cor-nered.

"Is perhaps sometime we make good possibility, eh?" He breathed cigar smoke and tooth decay. "Little flovver?"

Through the darkened glass, I could see woods flashing past, all sunlight and dappled leaves. If only I could throw myself out of the vehicle, roll down the grassy bank, and run in among the trees. But we were going too fast. I shut my eyes and pretended to be asleep.

We drove on in silence for maybe twenty minutes. Vulk lit another cigar. I watched him through my lowered lashes, puffing away, hunched over the wheel. Puff. Stink. Puff. Stink. How much farther could it be? Then there was a crunching of gravel under the wheels, and with one last violent lurch the mafia-machine came to a halt. I opened my eyes. We had pulled up in front of a pretty steep-roofed farmhouse set behind a summery garden where there were chairs and tables set out on the lawn that sloped down to a shallow glassy river. Just like England is supposed to be. Now at last, I thought, there will be normal people; they will talk to me in English; they will give me tea.

But they didn't. Instead, a pudgy red-faced man wearing dirty clothes and rubber boots came out of the house—the farmer, I guessed—and he helped me out of Vulk's vehicle, mumbling something I couldn't understand, but it was obviously not an invitation to tea. He looked me up and down in that same rude way, as though I were a horse he'd just bought. Then he and Vulk muttered to each other, too fast for me to follow, and exchanged envelopes.

"Bye-bye, little flovver," Vulk said, with that chip-fat smile. "Ve meet again. Maybe ve mekka possibility?"

"Maybe."

I knew it was the wrong thing to say, but by then I was just desperate to get away.

The farmer shoved my bag into his Land Rover and then he shoved me in too, giving my behind a good feel with his hand as he did so, which was quite unnecessary. He only had to ask and I would have climbed in by myself.

"I'll take you straight out to the field," he said, as we rattled along narrow winding lanes. "You can start picking this afternoon."

After some five kilometers, the Land Rover swung in through the gate, and I felt a rush of relief as at last I planted my feet on firm ground. The first thing I noticed was the light—the dazzling salty light dancing on the sunny field, the ripening strawberries, the little rounded trailer perched up on the hill and the oblong boxy trailer down in the corner of the field, the woods beyond, and the long, curving horizon, and I smiled to myself. So this is England.

DEEPAK UNNIKRISHNAN

From
TEMPORARY PEOPLE

CHABTER THREE: PRAVASIS

Expat. Worker.
Guest. Worker.
Guest Worker. Worker.
Foreigner. Worker.
Non-resident. Worker.
Non-citizens. Workers.
Workers. Visa.
People. Visas.
Workers. Worker.
A million. More.
Homeless. Visiting.
Residing. Born.
Brought. Arrived.
Acclimatizing. Homesick.
Lovelorn. Giddy.
Worker. Workers.
Tailor. Solderer.
Chauffeur. Maid.
Oil Man. Nurse.
Typist. Historian.
Shopkeeper. Truck driver.
Watchman. Gardener.
Secretary. Pilot.
Smuggler. Hooker.
Tea boy. Mistress.
Temporary. People.

Illegal. People.
Ephemeral. People.
Gone. People.
Deported. Left.
More. Arriving.

CHABTER FOUR: PRAVASIS?

Tailor. Hooker. Horse Looker. Maid. Camel Rider. Historian. Nurse. Oil Man. Shopkeeper. Chauffeur. Watchman. Porrota Maker. Secretary. Gardener. Smuggler. Solderer. Tea Boy. Mistress. Newspaper Walla. Truck Driver. Storekeeper. Manager. Computer Person. AC Repairman. Claark. TV Mechanic. Caar Mechanic. Bus Driver. Kadakaran. Accountant. Housewife. First Wife. Ex-wife. Barber. Delivery Boy. Electrician. Plumber. Security Guard. Housemaid. Nanny. Schoolteacher. Ayah. Perfume Seller. Philanderer. Husband. Bar Man. Bar Girl. Carpet Seller. Vet. Doc. Mr. Mrs. Sycophant. Laborer. Taxi Driver. Launderer. Money Lender. Murderer. Junk Dealer. Road Cleaner. Brick Layer. Bread Maker. Butcher. Teacher. Preacher. Fotographer. Stair Washer. Window Cleaner. Technician. Manager Person. Petro Lobbyist. Typist. Delivery Boy. Present Wrapper. Pill Pusher. Drug Pusher. Travel Agent. Bellhop. Marketing Man. Face Model. Administrator. Pet Groomer. Pilot. DJ. RJ. VJ. Groom. Bride. Lorry Driver. Shopping-Mall Cashier. Carpet Seller. Hitman. Junkie. Flunkie. Fishmonger. Floor Sweeper. Cement Mixer. Gas Man. Fixer. Usher. Waiter. Pizza Maker. Cook. Dish Washer. Valet. Robber. Ambulance Driver. Blood Donor. Driving Teacher. Computer Expert. Con Man. Checkout Girl. Language Translator. Receptionist. Carpenter. Furniture Repairman. Morgue Cleaner. Jeweler. Murderess. Business Lady. Mullah. Father. Optimist. Futurist. Golf Expert. Tennis Coach. Life Guard. Amusement-Park-Ride Operator. Costumer. Marketing Strategist. Water Expert. Desalination Consultant. Game-Park Investor. Gambler. Diamond Dealer. Interior Decorator. Diplomat. Doorman. Mercenary. Crane Operator. Kappalandi Vendor. Ship Boy. Pucchakari Seller. Supermarket Shelf Stocker. Pipe Fitter. Stone Mason. Knife Sharpener. Imported-Fruit Stowaway. Duty Free Employee. Paper Editor. Caar Washer. Forklift Driver. Video-Shooter. Organ Donor. Cadaver. Music Teacher. Tree Planter. Maalish Man. Chai Maker. Kaapi Stirrer. Lentil Seller. Carpet Cleaner. Table Wiper. Garbage Man. Watch Repairer. Kennel Sweeper.

Shawarma Slicer. Assistant Person. Peon. Iron Man. Forger.
Mithai Maker. Veed Builder. Cobbler. Food Supplier. Wall
Painter. Bar Dancer. Bra Salesman. Bank Teller. Telephone
Lineman. Dredger. Assembly-Line Worker. Toy Maker.
Welder. Moocher. Drifter. Breadwinner. Supermarket Bagger.
Fruit Hawker. Chicken Decapitator. Exterminator. Highway
Maker. Building Builder. Saleslady. Trolley Boy. Gold-Shop
Employee. Department-Store Mascot. Camera Guy. Ladies
Hairdresser. Pandit. Nun. Perfume Seller. Laundry Person.
Wall Painter. Factory Supervisor. Machinist. Glass Wiper. Grass
Mower. Plant Waterer. Warehouse Protector. Ambulance
Driver. Trash Picker. Camp Foreman. Cycle Mechanic. Brick
Layer. Raffle Seller. Currency Exchanger. Loan Shark. Mani-
curist. Pedicurist. Cafeteria Worker. Burger Maker. Masseur.
Masseuse. Florist. Dentist. Pool Cleaner. Water-Slide Inspec-
tor. Hostess. Hotel Concierge. Immigration Attorney. Morti-
cian. Sandwich Maker. Disco Bouncer. Crows. Continental
Cook. VCD Dealer. Letter Writer. Internet Explainer. Poster
Painter. Flower Potter. Stable Boy. Electrician. Mont Blanc
Salesman. Helicopter Pilot. Seamstress. Trouser Stocker. Chap-
pal Hawker. Imported-Caar-Tyre Fixer. Loan Signer. Debt
Defaulter. Escaper. Cash Hoarder. Money Spender. Rent Bor-
rower. Suicider. Raffle Winner. Breadloser. Roti Roller. Poori
Fryer. Bread Kneader. Bed Maker. Tongue Speaker. Coffin
Specialist. Coffee Pourer. Ice-Cream Server. Bootlegger. Shoe
Shiner. Front Door Greeter. Gym Instructor. Bookshop
Owner. Paper Shredder. Spice Dealer. Fireworks Specialist.
Wet Nurse. Elevator Repairman. Fountain Specialist. Scrap
Dealer. Dog Groomer. Tree Tender. Farm Hand. Mehendi Putter.
College Professor. Chartered Accountant. Marriage Broker.
Fact Checker. Customer-Service Representative. Tiler. Van
Driver. Mover. Nationalist. Atheist. Fundamentalist. Jingoist.
Scrap Collector. Garment Seller. Squeegee Wielder. Porno
Dealer. Plant Worker. Kitchen Assistant. House Liver. Camp
Resider. Homeless. Jobless. Hopeless. Clueless. Content. Festi-
val Consultant. Starlet. Smithy. Interior Designer. Electronics
Salesman. Stadium Builder. Metro Maker. Electrician. Dress-
maker. Food-Court Vendor. Gas Worker. Rig Worker. Driller.

Miller. Killer. Skyscraper Specialist. Engineer. Mechanical
Engineer. Beautician. Ladies Nurse. Ad Man. Bachelor.
Stringer. Football Coach. Football Player. Boat Hand. Cutlery
Representative. Cargo Hauler. Museum Director. Sculpture
Mover. Bulldozer Operator. Earth Digger. Stone Breaker.
Foundation Putter. Infrastructure Planner. Rule Follower.
House Builder. Camp Builder. Tube-Light Installer. Helmet
Wearer. Jumpsuit Sporter. Globetrotter. Daydreamer. City Maker.
Country Maker. Place Builder. Laborer. Cog. Cog? Cog.

CHABTER NINE: NALINAKSHI

My name is Nalinakshi. I am from Nadavaramba, Thrissur.
Yesterday, I turned eighty. My husband was fifty-eight when he
passed. My sisters are in their sixties. They live with their grand-
kids and daughters-in-law. I also have a boy, my only son, Hari-
das Menon, my Hari. Ever since Hari could crawl, I knew he'd
be a wanderer, destined to be a pravasi. And you know what, I
was right. As soon as he started to walk, he walked his skinny
ass all the way to Dubai. I suppose you're too young to under-
stand what pravasi means, young man, what it truly means.
Maybe that's why you singled me out for your research. What-
ever comes, speak into the recorder, you said. Maybe I've got
the look of an old crone with wisdom to spare, And you know
what, you're right, I feel like I'm going to be talkative in my
eighties. So let me tell you what pravasi means, but when my
voice gets played back to your teachers, tell them Nalinakshi
was of sound state and mind as she said her piece. Not a trace of
bitterness, not an ounce of pity.

Pravasi means foreigner, outsider. Immigrant, worker. Pravasi
means you've left your native place. Pravasi means you'll have
regrets. You'll want money, then more money. You'll want one
house with European shitters. And one car, one scooter. Pravasi
means you've left your loved ones because you're young, ambi-
tious, filled with confidence that you'll be back some day, and
you probably will. For a few weeks every year, you'll return for
vacations, but mind you, you return older. Blacker. News hun-
gry. Before you've had time to adjust to power cuts and pot-
holes, like they had in the old days when phones were luxuries
or glued to walls, someone's going to tell you so-and-so died.
And it'll be a shock, because you didn't know. And when you
go to this person's house to pay your respects, you'll discover
someone else has died. And as you continue to see people you
know you're required to see, you'll hear about more dead peo-
ple. Or ailments. Or needs. Then you'll see the new people, fat
babies or wives or husbands. And you'll look at what they've

got. Inevitably, you'll think about your own life, the choices you made. How far you've come, if paying for those shitters was worth it. And by the time you've done the math in your head, everything you've missed, what's been gained, you'll come to realize what the word pravasi really means: absence. That's what it means, absence. When you write your book, address my Hari personally, and tell my beautiful, beautiful boy, tell my son that's what it's always meant: absence.

DJAMILA IBRAHIM

HEADING SOMEWHERE

Omar types *domestic workers Syria* and waits for the page to load. Images swirl in his mind like a gutted photo album set to the wind: his old girlfriend Sara, his childhood friends Meseret and Naima, another girl or two whose names he can't remember. Young women who'd left Addis Ababa to work as maids in Saudi Arabia, Syria, and elsewhere, light on luggage and high on anticipation for a better life. Words chase these images like guided missiles—*isolation, beating, rape,* and *murder* (disguised as *suicide*)—but Omar doesn't want to think about these things right now. He wills his mind in another direction: Sara wading through Damascus's narrow, winding streets, past busy, dusty souks—a landscape he only knows from pictures he'd googled recently—to find a way out of Syria before civil war engulfs the city.

It's only 4:15 p.m. but the snow cloaking the quiet Ottawa neighbourhood is already turning to soft indigo. Omar hopes to find a lead into Sara's whereabouts or at least a contact number before his wife, Marianne, comes home from work in an hour.

The rebels have taken control of Douma, a city only ten kilometers away from Damascus, he'd heard announced on the news last night.

Sara might already be in one of the NGOs' makeshift shelters, waiting for a flight home. If only Ethiopia had an embassy in Syria . . . or maybe she's on her way to the Ethiopian consulate in Beirut. He keeps speculating, as he's been doing for the last two days, ever since Sara's mother called from Addis Ababa to ask him for help in getting her daughter out of Damascus.

When he was little, back in Addis Ababa, whenever he and his friends heard screams coming from the police station adjacent to their compound, they'd rush to stack up boxes, tires, or any piece of trash solid enough to stand on against the concrete wall separating the compound from the station so they could glimpse whomever was being interrogated that day. Sara would already be there beside him, her eyes sparkling eagerly. Together, they'd dare other children to join them. Serious interrogations were done behind closed doors so only screams and echoes of unintelligible words could be heard, but the kids would line up beside each other anyway, stand on tiptoe and crane their little heads over the wall, hoping to see some poor, petty criminal writhe and scream on the dusty court surrounded by police officers beating on him with batons and straps. Sometimes, an officer would catch them watching and threaten to lock them up, wagging a finger and cursing, or even flinging rocks at them. They'd all run away, clumsily tripping over their cobbled-together stands, down dirt paths riddled with potholes and sharp rocks half-buried in the soil, to their homes. Some would be on the verge of tears by the time they stopped, but not Sara. She would laugh, her mischievous eyes wild with exhilaration. Omar loved and hated that about her. He admired her fearlessness and yet lived in constant worry that in the eyes of their peers, she, a girl, might one day prove to be the braver of the two.

This childhood memory melts into a sadness in Omar's gut. He shakes his melancholy away, opens a link, and scans through the news:

We heard gunfire and we saw black smoke behind the buildings but our employer told us there was a celebration at the army barracks.

We wanted to return home but our employers left the country and we were locked inside their house.

Stranded migrant workers should contact their embassies or the International Organization for Migration (IOM) for repatriation assistance . . .

He spots a link to the IOM and learns they have an office in Damascus. He frantically clicks and clicks again until he finds their contact information. On a piece of paper he writes down the IOM's number, under the one Sara's mother had given him to reach her daughter at her employers' house. He adds the Ethiopian Consulate's number in Beirut to the list. He opens another link or two, then gives up. The news is too depressing to continue reading. He tucks the piece of paper in his shirt pocket. He'll call early tomorrow morning. It'll be afternoon in that part of the world by then. He'll also try Sara's employers' house again. He closes his laptop, picks up his winter coat from the hallway closet, closes the front door behind him, and heads to the grocery store a few blocks away.

Holding the corner post for balance, Sara climbs onto the patio chair. She wraps the bedsheet she's tied to the ledge like a rope around her arm and slowly climbs over her employers' second-floor balcony and down to the quiet street below. Unlike her Filipina neighbour who ran to her government's embassy in the city, Sara had to find a way out of Damascus and into Beirut where she could seek help from the Ethiopian consulate. A metre or so before her feet touch the ground, she loses her grip and falls on the asphalt. She gets up quickly, adjusts the duffle bag on her back, and looks up toward the house. The lights have not been turned on. She takes a deep breath and searches the dark street for the ride Mohamed, her employers' gate-keeper, had arranged for her. She spots an old van a few metres away. Its brake lights flash twice, as agreed upon. She walks toward it as fast as she can without running.

"Get in the back," the driver says from the half-open window before Sara has a chance to make eye contact.

"Cover yourself with that blanket and keep your head down," he orders with a rushed voice.

Panic takes over as she slides the van door shut. What if this is a trap? She trusts Mohamed. He didn't usually let her out of the compound alone for fear of losing his job but he was nice to her. And he has delivered on the promise of finding her someone who, for a fee, would help her. But this man could be taking her to the police station instead of the outskirts of

Damascus where she's supposed to meet another man who will take her to Beirut. She shakes the distressing thought away. There is nothing she can do now but hope for the best. She squeezes her slim body between two rows of seats as an extra precaution. Mohamed had said the military was intensifying its operations in the city and that soldiers have been stopping and searching cars often these days. She rests her head on her duffle bag and covers herself with the blanket. The man starts the car and heads toward Jawaher Lal Nahro.

For a while, she listens through the van's rattles for any changes in speed or signs of abnormal noise outside. Then, to ease her anxiety, she tries to think of happier times. Her earliest memory is of Ababa Tesfaye's children's TV show. Every Saturday at 6 p.m., she, Omar, and other neighbourhood kids would gather at the entrance of Emama Elsabet's living-room-turned-bar. Wriggling around each other to get to the front of the line, they'd watch Emama Elsabet as she heaved herself onto a short wooden stool, removed the crocheted doily from the small TV on the shelf in the corner above the glass bar, and turned the dial to on. The children would then rush to get the best spot by the side door, from where they could watch their favourite show without disturbing Emama Elsabet's customers. Some nights, there would be too many kids to fit in the tight space assigned to them. Fighting would erupt and the bar owner would shoo everybody home, cursing. On good days, though, they'd sit there, all senses glued to that TV, like seedlings turned to the sun, lost in Ababa Tesfaye's tales of smart foxes and gullible little children, of greedy humans and misunderstood snakes. They'd sit on the chilly red-and-black-checkered cement tiles for an hour, their scrawny little bodies huddled together for warmth against the cold air coming through the open door. They'd return Ababa Tesfaye's greetings, answer his questions, and cheer in unison when Good prevailed against Evil. Once in a while, Emama Elsabet or one of her waitresses would instruct them to keep quiet.

Back then, Omar wanted to follow in Ababa Tesfaye's footsteps, and Sara dreamed of becoming an actress or a singer, anything to get her on TV. Together, they would memorize Ababa

———

Tesfaye's stories and reenact them in front of their friends and families. How strange and remote that part of her life feels now, as though she's lived two consecutive lives connected only by brittle threads of memory.

Sara looks around hoping to find a familiar face. A dozen African and Asian men and women are sitting on the shabby linoleum floor, all staring at the dirty walls in front of them or at their own hands. None of them is *Habesha*. A piece of fabric that might once have served as a tablecloth curtains the only window in the room. A light bulb hanging low from the ceiling bathes the room with a dim orange hue. This apartment must be in one of Damascus's western suburbs, near the border into Lebanon. That's what Mohamed had told her, but her driver had only grunted when she asked him to confirm this as he dropped her off. She sits beside a Black woman with a dirty shawl around her shoulders and waits for the car that will clandestinely transport them into Lebanon.

"Where are you from?" Sara asks her neighbour. A tuft of hair has escaped from the woman's several-months-old braids as if someone had pulled her by the hair.

"Uganda," the woman replies without turning, her voice cracking a little.

Sara waits for a second. "I'm from Ethiopia," she volunteers.

The woman nods slightly without looking at her.

Sara leaves the woman to her silence, folds her legs closer to her chest, and discreetly takes out a piece of paper from her bra. She examines the portrait-size picture of Jesus in her palm, one of the few things the recruiters at the employment agency had not confiscated when she came to work in Damascus ten months ago. If only they hadn't taken her cellphone or the thin gold necklace Omar had given her before he left for Canada. She could have sold them and used the money now.

"You know, your saviour seems more in need of saving than the people he presides over," Omar had said once, pointing with his chin at a framed portrait of Jesus her mother hung on the wall above the credenza in their living room. Making fun of each other's religion was a subtle way they had of testing the parameters of a possible future together.

"I prefer him to your faceless Allah," she'd retorted.

Now, staring at Jesus's soft golden hair flowing like mead around His oval, blemish-free face, His big childish blue eyes, His delicate hand pointing at a heart that resembles the strawberries her madam reserved for important guests, Sara wonders if her innocent and fragile-looking God could indeed save her from the nightmare she's in. She quickly shakes the blasphemous thought away, cautiously crosses herself, and tucks the picture back into her bra.

Omar picks up a plastic basket from a pile by the grocery store's entrance and joins a crowd of after-work shoppers. He chooses a pack of whole-wheat spaghetti from the pasta and sauce aisle and heads to the organic produce section. He squeezes through a mostly white and middle-class group of people who are, with the seriousness of a physician examining patients, stroking ripe mangoes and pears or studying the crispiness of leafy vegetables. He grabs a bag of mixed greens and walks past other patrons comparing the nutritional values of condiments in tiny jars and takes his place at the end of the express lane.

He prefers regular pasta but Marianne is big on healthy eating except for her weekly indulgence of a Big Mac, poutine, and Diet Coke. He once or twice pointed out the irony of the Diet Coke in this meal, but to no avail. His wife can be stubborn sometimes, not very unlike Sara, except Marianne's unyielding nature comes from a life of comfort, free of wants and doubts. He admires Marianne's assurance, her deep-seated confidence that nothing is out of reach, that every broken thing or person is potentially repairable. That must be what she saw in him, his potential; he was someone she could save and fix.

It was pure chance, how he'd met Marianne. She, a Canadian foreign service officer on her first mission abroad, had accompanied the new Canadian consular officer to a function organized by the Ethiopian Tourism Commission to welcome new foreign diplomats; he, a third-year Addis Ababa University student, had escorted a distant aunt, a bureaucrat at the Ministry of Culture and Tourism, to the event in lieu of her ailing husband. Mari-anne would tell him later how she'd watched him from afar as he talked his way around the room, mesmerized by the ease with which he carried himself despite his apparent youth and the ill-fitting blazer he wore. And how a rush of curiosity and desire had taken her over, a wonderful stirring of the heart she hadn't felt in the year and a half she'd lived in Addis Ababa. And how, surprising even herself, she'd accepted his offer to show her around the city—even though she'd already seen all the tourist spots—to satisfy a sudden need to be wooed by a tall, handsome man.

The day he left Addis Ababa a married man, he'd stood out-side the bedroom he'd shared with his three brothers, his eyes travelling from one corner of the room to the next, trying to look at his childhood's landscape from the perspective of his future Canadian self, as he imagined a cartographer or an ar-cheologist would do upon discovering an ancient site. Would he recognize the way the sun's rays, nonchalant as only eternal things can afford to be, spread on his single bed, diluting the brown sheets to a soft caramel tone? Would he recognize the sandalwood smell that clung to every corner of the two-room house from his mother's daily incense burning to voracious spirits who'd never answer her prayers? Would he remember the names of the girls whose initials he and his brothers carved on the legs of their wooden beds when they were teenagers? He didn't want to forget these things. Others, he wished to erase: the ugliness of the newspaper-covered dirt walls, the paper brown and stiff in places from water damage; the smell of urine in the pink plastic chamber pot his mother kept under her bed for when it was too late to go to the communal bathroom at the other end of the compound; the misery and hunger that forced him and his siblings to work as shoe-shiners and street vendors before they were ten years old.

Rivulets of cold sweat had run down his armpits as he walked past rows of old, pastel-coloured houses and their run-down verandas on his way to the car that would take him to the airport. He'd felt a little dazed, like a prisoner stuck on the threshold between dream and reality, his mother's hold on his arm as she limped beside him the only weight constantly grounding him back into the tangible world.

On their way out of the compound, he'd stopped in front of the little house Sara shared with her parents. He'd stared at what must have once been deep bright red steps where Sara and other neighbourhood girls used to play marbles when they were little, now turned to the colour of raw beet skin. It was on these steps that he'd said goodbye to her the night before, and where he'd promised to send her sponsorship papers as soon as he could. He'd wished he had the power to fuse her body onto his then, melt flesh on flesh and mind to heart, so he could take something real of her with him, so he could reassure her of his love and commitment, convince her that Marianne meant nothing to him, was only a means to an end, a gateway to their future happiness in Canada. But he was never good at serious talk. His was the language of a street hustler and Sara knew all his tricks.

The woman in front of Omar in the grocery store's express lane leans her head to the side of the line then turns to him and says: "It's never going to stop, is it?" And to Omar's perplexed look, she adds, "The snow," pointing at a wall of white outside the store's sliding doors.

Omar nods.

"I wish I was in Jamaica right now. Or anywhere else but here."

"Be careful of what you wish for," Omar says with a sly smile.

The woman looks at him, puzzled for a moment. Then she says, "Well, not anywhere, but you know what I mean. Some place warm and pleasant."

Omar nods again and scrolls through his cellphone, looking for missed unknown or international calls.

The Canadian embassy has already closed its office in Damascus. Otherwise, he would have asked Marianne to contact one of her colleagues there to help him find Sara. His wife has always been a little touchy about his history with Sara, but this is too important. Marianne would have put her feelings aside, at least until Sara was out of harm's way. The tension, innuendos, and outright accusations might have started again later, the way they did last year when Omar, too busy planning his first trip back to Ethiopia, and too absorbed by the prospect of seeing Sara again, had neglected Marianne. Thankfully, his wife didn't go as far as threatening him with a divorce as he had feared. He resented Marianne her power—divorce meant the loss of his permanent resident card, maybe even deportation. More importantly, though, he was furious with himself for having let his guard down with her. However, things are different now between Sara and him, and his wife probably knows that.

Last year, after four years in Canada, Omar had finally made it to Addis Ababa for a month-long visit. And Sara had just returned home from a three-year stint in Dubai. At first, their reunion was all that Omar had hoped it would be. The outburst of contagious joy that was her laughter had become somehow dimmer, her manners more poised. Still, her face had retained the fullness of her teenage years and under the restrained demeanour she wore like a protective veil, he could discern the contours of the vivacious girl he grew up with. But it didn't take long before his excitement was shattered. In tightly knit communities like theirs, secrets rarely stay hidden. His best friend, Alemayehu, was the first to tell him what Sara had been up to in Dubai.

When he confronted her, to his surprise, she didn't deny the allegations nor did she try to repent.

"I did what I had to do . . . just as you did," she said.

He could taste the venom in her contained voice, the sarcasm in her dry laughter afterwards. He felt a gush of hatred toward her for implying that marrying Marianne for Canadian citizenship was akin to the life of prostitution she'd chosen. Why didn't she just return home after she'd run away from her abusive employers' house? He wished he could lay his hands on the nameless people that had pushed her into such degradation.

"I couldn't come home empty-handed," she'd said. "I went there to make money."

He should have known that Sara couldn't have allowed herself to give up on her responsibilities. If a lifetime of struggle teaches anything to someone as strong willed as Sara, it's perseverance.

What surprised him most later on was that their last confrontation was not infused with insults and tears the way their fights used to be; their final breakup was not inscribed in a specific, single instance that he could replay in his mind. Instead, the irreparability of the matter was felt rather than heard, the reality of it taken in slowly, like the smell of rot carried by a light breeze over a distance. Only recently did he realize why his anger had, for so long, felt muddied, unripe for outburst, his vexation rigged with confusion and despair: it hid his own shame. The shame of a man who'd failed to protect the woman he loved.

If only everyone he trusted had not joined the others in vilifying Sara. "City girls can't handle hard work. You'd never hear of village girls debasing themselves that way," said his old neighbour, a woman who'd known both Sara and him since they were babies.

"A Muslim girl would not have done that," his mother said.

But he can't blame anyone. No matter how modern he believed himself to be, he just couldn't shed the image of other men possessing Sara's warm, lithe body. It had damaged the truth of his love for her and sullied the dream he had for them.

For months after returning to Canada, he'd felt as though he was afflicted with permanent jet lag. Even the childhood memories he used to cherish turned to ashes in his mind. For a while, the only thing he clearly remembered about his trip was the clinking sound of the gold bracelets Sara wore daily as if to remind herself it was all worth it.

Now, surrounded by people who have never experienced the stink of abject poverty, a new truth reveals itself to him: Sara might pay for his ego with her life, caught in the crossfire of a civil war. Would he be able to live with himself if something happened to her in Syria? Why did she have to go to Syria any-way, as though Dubai was not bad enough?

The woman in front of him in the express lane interrupts his thoughts again. "I bet it's always warm where you're from."

"Yes," Omar says and turns his head left and right, pretend-ing to be searching for someone.

On any other day, he would have been more receptive. He would have told the woman about Addis Ababa's two-thousand-kilometre-high altitude, the blazing sun in January and the cold teeth-shattering early morning wind at the height of the rainy season in July. He would have told her about the hail, some-times as big as ping-pong balls, that crackled against his house's tin roof like popcorn. He would have told her how, when he was little, sometimes he'd collect hail from his neighbours' front yards in his mother's rusted enamel bucket then dump it in front of his house, spread it around quickly before it melted, and pre-tend he lived in America, which in his mind at that time encom-passed the whole of Europe and Canada. But not today. Today, he just wants to get to the cash register, pay for his groceries, and go home. He wants the churning in his stomach to stop. He wants the night to end so he can try to contact Sara tomorrow.

Sara brushes her arm against her small chest to feel the thin wad of cash in her bra. There's just enough money to cover the fare to Beirut and some food. She's going home empty-handed. She bites her lower lip hard to stifle the anger in her throat, then remembers her surroundings: she might not make it out of Syria at all. She realizes that she shouldn't have come to Da-mascus, but how could a poor girl with only a high school di-ploma and average looks achieve anything in a country of tens of millions of unemployed youth?

She imagines her mother counting and recounting what's left of the money she'd sent her four months earlier, devising ways to make it last until the next time. But there won't be a next time. The money Sara made in Dubai was supposed to have been enough to supplement her father's modest income. She had dreamed of her parents running a small business together, perhaps a pastry shop, working side by side, filled with a joy only a sense of recovered dignity and pride can bring. She had even fancied she'd have enough extra money to cover her flight to Canada when Omar sent her the sponsorship papers he'd promised. Instead, all that money and all the gold Abu Karim— the old Emirati widower whose mistress she'd been for a year before his sons kicked her out of his house—was spent on her father's medical bills when his diabetes suddenly attacked his vision and kidneys.

"My ma'am was killed when she was coming home from her friend's house. A bomb fell on the building next door and took her life," Sara hears a middle-aged woman sitting across from her say to her neighbour. "Everybody was running and crying. I went to my ma'am's room and took money from where she hides it and ran away."

"The taxi driver I paid to bring me here almost handed me over to the police," a young man said to the middle-aged woman. "I open the car door and run away when I saw the police station sign."

"My ma'am refused to give me food. She beat me until I was unconscious. I was not sorry she died," the middle-aged woman said, adjusting her shawl on her head.

Sara looks down at her sweat-stained clothes, her jeans dirty from when she fell as she jumped out of her employers' house, her fingernails chipped and dirty. How self-conscious she'd felt last year when she first saw Omar in Addis Ababa after four years. He had greeted her with open arms and the same boyish smile she remembered. He'd hugged her, too, but his embrace was tentative, as if he were suddenly unable to trust the memory of their intimacy. Although she didn't recognize his scent, she hoped he'd recall the perfume she wore, the one he'd bought her long before he'd left for Canada.

She sat across from him in one of the two wooden chairs in his mother's living room. In the dim light, she searched his face for signs of time's passage or the strains of distance that might have altered her knowledge of him. Omar's dark skin, which used to glow like freshly roasted coffee beans in the summer, had gotten lighter, his body fleshy, yet not fat. She thought it suited him, but these manifestations of comfort had proved her fear right: time and circumstances had erected an insurmountable barrier between them.

She'd tucked her dry hands between her thighs, rubbing them together in the folds of her skirt to smooth out their coarseness and, by the same token, the memories of the years spent in Dubai, first cooking, scrubbing floors, and washing eight people's clothes by hand. And then, after her employer made it a habit of forcing himself on her whenever his wife and children were away, of sleeping with men for pay.

"If you can't stop them, might as well have them pay for it," a girlfriend had said to her.

She had found it hard at first, but like anything else in life, only the first steps were unbearable. She was lucky to have attracted Abu Karim's eye. Within a month, she had gone from a battered maid to a prostitute to a live-in mistress. But some scars are hard to conceal. Omar's gaze was a burning sun melting her cover. If he ever saw her naked again, she was sure he'd be able to discern the outlines of Abu Karim's pale, spotty hands as the old man squeezed her thighs until they hurt in a pathetic attempt to summon his long-lost vigour, and the foul lust of all the others before him.

Only the state of Omar's mother's house quieted her fears a little. Nothing in the living room had been moved or replaced in decades. His mother's single bed with its thin mattress occupied one dark wall. Another corner housed the family's modest belongings, piled up under an old bedsheet. She was abashed by the fact that noticing these things improved her mood, made her think that perhaps Omar was not as out of reach as she had thought.

"How was Dubai?" he'd asked, with his usual playful tone, as if she'd only been away on a short vacation, with the same honeyed voice that sometimes made it hard for her to take him seriously. "I'm so relieved you're back for good," he'd added before she had time to respond, turning her irritation into a yearning in her throat—he had not yet heard about what had happened in Dubai.

Her eyes followed the fat vein above his left eyebrow, the only sign she knew of his nervousness. It travelled up in an uncertain path and forked right under his hairline, dividing his forehead into two, almost identical, flat planes. She ached to follow its path with her finger the way she used to. She wanted to tell him how, when she first moved to Dubai, often, when she found her employers' prayer rugs laid out on the floor, she'd think of him. When the whole family went out shopping or to visit with friends, she'd lie down on the floor beside the rug and, propped on her elbow, brush her palm against the velvety prints of minarets and the Kaaba, follow the intricate patterns of arabesque and mysterious words embroidered into the fabric, all the while dreaming of his fingers on her skin.

"Take your dirty hands off my prayer rug, *ya kafira*!" her madam had yelled at her once, bursting into the room and swinging her shopping bags at her. Sara knew not to touch the Quran but didn't know a rug could also be too precious for her Christian hands. Nevertheless, she'd felt such a perverse pleasure seeing her madam's reaction that she wished she could tell her about the sexual thoughts she'd just had. Later on, lying on her thin mattress on the kitchen floor where she slept, she'd wondered if Omar would have disapproved too.

Jealousy and competition are rife among those who manage to find work in the Middle East, so it was only a matter of time before her secret was out. She tried to tell Omar of the abuse that led her to prostitution. She wanted him to know that every time her employer attacked her, she fought him off with all her might, and that, when he invariably overpowered her, she refused to look at his face, keeping her eyes shut or on the ceiling to deny him the acknowledgement he sought. But she couldn't find words to describe her ordeal.

Once Omar found out what had happened, he couldn't look her in the eye or touch her, as though she had become a leper overnight. At least in the eyes of the other neighbours, she could see envy mixed with disapproval as they ogled her foreign-made clothes and gold jewellery. His attitude enraged her. She snickered at his discomfort, donning the protective mask of an only girl-child who'd learned at an early age that laughter can be as powerful an arsenal against fear or shame as a fist. What did he expect her to do? Run back home and wait for him to rescue her? Yet, after the heat of the moment had passed, she wished Omar would see through her facade and that, once the shock of the news had subsided from his mind, he'd come back to her.

She should have known better. No matter how much things have changed from the time of her parents, women will always bear the brunt of any transgression. "The markings of Eve's daughters," her mother would have said. Why did she expect Omar to be above this?

She only admitted her defeat after he'd left for Canada again, this time with just a vague promise to keep in touch. How naive she'd been for thinking that they could someday pick up from where they'd left off four years earlier when, for months, she'd lived spellbound by Omar's vivid aspirations for their future together. The way he held her close that night on her parents' doorstep, dragging out the moment of separation before he'd left. In spite of herself, she'd believed in his power to whisk her away from that miserable neighbourhood, that dead-end of a life.

"Good riddance. What did you expect from a Muslim?" her mother had said in an attempt at consolation, but both women knew that what Sara had done would always cling to her, staining her chances of marriage to any man, Muslim or Christian. Her only choice was to go back to the Middle East, make good money, and support her family, not wallow in self-pity.

Omar takes the spaghetti sauce he and Marianne had prepared on the weekend out of the freezer and places it in the microwave. He leans on the granite countertop and watches the day die outside his window, the suburban desolation turn into a dim crescent moon of serenity. He opens the box of whole-wheat spaghetti he bought and adds the contents to the hot water on the stove. With his palm, he slowly pushes the tips of the dry pasta into the water as the submerged parts soften and curve.

His cellphone rings.

"Hon, can you run and pick up some salad and a dessert? I'm stuck in traffic," his wife says through an ambulance siren in the distance.

"I got the salad but not dessert."

"You know how much my mom loves cake . . . Please?"

He had forgotten his in-laws were coming to dinner tonight. Irritation mounts in him. He has always been good at massaging people's egos into liking him, except for his in-laws. In five years, he hasn't been able to get through to them. Whenever they show interest in him, it feels suspect, their insinuations just out of reach of his rugged English. His mother-in-law annoys him: her perfectly coiffed salt-and-pepper hair, stiff and flat on her head, her big inquisitive eyes and non-stop chatter. She makes him think of a grey parrot. She uses words such as "marvellous" or "extraordinary" after every sentence he utters, equally impressed by his ability to remove stains from carpets as she is by his answers to questions about his life back home. His father-in-law's approach is more direct, more directly aimed at emasculating him.

"Trust me, baby, it might come off wrong to you but they don't mean any harm," Marianne would say once they're alone, wrapping her plump arms around his neck. "They're just old and set in their old ways, you know? Anyway, you'll graduate soon, get a good job, and make Daddy proud, okay?" she'd tease, guiding his hands to her ample breasts.

He can't complain, though. Marianne has been good to him. After his trip to Ethiopia, he'd decided to leave his stained past with Sara behind and fully embrace the comfortable and uncomplicated life Marianne offered. "Home is what you make it," he'd heard someone say on the bus once. And this saying had stayed with him. After all, he'd come a long way, so why provoke fate by wanting to have it all? And until now, this thought had sustained him.

The clock above the hickory kitchen cabinets chimes 6 p.m. He turns the stove off and strains the cooked noodles in a colander. He should have just waited until Marianne was home to boil the pasta.

As he picks up his winter coat from the hallway closet again, he catches a glimpse of his reflection in the hallway mirror. His mind leaps toward Sara again. The little girl who laughed off the officers' threats at the police station next to their compound. Her devilish glee. And the other, grown one, who stood up to his condemnation with fortitude and pride. He decides to call Sara one more time before he heads out to the grocery store. He puts his winter coat down on a stool in the kitchen and reaches in his shirt pocket for the piece of paper where he'd written Sara's employers' number and a calling card. He dials the numbers on the calling card first, then Sara's employers'.

"May I speak to Sara, please," he says, surprised that the line connected on the first try this time. "I'm her cousin, calling from Canada," he continues, as Sara's mother had instructed him to do to avoid raising any suspicion.

"From Canada?" the man on the other end asks, his voice full of sleep. "Wait."

Omar hears grumbling in the background. He imagines the man explaining the late-night call to his wife. He pictures Sara apologizing to them as she hurries to the phone. He feels a nervous rush overcome his body. He takes a deep breath and tries to rehearse what he will say to her but the sentences disappear before he's done forming them.

The voices at the other end of the line become louder. He hears a man and a woman arguing but he can't understand what they're saying. After what seems like an hour, the man picks up the phone and with an accusatory tone says: "She's not here. She is gone."

Before Omar has time to ask any more questions, the man yells at him in Arabic and hangs up.

Omar stares at the phone in his hand, trying to understand what just happened. He starts to dial the number again. Then it dawns on him: Sara has managed to escape from her employers' house.

He picks up his winter jacket again, closes the door behind him, and faces the shimmering snow dancing in the wind. What really bothers him is not so much what she'd done but what others had done to her body. This knowledge still digs into his chest like a crooked rib and there isn't much he can do about it. He stands in the doorway for a moment. He focuses on a thought forming in the back of his consciousness, the way a photographer sharpens the contours of an image by manipulating the lens. Maybe it's the fresh cold air that clears his mind a little or maybe it's the small piece of good news he'd just heard, but he feels hope, a small and shrivelled hope that's true, but one that's as flammable as tinder. Perhaps with time, he'll learn to live with that nudging in his chest the way people accept their wounds when they realize they won't die from them. Another hope he nurses is that Sara will forgive him for having broken his promise to sponsor her and for having shunned her for doing what she had to do. This one is the most fragile of his aspirations.

He touches his chest on the side where the piece of paper with Sara's contact numbers is tucked in his shirt pocket as if this gesture might nudge events toward a favourable outcome. He takes a deep breath to alleviate the guilt, worry, and longing inside then walks into the dark night to the same grocery store, thinking of how ludicrous the idea of a grown person demanding dessert after each meal would sound to anyone back home.

Sara's employers will soon notice she's gone. They have treated her fairly; they even took her on a vacation to their village by the sea once, although she would have preferred a few days off instead. Nonetheless, they'd refused to give her her passport back when she told them last week she wanted to return home. Instead, they dismissed her worries and tried to appease her, promising that if the rebels pushed any closer to Damascus, they'd take her out of Syria themselves. If she'd learned anything from her time in the Middle East, it was not to trust any Arab. Even her friend Lily, who is lucky enough to work for a nice couple in Kuwait that let her call long distance for free, had agreed with her.

She wonders if Omar is worrying about her at this instant, as she waits in a filthy room for a van that might or might not come. Or if he is leading the life of a Canadian man with his Canadian wife in a safe and comfortable Canadian home, oblivious to the misery or dangers of a world thousands of kilometres away from his. She tries in vain to imagine him at a dinner table with his wife. Her memory of his physique is frozen in a picture he'd sent her a few months after he'd moved to Ottawa: the wide collars of his winter jacket turned up to his ears, his slender body scrunched up, his smile like a grimace of pain. He looked as if he were being swallowed by the whitewashed Canadian landscape of clouds and snow and imploring the viewer to rescue him. She'd felt such anguish for him then. It's his turn now. She wants him to be worried sick for her. She wants him gutted by guilt and remorse. After all, it's his fault she's in this mess.

She stretches her legs in front of her and pulls a water bottle out of her bag. She takes a few sips and passes it to her neighbour, examining the woman as she gulps down the rest. She wonders if this woman is thinking about some man too. And if she's despising herself for thinking of him at a time like this. For caring about what he thought, what he did, if he'd come back to her or wait for her, whatever the case may be.

She gets up and paces back and forth, unconcerned with her travel companions' stares, then stops in her tracks to listen to the muffled voices of men outside the closed door. A man wearing a heavy wool jacket with a few buttons missing opens the door and with the urgency of the hunted yells: "*Yalla,* get up, the car is here!"

The Ugandan woman jerks her head right to left and again but remains seated, as though she has been tricked one too many times to trust her luck now. Sara picks up her duffle bag with one hand and extends an arm to help the woman up. She attempts an encouraging smile even though her own heart is beating so violently she fears it might break out of her chest, taking her life with it. But if she has to die, she would rather die on the move, heading somewhere.

Everyone shuffles through the apartment door. The freezing strong January wind washes over Sara's face, dousing her nervousness. In the distance, a muezzin calls the faithful to prayer. The travellers hand their fare to the man in the wool jacket and one by one take their seats in an old Toyota HiAce that reminds Sara of the minivan taxis that are ubiquitous in Addis Ababa's streets. She takes her seat in the tightly packed, beat-up van for the hour or so ride to Beirut. As the vehicle starts to move, she leans her head against the headrest and covers her nose and mouth with her scarf against the smell of sweat and exhaust fumes.

She thinks of what could happen if they get caught after they cross the border. Would the Lebanese hand them over to the Syrians? She thinks of the possibility of dying here. The thought of leaving this earth without seeing Omar again, without any hope for reconciliation, digs a hole in her heart. She thinks of all the ways people have of hurting each other. She'd practised letting Omar fade from her consciousness, piece by piece. *Eventually I'll just go on living, as people always do,* she'd told herself time and again. Was she wrong to have sneered at his reaction? Was she too selfish, too hard-headed? They have been a part of each other's lives since childhood. All that entangled history, all the memories: some hard and painful like ice, others as warm and nourishing as summer rain. Some of it might eventually dissipate but she knows Omar will endure in her mind and body for a very long time. And if she dies before she makes it home, she knows she will linger in Omar's memories as well. Of this much she is certain. But she can't indulge in regrets and hope for a future with him right now. What's important, what has so far stood the test of time, is her will to fight, her determination to hold herself together. And to make it home, to her parents'. The other home, the one she once dreamed up with Omar, might have after all only been just that: a dream.

Sara feels someone shaking her by the arm. She opens her eyes and looks at the Ugandan woman beside her. The woman points at dim lights in the distance: "Lebanon?" she asks, suddenly realizing it was possible to make it out of Syria.

Sara rubs her eyes to clear her mind of sleep, surprised that she'd dozed off. She checks her watch: it has been forty minutes since they left the apartment in Damascus. At the horizon, the pink dusty sky has started to extract itself from the dark mountains.

"Should be. But I don't know," she says. "Did the driver stop anywhere? A checkpoint?"

The woman gives Sara a puzzled look.

"Are we in Lebanon?" Sara asks the Indian-looking man in front of her.

"Yes," the man whispers, but with doubt in his eyes. Or is it disbelief? Sara is not sure. The other passengers are all searching the misty darkness outside for signs of deliverance, their backs and necks stiff with suspense, their hands clasping their meagre possessions. Whatever comes next, Sara realizes she won't be facing it alone and this awareness of a shared destiny gives her the strength she needs to keep calm.

She turns to the Ugandan woman and offers her the most reassuring smile she can muster.

GENERATIONS

*defining myself my own way any way many
many ways*
—TATO LAVIERA, "AMERÍCAN"

MENA ABDULLAH

THE TIME OF THE PEACOCK

When I was little everything was wonderful; the world was our farm and we were all loved. Rashida and Lal and I, Father and our mother, Ama: we loved one another and everything turned to good.

I remember in autumn, how we burned the great baskets of leaves by the Gwydir and watched the fires burning in the river while Ama told us stories of Krishna the Flute-player and his moving mountains. And when the fires had gone down and the stories were alive in our heads we threw cobs of corn into the fires and cooked them. One for each of us—Rashida and Lal and I, Father and our mother.

Winter I remember, when the frost bit and stung and the wind pulled our hair. At night by the fire in the warmth of the house, we could hear the dingoes howling.

Then it was spring and the good year was born again. The sticks of the jasmine vine covered themselves with flowers.

One spring I remember was the time of the peacock when I learnt the word *secret* and began to grow up. After that spring everything somehow was different, was older. I was not little any more, and the baby came.

I had just learnt to count. I thought I could count anything. I counted fingers and toes, the steps and the windows, even the hills. But this day in spring the hills were wrong.

There should have been five. I knew that there should have been five. I counted them over and over—"*Ek, do, tin, panch*"—but it was no good. There was one too many, a strange hill, a leftover. It looked familiar, and I knew it, but it made more than five and worried me. I thought of Krishna and the mountains that moved to protect the cow-herds, the travellers lost because of them, and I was frightened because it seemed to me that our hills had moved.

I ran through the house and out into the garden to tell Ama the thing that Krishna had done and to ask her how we could please him. But when I saw her I forgot all about them; I was as young as that. I just stopped and jumped, up and down.

She was standing there, in her own garden, the one with the Indian flowers, her own little walled-in country. Her hands were joined together in front of her face, and her lips were moving. On the ground, in front of the Kashmiri rosebush, in front of the tuberoses, in front of the pomegranate-tree, she had placed little bowls of shining milk. I jumped to see them. Now I knew why I was running all the time and skipping, why I wanted to sing out and to count everything in the world.

"It is spring," I shouted to Ama. "Not nearly-spring! Not almost-spring! But really-spring! Will the baby come soon?" I asked her. "Soon?"

"Soon, Impatience, soon."

I laughed at her and jumped up and clapped my hands together over the top of my head.

"I am as big as that," I said. "I can do anything." And I hopped on one leg to the end of the garden where the peacock lived. "Shah-Jehan!" I said to him—that was his name. "It is spring and the baby is coming, pretty Shah-Jehan." But he didn't seem interested. "Silly old Shah-Jehan," I said. "Don't you know anything? I can count ten."

He went on staring with his goldy eye at me. He *was* a silly bird. Why, he had to stay in the garden all day, away from the rooster. He couldn't run everywhere the way that I could. He couldn't do anything.

"Open your tail," I told him. "Go on, open your tail." And we went on staring at one another till I felt sad.

"Rashida is right," I said to him. "You will never open your tail like the bird on the fan. But why don't you try? Please, pretty Shah-Jehan." But he just went on staring as though he would never open his tail, and while I looked at him sadly I remembered how he had come to us.

He could lord it now and strut in the safety of the garden, but I remembered how the Lascar brought him to the farm, in a bag, like a cabbage, with his feathers drooping and his white tail dirty.

The Lascar came to the farm, a seaman on the land, a dark face in a white country. How he smiled when he saw us—Rashida and me swinging on the gate. How he chattered to Ama and made her laugh and cry. How he had shouted about the curries that she gave him.

And when it was time to go, with two basins of curry tied up in cloth and packed in his bag, he gave the bird to Ama, gave it to her while she said nothing, not even "thank you." She only looked at him.

"What is it?" we said as soon as he was far enough away. "What sort of bird?"

"It is a peacock," said Ama, very softly. "He has come to us from India."

"It is not like the peacock on your Kashmiri fan," I said. "It is only a sort of white."

"The peacock on the fan is green and blue and gold and has a tail like a fan," said Rashida. "This is not a peacock at all. Anyone can see that."

"Rashida," said Ama, "Rashida! The eldest must not be too clever. He is a white peacock. He is too young to open his tail. He is a peacock from India."

"Ama," I said, "make him, make him open his tail."

"I do not think," she said, "I do not think he will ever open his tail in this country."

"No," said Father that night, "he will never open his tail in Australia."

"No," said Uncle Seyed next morning, "he will never open his tail without a hen-bird near."

But we had watched him—Rashida and Lal and I—had watched him for days and days until we had grown tired of watching and he had grown sleek and shiny and had found his place in the garden.

"Won't you ever open your tail?" I asked him again. "Not now that it's spring?" But he wouldn't even try, not even try to

look interested, so I went away from him and looked for some-
one to talk to.

The nurse-lady who was there to help Ama and who was
pink like an apple and almost as round was working in the
kitchen.

"The baby is coming soon," I told her. "Now that it's spring."

"Go on with you," she laughed. "Go on."

So I did, until I found Rashida sitting in a windowsill with a
book in front of her. It was the nurse-lady's baby-book.

"What are you doing?"

"I am reading," she said. "This is the baby-book. I am read-
ing how to look after the baby."

"You can't read," I said. "You know you can't read."

Rashida refused to answer. She just went on staring at the
book, turning pages.

"But you can't read!" I shouted at her. "You can't."

She finished running her eye down the page. "I am not read-
ing words," she said. "I know what the book tells. I am read-
ing things."

"But you know, you know you can't read." I stamped away
from her, cranky as anything, out of the house, past the window
where Rashida was sitting—so cleverly—down to the vegetable
patch where I could see Lal. He was digging with a trowel.

"What are you doing?" I said, not very pleasantly.

"I am digging," said Lal. "I am making a garden for my new
baby brother."

"How did you know? How did you all know? I was going to
tell *you*." I was almost crying. "Anyway," I said, "it might not
be a brother."

"Oh yes, it will," said Lal. "We have girls."

"I'll dig, too," I said, laughing, and suddenly happy again.
"I'll help you. We'll make a big one."

"Digging is man's work," said Lal. "I'm a man. You're a girl."

"You're a baby," I said. "You're only four." And I threw some
dirt at him, and went away.

Father was making a basket of sticks from the plum-tree. He
used to put crossed sticks on the ground, squat in the middle of
them, and weave other sticks in and out of them until a basket

had grown up round him. All I could see were his shoulders and the back of his turban as I crept up behind him, to surprise him.

But he was not surprised. "I knew it would be you," he said. I scowled at him then, but he only laughed the way that he always did.

"Father—" I began in a questioning voice that made him groan. Already I was called the Australian one, the questioner. "Father," I said, "why do peacocks have beautiful tails?"

He tugged at his beard. "Their feet are ugly," he said. "Allah has given them tails so that no one will look at their feet."

"But Shah-Jehan," I said, and Father bent his head down over his weaving. "Everyone looks at his feet. His tail never opens."

"Yes," said Father definitely, as though that explained everything, and I began to cry: it was that sort of day, laughter and tears. I suppose it was the first day of spring.

"What is it, what is it?" said Father.

"Everything," I told him. "Shah-Jehan won't open his tail, Rashida pretends she can read, Lal won't let me dig. I'm nothing. And it's spring, Ama is putting out the milk for the snakes, and I counted—" But Father was looking so serious that I never told him what I had counted.

"Listen," he said. "You are big now, Nimmi. I will tell you a secret."

"What is secret?"

He sighed. "It is what is ours," he said. "Something we know but do not tell, or share with one person only in the world."

"With me!" I begged. "With me!"

"Yes," he said, "with you. But no crying or being nothing. This is to make you a grown-up person."

"Please," I said to him, "please." And I loved him then so much that I wanted to break the cage of twigs and hold him.

"We are Muslims," he said. "But your mother has a mark on her forehead that shows that once she was not. She was a Brahmin and she believed all the stories of Krishna and Siva."

"I know that," I said, "and the hills—"

"Monkey, quiet," he commanded. "But now Ama is a Muslim, too. Only, she remembers her old ways. And she puts out the milk in the spring."

"For the snakes," I said. "So they will love us, and leave us from harm."

"But there are no snakes in the garden," said Father.

"But they drink the milk," I told him. "Ama says——"

"If the milk were left, the snakes would come," said Father. "And they must not come, because there is no honour in snakes. They would strike you or Rashida or little Lal or even Ama. So— and this is the secret that no one must know but you and me—I go to the garden in the night and empty the dishes of milk. And this way I have no worry and you have no harm and Ama's faith is not hurt. But you must never tell."

"Never, never tell," I assured him.

All that day I was kind to Lal, who was only a baby and not grown up, and I held my head up high in front of Rashida, who was clever but had no secret. All of that day I walked in a glory full of my secret. I even felt cleverer than Ama, who knew everything but must never, never know this.

She was working that afternoon on her quilt. I looked at the crochet pictures in the little squares of it.

"Here is a poinsettia," I said.

"Yes," said Ama. "And here is——"

"It's Shah-Jehan! With his tail open."

"Yes," said Ama, "so it is, and here is a rose for the baby."

"When will the baby come?" I asked her. "Not soon, but when?"

"Tonight, tomorrow night," said Ama, "the next."

"Do babies always come at night?"

"Mine, always," said Ama. "There is the dark and the waiting, and then the sun on our faces. And the scent of jasmine, even here." And she looked at her garden.

"But, Ama——"

"No questions, Nimmi. My head is buzzing. No questions today."

That night I heard a strange noise, a harsh cry. "Shah-Jehan!" I said. I jumped out of bed and ran to the window. I stood on a chair and looked out to the garden.

It was moonlight, the moon so big and low that I thought I

could lean out and touch it, and there—looking sad, and white as frost in the moonlight—stood Shah-Jehan.

"Shah-Jehan, little brother," I said to him, "you must not feel about your feet. Think of your tail, pretty one, your beautiful tail."

And then, as I was speaking, he lifted his head and slowly, slowly opened his tail—like a fan, like a fan of lace that was as white as the moon. O Shah-Jehan! It was as if you had come from the moon.

My throat hurt, choked, so that my breath caught and I shut my eyes. When I opened them it was all gone: the moon was the moon, and Shah-Jehan was a milky-white bird with his tail drooping and his head bent.

In the morning the nurse-lady woke us. "Get up," she said. "Guess what? In the night, a sister! The dearest, sweetest, baby sister. . . . Now, up with you."

"No brother," said Lal. "No baby brother."

We laughed at him, Rashida and I, and ran to see the baby. Ama was lying, very still and small, in the big bed. Her long plait of black hair stretched out across the white pillow. The baby was in the old cradle and we peered down at her. Her tiny fists groped on the air towards us. But Lal would not look at her. He climbed onto the bed and crawled over to Ama.

"No boy," he said sadly. "No boy to play with."

Ama stroked his hair. "My son," she said. "I am sorry, little son."

"Can we change her?" he said. "For a boy?"

"She is a gift from Allah," said Ama. "You can never change gifts."

Father came in from the dairy, his face a huge grin, he made a chuckling noise over the cradle and then sat on the bed.

"Missus," he said in the queer English that always made the nurse-lady laugh, "this one little fellow, eh?"

"Big," said Ama. "Nine pounds." And the nurse-lady nodded proudly.

"What wrong with this fellow?" said Father, scooping Lal up in his arm. "What wrong with you, eh?"

"No boy," said Lal. "No boy to talk to."

"*Ai! Ai!*" lamented Father, trying to change his expression. "Too many girls here," he said. "Better we drown one. Which one we drown, Lal? Which one, eh?"

Rashida and I hurled ourselves at him, squealing with delight. "Not me! Not me!" we shouted while the nurse-lady tried to hush us.

"You are worse than the children," she said to Father. "Far worse." But then she laughed, and we all did—even the baby made a noise.

But what was the baby to be called? We all talked about it. Even Uncle Seyed came in and leant on the doorpost while names were talked over and over.

At last Father lifted the baby up and looked into her big dark eyes. "What was the name of your sister?" he asked Uncle Seyed. "The little one, who followed us everywhere? The little one with the beautiful eyes?"

"Jamila," said Uncle Seyed. "She was Jamila."

So that was to be her first name, Jamila, after the little girl who was alive in India when Father was a boy and he and Uncle Seyed had decided to become friends like brothers. And her second name was Shahnaz, which means the Heart's Beloved.

And then I remembered. "Shah-Jehan," I said. "He can open his tail. I saw him last night, when everyone was asleep."

"You couldn't see in the night," said Rashida. "You dreamt it, baby."

"No, I didn't. It was bright moon."

"You dreamt it, Nimmi," said Father. "A peacock wouldn't open his tail in this country."

"I didn't dream it," I said in a little voice that didn't sound very certain: Father was always right. "I'll count Jamila's fingers," I said before Rashida could say anything else about the peacock. "*Ek, do, tin, panch,*" I began.

"You've left out *cha*," said Father.

"Oh yes, I forgot. I forgot it. *Ek, do, tin, cha, panch*—she has five," I said.

"Everyone has five," said Rashida.

"Show me," said Lal. And while Father and Ama were showing

him the baby's fingers and toes and telling him how to count them, I crept out on the veranda where I could see the hills.

I counted them quickly. *"Ek, do, tin, cha, panch."* There were only five, not one left over. I was so excited that I felt the closing in my throat again. "I didn't dream it," I said. "I couldn't dream the pain. I did see it, I did. I have another secret now. And only five hills. *Ek, do, tin, cha, panch."*

They never changed again. I was grown up.

From
TEA IN THE HAREM

Majid takes off his shoes and heads straight down the corridor
to his room. His is a large family, and his brothers and sisters
are round the front-room table arguing over their homework.
His mother—Malika—is a solidly-built Algerian woman. As
she stands in the kitchen, she sees her son sneaking down the
corridor.

'Majid!'

Without turning round he goes straight into his room. 'Yeah?'

'Go and get your father.'

'In a minute!'

Malika bangs her pan down on the draining-board and shouts:
'Straight away!'

He puts the Sex Pistols on the record player and plays *God
Save the Queen* at full blast. Punk rock. That way he doesn't
have to listen to his mother. He lies back on the bed, hands be-
hind his head, and shuts his eyes to listen to the music. But his
mum isn't giving up so easily:

'Did you hear what I said?'

She speaks lousy French, with a weird accent, and gesticu-
lates like an Italian. Majid raises his eyes to the ceiling, with
the air of a man just returned from a hard day's work, and in
a voice of tired irritation he replies:

'Lay off, ma, I'm whacked!'

Since she only half understands what he's saying, she goes
off the deep end. She loses her temper, and her African origins
get the upper hand. She starts ranting at him in Arabic.

She comes up to the end of the bed and shakes him, but he doesn't budge. She dries her hands on the apron which is forever about her waist, switches off the stereo, tucks back the tuft of greying hair that hangs across her forehead, and begins abusing her son with all the French insults she can muster—'Layabout . . . Hooligan . . . Oaf . . .' and suchlike, all in her weird pronunciation. Majid pretends he doesn't understand. He answers coolly, just to irritate her:

'What'd you say? I didn't understand a word.'

By now his mother is beside herself. 'Didn't understand, didn't understand . . . Oh, God . . . !' and she slaps her thighs.

She tries to grab him by the ear, but he ducks out of range. Finally he admits defeat and gets off the bed, scratching his head.

His mother follows him:

'Yes. Layabout! Hooligan!'

While she continues ranting at him and calling him every name under the sun, he puts the Sex Pistols back in their sleeve and gives a long-suffering sigh.

Then Malika informs her son, in Arabic, that she's going to see the Algerian consul. 'They'll come and get you, and you'll have to do your military service. *That* way you'll learn about your country . . . *and* you'll learn the language . . . *that'll* make a man of you. You say you won't do your military service like all your friends have to, but if you don't you'll never get your papers, and me neither. You'll lose your citizenship, and you'll never be able to go to Algeria because you'll end up in prison. *That's* where you'll end up. No country, no roots, no nothing. You'll be finished.'

Majid understands the occasional phrase here and there, and his reply is subdued, because whatever he says is bound to hurt her.

'I never asked to come here. If you hadn't decided to come to France, I wouldn't be "finished", would I, eh? So leave me alone, will you?'

She continues haranguing him, unleashing all the bitterness that is locked in her heart. It's not unusual for her to end up crying.

Someone knocks at the front door.

'Who is it?' she shouts, still furious.

She leaves the room and Majid flops down on the bed, reflecting that for a long time he's been neither French nor Arab. He's the son of immigrants—caught between two cultures, two histories, two languages, and two colours of skin. He's neither black nor white. He has to invent his own roots, create his own reference points. For the moment, he's waiting . . . waiting . . . He doesn't want to have to think about it . . .

(TRANSLATED FROM THE FRENCH
BY ED EMERY)

JOSEPH BRUCHAC

ELLIS ISLAND

Beyond the red brick of Ellis Island
where the two Slovak children
who became my grandparents
waited the long days of quarantine,
after leaving the sickness,
the old Empires of Europe,
a Circle Line ship slips easily
on its way to the island
of the tall woman, green
as dreams of forests and meadows
waiting for those who'd worked
a thousand years
yet never owned their own.

Like millions of others,
I too come to this island,
nine decades the answerer
of dreams.

Yet only part of my blood loves that memory.
Another voice speaks
of native lands
within this nation.
Lands invaded
when the earth became owned.
Lands of those who followed
the changing Moon,
knowledge of the seasons
in their veins.

DAVID DABYDEEN

COOLIE MOTHER

Jasmattie live in bruk-
Down hut big like Bata shoe box,
Beat clothes, weed yard, chop wood, feed fowl
For this body and that body and every blasted body,
Fetch water, all day fetch water like if the
Whole slow-flowing Canje River God create
Just for she one bucket.

Till she foot bottom crack and she hand cut up
And curse swarm from she mouth like red ants
And she cough blood on the ground but mash it in:
Because Jasmattie heart hard, she mind set hard.

To hustle save she one-one slow penny,
Because one-one dutty make dam cross the Canje
And she son Harilall got to go to school in Georgetown,
Must wear clean starch pants, or they go laugh at he,
Strap leather on he foot, and he must read book,
Learn talk proper, take exam, go to England university,
Not turn out like he rum-sucker chamar dadee.

COOLIE SON
(THE TOILET ATTENDANT
WRITES HOME)

Taana boy, how you do?
How Shantri stay? And Sukhoo?
Mosquito still a-bite all-you?
Juncha dead true-true?
Mala bruk-foot set?
Food deh foh eat yet?

Englan nice, snow an dem ting,
A land dey say fit for a king,
Iceapple plenty on de tree and bird a-sing—
Is de beginning of what dey call "The Spring."

And I eating enough for all all-we
And reading book bad bad.

But is what make Matam wife fall sick
And Sonnel cow suck dry wid tick?

Soon, I go turn lawya or dacta,
But, just now, passage money run out
So I tek lil wuk—
I is a Deputy Sanitary Inspecta,
Big-big office, boy! Tie roun me neck!
Brand new uniform, one big bunch keys!
If Ma can see me now how she go please . . .

SHANI MOOTOO

OUT ON MAIN STREET

I.

Janet and me? We does go Main Street to see pretty pretty sari and bangle, and to eat we belly full a burfi and gulub jamoon, but we doh go too often because, yuh see, is dem sweets self what does give people like we a presupposition for untameable hip and thigh.

Another reason we shy to frequent dere is dat we is watered-down Indians—we ain't good grade A Indians. We skin brown, is true, but we doh even think 'bout India unless something happen over dere and it come on de news. Mih family remain Hindu ever since mih ancestors leave India behind, but nowadays dey doh believe in praying unless things real bad, because, as mih father always singing, like if is a mantra: "Do good and good will be bestowed unto you." So he is a veritable saint cause he always doing good by his women friends and dey children. I sure some a dem must be mih half sister and brother, oui!

Mostly, back home, we is kitchen Indians: some kind a Indian food every day, at least once a day, but we doh get carda-mom and other fancy spice down dere so de food not spicy like Indian food I eat in restaurants up here. But it have one thing we doh make joke 'bout down dere: we like we meethai and sweetrice too much, and it remain overly authentic, like de day Naana and Naani step off de boat in Port of Spain harbour over a hundred and sixty years ago. Check out dese hips here nah, dey is pure sugar and condensed milk, pure sweetness!

But Janet family different. In de ole days when Canadian mis-sionaries land in Trinidad dey used to make a bee-line straight for Indian from down South. And Janet great grandparents is one a de first South families dat exchange over from Indian to Presbyterian. Dat was a long time ago.

When Janet born, she father, one Mr. John Mahasc, insist on asking de Reverend MacDougal from Trace Settlement Church, a leftover from de Canadian Mission, to name de baby girl. De good Reverend choose de name Constance cause dat was his mother name. But de mother a de child, Mrs. Savitri Mahase, wanted to name de child sheself. Ever since Savitri was a lil girl she like de yellow hair, fair skin and pretty pretty clothes Janet and John used to wear in de primary school reader—since she lil she want to change she name from Savitri to Janet but she own father get vex and say how Savitri was his mother name and how she will insult his mother if she gone and change it. So Savitri get she own way once by marrying this fella name John, and she do a encore, by calling she daughter Janet, even doh husband John upset for days at she for insulting de good Reverend by throwing out de name a de Reverend mother.

So dat is how my girlfriend, a darkskin Indian girl with thick black hair (pretty fuh so!) get a name like Janet.

She come from a long line a Presbyterian school teacher, headmaster and headmistress. Savitri still teaching from de same Janet and John reader in a primary school in San Fernando, and John, getting more and more obtuse in his ole age, is headmaster more dan twenty years now in Princes Town Boys' Presbyterian High School. Everybody back home know dat family good good. Dat is why Janet leave in two twos. Soon as A Level finish she pack up and take off like a jet plane so she could live without people only shoo-shooing behind she bark . . . "But A A! Yuh ain't hear de goods 'bout John Mahase daughter, gyul? How yuh mean yuh ain't hear? Is a big thing! Everybody talking 'bout she. Hear dis, nah! Yuh ever see she wear a dress? Yes! Doh look at mih so. Yuh reading mih right!"

Is only recentish I realize Mahase is a Hindu last name. In de ole days every Mahase in de country turn Presbyterian and now de name doh have no association with Hindu or Indian whatsoever. I used to think of it as a Presbyterian Church name until some days ago when we meet a Hindu fella fresh from India name Yogdesh Mahase who never even hear of Presbyterian.

De other day I ask Janet what she know 'bout Divali. She say, "It's the Hindu festival of lights, isn't it?" like a line straight out a dictionary. Yuh think she know anything 'bout how lord Rama get himself exile in a forest for fourteen years, and how when it come time for him to go back home his followers light up a pathway to help him make his way out, and dat is what Divali lights is all about? All Janet know is 'bout going for drive in de country to see light, and she could remember looking forward, around Divali time, to the lil brown paper-bag packages full a burfi and parasad that she father Hindu students used to bring for him.

One time in a Indian restaurant she ask for parasad for dessert. Well! Since den I never go back in dat restaurant, I embarrass fuh so!

I used to think I was a Hindu *par excellence* until I come up here and see real flesh and blood Indian from India. Up here, I learning 'bout all kind a custom and food and music and clothes dat we never see or hear 'bout in good ole Trinidad. Is de next best thing to going to India, in truth, oui! But Indian store clerk on Main Street doh have no patience with us, specially when we talking English to dem. Yah ask dem a question in English and dey insist on giving de answer in Hindi or Punjabi or Urdu or Gujarati. How I suppose to know de difference even! And den dey look at yuh disdainful disdainful—like yuh disloyal, like yuh is a traitor.

But yuh know, it have one other reason I real reluctant to go Main Street. Yuh see, Janet pretty fuh so! And I doh like de way men does look at she, as if because she wearing jeans and T-shirt and high-heel shoe and make-up and have long hair loose and flying about like she is a walking-talking shampoo ad, dat she easy. And de women always looking at she beady eye, like she loose and going to thief dey man. Dat kind a thing always make me want to put mih arm round she waist like, she is my woman, take yuh eyes off she! and shock de false teeth right out dey mouth. And den is a whole other story when dey see me with mih crew cut and mih blue jeans tuck inside mih jim-boots. Walking next to Janet, who so femme dat she redundant, tend to make me look like a gender dey forget to classify. Before going Main Street I does parade in front de mirror practicing a jiggly-wiggly kind a walk. But if I ain't walking like a strong-man monkey I doh exactly feel right and I always revert back to mih true colours. De men dem does look at me like if dey is exactly what I need a taste of to cure me good and proper. I could see dey eyes watching Janet and me, dey face growing dark as dey imagining all kind a situation and position. And de women dem embarrass fuh so to watch me in mih eye, like dey fraid I will jump up and try to kiss dem, or make pass at dem. Yuh know, sometimes I wonder if I ain't mad enough to do it just for a little bacchanal, nah!

Going for a outing with mih Janet on Main Street ain't easy! If only it wasn't for burfi and gulub jamoon! If only I had a learned how to cook dem kind a thing before I leave home and come up here to live!

2.

In large deep-orange Sanskrit-style letters, de sign on de saffron-colour awning above de door read "Kush Valley Sweets." Underneath in smaller red letters it had "Desserts Fit For The Gods." It was a corner building. The front and side was one big glass wall. Inside was big. Big like a gymnasium. Yuh could see in through de brown tint windows: dark brown plastic chair, and brown table, each one de length of a door, line up stiff and straight in row after row like if is a school room.

Before entering de restaurant I ask Janet to wait one minute outside with me while I rumfle up mih memory, pulling out all de sweet names I know from home, besides burfi and gulub jamoon: meethai, jilebi, sweetrice (but dey call dat kheer up here), and ladhoo. By now, of course, mih mouth watering fuh so! When I feel confident enough dat I wouldn't make a fool a mih Brown self by asking what dis one name? and what dat one name? we went in de restaurant. In two twos all de spice in de place take a flying leap in our direction and give us one

big welcome hug up, tight fuh so! Since den dey take up per-
manent residence in de jacket I wear dat day!

Mostly it had women customers sitting at de tables, chatting
and laughing, eating sweets and sipping masala tea. De only
men in de place was de waiters, and all six waiters was men. I
figure dat dey was brothers, not too hard to conclude, because
all a dem had de same full round chin, round as if de chin
stretch tight over a ping-pong ball, and dey had de same big
roving eyes. I know better dan to think dey was mere waiters
in de employ of a owner who chook up in a office in de back. I
sure dat dat was dey own family business, dey stomach proudly
preceeding dem and dey shoulders throw back in de confi-
dence of dey ownership.

It ain't dat I paranoid, yuh understand, but from de moment
we enter de fellas dem get over-animated, even armorously agi-
tated, Janet again! All six pair a eyes land up on she, following
she every move and body part. Dat in itself is something dat
does madden me, oui! but also a kind a irrational envy have a
tendency to manifest in me. It was like I didn't exist. Some-
times it could be a real problem going out with a good-looker,
yes! While I ain't remotely interested in having a squeak of a
flirtation with a man, it doh hurt a ego to have a man notice
yuh once in a very long while. But with Janet at mih side, I doh
have de chance of a penny shave-ice in de hot sun. I tuck mih
elbows in as close to mih sides as I could so I wouldn't look like
a strong man next to she, and over to de l-o-n-g glass case jam
up with sweets I jiggle and wiggle in mih best imitation a some
a dem gay fellas dat I see downtown Vancouver, de ones who
more femme dan even Janet. I tell she not to pay de brothers no
attention, because if any a dem flirt with she I could start a
fight right dere and den. And I didn't feel to mess up mih crew
cut in a fight.

De case had sweets in every nuance of colour in a rainbow.
Sweets I never before see and doh know de names of. But dat
was alright because I wasn't going to order dose ones anyway.

Since before we leave home Janet have she mind set on a nice
thick syrupy curl a jilebi and a piece a plain burfi so I order dose

for she and den I ask de waiter-fella, resplendent with thick thick bright-yellow gold chain and ID bracelet, for a stick a meethai for mihself. I stand up waiting by de glass case for it but de waiter/owner lean up on de back wall behind de counter watching me like he ain't hear me. So I say loud enough for him, and every body else in de room to hear, "I would like to have one piece a meethai please," and den he smile and lift up his hands, palms open-out motioning across de vast expanse a glass case, and he say, "Your choice! Whichever you want, Miss." But he still lean up against de back wall grinning. So I stick mih head out and up like a turtle and say louder, and slowly, "One piece a meethai—dis one!" and I point sharp to de stick a flour mix with ghee, deep fry and den roll up in sugar. He say, "That is koorma, Miss. One piece only?"

Mih voice drop low all by itself. "Oh ho! Yes, one piece. Where I come from we does call dat meethai." And den I add, but only loud enough for Janet to hear, "And mih name ain't 'Miss.'"

He open his palms out and indicate de entire panorama a sweets and he say, "These are all meethai, Miss. Meethai is Sweets. Where are you from?"

I ignore his question and to show him I undaunted, I point to a round pink ball and say, "I'll have one a dese sugarcakes too please." He start grinning broad broad like if he half-pitying, half-laughing at dis Indian-in-skin-colour-only, and den he tell me, "That is called chum-chum, Miss." I snap back at him, "Yeh, well back home we does call dat sugarcake, Mr. Chum-chum."

At de table Janet say, "You know, Pud [Pud, short for Pudding; is dat she does call me when she feeling close to me, or sorry for me], it's true that we call that 'meethai' back home. Just like how we call 'siu mai' 'tim sam.' As if 'dim sum' is just one little piece a food. What did he call that sweet again?"

"Cultural bastards, Janet, cultural bastards. Dat is what we is. Yuh know, one time a fella from India who living up here call me a bastardized Indian because I didn't know Hindi. And now look at dis, nah! De thing is: all a we in Trinidad is cultural bastards, Janet, all a we. *Toutes bagailles!* Chinese people, Black people, White people. Syrian. Lebanese. I looking forward to de day I find out dat place inside me where I am nothing else but Trinidadian, whatever dat could turn out to be."

I take a bite a de chum-chum, de texture was like grind-up coconut but it had no coconut, not even a hint a coconut taste in it. De thing was juicy with sweet rose water oozing out a it. De rose water perfume enter mih nose and get trap in mih cranium. Ah drink two cup a masala tea and a lassi and still de rose water perfume was on mih tongue like if I had a overdosed on Butchart Gardens.

Suddenly de door a de restaurant spring open wide with a strong force and two big burly fellas stumble in, almost rolling over on to de ground. Dey get up, eyes red and slow and dey skin burning pink with booze. Dey straighten up so much to over-compensate for falling forward, dat dey find deyself leaning backward. Everybody stop talking and was watching dem. De guy in front put his hand up to his forehead and take a deep Walter Raleigh bow, bringing de hand down to his waist in a rolling circular movement. Out loud he greet everybody with "Alarm o salay koom." A part a me wanted to bust out laughing. Another part make mih jaw drop open in disbelief. De calm in de place get rumfle up. De two fellas dem, feeling chupid now because nobody reply to dey greeting, gone up to de counter to Chum-chum trying to make a little conversation with him. De same booze-pink alarm-o-salay-koom-fella say to Chum-chum, "Hey, howaryah?"

Chum-Chum give a lil nod and de fella carry right on, "Are you Sikh?"

Chum-chum brothers converge near de counter, busying dey-selves in de vicinity. Chum-chum look at his brothers kind a quizzical, and he touch his cheek and feel his forehead with de back a his palm. He say, "No, I think I am fine, thank you. But I am sorry if I look sick, Sir."

De burly fella confuse now, so he try again.

"Where are you from?"

Chum-chum say, "Fiji, Sir."

"Oh! Fiji, eh! Lotsa palm trees and beautiful women, eh! Is it true that you guys can have more than one wife?"

De exchange make mih blood rise up in a boiling froth. De restaurant suddenly get a gruff quietness 'bout it except for a woman I hear whispering angrily to another woman at de table behind us, "I hate this! I just hate it! I can't stand to see our men humiliated by them, right in front of us. He should refuse to serve them, he should throw them out. Who on earth do they think they are? The awful fools!" And de friend whisper back, "If he throws them out all of us will suffer in the long run."

I could discern de hair on de back a de neck a Chum-chum brothers standing up, annoyed, and at de same time de brothers look like dey was shrinking in stature. Chum-chum get serious, and he politely say, "What can I get for you?"

Pinko get de message and he point to a few items in de case and say, "One of each, to go please."

Holding de white take-out box in one hand he extend de other to Chum-chum and say, "How do you say 'Excuse me, I'm sorry' in Fiji?"

Chum-chum shake his head and say, "It's okay. Have a good day."

Pinko insist, "No, tell me please. I think I just behaved badly, and I want to apologize. How do you say 'I'm sorry' in Fiji?"

Chum-chum say, "Your apology is accepted. Everything is okay." And he discreetly turn away to serve a person who had just entered de restaurant. De fellas take de hint dat was broad like daylight, and back out de restaurant like two little mouse.

Everybody was feeling sorry for Chum-chum and Brothers. One a dem come up to de table across from us to take a order from a woman with a giraffe-long neck who say, "Brother, we mustn't accept how these people think they can treat us. You men really put up with too many insults and abuse over here. I really felt for you."

Another woman gone up to de counter to converse with Chum-chum in she language. She reach out and touch his hand, sympathy-like. Chum-chum hold the one hand in his two and make a verbose speech to her as she nod she head in agreement generously. To italicize her support, she buy a take-out box a two burfi, or rather, dat's what I think dey was.

De door a de restaurant open again, and a bevy of Indian-
looking women saunter in, dress up to weaken a person's deco-
rum. De Miss Universe pageant traipse across de room to a
table. Chum-chum and Brothers start smoothing dey hair back,
and pushing de front a dey shirts neatly into dey pants. One
brother take out a pack a Dentyne from his shirt pocket and
pop one in his mouth. One take out a comb from his back
pocket and smooth down his hair. All a dem den converge on
dat single table to take orders. Dey begin to behave like young
pups in mating season. Only, de women dem wasn't impress by
all this tra-la-la at all and ignore dem except to make dey order,
straight to de point. Well, it look like Brothers' egos were hav-
ing a rough day and dey start roving 'bout de room, dey egos
and de crotch a dey pants leading far in front dem. One brother
gone over to Giraffebai to see if she want anything more. He
call she "dear" and put his hand on she back. Giraffebai
straighten she back in surprise and reply in a not-too friendly
way. When he gone to write up de bill she see me looking at she
and she say to me, "Whoever does he think he is! Calling me
dear and touching me like that! Why do these men always
think that they have permission to touch whatever and wher-
ever they want! And you can't make a fuss about it in public,
because it is exactly what those people out there want to hear
about so that they can say how sexist and uncivilized our cul-
ture is."

I shake mih head in understanding and say, "Yeah. I know.
Yuh right!"

De atmosphere in de room take a hairpin turn, and it was
man aggressing on woman, woman warding off a herd a man
who just had dey pride publicly cut up a couple a times in just
a few minutes.

One brother walk over to Janet and me and he stand up fac-
ing me with his hands clasp in front a his crotch, like if he pro-
tecting it. Stiff stiff, looking at me, he say, "Will that be all?"

Mih crew cut start to tingle, so I put on mih femmest smile
and say, "Yes, that's it, thank you. Just the bill please." De smart-
ass turn to face Janet and he remove his hands from in front a his
crotch and slip his thumbs inside his pants like a cowboy 'bout

to do a square dance. He smile, looking down at her attentive
fuh so, and he say, "Can I do anything for you?"

I didn't give Janet time fuh his intent to even register before
I bulldoze in mih most un-femmest manner, "She have every-
thing she need, man, thank you. The bill please." Yuh think he
hear me? It was like I was talking to thin air. He remain smil-
ing at Janet, but she, looking at me, not at him, say, "You
heard her. The bill please."

Before he could even leave de table proper, I start mih ti-
rade. "But A A! Yuh see dat? Yuh could believe dat! De effing
so-and-so! One minute yuh feel sorry fuh dem and next min-
ute dey harassing de heck out a you. Janet, he crazy to mess
with my woman, yes!" Janet get vex with me and say I over-
reacting, and is not fuh me to be vex, but fuh she to be vex. Is
she he insult, and she could take good enough care a sheself.

I tell she I don't know why she don't cut off all dat long hair,
and stop wearing lipstick and eyeliner. Well, who tell me to say
dat! She get real vex and say dat nobody will tell she how to
dress and how not to dress, not me and not any man. Well I
could see de potential dat dis fight had coming, and when Janet
get fighting vex, watch out! It hard to get a word in edgewise,
yes! And she does bring up incidents from years back dat have
no bearing on de current situation. So I draw back quick quick
but she don't waste time; she was already off to a good start. It
was best to leave right dere and den.

Just when I stand up to leave, de doors dem open up and in
walk Sandy and Lise, coming for dey weekly hit a Indian sweets.
Well, with Sandy and Lise is a dead giveaway dat dey not dress-
ing fuh any man, it have no place in dey life fuh man-vibes, and
dat in fact dey have a blatant penchant fuh women. Soon as dey
enter de room yuh could see de brothers and de couple men cus-
tomers dat had come in minutes before stare dem down from
head to Birkenstocks, dey eyes bulging with disgust. And de
women in de room start shoo-shooing, and putting dey hand in
front dey mouth to stop dey surprise, and false teeth, too, from
falling out. Sandy and Lise spot us instantly and dey call out to
us, shameless, loud and affectionate. Dey leap over to us, eager
to hug up and kiss like if dey hadn't seen us for years, but it was

really only since two nights aback when we went out to dey favourite Indian restaurant for dinner. I figure dat de display was a genuine happiness to be seen wit us in dat place. While we stand up dere chatting, Sandy insist on rubbing she hand up and down Janet back—wit friendly intent, mind you, and same time Lise have she arm round Sandy waist. Well, all cover get blown. If it was even remotely possible dat I wasn't noticeable before, now Janet and I were over-exposed. We could a easily suffer from hypothermia, specially since it suddenly get cold cold in dere. We say goodbye, not soon enough, and as we were leaving I turn to acknowledge Giraffebai, but instead a any recognition of our buddiness against de fresh brothers, I get a face dat look like it was in de presence of a very foul smell.

De good thing, doh, is dat Janet had become so incensed 'bout how we get scorned, dat she forgot I tell she to cut she hair and to ease up on de make-up, and so I get save from hearing 'bout how I too jealous, and how much I inhibit she, and how she would prefer if I would grow *my* hair, and wear lipstick and put on a dress sometimes. I so glad, oui! dat I didn't have to go through hearing how I too demanding a she, like de time, she say, I prevent she from seeing a ole boyfriend when he was in town for a couple hours *en route* to live in Australia with his new bride (because, she say, I was jealous dat ten years ago dey sleep together). Well, look at mih crosses, nah! Like if I really so possessive and jealous!

So tell me, what yuh think 'bout dis nah, girl?

HANIF KUREISHI

MY SON THE FANATIC

Surreptitiously the father began going into his son's bedroom. He would sit there for hours, rousing himself only to seek clues. What bewildered him was that Ali was getting tidier. Instead of the usual tangle of clothes, books, cricket bats, video games, the room was becoming neat and ordered; spaces began ap pearing where before there had been only mess.

Initially Parvez had been pleased: his son was outgrowing his teenage attitudes. But one day, beside the dustbin, Parvez found a torn bag which contained not only old toys, but computer discs, video tapes, new books and fashionable clothes the boy had bought a few months before. Also without explanation, Ali had parted from the English girlfriend who used to come often to the house. His old friends stopped ringing.

For reasons he didn't himself understand, Parvez wasn't able to bring up the subject of Ali's unusual behaviour. He was aware that he had become slightly afraid of his son, who, alongside his silences, was developing a sharp tongue. One remark Parvez did make, 'You don't play your guitar any more,' elicited the mysterious but conclusive reply, 'There are more important things to be done.'

Yet Parvez felt his son's eccentricity as an injustice. He had always been aware of the pitfalls which other men's sons had fallen into in England. And so, for Ali, he worked long hours and spent a lot of money paying for his education as an accountant. He had bought him good suits, all the books he required and a computer. And now the boy was throwing his possessions out!

The TV, video and sound system followed the guitar. Soon the room was practically bare. Even the unhappy walls bore marks where Ali's pictures had been removed.

Parvez couldn't sleep; he went more to the whisky bottle, even when he was at work. He realised it was imperative to discuss the matter with someone sympathetic.

Parvez had been a taxi driver for twenty years. Half that time he'd worked for the same firm. Like him, most of the other drivers were Punjabis. They preferred to work at night, the roads were clearer and the money better. They slept during the day, avoiding their wives. Together they led almost a boy's life in the cabbies' office, playing cards and practical jokes, exchanging lewd stories, eating together and discussing politics and their problems.

But Parvez had been unable to bring this subject up with his friends. He was too ashamed. And he was afraid, too, that they would blame him for the wrong turning his boy had taken, just as he had blamed other fathers whose sons had taken to running around with bad girls, truanting from school and joining gangs.

For years Parvez had boasted to the other men about how Ali excelled at cricket, swimming and football, and how attentive a scholar he was, getting straight 'A' in most subjects. Was it asking too much for Ali to get a good job now, marry the right girl and start a family? Once this happened, Parvez would be happy. His dreams of doing well in England would have come true. Where had he gone wrong?

But one night, sitting in the taxi office on busted chairs with his two closest friends watching a Sylvester Stallone film, he broke his silence.

'I can't understand it!' he burst out. 'Everything is going from his room. And I can't talk to him any more. We were not father and son—we were brothers! Where has he gone? Why is he torturing me!'

And Parvez put his head in his hands.

Even as he poured out his account the men shook their heads and gave one another knowing glances. From their grave looks Parvez realised they understood the situation.

'Tell me what is happening!' he demanded. The reply was almost triumphant. They had guessed something was going wrong. Now it was clear: Ali was taking drugs and selling his possessions to pay for them. That was why his bedroom was emptying.

'What must I do then?'

Parvez's friends instructed him to watch Ali scrupulously and then be severe with him, before the boy went mad, overdosed or murdered someone.

Parvez staggered out into the early morning air, terrified they were right. His boy—the drug addict killer!

To his relief he found Bettina sitting in his car.

Usually the last customers of the night were local 'brasses' or prostitutes. The taxi drivers knew them well, often driving them to liaisons. At the end of the girls' night, the men would ferry them home, though sometimes the women would join them for a drinking session in the office. Occasionally the drivers would go with the girls. 'A ride in exchange for a ride', it was called.

Bettina had known Parvez for three years. She lived outside the town and on the long drive home, where she sat not in the passenger seat but beside him, Parvez had talked to her about his life and hopes, just as she talked about hers. They saw each other most nights.

He could talk to her about things he'd never be able to discuss with his own wife. Bettina, in turn, always reported on her night's activities. He liked to know where she was and with whom. Once he had rescued her from a violent client, and since then they had come to care for one another.

Though Bettina had never met the boy, she heard about Ali continually. That late night, when he told Bettina that he suspected Ali was on drugs, she judged neither the boy nor his father, but became businesslike and told him what to watch for.

'It's all in the eyes,' she said. They might be blood-shot; the pupils might be dilated; he might look tired. He could be liable to sweats, or sudden mood changes. 'Okay?'

Parvez began his vigil gratefully. Now he knew what the problem might be, he felt better. And surely, he figured, things couldn't have gone too far? With Bettina's help he would soon sort it out.

He watched each mouthful the boy took. He sat beside him at every opportunity and looked into his eyes. When he could he took the boy's hand, checking his temperature. If the boy wasn't at home Parvez was active, looking under the carpet, in his drawers, behind the empty wardrobe, sniffing, inspecting, probing. He knew what to look for: Bettina had drawn pictures of capsules, syringes, pills, powders, rocks.

Every night she waited to hear news of what he'd witnessed.

After a few days of constant observation, Parvez was able to report that although the boy had given up sports, he seemed healthy, with clear eyes. He didn't, as his father expected, flinch guiltily from his gaze. In fact the boy's mood was alert and steady in this sense: as well as being sullen, he was very watchful. He returned his father's long looks with more than a hint of criticism, of reproach even, so much so that Parvez began to feel that it was he who was in the wrong, and not the boy!

'And there's nothing else physically different?' Bettina asked.

'No!' Parvez thought for a moment. 'But he is growing a beard.'

One night, after sitting with Bettina in an all-night coffee shop, Parvez came home particularly late. Reluctantly he and Bettina had abandoned their only explanation, the drug theory, for Parvez had found nothing resembling any drug in Ali's room. Besides, Ali wasn't selling his belongings. He threw them out, gave them away or donated them to charity shops.

Standing in the hall, Parvez heard his boy's alarm clock go off. Parvez hurried into his bedroom where his wife was still awake, sewing in bed. He ordered her to sit down and keep quiet, though she had neither stood up nor said a word. From this post, and with her watching him curiously, he observed his son through the crack of the door.

The boy went into the bathroom to wash. When he returned to his room Parvez sprang across the hall and set his ear at Ali's door. A muttering sound came from within. Parvez was puzzled but relieved.

Once this clue had been established, Parvez watched him at

other times. The boy was praying. Without fail, when he was at home, he prayed five times a day.

Parvez had grown up in Lahore where all the boys had been taught the Koran. To stop him falling asleep when he studied, the Moulvi had attached a piece of string to the ceiling and tied it to Parvez's hair, so that if his head fell forward, he would instantly awake. After this indignity Parvez had avoided all religions. Not that the other taxi drivers had more respect. In fact they made jokes about the local mullahs walking around with their caps and beards, thinking they could tell people how to live, while their eyes roved over the boys and girls in their care.

Parvez described to Bettina what he had discovered. He informed the men in the taxi office. The friends, who had been so curious before, now became oddly silent. They could hardly condemn the boy for his devotions.

Parvez decided to take a night off and go out with the boy. They could talk things over. He wanted to hear how things were going at college; he wanted to tell him stories about their family in Pakistan. More than anything he yearned to understand how Ali had discovered the 'spiritual dimension', as Bettina described it.

To Parvez's surprise, the boy refused to accompany him. He claimed he had an appointment. Parvez had to insist that no appointment could be more important than that of a son with his father, and, reluctantly, Ali accompanied him.

The next day, Parvez went immediately to the street where Bettina stood in the rain wearing high heels, a short skirt and a long mac on top, which she would hopefully open at passing cars.

'Get in, get in!' he said.

They drove out across the moors and parked at the spot where, on better days, with a view unimpeded for many miles by nothing but wild deer and horses, they'd lie back, with their eyes half-closed, saying 'this is the life'. This time Parvez was trembling.

Bettina put her arms around him.

'What's happened?'

'I've just had the worst experience of my life.'

As Bettina rubbed his head Parvez told her that the previous evening, as he and his son studied the menu, the waiter, whom Parvez knew, brought him his usual whisky and water. Parvez was so nervous he had even prepared a question. He was going to ask Ali if he was worried about his imminent exams. But first, wanting to relax, he loosened his tie, crunched a popadom and took a long drink.

Before Parvez could speak, Ali made a face.

'Don't you know it's wrong to drink alcohol?' he said.

'He spoke to me very harshly,' Parvez said to Bettina. 'I was about to castigate the boy for being insolent, but managed to control myself.'

He had explained patiently that for years he had worked more than ten hours a day, had few enjoyments or hobbies and never went on holiday. Surely it wasn't a crime to have a drink when he wanted one?

'But it is forbidden,' the boy said.

Parvez shrugged, 'I know.'

'And so is gambling, isn't it?'

'Yes. But surely we are only human?'

Each time Parvez took a drink, the boy made, as an accompaniment, some kind of wince or fastidious face. This made Parvez drink more quickly. The waiter, wanting to please his friend, brought another glass of whisky. Parvez knew he was getting drunk, but he couldn't stop himself. Ali had a horrible look, full of disgust and censure. It was as if he hated his father.

Halfway through the meal Parvez suddenly lost his temper and threw a plate on the floor. He felt like ripping the cloth from the table, but the waiters and other customers were staring at him. Yet he wouldn't stand for his own son telling him the difference between right and wrong. He knew he wasn't a bad man. He had a conscience. There were a few things of which he was ashamed, but on the whole he had lived a decent life.

'When have I had time to be wicked?' he told Ali.

In a low monotonous voice the boy explained that Parvez had not, in fact, lived a good life. He had broken countless rules of the Koran.

'For instance?' Parvez demanded.

Ali didn't need to think. As if he had been waiting for this moment, he asked his father if he didn't relish pork pies.

'Well?'

Parvez couldn't deny that he loved crispy bacon smothered with mushrooms and mustard and sandwiched between slices of fried bread. In fact he ate this for breakfast every morning.

Ali then reminded him that Parvez had ordered his own wife to cook pork sausages, saying to her, 'You're not in the village now, this is England. We have to fit in!'

Parvez was so annoyed and perplexed by this attack that he called for more drink.

'The problem is this,' the boy said. He leaned across the table. For the first time that night his eyes were alive. 'You are too implicated in Western civilisation.'

Parvez burped; he thought he was going to choke. 'Implicated!' he said. 'But we live here!'

'The Western materialists hate us,' Ali said. 'Papa, how can you love something which hates you?'

'What is the answer then?' Parvez said miserably, 'According to you.'

Ali addressed his father fluently, as if Parvez were a rowdy crowd that had to be quelled and convinced. The Law of Islam would rule the world; the skin of the infidel would burn off again and again; the Jews and Christers would be routed. The West was a sink of hypocrites, adulterers, homosexuals, drug takers and prostitutes.

As Ali talked, Parvez looked out of the window as if to check that they were still in London.

'My people have taken enough. If the persecution doesn't stop there will be jihad. I, and millions of others, will gladly give our lives for the cause.'

'But why, why?' Parvez said.

'For us the reward will be in paradise.'

'Paradise!'

Finally, as Parvez's eyes filled with tears, the boy urged him to mend his ways.

'How is that possible?' Parvez asked.

'Pray,' said Ali. 'Pray beside me.'

Parvez called for the bill and ushered his boy out of there as soon as he was able. He couldn't take any more. Ali sounded as if he'd swallowed someone else's voice.

On the way home the boy sat in the back of the taxi as if he were a customer.

'What has made you like this?' Parvez asked him, afraid that somehow he was to blame for all this. 'Is there a particular event which has influenced you?'

'Living in this country.'

'But I love England,' Parvez said, watching his boy in the mirror. 'They let you do almost anything here.'

'That is the problem,' he replied.

For the first time in years Parvez couldn't see straight. He knocked the side of the car against a lorry, ripping off the wing mirror. They were lucky not to have been stopped by the police: Parvez would have lost his licence and therefore his job.

Getting out of the car back at the house, Parvez stumbled and fell in the road, scraping his hands and ripping his trousers. He managed to haul himself up. The boy didn't even offer him his hand.

Parvez told Bettina he was willing to pray, if that was what the boy wanted, if it would dislodge the pitiless look from his eyes.

'But what I object to,' he said, 'is being told by my own son that I am going to hell!'

What finished Parvez off was that the boy had said he was giving up accountancy. When Parvez had asked why, Ali said sarcastically that it was obvious.

'Western education cultivates an anti-religious attitude.'

And, according to Ali, in the world of accountants it was usual to meet women, drink alcohol and practise usury.

'But it's well-paid work,' Parvez argued. 'For years you've been preparing!'

Ali said he was going to begin to work in prisons, with poor Muslims who were struggling to maintain their purity in the face of corruption. Finally, at the end of the evening, as Ali went up to bed, he had asked his father why he didn't have a beard, or at least a moustache.

'I feel as if I've lost my son,' Parvez told Bettina. 'I can't bear to be looked at as if I'm a criminal. I've decided what to do.'

'What is it?'

'I'm going to tell him to pick up his prayer mat and get out of my house. It will be the hardest thing I've ever done, but tonight I'm going to do it.'

'But you mustn't give up on him,' said Bettina. 'Many young people fall into cults and superstitious groups. It doesn't mean they'll always feel the same way.'

She said Parvez had to stick by his boy, giving him support, until he came through.

Parvez was persuaded that she was right, even though he didn't feel like giving his son more love when he had hardly been thanked for all he had already given.

Nevertheless, Parvez tried to endure his son's looks and reproaches. He attempted to make conversation about his beliefs. But if Parvez ventured any criticism, Ali always had a brusque reply. On one occasion Ali accused Parvez of 'grovelling' to the whites; in contrast, he explained, he was not 'inferior'; there was more to the world than the West, though the West always thought it was best.

'How is it you know that,' Parvez said, 'seeing as you've never left England?'

Ali replied with a look of contempt.

One night, having ensured there was no alcohol on his breath, Parvez sat down at the kitchen table with Ali. He hoped Ali would compliment him on the beard he was growing but Ali didn't appear to notice.

The previous day Parvez had been telling Bettina that he thought people in the West sometimes felt inwardly empty and that people needed a philosophy to live by.

'Yes,' said Bettina. 'That's the answer. You must tell him what your philosophy of life is. Then he will understand that there are other beliefs.'

After some fatiguing consideration, Parvez was ready to begin. The boy watched him as if he expected nothing.

Haltingly Parvez said that people had to treat one another with respect, particularly children their parents. This did seem, for a moment, to affect the boy. Heartened, Parvez continued. In his view this life was all there was and when you died you rotted in the earth. 'Grass and flowers will grow out of me, but something of me will live on.'

'How?'

'In other people. I will continue—in you.' At this the boy appeared a little distressed.

'And your grandchildren,' Parvez added for good measure. 'But while I am here on earth I want to make the best of it. And I want you to, as well!'

'What d'you mean by "make the best of it"?' asked the boy.

'Well,' said Parvez. 'For a start . . . you should enjoy yourself. Yes. Enjoy yourself without hurting others.'

Ali said enjoyment was a 'bottomless pit'.

'But I don't mean enjoyment like that!' said Parvez. 'I mean the beauty of living!'

'All over the world our people are oppressed,' was the boy's reply.

'I know,' Parvez replied, not entirely sure who 'our people' were, 'but still life is for living!'

Ali said, 'Real morality has existed for hundreds of years. Around the world millions and millions of people share my beliefs. Are you saying you are right and they are all wrong?'

Ali looked at his father with such aggressive confidence that Parvez could say no more.

One evening Bettina was sitting in Parvez's car, after visiting a client, when they passed a boy on the street.

'That's my son,' Parvez said suddenly. They were on the other side of town, in a poor district, where there were two mosques.

Parvez set his face hard.

Bettina turned to watch him. 'Slow down then, slow down!' She said, 'He's good-looking. Reminds me of you. But with a more determined face. Please, can't we stop?'

'What for?'

'I'd like to talk to him.'

Parvez turned the cab round and stopped beside the boy.

'Coming home?' Parvez asked. 'It's quite a way.'

The sullen boy shrugged and got into the back seat. Bettina sat in the front. Parvez became aware of Bettina's short skirt, gaudy rings and ice-blue eye-shadow. He became conscious that the smell of her perfume, which he loved, filled the cab. He opened the window.

While Parvez drove as fast as he could, Bettina said gently to Ali, 'Where have you been?'

'The mosque,' he said.

'And how are you getting on at college? Are you working hard?'

'Who are you to ask me these questions?' he said, looking out of the window. Then they hit bad traffic and the car came to a standstill.

By now Bettina had inadvertently laid her hand on Parvez's shoulder. She said, 'Your father, who is a good man, is very worried about you. You know he loves you more than his own life.'

'You say he loves me,' the boy said.

'Yes!' said Bettina.

'Then why is he letting a woman like you touch him like that?'

If Bettina looked at the boy in anger, he looked back at her with twice as much cold fury.

She said, 'What kind of woman am I that deserves to be spoken to like that?'

'You know,' he said. 'Now let me out.'

'Never,' Parvez replied.

'Don't worry, I'm getting out,' Bettina said.

'No, don't!' said Parvez. But even as the car moved she opened the door, threw herself out and ran away across the road. Parvez shouted after her, several times called after her, but she had gone.

Parvez took Ali back to the house, saying nothing more to him. Ali went straight to his room. Parvez was unable to read the paper, watch television or even sit down. He kept pouring himself drinks.

At last he went upstairs and paced up and down outside Ali's room. When, finally, he opened the door, Ali was praying. The boy didn't even glance his way.

Parvez kicked him over. Then he dragged the boy up by his shirt and hit him. The boy fell back. Parvez hit him again. The boy's face was bloody. Parvez was panting, he knew the boy was unreachable, but he struck him nonetheless. The boy neither covered himself nor retaliated; there was no fear in his eyes. He only said, through his split lip: 'So who's the fanatic now?'

From
WHITE TEETH

There was a lamppost, equidistant from the Jones house and Glenard Oak Comprehensive, that had begun to appear in Irie's dreams. Not the lamppost exactly, but a small, hand-made ad that was taped round its girth at eye level. It said:

LOSE WEIGHT TO EARN MONEY
081 555 6752

Now, Irie Jones, aged fifteen, was big. The European proportions of Clara's figure had skipped a generation, and she was landed instead with Hortense's substantial Jamaican frame, loaded with pineapples, mangoes, and guavas; the girl had weight; big tits, big butt, big hips, big thighs, big teeth. She was 182 pounds and had thirteen pounds in her savings account. She knew she was the target audience (if ever there was one), she knew full well, as she trudged schoolward, mouth full of dough-nut, hugging her spare tires, that the ad was speaking to her. It was *speaking* to her. LOSE WEIGHT (it was saying) TO EARN MONEY. You, you, *you*, Miss Jones, with your strategically placed arms and cardigan, tied around the arse (the endless mystery: how to diminish that swollen enormity, the Jamaican posterior?), with your belly-reducing panties and breast-reducing bra, with your meticulous Lycra corseting—the much-lauded nineties answer to whalebone—with your elasticized waists. She knew the ad was talking to *her*. But she didn't know quite what it was saying. What were we talking about here? Sponsored slim? The earning capacity of thin people? Or something altogether more Jacobean, the brainchild of some sordid Willesden Shylock, a pound of flesh for a pound of gold: *meat for money*?

Rapid. Eye. Movement. Sometimes she'd be walking through school in a bikini with the lamppost enigma written in chalk over her brown bulges, over her various ledges (shelf space for books, cups of tea, baskets, or, more to the point, children, bags of fruit, buckets of water), ledges genetically designed with another country in mind, another climate. Other times, the sponsored slim dream: knocking on door after door, butt-naked with a clipboard, drenched in sunlight, trying to encourage old men to pinch-an-inch and pledge-a-pound. Worst times? Tearing off loose, white-flecked flesh and packing it into those old curvaceous Coke bottles; she is carrying them to the corner shop, passing them over a counter; and Millat is the bindi-wearing, V-necked shopkeeper, he is adding them up, grudgingly opening the till with blood-stained paws, handing over the cash. *A little Caribbean flesh for a little English change*.

Irie Jones was obsessed. Occasionally her worried mother cornered her in the hallway before she slunk out of the door, picked at her elaborate corsetry, asked, "What's up with you? What in the Lord's name are you wearing? How can you breathe? Irie, my love, you're fine—you're just built like an honest-to-God Bowden—don't you know you're fine?"

But Irie didn't know she was fine. There was England, a gigantic mirror, and there was Irie, without reflection. A stranger in a stranger land.

Nightmares and daydreams, on the bus, in the bath, in class. Before. After. Before. After. Before. *After*. The mantra of the makeover junkie, sucking it in, letting it out; unwilling to settle for genetic fate; waiting instead for her transformation from Jamaican hourglass heavy with the sands that gather round Dunns River Falls, to *English Rose*—oh, you know her—she's a

slender, delicate thing not made for the hot sun, a surfboard
rippled by the wave:

Before: After:

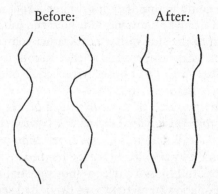

Mrs. Olive Roody, English teacher and expert doodle-spotter
at distances of up to twenty yards, reached over her desk to
Irie's notebook and tore out the piece of paper in question.
Looked dubiously at it. Then inquired with melodious Scottish
emphasis, "Before and after *what*?"

"Er . . . what?"

"Before and after *what*?"

"Oh. Nothing, miss."

"Nothing? Oh, come now, Ms. Jones. No need for modesty.
It is obviously more interesting than Sonnet 127."

"Nothing. It's *nothing*."

"Absolutely certain? You don't wish to delay the class any-
more? Because . . . some of the class need to listen to—are even
a wee bit *interested in*—what I have to say. So if you could
spare some time from your dooooodling—"

No one but no one said "doodling" like Olive Roody.

"—and join the rest of us, we'll continue. Well?"

"Well what?"

"Can you? Spare the time?"

"Yes, Mrs. Roody."

"Oh, *good*. That's cheered me up. Sonnet 127, please."

"In the old age black was not counted fair," continued Fran-
cis Stone in the catatonic drone with which students read Eliz-
abethan verse. *"Or if it were, it bore not beauty's name."*

Irie put her right hand on her stomach, sucked in, and tried to catch Millat's eye. But Millat was busy showing pretty Nikki Tyler how he could manipulate his tongue into a narrow roll, a flute. Nikki Tyler was showing him how the lobes of her ears were attached to the side of her head rather than loose. Flirtatious remnants of this morning's science lesson: *Inherited characteristics. Part One (a). Loose. Attached. Rolled. Flat. Blue eye. Brown eye. Before. After.*

"Therefore my mistress' eyes are raven black, her brows so suited, and they mourners seem . . . My mistress' eyes are nothing like the sun; Coral is far more red than her lips' red. If snow be white, why then her breasts are dun . . ."

Puberty, real full-blown puberty (not the slight mound of a breast, or the shadowy emergence of fuzz), had separated these old friends, Irie Jones and Millat Iqbal. Different sides of the school fence. Irie believed she had been dealt the dodgy cards: mountainous curves, buckteeth and thick metal retainer, impossible Afro hair, and to top it off mole-ish eyesight that in turn required Coke-bottle spectacles in a light shade of pink. (Even those blue eyes—the eyes Archie had been so excited about—lasted two weeks only. She had been born with them, yes, but one day Clara looked again and there were brown eyes staring up at her, like the transition between a closed bud and an open flower, the exact moment of which the naked, waiting eye can never detect.) And this belief in her ugliness, in her *wrongness,* had subdued her; she kept her smart-ass comments to herself these days, she kept her right hand on her stomach. She was all *wrong.*

Whereas Millat was like youth remembered in the nostalgic eyeglass of old age, beauty parodying itself: broken Roman nose, tall, thin; lightly veined, smoothly muscled; chocolate eyes with a reflective green sheen like moonlight bouncing off a dark sea; irresistible smile, big white teeth. In Glenard Oak Comprehensive, black, Pakistani, Greek, Irish—these were races. But those with sex appeal lapped the other runners. They were a species all of their own.

"If hairs be wires, black wires grow on her head . . ."

She loved him, of course. But he used to say to her: "Thing is, people rely on me. They need me to be Millat. Good old Millat. Wicked Millat. Safe, sweet-as, Millat. They need me to be cool. It's *practically* a responsibility."

And it practically was. Ringo Starr once said of the Beatles that they were never bigger than they were in Liverpool, late 1962. They just got more countries. And that's how it was for Millat. He was so big in Cricklewood, in Willesden, in West Hampstead, the summer of 1990, that nothing he did later in his life could top it. From his first Raggastani crowd, he had expanded and developed tribes throughout the school, throughout North London. He was simply too big to remain merely the object of Irie's affection, leader of the Raggastanis, or the son of Samad and Alsana Iqbal. He had to please all of the people all of the time. To the Cockney wide-boys in the white jeans and the colored shirts he was the joker, the risk-taker, respected lady-killer. To the black kids he was fellow weed-smoker and valued customer. To the Asian kids, hero and spokesman. Social chameleon. And underneath it all, there remained an ever-present anger and hurt, the feeling of belonging nowhere that comes to people who belong everywhere. It was this soft underbelly that made him most beloved, most adored by Irie and the nice oboe-playing, long-skirted middle-class girls, most treasured by these hair-flicking and fugue-singing females; he was their dark prince, occasional lover or impossible crush, the subject of sweaty fantasy and ardent dreams . . .

And he was also their *project*: what *was* to be done about Millat? He simply *must* stop smoking weed. We *have* to try and stop him walking out of class. They worried about his "attitude" at sleep-overs, discussed his education hypothetically with their parents (*Just say there was this Indian boy, yeah, who was always getting into* . . .), even wrote poems on the subject. Girls either wanted him or wanted to improve him, but most often a combination of the two. They wanted to improve him until he justified the amount they wanted him. Everybody's bit of rough, Millat Iqbal.

"But you're different," Millat Iqbal would say to the martyr

Irie Jones, "you're *different*. We go way back. We've got history. You're a *real* friend. They don't really *mean* anything to me."

Irie liked to believe that. That they had history, that she was different in a good way.

"Thy black is fairest in my judgement's place . . ."

Mrs. Roody silenced Francis with a raised finger. "Now, what is he saying there? Annalese?"

Annalese Hersh, who had spent the lesson so far braiding red and yellow thread into her hair, looked up in blank confusion.

"Anything, Annalese, dear. Any little idea. No matter how small. No matter how paltry."

Annalese bit her lip. Looked at the book. Looked at Mrs. Roody. Looked at the book.

"Black? . . . Is? . . . Good?"

"Yes . . . well, I suppose we can add that to last week's contribution: Hamlet? . . . Is? . . . Mad? Anybody else? What about this? *For since each hand hath put on nature's power, Fairing the foul with art's false borrow'd face.* What might that mean, I wonder?"

Joshua Chalfen, the only kid in class who volunteered opinions, put his hand up.

"Yes, Joshua?"

"Makeup."

"Yes," said Mrs. Roody, looking close to orgasm. "Yes, Joshua, that's it. What about it?"

"She's got a dark complexion that she's trying to lighten by means of makeup, artifice. The Elizabethans were very keen on a pale skin."

"They would've loved you, then," sneered Millat, for Joshua was pasty, practically anemic, curly-haired, and chubby, "you would have been Tom bloody Cruise."

Laughter. Not because it was funny, but because it was Millat putting a nerd where a nerd should be. In his place.

"One more word from you, Mr. Ick-Ball, and you are out!"

"Shakespeare. Sweaty. Bollocks. That's three. Don't worry, I'll let myself out."

This was the kind of thing Millat did so expertly. The door slammed. The nice girls looked at each other in *that* way. (He's just *so* out of control, *so* crazy . . . he *really* needs some help, some close one-to-one *personal* help from a *good friend* . . .) The boys belly-laughed. The teacher wondered if this was the beginning of a mutiny. Irie covered her stomach with her right hand.

"Marvelous. Very adult. I suppose Millat Iqbal is some kind of hero." Mrs. Roody, looking round the gormless faces of 5F, saw for the first time and with dismal clarity that this was exactly what he was.

"Does anyone else have anything to say about these sonnets? Ms. Jones! Will you *stop* looking mournfully at the door! He's gone, all right? Unless you'd like to join him?"

"No, Mrs. Roody."

"All right, then. Have you anything to say about the sonnets?"

"Yes."

"What?"

"Is she black?"

"Is who black?"

"The dark lady."

"No, dear, she's *dark*. She's not black in the modern sense. There weren't any . . . well, Afro-Carri-bee-yans in England at that time, dear. That's more a modern phenomenon, as I'm sure you know. But this was the 1600s. I mean I can't be sure, but it does seem terribly unlikely, unless she was a slave of some kind, and he's unlikely to have written a series of sonnets to a lord and then a slave, is he?"

Irie reddened. She had thought, just then, that she had seen something like a reflection, but it was receding; so she said, "Don't know, miss."

"Besides, he says very clearly, *In nothing art thou black, save in thy deeds* . . . No, dear, she just has a dark complexion, you see, as dark as mine, probably."

Irie looked at Mrs. Roody. She was the color of strawberry mousse.

"You see, Joshua is quite right: the preference was for women to be excessively pale in those days. The sonnet is about the debate between her natural coloring and the makeup that was the fashion of the time."

"I just thought . . . like when he says, here: *Then will I swear, beauty herself is black* . . . And the curly hair thing, black wires—"

Irie gave up in the face of giggling and shrugged.

"No, dear, you're reading it with a modern ear. Never read what is old with a modern ear. In fact, that will serve as today's principle—can you all write that down, please."

5F wrote that down. And the reflection that Irie had glimpsed slunk back into the familiar darkness. On the way out of class, Irie was passed a note by Annalese Hersh, who shrugged to signify that she was not the author but merely one of many handlers. It said: "By William Shakespeare: ODE TO LETITIA AND ALL MY KINKY-HAIRED BIG-ASS BITCHEZ."

TATO LAVIERA

AMERÍCAN

we gave birth to a new generation,
AmeRícan, broader than lost gold
never touched, hidden inside the
puerto rican mountains.

we gave birth to a new generation
AmeRícan, it includes everything
imaginable you-name-it-we-got-it
society.

we gave birth to a new generation,
AmeRícan salutes all folklores,
european, indian, black, spanish
and anything else compatible:

AmeRícan,   singing to composer pedro flores' palm
           trees up high in the universal sky!

AmeRícan,   sweet soft spanish danzas gypsies
           moving lyrics la española cascabelling
           presence always singing at our side!

AmeRícan,   beating jíbaro modern troubadours
           crying guitars romantic continental
           bolero love songs!

AmeRícan,   across forth and across back
           back across and forth back
           forth across and back and forth
           our trips are walking bridges!

it all dissolved into itself, an attempt
was truly made, the attempt was truly
absorbed, digested, we spit out
the poison, we spit out in malice,
we stand, affirmative in action,
to reproduce a broader answer to the
marginality that gobbled us up abruptly!

AmeRícan,   walking plena-rhythms in new york,
                 strutting beautifully alert, alive
                 many turning eyes wondering,
                 admiring!

AmeRícan,   defining myself my own way any way many
                 many ways Am e Rícan, with the big
                 R and the accent on the í!

AmeRícan,   like the soul gliding talk of gospel
                 boogie music!

AmeRícan,   speaking new words in spanglish tenements,
                 fast tongue moving street corner "que
                 corta" talk being invented at the
                 insistence of a smile!

AmeRícan,   abounding inside so many ethnic english
                 people, and out of humanity, we blend
                 and mix all that is good!

AmeRícan,   integrating in new york and defining our
                 own destino, our own way of life,

AmeRícan,   defining the new america, humane america,
                 admired america, loved america,
                 harmonious america, the world in peace,
                 our energies collectively invested to find
                 other civilizations, to touch God,

further and further, to dwell in the
spirit of divinity!

AmeRícan,   yes, for now, for i love this, my second
land, and i dream to take the accent from
the altercation, and be proud to call
myself american, in the u.s. sense of the
word, AmeRícan, America!

SEFI ATTA

GREEN

This is going to be really boring. I forgot my book in the car. We are in the immigration office in New Orleans. The television is on CNN not Disney. A news woman is talking about the elections again. I don't vote. I'm only nine.

We sit in plastic purple chairs joined together, Mom and me. Dad stands in line for one of the booths. The booth curtains are purple too. They are open like a puppet show is about to begin, but real people sit behind the glass windows, stamping and checking. I hope my parents get their green cards. I really hope we can drive back to Mississippi in time for my soccer game.

Booth A is for information and questions. Booth B is for applications. Booth C is for replacement cards. D is for forms and E is for adjudications. I know these words because I read, especially when I'm bored. What I don't understand is why must they explain the rules in different languages here?

No Smoking is *No Fumar*.

No Drinking is *Khong Duoc Uong*.

No Eating is *No Comer* and *Khong Duoc An*.

I ask Mom, "What language is that?"

"Spanish," she says. She is not wearing her glasses so she can't see far. She is holding the yellow envelope for their passports.

I should have guessed Spanish. I take lessons in our after school program. Mr. Gonzalez won't let us leave until we get our words right. He is always telling us to shut our mouths or else. Then you should see him at mass on Thursdays, eating the body of Christ and drinking the blood of Christ.

There are people here who look like Mr. Gonzalez. Indian

looking people too, like my friend Areeba who left our school because Catholic religion was confusing her. There are people who look Chinese to me, but whenever I say this, Mom says, They're not all Chinese! Sometimes she gets on my last nerve. I'm just a kid. There is one family who looks African like us, but Mom says they must be Haitian because a man next to them keeps speaking French to their son.

A pretty woman comes out of a wooden door. "Mr. Murphy?" she says. "Enrique Morales?" The third name she says sounds like Hung Who Win?

Mr. Murphy is the French speaking man. *"À bientôt,"* he says, when he gets up. No one in the Haitian family answers him. Maybe they are too tired to be polite.

I tell Mom, "Bet that's where the green cards are hidden. Behind that wooden door."

"Like lost treasure," she says.

"Why green?" I ask.

"I don't know."

"Maybe because green is for go?"

"Maybe."

"Remember when you ran a red light, Mom?"

"When did I ever run a red light?"

She did. She ran one and said it was too late to stop. I was small and I yelled, "Oo, that's begainst the law."

"Can I please go and get my book from the car?" I ask. "Please?"

"No," she says. "Absolutely not. What if they go and call us?"

Green is for vegetables. I will never eat mine. Green is for Northeast soccer field, especially when it rains. Green is for envy. My best friend Celeste is trying to make a move on my man, just because their names both start with C. His name is Chance. I told Mom my true feelings when she forced me to share. She said if two women are fighting over a man they've already lost. "What if your best friend makes a move on your man?" I asked. *"Kai,"* she said and bit her finger. "I blame that Britney Spears."

Dad hands over their passports to an old woman with orangey lipstick in the booth. When he comes back, he sits next to me.

"How long will it take?" I ask.

"You never know," he says.

"What if it takes all day?"

"We'll wait."

"Aw, man."

"'Aw man,' what?"

"Nothing."

Last year, when Grandpa died, Dad couldn't go for the funeral in Africa. Mom said this was because they were out of status waiting for their green cards. If Dad went to Africa, he wouldn't be able to come back to America. Dad cried. Mom said people didn't know the sacrifices we had to make. Then on the day of Grandpa's funeral, a white pigeon landed on our roof. She said that it was Grandpa coming to tell Dad his spirit was at peace, which made me scared, so I sneaked into their bed again, in the middle of the night, even though I really didn't believe that pigeon on the roof was my Grandpa.

"How I wish we can get back to Mississippi before six," I say.

"What's on at six?" Dad asks. "Some Disney rubbish?"

"Never mind," I say.

If I tell him, he'll think I'm selfish. I want to get back to Mississippi in time for soccer. Already he is watching the elections on CNN.

Green is for my parents' passports. Green white green is the color of the flag of their country in Africa, Nigeria.

***

The pretty woman comes out of the door again. What she says sounds like Oloboga? Ologoboga?

"That's you," I say, pulling Dad's jacket. "Come on. Come on."

"Ah-ah, what's wrong with you?" he asks.

"Calm down," Mom says.

Sometimes my parents act like I'm bothering them all the time. I walk behind them. I don't even want to be in the same footsteps with them. The pretty woman says, "Hey Sweetie."

"Stop sulking," Mom says.

"Are we getting your thumb print today, Sweetie?" the pretty woman asks me.

"No, she's the American in the family," Mom says and smiles.

On the other side of the door, I don't see any green cards, only a room with a table and a copier. The pretty woman does Dad's thumb print, then Mom's, and then she writes our address in Mississippi to send their green cards. Mom won't stop thanking her.

"You have no idea. We waited so long. When will they come?"

The woman leads us to the door saying, "By regular post. Yes, you can travel as you like. Yes, yes, you're officially permanent residents." I don't think she cares.

"Can we go now?" I ask, after she shuts the door.

The Haitian family is still sitting out there. The lines for the booths are longer. An Indian boy spreads his arms like plane wings and makes engine sounds with his lips. Brr! Brr!

We walk to the elevators.

"Mardi Gras parade," Dad says.

"Is there one this afternoon?" Mom asks.

"Shall we?" he says. "To celebrate?"

"Do you want to stay for a Mardi Gras parade?" Mom asks me.

Dad is dancing. Limbo. The yellow envelope with their passports is under his armpit. It's so embarrassing.

"Em," I say. "No."

Last year we came for Mardi Gras in New Orleans. The weather was sunny. We watched the Oshun Parade on Canal Street. I was trying to catch the beads people were throwing from the floats. I preferred the golds. My neck was weighed down. Mom kept yelling in my ear, "Oshun is African. People here don't know. She is the Yoruba goddess of love." Her breath smelled of the beignets we ate for breakfast. Dad was saying, "Don't just reach out like that. That's why you keep missing them. See, there is a technique to catching the beads." "What technique?" Mom asked and Dad stepped in front to show us and a huge black bead smacked him in the face. Then we had to eat lunch. I said I wanted Chinese. They said they wanted

Thai. Mom said it was all the same. "Chinese is not Thai!" I said, and Mom asked, "How come you know the difference when it comes to food?" We ate King Cake on our way back to Mississippi. It was creamy and glorious. I got the pink plastic baby Jesus inside and Dad said, "That's great," and Mom asked, "What if she choked on it?"

"It's too wet for Mardi Gras," I say.

Mom says, "The American has spoken. Back to Mississippi for us."

Green is for Mardi Gras beads. Green is for sugar sprinkles on King Cake. Green is for green onions in Pad Thai. I had to pick them out last year.

***

There is a big lake in New Orleans called Pontchartrain with little bungalows on sticks. Whenever we drive over it, on a roller coaster type of bridge, I know we'll soon be in Mississippi. The car is warm. Dad is going on about the elections again. Gay marriages won't make a blind bit of difference, blah, blah. Mom is yawning. I know exactly what she will say very soon. She will call out the names of creeks and rivers we pass: Pearl, Wolf, Little Black, Bowie, Hobolochitto, Tallahala, Chunky. Then she will say, "It's terrible. Names are all we ever see of Native Americans."

My parents are predictable. Whenever I say this they laugh, but they are. My mom is for woman power. Everything in the world is her right. Even shopping is her right. In Mississippi, she argues in the mall whenever they ask her to show her ID. "That's discrimination," she'll say. "That is dis-cri-mi-nation." In JC Penney, too. At home, she acts like she's the boss of me and Dad. "Eat up. What's this doing here? Can't you flush?" My dad says that's because she is a lecturer. He is a doctor. He gets mad with the President, and still he wants the President to win the elections, to teach the people who are against the President a lesson, because they are not getting it together, especially with Health. Every day, when he comes home from work, he yells at the television because of the elections. Whenever the

President comes on Mom says, "Ugh, turn him off. That man can't string two words together." Yet she tells me it's not right to be rude to people who can't speak English.

Last election, we voted in school. All my friends voted for the President—before he became president—because the other guy killed babies. "Who said he kills babies?" Mom asked when I told her. Your teacher? Your friend? What kind of parent says such a horrible thing to their kid. Well, they must have heard it from somewhere. Well, I think grown ups should keep their political opinions to themselves." I told her I voted for the President. She said, "What! Why?" "Everyone else did," I said. She said, "Listen, I brought you up to stand your ground. To stick up for what you believe in." I said, "Oh, please." First of all, it was her ground not mine. Number B, I believe in fitting in.

"What's it like being African?" my friend Celeste asked when we used to be friends. "I don't know," I told her. I was protecting my parents. I didn't want Celeste to know the secret about Africans. Bones in meat are very important to them. They suck the bones and it's so frustrating I could cry. My mom is the worst, especially when she eats okra stew. Afterwards she chews the bones to a mush and my dad laughs and asks, "What was that before your teeth got to it? Oxtail? Chicken Wings? Red Snapper? Crab?" I'm like, get some manners.

Being African was being frustrated again when my teacher showed pictures of clothes from all over the world. When she showed the pictures of Africans, that lame Daniel Dawson asked, "Why are they wearing those funny hats?" and everyone in class laughed.

Green is for the color I like most—yellow. Green is for a color I can't stand—blue. Green is a mixture of blue and yellow. Green is for confusion.

Dad is still talking about the elections. "Where are the weapons of mass destruction?" he asks.

Mom points out of the window and says, "Pearl River."

"You guys," I say. "I have a soccer game tonight."

They start yelling.

"For goodness sake!"

"Again?"

"I don't remember that being in my calendar . . ."

"Why didn't you tell us before?"

"Soccer is meant for the summer. Only the British play in the spring . . ."

"Only Americans call football soccer."

My parents are so predictable.

"These people are crazy," Dad says. "The weather is not conducive."

Mom says, "What people? Don't put prejudice in my daughter's heart."

"I didn't mention any race," Dad says.

I'm like, what in the world right now? "You guys," I say. "If you're going to live in this country you might as well get used to soccer. It's part of life. I'm American. How do you expect me to feel?"

"You know," Dad says. "She's right."

I can't believe he fell for that.

"What time's the game anyway?" Mom asks.

"Six."

"Shit."

"Don't cuss, Mom."

"Sorry, baby, but I hated sports in Africa and I hate them here."

***

We've passed Chunky River. I've finished my book. I think we'll make it in time for my game. Mom asks, "Are you still mad with us?"

"A little," I say.

"Sorry. Today has been a bit . . ."

"I know. Are you happy about your green cards?"

"You have no idea."

"America will soon be number one in the world for soccer," Dad says. "You wait and see. Look at the way they organize themselves. From the grassroots level. Everyone involved."

"Girls too," Mom says, and raises her thumb at me.

I'm not into all that. I know what girls like Celeste can do.

"Even if they don't have any talent," Dad says, rubbing his chin. "They have the money to import talent. Did you hear of that fourteen year old? Highest paid in the soccer leagues. Freddy Adu. His family came from Ghana. Immigration will save America."

"Because of soccer?" Mom asks.

Green is for the Comets color. I hope we beat the Comets tonight. I really hope we beat them.

***

We made it to the game. Mom and Dad stayed, maybe because of guilt.

You should see me. My color is red. My number is oo. I'm ready to blast those Comets to kingdom come. I'm dribbling down the field. The lights are like stars. The grass is wet. I have to be careful because Mississippi mud can make you slip and slide. Everyone is cheering, "Come on! Get on it! Get on it!"

I kick that sucker. It zooms like a jet, lands in the corner of the goal post, neat as my bedroom when I get two dollars for cleaning up. Girls in my team are slapping my back, "Way to go! Good one!" My parents are cheering with other parents. This is it. Me, scoring. My mom looking like she loves soccer. My dad looking like he really loves the President. Three of us, looking like we really belong. It's better than finding the baby in King Cake, and my team hasn't even won yet.

SAFIA ELHILLO

ORIGIN STORIES (REPRISE)

i was born in the winter in 1990 in a country not my own
i was born with my father's eyes maybe i stole them he
doesn't look like that   anymore   i was born
in seven countries   i was born carved up by borders
i was born with a graveyard of languages for teeth   i was
born to be a darkness in an american boy's bed   or   i
was born with many names   to fill the quiet   i forget
which one is mine   i forget   what is silence   &
what   is a language i cannot speak   i was born
crookedhearted   born ticking   born on the
subway platform at 103rd st   fainting   blood sliding
around thin as water in my body   i was born
to the woman who caught me   floating into the train   & to
every pair of hands keeping me from dying   my mother's
cool fingers snaking my hair into braids   my grandmother's
thick knuckles collecting my feet in her lap   & my own
cupped for rainwater   raising every day to my own mouth
to drink

RETURNS

PAULINE KALDAS

A CONVERSATION

"You want me to go back? I'm sixty-five years old."

My hair is gray, and my body has grown into its age. I have settled into myself. No longer the young girl you met, the one who flirted and teased, who wore her black hair like a shield, enticing you to ask for her hand. No longer the one who agreed to wrap herself around you and fly across the ocean, willing to release each strand that held me close to family and home, believing in this miracle of America. I'm old, and my steps are solid on this land where I have learned to live; they cannot turn around now and go in a different direction.

"We can retire there. Do you know how much our money is worth? I can buy a beautiful apartment. We can live on the corniche and look at the Nile every day."

I left, only a young man with little in my pocket. My family held me back, ridiculed my dreams, told me I would never make it in America: that my life could only be wrapped in this place with a job pushing me each day to make only enough to feed us and hold a roof up, that I was a fool to imagine myself in the open space of a new land, that I would return to beg for a morsel of food. Now my money can take me back to every ice cream my mouth drooled for as a young child. These dollars I have bought and sold will multiply till they're an endless chain of pearls. Like the rich, we can buy an apartment, two stories, with marble floors and gold faucets, and a balcony that lifts us above the city so our eyes can stretch over the Nile each day.

"We've been in this country for forty years."

Forty years is a lifetime. Your mother died before she turned fifty; her heart failed after we left. You could not even tell her the truth about our immigration, trying to convince her it was only a short excursion, a youthful desire to see the magic of the other side of the world. But she looked at our faces, the anxiety of our anticipation, and she knew that her only son was leaving. My father died only years later, barely reaching the age of sixty. We could not even return so I could stand by mother's side as she buried him. Forty years we have built a life and left one behind.

"You can have everything there. I'll buy you whatever you want."

Those early years, every penny we had to hold tight in our fists. I watched you cut coupons, squint your eyes at the price tags, and stretch each pound of meat with bread. Every birthday I failed you, and even a single rose was an extravagance I held back. There I can buy you dresses to sparkle on your body, jewels to circle your wrists; whatever your eye rests on, I'll offer you as my gift. Don't you want to enter a store and lay your finger on any item, to have it be yours like the magic of wishes coming true?

"And do you have enough money to get rid of the pollution and the crowds too?"

When we decided to go and everyone's talk of foolish dreams and the struggle of America failed to keep our feet still, my father sold his land by the pyramids so we could have something to hold us as we began our new lives. My mother took off her gold bracelet with its snakes intertwining around her wrist and sold it so there was enough to buy the tickets. What can your money buy for us now? The streets in Egypt are brimming with the poor and hopeful, and their dreams release the stench caught in our nostrils. You can't walk without the weight of people bumping against you and inhaling the smoke and garbage that fumes the city. Our money will not release us from its grabbing fist.

"We can go to the Red Sea. We'll buy a chalet, and we can go when we like."

Do you remember our honeymoon in Hurghada? We rented a small chalet, and each morning the slender waves lapped at our door. I held your hand as we crossed the sand, and we walked toward the corals beneath the surface, laughing when the tiny fish nibbled at our ankles. I unfolded my arms like a hammock to hold your body so the sea could carry you. And at night, the sand winds whistled at our door as we floated inside each other, my body surprised by the softness of your skin like the caress of each wave. The beach was almost empty that October, and we owned each grain of sand as we spoke our dreams like the drops of water glistening on our skin. We'll buy a chalet to make it our own, a place we can inhabit at our will. We'll own the corals and the waves and the sun's dreams, walk across the edge of sand, marking our ground.

"After we've come here and struggled and built a life?"

You couldn't find a job, and when you came home, I saw your face like a stone engraved in silence. You took a job washing dishes. Your hands became red and brittle, the fingers bending in and your knuckles hardening against the harsh soap. A year until finally you found something in a small company, each day sitting at your desk. But I knew the boss looked over your shoulder, touching his pen to your work, marking corrections. You stooped over that desk for years, the fear of losing the job etched in your eyes. I found work, punching in time cards, leaving my children in day care centers, afraid I would forget their faces. It took years till we saved enough that you could shrug off the choke of having a boss and strike out on your own. We have built this life with our hands; each stone in this house we have carried on our backs.

"We can live like royalty there."

What do we have here? Our house we pay for each month, the bank looming over us. It is empty space, the walls turning their corners, tucking us inside their angles, keeping us cloistered. We live like monks, our lives restricted. In Egypt, our hands would touch nothing. We can purchase each task: a servant to clean the house, a man to deliver the groceries, a cook to stand in the kitchen. And we would be free to come and go as we please. We can stay at the Oberoi hotel in Giza, lounge at the pool, and watch the sun set over the pyramids, each drink and each plate delivered to us. Imagine your life at your fingertips, only making the request to have it be granted.

"These are dreams. No one lives like a king there."

You remember only the beauty of things; maybe that is why I married you. Your eyes have always stretched their vision beyond the boundaries of the horizon; you follow a dream that no one else can see. Egypt has no more kings or queens. Its days of glory are over. The country is crowded only with leftover peasants. The kings gathered their wealth and ran, leaving only those who know how to struggle for the same bread they eat daily. Their bare feet are caked with the mud of the Nile as they carry their loads and scrape their few piasters each day. The river's water has become poisonous and the land abandoned to those who cannot nurture it.

"Over there life is good, and the people have morals."

A sense of decency. People look in your face. Greet you with respect. We take care of each other—not like here, abandoned, every man for himself and no one stops to help lift those who fall. People can still feel with their hearts. There, even those who have nothing share their bite of food.

"Over there people are eating each other and everyone is just for himself. You've forgotten why we came."

The corruption. The bribes. The connections you need to

take even a small step. The poor scramble for a few scraps of nourishment, while the rich play their Monopoly with real money. There is nothing but the hardship of each day. Each man tumbling over the next to win.

"We'll have everything. At least people will respect us. Not like here. Forty years and the Americans still look at us as if we were cockroaches walking on their land."

I have learned their language, their slang, their clothing, how to eat their food, how to laugh at their jokes, how to make their money. Still they grimace when they meet me, they scratch their heads instead of shaking my hand, they scowl when they learn I live in the best neighborhood. I changed my name, so I could erase the sour look on their faces when I introduce myself. America welcomes you into its land so you can mop its floors. I want to hold my head up high again, to breathe my name and have it heard.

"What are you saying? We found good work, and we bought a house. Our children got educated here. You want me to go back and not see them?"

Look, look at what we have. This house that is large and grand. In Egypt, we would have stayed in that two-bedroom apartment. I found a job here and went in each day to earn our living. No one harassed me, and no one told me I wasn't smart enough. We raised our sons in this house instead of cramming them between the walls and the alleys. We paid for their education with our blood, and one is a doctor and one is an engineer. In that country, they would have stepped on them like vermin because they're Christian; every door shut in their faces till we would have been lucky to see them sweep the streets for a living.

"They'll come visit us."

We'll bring them to see us. They will know where they are from, and they will be part of their family. They will bring their children to play on the sand and bounce in the waves of

the sea like you and I did when we were young. We will pull
our family together again and loosen the tight grip of isola-
tion. We will all return to settle our feet into the sand and
water of our homeland.

"You're dreaming. Our children will never leave this country."
Your thoughts are like a fairy tale; you weave light and air
to make a tapestry of magic colors. Our sons have settled their
lives in this country. They have found a place for themselves,
and already they are piling the stones to build a home for their
children. From their birth, they claimed this land as their own,
and the thread that ties them to Egypt has become a thin sliver
too invisible to follow back.

"I want to live the rest of my life in peace without struggling."
To look out on the sea and own the world.

"I came here, and I'm going to die here."
This life I have built, I will not let it go.

About the Authors

Mena Abdullah was born in Bundarra, Australia, in 1930 to a Punjabi immigrant family. Her best-known work is the short story collection *The Time of the Peacock*. As well as writing fiction, she has worked for the Commonwealth Scientific and Industrial Research Organisation.

Sefi Atta was born in Lagos, Nigeria, in 1964, and currently divides her time among the United States, the UK, and Nigeria. Her novels include *Everything Good Will Come, Swallow*, and *A Bit of Difference*; she has also written a short story collection and several stage and radio plays.

Born in Montreal, Canada, in 1962, **Shauna Singh Baldwin** holds degrees from universities in India, the United States, and Canada. She is the author of three novels, two short story collections, a nonfiction collection, and a play, and coauthor of *A Foreign Visitor's Survival Guide to America*.

E. R. Braithwaite was born in Georgetown, Guyana, in 1912. His writings include *To Sir, With Love; Paid Servant*; and *A Kind of Homecoming*. He taught high school in the UK and college in the United States, and served as Guyana's ambassador to Venezuela. Braithwaite died in 2016 at the age of 104.

Joseph Bruchac was born in 1942 in the United States. He is the author of several works of fiction, poetry, and nonfiction depicting the life of Native Americans. He is also a storyteller and musician, and, with his sister and two sons, has been heavily involved in preserving and disseminating the language, culture, and music of the Abenaki people.

Mehdi Charef was born in 1952 in Algeria and immigrated to France with his family in 1964. In addition to writing *Tea in the Harem* and two other novels, Charef has directed several films.

David Dabydeen was born in 1955 in Berbice, Guyana, and moved to the UK as a teenager. The author of several novels, poetry collections, and works of nonfiction and criticism, he is director of the Yesu Persaud Centre for Caribbean Studies at the University of Warwick, as well as Guyana's ambassador-at-large.

Edwidge Danticat was born in Port-au-Prince, Haiti, in 1969, and moved to Brooklyn, USA, at age twelve. She has written many novels and short story collections, a travel narrative, a memoir, and six books for children and young adults, and has edited three collections of stories and essays.

Safia Elhillo was born in 1990 in the United States to Sudanese parents. Her poetry has appeared in multiple journals and anthologies; she also coedited the collection *Halal If You Hear Me* (The Break-Beat Poets, volume 3).

Olaudah Equiano was born around 1745 in what is now Anambra State, Nigeria. As he recounts in his autobiography *The Interesting Narrative of the Life of Olaudah Equiano*, he was enslaved as a child and transported to Barbados and then the United States. After earning his freedom in 1766, he became a writer and activist against transatlantic slavery. Equiano died in 1797 in London.

Mohsin Hamid was born in 1971 in Lahore, Pakistan. He is the author of four novels, *Moth Smoke*, *The Reluctant Fundamentalist*, *How to Get Filthy Rich in Rising Asia*, and *Exit West*, and a book of essays, *Discontent and Its Civilizations: Dispatches from Lahore, New York, and London*.

Eva Hoffman was born in Kraków, Poland, in 1945, to parents who had recently survived the Holocaust. She emigrated to Canada with her family at age thirteen. The author of several works of fiction and nonfiction, Hoffman has taught literature and creative writing at various universities in the United States. She now lives in London.

Born in Addis Ababa, Ethiopia, **Djamila Ibrahim** moved to Canada in 1990. She worked as an immigration and citizenship advisor for the Canadian government while also writing fiction. Her debut short story collection, *Things Are Good Now*, appeared in 2018.

Francisco Jiménez was born in Tlaquepaque, Mexico, in 1943, and moved to the United States as a child for farmwork. A professor and former director of the Ethnic Studies program at Santa Clara University, he has written a memoir series in four installments, as well as several critical studies of Mexican and Mexican American literature.

Pauline Kaldas, born in Egypt in 1961, emigrated to the United States as a child in 1969. She has taught at Rhode Island College, Rhode Island School of Design, and the American University in Cairo. The author of several books of fiction, poetry, and nonfiction, she is currently a professor of literature and creative writing at Hollins University.

Hanif Kureishi was born in South London, UK, in 1954—like the protagonist of his novel *The Buddha of Suburbia*, to a South Asian father and a white English mother. Along with several novels, he has written short stories, plays, nonfiction, and screenplays, including the groundbreaking *My Beautiful Laundrette*.

Tato Laviera was born in San Juan, Puerto Rico, in 1950, and moved to New York in 1960. He was a founder of the Nuyorican poetry movement and the author of several poetry collections and plays. Laviera died in 2013.

Marina Lewycka was born in 1946 to a Ukrainian refugee family in Kiel, Germany, and moved to the UK as an infant. She has written five novels, as well as a nonfiction book on elder care.

Claude McKay was born in Clarendon Parish, Jamaica, in 1889. He began writing poetry as a young adult, and published two collections in 1912, the same year he moved to the United States. Until his death in 1948, McKay continued to write poetry, as well as fiction, memoir, and nonfiction.

Dinaw Mengestu was born in 1978 in Addis Ababa, Ethiopia. He and his family moved to the United States to escape civil war when he was two years old. He is the author of three novels, as well as nonfiction accounts of conflict in Uganda and Sudan. A MacArthur Fellowship recipient, Mengestu currently lives in New York.

Dunya Mikhail was born in 1965 in Baghdad, Iraq. She worked as a journalist and translator before fleeing the country under government pressure, first to Jordan and then the United States. She writes poetry in Arabic and English, and teaches Arabic at Oakland University.

Shani Mootoo was born in Dublin, Ireland, in 1957, grew up in Trinidad and Tobago, and moved to Canada at age nineteen. She is a writer, painter, photographer, and video artist whose work includes the novels *Cereus Blooms at Night* and *Moving Forward Sideways Like a Crab*.

Julie Otsuka was born in Palo Alto, USA, in 1962. After studying art and pursuing a career as a painter, she began writing fiction at age thirty. Her novels *The Buddha in the Attic* and *When the Emperor Was Divine* depict Japanese emigration to the United States and internment during World War II.

Emine Sevgi Özdamar was born in Malatya, Turkey, in 1946. In 1965 she moved to West Germany, where, like the characters in her 1998 novel *The Bridge of the Golden Horn*, she worked in a factory and lived in a large residence for Turkish women. She returned to Turkey to study acting; she currently lives in Berlin, where she acts, directs, and writes fiction and poetry.

M. NourbeSe Philip was born in Moriah, Trinidad and Tobago, in 1947, and moved to Canada as a young adult to study political science and law. After writing and practicing law for seven years, she became a full-time writer in 1983, and has since produced fiction for adults and children, three essay collections, two plays, and several poetry collections.

Paulette Ramsay grew up in Hanover Parish, Jamaica. She received her PhD in Spanish from the University of the West Indies and has also studied in the Dominican Republic, Spain, the United States, and Venezuela. She has published a novel, three poetry collections, and several academic studies on Afro-Mexican and other Afro-Latinx culture and history.

Salman Rushdie was born in 1947 in Mumbai (then called Bombay), India. He moved to the UK at age fourteen and later worked in advertising while writing his first two novels, *Grimus* and *Midnight's*

Children. He is the author of many other novels, a short story collection, and two essay collections.

Marjane Satrapi was born in Rasht, Iran, in 1969. As portrayed in the second volume of her graphic memoir *Persepolis*, Satrapi attended boarding school in Austria. She returned to Iran for college and graduate school, and now resides in France.

Sam Selvon was born in San Fernando, Trinidad and Tobago, in 1923. He worked as a telegraph operator and newspaper reporter, while also writing fiction and poetry, before moving to London in 1950. There he wrote many novels set in Trinidad and London, including *A Brighter Sun*, *The Lonely Londoners*, and *The Housing Lark* (newly reissued as a Penguin Classic). Selvon relocated to Canada in 1978, and died during a trip to Trinidad in 1994.

Warsan Shire was born in 1988 in Kenya to Somali parents, and moved to the UK at age one. London's inaugural Young Poet Laureate, she has published widely and has read her poetry at venues around the world.

Zadie Smith was born in London, UK, in 1975. She has written many works of fiction and nonfiction, several of which (such as her novels *White Teeth*, *NW*, and *Swing Time*) take place in the immigrant-rich NW area of London.

Deepak Unnikrishnan was born in Kerala, India, in 1980, and moved to Abu Dhabi as an infant. His surreal multigenre novel *Temporary People* appeared in 2017. Unnikrishnan currently teaches creative writing in Abu Dhabi.

Born in the Senegambia region of West Africa around 1753, **Phillis Wheatley** was enslaved and transported to Massachusetts around age eight. She began writing poetry as a teenager and published her first collection—also the first collection by an African American poet—in 1773. She became a spokesperson for both revolutionary and abolitionist causes before her death in 1784.

Suggestions for Further Reading and Viewing

* = available from Penguin Classics

FICTION AND DRAMA

Chris Abani, *Becoming Abigail* (Nigeria → UK)

Atia Abawi, *A Land of Permanent Goodbyes* (Syria → Turkey → Greece)

Randa Abdel-Fattah, *The Lines We Cross* (Afghanistan → Australia); *Ten Things I Hate About Me* (Lebanon → Australia)

Azhar Abidi, *The House of Bilqis* (Australia → Pakistan); *Passarola Rising* (multiple migrations)

Leila Aboulela, *Minaret* (Sudan → UK); *Lyrics Alley* (Sudan → Egypt → UK); *The Translator* (Sudan → Scotland)

Chantel Acevedo, *The Living Infinite* (Spain → Cuba → USA)

Elizabeth Acevedo, *The Poet X* (first generation USA)

Chimamanda Ngozi Adichie, *Americanah* (Nigeria → USA → Nigeria)

Ama Ata Aidoo, *Our Sister Killjoy* (Ghana → Germany → Ghana)

Yelena Akhtiorskaya, *Panic in a Suitcase* (Ukraine → USA)

Hanan al-Shaykh, *Only in London* (Iraq/Lebanon/Morocco → UK)

*Shalom Aleichem, *Motl the Cantor's Son* (Russian Empire → USA); *Tevye the Dairyman* (Russian Empire → Palestine)

Meena Alexander, *Nampally Road* (India → UK → India)

William Alexander, *Ambassador* (Mexico → USA)

Monica Ali, *Brick Lane* (Bangladesh → UK)

Sabahattin Ali, *Madonna in a Fur Coat* (Turkey → Germany)

Julia Alvarez, *How the García Girls Lost Their Accents* (Dominican Republic → USA)

Hala Alyan, *Salt Houses* (Palestine → Kuwait and elsewhere)

*Mary Antin, *The Promised Land* (Russian Empire [present-day Belarus] → USA)

Nathacha Appanah, *The Last Brother* (Czechoslovakia → Mauritius); *Waiting for Tomorrow* (Mauritius → France)

Alexia Arthurs, *How to Love a Jamaican: Stories* (Jamaica → USA → Canada)

Sefi Atta, *A Bit of Difference* (Nigeria → UK); *News from Home* (Nigeria → various destinations)

Juan Tomás Ávila Laurel, *The Gurugu Pledge* (various countries in Africa → Spain)

Mariama Bâ, *Scarlet Song* (Senegal → France)

Anita Rau Badami, *The Hero's Walk* (India → Canada → India); *Tamarind Woman* (India → Canada)

Sharon Bala, *The Boat People* (Sri Lanka → Canada)

James Baldwin, *Giovanni's Room* (USA → France)

Shauna Singh Baldwin, *English Lessons and Other Stories* (India → Canada/USA)

Azouz Begag, *Shantytown Kid* (*Le Gone du Chaâba*) (Algeria → France)

*Aphra Behn, *Oroonoko* (West Africa → Surinam)

Tahar Ben Jelloun, *Leaving Tangier* (Morocco → Spain)

Benyamin, *Goat Days* (India → Saudi Arabia)

David Bezmozgis, *The Free World* (Latvia → USA); *Natasha and Other Stories* (Latvia → Canada)

Joseph Boyden, *Three Day Road* (Canadian First Nations → France → Belgium)

Dionne Brand, *At the Full and Change of the Moon*; *Sans Souci and Other Stories* (Trinidad and Tobago, and other Caribbean → Canada); *What We All Long For* (Vietnam → Canada)

Lily Brett, *Things Could Be Worse* (Poland → Australia); *Too Many Men* (USA → Poland)

NoViolet Bulawayo, *We Need New Names* (Zimbabwe → USA)

*Frances Hodgson Burnett, *The Secret Garden* (India → UK)

*Abraham Cahan, *The Rise of David Levinsky* (Russian Empire [present-day Lithuania] → USA)

Rosa R. Cappiello, *Oh Lucky Country* (Italy → Australia)

Jennifer Davis Carey, *Near the Hope* (Barbados → USA)

Gianrico Carofiglio, *Involuntary Witness* (Senegal → Italy)

Ana Castillo, *The Guardians* (USA → Mexico)

Elaine Castillo, *America Is Not the Heart* (Philippines → USA)

*Willa Cather, *O Pioneers!* (Sweden → USA)

May-lee Chai, *Tiger Girl* (Cambodia → USA); *Useful Phrases for Immigrants: Stories* (China → USA)

Myriam J. A. Chancy, *The Loneliness of Angels* (multiple migrations); *The Scorpion's Claw* (Haiti → Canada)

David Chariandy, *Brother*; *Soucouyant* (Trinidad and Tobago → Canada)

Kirstin Chen, *Bury What We Cannot Take* (China → USA)

Melanie Cheng, *Australia Day* (multiple migrations)

Wayson Choy, *All That Matters* (China → Canada)

Sandra Cisneros, *Caramelo*; *The House on Mango Street*; *Woman Hollering Creek and Other Stories* (Mexico → USA)

Austin Clarke, *Choosing His Coffin: The Best Stories of Austin Clarke*; *More*; *The Origin of Waves*; *There Are No Elders* (Barbados → Canada)

Maxine Beneba Clarke, *Carrying the World*; *Foreign Soil and Other Stories* (multiple migrations)

Michelle Cliff, *No Telephone to Heaven* (Jamaica → USA → UK → Jamaica)

Teju Cole, *Every Day Is for the Thief*; *Open City* (Nigeria → USA → Nigeria)

Maryse Condé, *Heremakhonon* (Guadeloupe → France → West Africa); *I, Tituba, Black Witch of Salem* (Barbados → North America); *Segu* (Mali → Morocco/Brazil)

*Joseph Conrad, *Heart of Darkness* and *The Congo Diary* (Belgium → Belgian Congo); *Victory: An Island Tale* (Sweden → Indonesia)

Edwidge Danticat, *Breath, Eyes, Memory*; *Brother, I'm Dying*; *The Dew Breaker*; *The Farming of Bones* (Haiti → USA)

Michelle de Kretser, *The Life to Come* (Sri Lanka → Australia → France); *Questions of Travel* (Sri Lanka → Australia)

Nicole Dennis-Benn, *Patsy* (Jamaica → USA)

Kiran Desai, *The Inheritance of Loss* (Nepal → India and India → USA)

Junot Díaz, *The Brief Wondrous Life of Oscar Wao*; *Drown* (Dominican Republic → USA)

Chitra Banerjee Divakaruni, *Oleander Girl*; *Sister of My Heart*; *Before We Visit the Goddess*; *The Vine of Desire* (India → USA)

Négar Djavadi, *Disoriental* (Iran → France)

Michael Donkor, *Housegirl* (Ghana → UK)

Marguerite Duras, *The Lover* (Vietnam → France)

Edith Eaton / Sui Sin Far, *A Chinese Ishmael and Other Stories* (China → USA); *Mrs. Spring Fragrance* (China → UK → Canada → USA)

Winnifred Eaton, *Me: A Book of Remembrance* (Canada → Jamaica → USA)

Esi Edugyan, *Half-Blood Blues* (USA/Germany → France); *The Second Life of Samuel Tyne* (Ghana → UK → Canada); *Washington Black* (Barbados → USA → Arctic)

Buchi Emecheta, *In the Ditch*; *Second Class Citizen* (Nigeria → UK)

Ramabai Espinet, *The Swinging Bridge* (Trinidad and Tobago → Canada)

Diana Evans, *26a* (Nigeria → UK)

Bernardine Evaristo, *Mr. Loverman* (Antigua → UK)

Nuruddin Farah, *Hiding in Plain Sight* (Italy → Kenya)

Brenda Flanagan, *In Praise of Island Women & Other Crimes* (Trinidad and Tobago → USA)

Jonathan Safran Foer, *Everything Is Illuminated* (USA → Ukraine → Poland)

Aminatta Forna, *Ancestor Stones* (UK → fictional West African country); *Happiness* (Ghana → UK)

Cecil Foster, *No Man in the House* (Barbados → UK); *Slammin' Tar* (Barbados → Canada); *Sleep On, Beloved* (Jamaica → Canada)

Cristina García, *Dreaming in Cuban; King of Cuba* (Cuba → USA); *Monkey Hunting* (China → Cuba → USA)

Roxane Gay, *An Untamed State* (USA → Haiti → USA)

Amitav Ghosh, *The Glass Palace* (India → Burma); *Sea of Poppies* (India → Mauritius); *The Shadow Lines* (India → UK)

Yasmine Gooneratne, *A Change of Skies* (Sri Lanka → Australia)

Reyna Grande, *Across a Hundred Mountains* (Mexico → USA)

Kate Grenville, *The Secret River* (UK → Australia)

Faïza Guène, *Kiffe Kiffe Tomorrow* (Morocco → France)

Xiaolu Guo, *A Concise Chinese-English Dictionary for Lovers* (China → UK)

Yaa Gyasi, *Homegoing* (Ghana → USA)

Rawi Hage, *Cockroach* (Lebanon → Canada)

Mohsin Hamid, *Exit West* (unnamed country very much like Pakistan → Greece → UK → USA); *The Reluctant Fundamentalist* (Pakistan → USA → Pakistan)

Bessie Head, *A Question of Power; When Rain Clouds Gather* (South Africa → Botswana)

Cristina Henríquez, *The Book of Unknown Americans* (Mexico/Panama → USA)

Yuri Herrera, *Signs Preceding the End of the World* (Mexico →
USA)

Lawrence Hill, *The Book of Negroes* (Niger → USA → Canada →
Sierra Leone → UK)

Nalo Hopkinson, *Brown Girl in the Ring* (unspecified Caribbean →
dystopian future Canada); *Midnight Robber* (fictional Afro-
futuristic planet colonized by Caribbean settlers); *The Salt
Roads* (African diaspora); *Skin Folk: Stories* (Jamaica and other
Caribbean → Canada)

Vanessa Hua, *A River of Stars* (China → USA)

Yang Huang, *My Old Faithful: Stories* (China → USA)

Djamila Ibrahim, *Things Are Good Now* (Ethiopia and elsewhere →
Canada and elsewhere)

Laila Ibrahim, *Paper Wife* (China → USA)

*Gilbert Imlay, *The Emigrants* (UK → USA)

Uzodinma Iweala, *Speak No Evil* (USA → Nigeria)

Naomi Jackson, *The Star Side of Bird Hill* (USA → Barbados)

*Henry James, *The Europeans* (Europe → USA)

Ha Jin, *A Free Life*; *A Good Fall* (China → USA); *A Map of Be-
trayal*; *Nanjing Requiem* (USA → China)

*James Weldon Johnson, *The Autobiography of an Ex-Colored
Man* (USA → France)

Jennifer Zeynab Joukhadar, *The Map of Salt and Stars* (Syria →
USA → Syria)

Jonas Hassen Khemiri, *Montecore* (Tunisia → Sweden / Sweden →
USA)

Jamaica Kincaid, *Lucy* (Antigua → USA)

*Rudyard Kipling, *Kim* (first generation India)

Christina Baker Kline, *Orphan Train* (Ireland → USA)

Joy Nozomi Kogawa, *Itsuka*; *Obasan* (Japan → Canada)

Amitava Kumar, *Immigrant, Montana* (India → USA)

Akil Kumarasamy, *Half Gods* (multiple migrations)

Hari Kunzru, *Transmission* (India → USA/global migrations)

Hanif Kureishi, *The Buddha of Suburbia* (first generation UK)

Harold Sonny Ladoo, *No Pain Like This Body* (India → Trinidad and Tobago)

Dany Laferrière, *The Enigma of the Return* (Haiti → Canada)

Jhumpa Lahiri, *Interpreter of Maladies*; *The Lowland*; *The Namesake* (India → USA)

Thanhha Lai, *Inside Out & Back Again* (Vietnam → USA)

Laila Lalami, *Hope and Other Dangerous Pursuits* (Morocco → Spain); *The Moor's Account* (Morocco → North America)

George Lamming, *The Emigrants*; *Of Age and Innocence* (Barbados → UK)

Nella Larsen, *Quicksand* (USA → Denmark)

Chang-rae Lee, *Native Speaker* (first generation USA)

Jen Sookfong Lee, *The End of East* (China → Canada)

Andrea Levy, *Every Light in the House Burnin'*; *The Long Song*; *Fruit of the Lemon*; *Never Far from Nowhere*; *Six Stories and an Essay*; *Small Island* (first generation UK)

Earl Lovelace, *Jestina's Calypso* (Trinidad and Tobago → USA)

Michael David Lukas, *The Last Watchman of Old Cairo* (USA → Egypt)

Sindiwe Magona, *Push-Push! and Other Stories* (South Africa → USA)

Gautam Malkani, *Londonstani* (first generation UK)

David Malouf, *Remembering Babylon* (UK → Australia)

*Thomas Mann, *Death in Venice and Other Tales* (Germany → Italy)

Dambudzo Marechera, *The House of Hunger* (Rhodesia [present-day Zimbabwe] → UK)

Paule Marshall, *Brown Girl, Brownstones*; *Daughters* (first generation USA)

Demetria Martínez, *Mother Tongue* (El Salvador → USA)

Hisham Matar, *Anatomy of a Disappearance* (unnamed country →
Egypt)

Imbolo Mbue, *Behold the Dreamers* (Cameroon → USA)

Colum McCann, *Dancer* (Russia → USA); *Songdogs* (Ireland →
Spain → Mexico → USA → Ireland); *TransAtlantic* (multiple
migrations)

*Herman Melville, *Israel Potter: His Fifty Years of Exile*; *Moby-Dick*;
Omoo; *Typee* (USA → various places)

Dinaw Mengestu, *The Beautiful Things That Heaven Bears* (Ethiopia
→ USA); *How to Read the Air* (Ethiopia → USA → Ethiopia)

Rohinton Mistry, *Tales from Firozsha Baag* (India → Canada)

Shani Mootoo, *Cereus Blooms at Night* (Lantanacamara [fictionalized
version of Trinidad] → UK → Lantanacamara); *Out on Main
Street and Other Stories* (Trinidad and Tobago → Canada)

Bharati Mukherjee, *Darkness*; *Jasmine*; *The Middleman and Other
Stories*; *The Tiger's Daughter*; *Wife* (India → USA)

*Multatuli, *Max Havelaar: Or The Coffee Auctions of the Dutch
Trading Company* (Netherlands → Java)

Nayomi Munaweera, *Island of a Thousand Mirrors* (Sri Lanka →
USA)

Vladimir Nabokov, *Lolita* (France → USA); *Pale Fire* (fictional East-
ern European country → USA); *Pnin* (Russia → USA)

V. S. Naipaul, *The Enigma of Arrival* (Trinidad and Tobago → UK);
The Mimic Men (fictional Caribbean country → UK)

Shenaaz Nanji, *Child of Dandelions* (India → Uganda)

Marie NDiaye, *Three Strong Women* (Senegal → France)

Viet Thanh Nguyen, *The Refugees* (various migrations); *The Sympa-
thizer* (Vietnam → USA)

Elizabeth Nunez, *Anna In-Between*; *Boundaries*; *Grace* (Trinidad
and Tobago → USA)

Nnedi Okorafor, *Akata Witch* (USA → Nigeria); *Binti* and *Binti:
Home* (fictional interplanetary migration)

Ben Okri, *Incidents at the Shrine* (Nigeria → UK)

Azareen Van der Vliet Oloomi, *Call Me Zebra* (Iran → USA → Spain)

Joseph O'Neill, *Netherland* (Netherlands → USA)

Emine Sevgi Özdamar, *Mother Tongue* (Turkey → Germany)

George Papaellinas, *The Trip* (Greece → Australia)

A. S. Patrić, *Black Rock White City* (Yugoslavia/Serbia → Australia)

Sasenarine Persaud, *Canada Geese and Apple Chatney: Stories* (Guyana → Canada/USA)

Marlene NourbeSe Philip, *Harriet's Daughter* (Trinidad and Tobago → Canada)

Caryl Phillips, *Crossing the River* (African diaspora); *A Distant Shore* (unnamed African country → UK); *A View of the Empire at Sunset* (Dominica → UK)

Velma Pollard, *Homestretch* (UK → Jamaica)

Zia Haider Rahman, *In the Light of What We Know* (Afghanistan → UK, and other migrations)

Ahmad Danny Ramadan, *The Clothesline Swing* (Syria → Canada)

Shobha Rao, *Girls Burn Brighter* (India → USA); *An Unrestored Woman* (India → Pakistan → USA/Europe)

Jean Rhys, *Voyage in the Dark* (Dominica → UK)

*José Rizal, *Noli Me Tangere* (Philippines → Spain → Philippines)

Rahna Reiko Rizzuto, *Shadow Child* (Japan → USA)

Ivelisse Rodriguez, *Love War Stories* (Puerto Rico → mainland USA)

Sandip Roy, *Don't Let Him Know* (India → USA)

*María Amparo Ruiz de Burton, *Who Would Have Thought It?* (Mexico → USA)

Salman Rushdie, *East, West: Stories*; *Fury*; *The Satanic Verses* (India → UK, and other migrations)

Anjali Sachdeva, *All the Names They Used for God: Stories* (multiple migrations)

Sunjeev Sahota, *The Year of the Runaways* (India → UK)

Kerri Sakamoto, *The Electrical Field* (Japan → Canada)

Tayeb Salih, *Season of Migration to the North* (Sudan → UK → Sudan)

Kim Scott, *Taboo* (Indigenous Australian internal migration); *That Deadman Dance* (indigenous view of Australian colonial migration)

*Catharine Maria Sedgwick, *Hope Leslie: or, Early Times in the Massachusetts* (UK → North America)

Taiye Selasi, *Ghana Must Go* (Ghana → UK/USA)

Shyam Selvadurai, *Funny Boy*; *The Hungry Ghosts* (Sri Lanka → Canada)

Sam Selvon, *The Housing Lark*; *The Lonely Londoners*; *Moses Ascending*; *Moses Migrating* (various Caribbean → UK)

Kamila Shamsie, *Home Fire* (Pakistan → UK → USA/Syria)

Gary Shteyngart, *The Russian Debutante's Handbook* (Russia → USA)

Makeda Silvera, *The Heart Does Not Bend* (Jamaica → Canada)

*Upton Sinclair, *The Jungle* (Lithuania → USA)

Isaac Bashevis Singer, *The Collected Stories*; *Enemies: A Love Story* (Eastern Europe → USA)

Khushwant Singh, *Train to Pakistan* (India → Pakistan)

*Zadie Smith, *The Embassy of Cambodia* (Ivory Coast → UK); *Swing Time* (first generation UK)

Wole Soyinka, *Death and the King's Horseman* (Nigeria → UK → Nigeria)

*John Steinbeck, *The Grapes of Wrath* (USA internal migration)

Misa Sugiura, *It's Not Like It's a Secret* (first generation USA)

Miguel Syjuco, *Ilustrado* (Philippines → USA → Philippines)

Natalia Sylvester, *Everyone Knows You Go Home* (Mexico → USA)

Nafcote Tamirat, *The Parking Lot Attendant* (Ethiopia → USA → fictional island commune)

Amy Tan, *The Joy Luck Club* (China → USA)

Lucy Tan, *What We Were Promised* (China → USA)

H. Nigel Thomas, *Lives: Whole and Otherwise* (various Caribbean → Canada); *No Safeguards* (St. Vincent → Canada); *When the Bottom Falls Out: And Other Stories* (fictional Caribbean island → Canada)

Colm Tóibín, *Brooklyn* (Ireland → USA); *The Master* (USA → Europe); *The South* (Ireland → Spain)

Monique Truong, *The Book of Salt* (Vietnam → France)

Katia D. Ulysse, *Drifting* (Haiti → USA); *Mouths Don't Speak* (USA → Haiti)

Thrity Umrigar, *The Weight of Heaven* (USA → India)

Luis Alberto Urrea, *The House of Broken Angels*; *Into the Beautiful North* (Mexico → USA)

M. G. Vassanji, *The Assassin's Song* (India → Canada); *The Book of Secrets* (India → Tanzania); *The In-Between World of Vikram Lall* (India → Kenya); *The Magic of Saida* (Tanzania → Uganda → Canada); *No New Land* (Tanzania → Canada)

Ruvanee Pietersz Vilhauer, *The Water Diviner and Other Stories* (Sri Lanka → USA)

Eric Walrond, *Tropic Death* (various Caribbean → Panama Canal Zone)

Timberlake Wertenbaker, *Our Country's Good* (UK → Australia)

Zoë Wicomb, *October* (Scotland → South Africa); *The One That Got Away: Short Stories* (South Africa → Scotland); *You Can't Get Lost in Cape Town* (South Africa → UK)

Tara June Winch, *After the Carnage* (multiple migrations)

Alexis Wright, *Carpentaria* (Indigenous Australian internal migration)

Gene Luen Yang, *American Born Chinese* (China → USA)

Tiphanie Yanique, *Land of Love and Drowning* (St. Thomas → USA)

Anzia Yezierska, *Bread Givers*; *Hungry Hearts*; *Salome of the Tenements* (Poland/Russia → USA)

Mia Yun, *Translations of Beauty* (South Korea → USA)

Xu Xi, *Habit of a Foreign Sky* (Hong Kong → USA)

Arnold Zable, *Cafe Scheherazade* (Eastern Europe → Australia)

POETRY

Chris Abani, *Sanctificum* (Nigeria → USA)

Kaveh Akbar, *Calling a Wolf a Wolf* (Iran → USA)

Meena Alexander, *Atmospheric Embroidery* (multiple migrations); *Illiterate Heart* (India → USA)

Dionne Brand, *No Language Is Neutral* (Trinidad and Tobago, and other Caribbean → Canada)

Joseph Brodsky, *Selected Poems* (Russia → USA)

Wayde Compton, *49th Parallel Psalm* (USA → Canada)

Yrsa Daley-Ward, *bone* (first generation UK)

Tsering Wangmo Dhompa, *Rules of the House* (Tibet → India/Nepal)

Ali Cobby Eckermann, *Inside My Mother* (Indigenous Australian internal migration)

Federico García Lorca, *Poet in New York* (Spain → USA)

Lorna Goodison, *Supplying Salt and Light*; *Travelling Mercies*; *Turn Thanks* (multiple migrations)

Nathalie Handal, *Poet in Andalucía*; *The Republics* (multiple migrations)

Lawson Fusao Inada, *Drawing the Line*; *Legends from Camp* (USA internment)

Linton Kwesi Johnson, *Dread Beat and Blood*; *Mi Revalueshanary Fren* (Jamaica → UK)

Canisia Lubrin, *Voodoo Hypothesis* (multiple migrations)

Grace Nichols, *I Have Crossed an Ocean* (Guyana → UK); *I Is a Long Memoried Woman* (West Africa → Caribbean)

Sasenarine Persaud, *In a Boston Night: Poems*; *Love in a Time of Technology: Poems*; *Monsoon on the Fingers of God: Poems* (Guyana → Canada/USA)

Andy Quan, *Bowling Pin Fire* (first generation Canada); *Slant* (China → various places)

Lalbihari Sharma, *I Even Regret Night: Holi Songs of Demerara*, translated by Rajiv Mohabir (India → Guyana)

H. Nigel Thomas, *Moving Through Darkness* (St. Vincent and other Caribbean → Canada)

Tenzin Tsundue, *Crossing the Border* (Tibet → India)

*Marina Tsvetaeva, *Selected Poems* (Russia → Germany → Czechoslovakia → Russia)

Gina Athena Ulysse, *Because When God Is Too Busy: Haïti, me, & THE WORLD* (USA → Haiti)

*César Vallejo, *"Spain, Take This Chalice from Me" and Other Poems* (Peru → Spain/France)

Ocean Vuong, *Night Sky with Exit Wounds* (Vietnam → USA)

*Phillis Wheatley, *Complete Writings* (West Africa → North America)

Mitsuye Yamada, *Camp Notes and Other Writings* (Japan → USA)

Ouyang Yu, *Moon Over Melbourne & Other Poems* (China → Australia)

MEMOIR/NONFICTION/MULTIGENRE

Meena Alexander, *Fault Lines* (India → Sudan → UK → USA); *The Shock of Arrival: Reflections on Postcolonial Experience* (India → USA)

Gaiutra Bahadur, *Coolie Woman: The Odyssey of Indenture* (India → Guyana)

Dionne Brand, *A Map to the Door of No Return: Notes to Belonging* (West Africa → Trinidad and Tobago → Canada)

Carlos Bulosan, *America Is in the Heart: A Personal History* (Philippines → USA)

Staceyann Chin, *The Other Side of Paradise* (Jamaica → USA)

Michelle Cliff, *If I Could Write This in Fire* (Jamaica → UK)

*Quobna Ottobah Cugoano, *Thoughts and Sentiments on the Evil of Slavery* (Ghana → West Indies → UK)

Yrsa Daley-Ward, *The Terrible: A Storyteller's Memoir* (first generation UK)

Tsering Wangmo Dhompa, *Coming Home to Tibet: A Memoir of Love, Loss, and Belonging* (India → Tibet)

*Frederick Douglass, *My Bondage and My Freedom*; *Narrative of the Life of Frederick Douglass, an American Slave* (USA internal migration)

Ali Cobby Eckermann, *Too Afraid to Cry: Memoir of a Stolen Childhood* (Indigenous Australian internal migration)

*Olaudah Equiano, *The Interesting Narrative and Other Writings* (West Africa → Barbados → UK)

Aminatta Forna, *The Devil That Danced on the Water: A Daughter's Quest* (Sierra Leone → UK)

Mohandas K. Gandhi, *An Autobiography: The Story of My Experiments with Truth* (India → South Africa → UK → India)

*Emma Goldman, *Living My Life* (Russia → USA)

Stuart Hall, *Familiar Stranger: A Life Between Two Islands* (Jamaica → UK)

Saidiya Hartman, *Lose Your Mother: A Journey Along the Atlantic Slave Route* (African diaspora)

Abeer Y. Hoque, *Olive Witch: A Memoir* (Nigeria → USA → Bangladesh)

Zora Neale Hurston, *Barracoon: The Story of the Last "Black Cargo"* (West Africa [present-day Benin] → USA)

*Elspeth Huxley, *The Flame Trees of Thika: Memories of an African Childhood* (UK → Kenya)

Francisco Jiménez, *Breaking Through*; *Reaching Out*; *Taking Hold: From Migrant Childhood to Columbia University* (Mexico → USA)

Ha Jin, *The Writer as Migrant* (China → USA)

Judith Kerr, *Bombs on Aunt Dainty*; *When Hitler Stole Pink Rabbit*; *A Small Person Far Away* (Germany → UK)

Jamaica Kincaid, *My Garden (Book)* (Antigua → USA)

Maxine Hong Kingston, *China Men*; *The Woman Warrior: Memoirs of a Girlhood Among Ghosts* (China → USA)

Chelene Knight, *Dear Current Occupant* (first generation Canada)

Tété-Michel Kpomassie, *An African in Greenland* (Togo → Greenland)

Amitava Kumar, *Passport Photos* (India → USA)

Murat Kurnaz, *Five Years of My Life: An Innocent Man in Guantánamo* (Germany → Pakistan → Guantánamo → Germany)

George Lamming, *The Pleasures of Exile* (Caribbean → UK)

Valeria Luiselli, *Tell Me How It Ends: An Essay in Forty Questions* (Mexico → USA)

Paule Marshall, *Triangular Road: A Memoir* (first generation USA)

*José Martí, *Selected Writings*; *Our America: Writings on Latin America and the Struggle for Cuban Independence* (Cuba → USA)

Hisham Matar, *The Return: Fathers, Sons and the Land in Between* (Libya → Kenya → Egypt → UK → USA → Libya)

Frank McCourt, *Angela's Ashes*; *Teacher Man*; *'Tis* (Ireland → USA)

Malachy McCourt, *A Monk Swimming*; *Singing My Him Song* (Ireland → USA)

Dhan Gopal Mukerji, *Caste and Outcast* (India → USA)

Vladimir Nabokov, *Speak, Memory: An Autobiography Revisited* (Russia → UK → USA)

*Shiva Naipaul, *North of South: An African Journey* (Trinidad and Tobago → East Africa)

Shoba Narayan, *Monsoon Diary: A Memoir with Recipes* (India → USA)

*Solomon Northup, *Twelve Years a Slave* (USA internal migration)

Elizabeth Nunez, *Not for Everyday Use* (Trinidad and Tobago → USA)

Dan-El Padilla Peralta, *Undocumented: A Dominican Boy's Odyssey from a Homeless Shelter to the Ivy League* (Dominican Republic → USA)

Shailja Patel, *Migritude* (Kenya → UK → USA)

Caryl Phillips, *Colour Me English: Reflections on Migration and Belonging* (St. Kitts → UK)

*Mary Prince, *The History of Mary Prince* (Bermuda → UK)

Jacob G. Rosenberg, *Sunrise West* (Poland → Australia)

*Mary Seacole, *Wonderful Adventures of Mrs Seacole in Many Lands* (Jamaica → UK and elsewhere)

Gary Shteyngart, *Little Failure* (Russia → USA)

Art Spiegelman, *Maus* (Poland → USA)

*Nikola Tesla, *My Inventions and Other Writings* (Croatia → USA)

*John Thompson, *The Life of John Thompson, a Fugitive Slave* (USA internal migration)

*Sojourner Truth, *Narrative of Sojourner Truth* (USA internal migration)

*Phillis Wheatley, *Complete Writings* (West Africa → North America)

ANTHOLOGIES

Bruce Bennett and Susan Hayes, eds., *Home and Away: Australian Stories of Belonging and Alienation* (various places → Australia)

James Berry, ed., *News for Babylon: The Chatto Book of Westindian-British Poetry* (Caribbean → UK)

Frank Birbalsingh, ed., *Jahaji: An Anthology of Indo-Caribbean Fiction* (India → Guyana/Trinidad and Tobago)

Meri Nana-Ama Danquah, ed., *Becoming American: Personal Essays by First Generation Immigrant Women* (first generation USA)

Edwidge Danticat, ed., *The Butterfly's Way: Voices from the Haitian Dyaspora in the United States* (Haiti → USA)

Jane Joritz-Nakagawa, ed., *Women: Poetry: Migration, an Anthology* (various migrations)

Louis Mendoza and Subramanian Shankar, eds., *Crossing into America: The New Literature of Immigration* (various places → USA)

Viet Thanh Nguyen, ed., *The Displaced: Refugee Writers on Refugee Lives* (various migrations)

Achy Obejas and Megan Bayles, eds., *Immigrant Voices: 21st Century Stories* (various places → USA)

Caryl Phillips, ed., *Extravagant Strangers: A Literature of Belonging* (various places → UK)

Shyam Selvadurai, ed., *Story-Wallah: Short Fiction from South Asian Writers* (South Asia → various destinations)

Paul Sharrad and Meeta Chatterjee Padmanabhan, eds., *Of Indian Origin: Writings from Australia* (India → Australia)

FILM/MULTIMEDIA

Ae Fond Kiss . . . , dir. Ken Loach (Pakistan/Ireland → Scotland)

Africa Paradis, dir. Sylvestre Amoussou (future Europe → Africa)

Ali's Wedding, dir. Jeffrey Walker (Iraq → Australia)

Amreeka, dir. Cherien Dabis (Palestine → USA)

Auntie, dir. Lisa Harewood (Barbados → UK)

Beautiful People, dir. Jasmin Dizdar (Bosnia → UK)

Bend It Like Beckham, dir. Gurinder Chadha (India → UK)

Bhaji on the Beach, dir. Gurinder Chadha (India → UK)

Black Girl / La noire de . . . , dir. Ousmane Sembène (Senegal → France)

Brooklyn, dir. John Crowley (Ireland → USA)

Cambodian Son, dir. Kosal Khiev (Cambodia → USA → Cambodia)

Children of the Crocodile, dir. Marsha Emerman (East Timor → Australia)

Daughter of Keltoum, dir. Mehdi Charef (Switzerland → Algeria)

Dirty Pretty Things, dir. Stephen Frears (Nigeria/Turkey → UK)

Dreaming Rivers, dir. Martina Attille (St. Lucia → UK)

East Is East, dir. Damien O'Donnell (Pakistan → UK)

Eat a Bowl of Tea, dir. Wayne Wang (China → USA)

Eden Is West, dir. Costa-Gavras (Greece → France)

El Norte, dir. Gregory Nava (Mexico → USA)

Europlex, dir. Ursula Biemann and Angela Sanders (Morocco → Spain)

Hate / La Haine, dir. Mathieu Kassovitz (first generation France)

Head On, dir. Ana Kokkinos (Greece → Australia)

Head-on, dir. Fatih Akin (Turkey → Germany)

Journey of Hope, dir. Xavier Koller (Turkey → Switzerland)

Kim's Convenience (TV series; Korea → Canada)

Latcho Drom, dir. Tony Gatlif (India → Europe Roma migration)

Layla M., dir. Mijke de Jong (Morocco → Netherlands)

Maria in Nobody's Land, dir. Marcela Zamora Chamorro (El Salvador → USA)

Mississippi Masala, dir. Mira Nair (Uganda → USA)

Motherland: Cuba Korea USA, dir. Dai Sil Kim-Gibson (Korea → Cuba → USA)

My Beautiful Laundrette, dir. Stephen Frears (first generation UK)

The Namesake, dir. Mira Nair (India → USA)

The Other Side of Immigration, dir. Roy Germano (Mexico ↔ USA)

Princesas, dir. Fernando León de Aranoa (Dominican Republic → Spain)

The Promise / La Promesse, dir. Luc and Jean-Pierre Dardenne (various places → Belgium)

Remote Sensing, dir. Ursula Biemann (various migrations)

The Secret of the Grain, dir. Abdellatif Kechiche (Tunisia → France)

Shouf Shouf Habibi! / Hush Hush Baby, dir. Albert ter Heerdt (Morocco → Netherlands)

Siberian Love, dir. Olga Delane (Siberia → Germany)

Sin Nombre, dir. Cary Joji Fukunaga (Mexico/Honduras → USA)

Small Island, dir. John Alexander (Jamaica → UK)

Sound of Torture, dir. Keren Shayo (Egypt → Eritrea)

Sunday God Willing / Inch'Allah Dimanche, dir. Yamina Benguigui (Algeria → France)

Tea in the Harem / Le Thé au Harem d'Archimède, dir. Mehdi Charef (Algeria → France)

To Sir, With Love, dir. James Clavell (Guyana → UK)

Under the Same Moon, dir. Patricia Riggen (Mexico → USA)

Which Way Home, dir. Rebecca Cammisa (El Salvador/Honduras → Mexico → USA)

http://www.global-migration.info: The Global Flow of People

http://peoplemov.in: Migration Flows Around the World

https://www.migrationpolicy.org: Migration Policy Institute

https://barrelstories.org: Barrel Stories Project

https://migrationliterature.weebly.com: Comparative Migration Literature

Acknowledgments

Like my previous anthology *Rotten English*, this one began as a course at St. John's University, where I remain grateful for the congenial atmosphere, supportive colleagues, open-minded students, and the freedom to design and teach unconventional courses. Students in two successive iterations of Comparative Migration Literature enthusiastically and helpfully advised me on many of the selections included here. I received invaluable text suggestions from many people, including Akelah Adams, Sonia Adams, Tanya Agathocleous, Eliya Ahmad, Melina Ahmad, Kaveh Akbar, Syed Ali, Baher Azmi, Yasmin Badin, Tabitha Benitez, Holly-Rose Boruta, Tuli Chatterji, Cora Diamond, Julie Diamond, J. Daniel Elam, Josh Fellman, Inderpal Grewel, Nadia Guessous, Orin Herskowitz, Anjuli Raza Kolb, Shondel Nero, Kristina Olsen, Lisa Outar, Marisa Parham, Supriya Pillai, Laila Shikaki, Abby Sider, Brandin Stone, Robin Varghese, and Wendy Walters. Julie Diamond and Orin Herskowitz provided general support: emotional, intellectual, and logistical. Sophie Bell and Orin Herskowitz gave thoughtful and encouraging feedback on the introduction. It was a delight to work with Elda Rotor, a visionary editor who has changed the public understanding of "classic." Tanya Agathocleous introduced me to Elda and championed the idea for the anthology. Finally, I'm extraordinarily grateful to Edwidge Danticat for her beautiful and moving foreword.